BOOKS BY ERNEST HEMINGWAY

True at First Light
The Complete Short Stories
The Garden of Eden
Dateline: Toronto
The Dangerous Summer
Selected Letters
The Enduring Hemingway
The Nick Adams Stories
Islands in the Stream
The Fifth Column and Four Stories of the Spanish Civil War
By-Line: Ernest Hemingway
A Moveable Feast
Three Novels
The Snows of Kilimanjaro and Other Stories
The Hemingway Reader
The Old Man and the Sea
Across the River and Into the Trees
For Whom the Bell Tolls
The Short Stories of Ernest Hemingway
To Have and Have Not
Green Hills of Africa
Winner Take Nothing
Death in the Afternoon
In Our Time
A Farewell to Arms
Men Without Women
The Sun Also Rises
The Torrents of Spring

Ernest Hemingway

———◆———

TRUE AT
FIRST LIGHT

*Edited with an Introduction
by Patrick Hemingway*

SCRIBNER

SCRIBNER
1230 Avenue of the Americas
New York, NY 10020

SCRIBNER and design are trademarks of Jossey-Bass, Inc., used
under license by Simon & Schuster, the publisher of this work.

Designed by Brooke Zimmer
Set in Sabon
Manufactured in the United States of America

1 3 5 7 9 10 8 6 4 2

Library of Congress Cataloging-in-Publication Data
Hemingway, Ernest, 1899–1961.
True at first light: a fictional memoir/Ernest Hemingway;
edited with an introduction by Patrick Hemingway.
p. cm.
(large print)
1. Large type books. I. Hemingway, Patrick. II. Title
[PS3515.E37T78 1999b]
813'.52—dc21 99-18195
CIP

ISBN 0-684-86448-7

Portions of this work were previously published, in different
form, in *Sports Illustrated*.

"In Africa a thing is true at first light and a lie by noon and you have no more respect for it than for the lovely, perfect weed-fringed lake you see across the sun-baked salt plain. You have walked across that plain in the morning and you know that no such lake is there. But now it is there absolutely true, beautiful and believable."

—ERNEST HEMINGWAY

INTRODUCTION

THIS STORY opens in a place and at a time which for me, at least, remains highly significant. I spent the first half of my grown-up life in East Africa and have read extensively the history and literature of the British and German minorities who lived there for a brief two and a half generations. The first five chapters may be hard to follow today without some explanation of what was going on in Kenya in the Northern Hemisphere winter of 1953–54.

Jomo Kenyatta, a well-educated and widely traveled black African, a Kikuyu who had married an Englishwoman when he lived in that country, had, according to the British colonial administration of the time, returned to his native Kenya and unleashed there a black farm laborers' insurgency called Mau Mau against the landowning immigrant farmers from Europe whom the Kikuyu believed had stolen the land from them. It's Caliban's grievance in *The Tempest:*

> *This island's mine by Sycorax my mother,*
> *Which thou tak'st from me! When thou*
>   *camest first*
> *Thou strok'st me, and made much of me,*
>   *wouldst give me*
> *Water with berries in't, and teach me how*
> *To name the bigger light and how the less,*
> *That burn by day and night; and then I*
>   *lov'd thee*
> *And show'd thee all the qualities o' th' isle,*
> *The fresh springs, brine pits, barren place*
>   *and fertile.*

Mau Mau was not the Pan-African independence movement that forty years later has finally achieved black African majority rule in the whole of the sub-Saharan continent but something, for the most part, specific to the anthropology of the Kikuyu tribe. A Kikuyu became a Mau Mau by taking a sacrilegious oath that separated him from his normal life and turned him into a kamikaze human missile aimed at his employer, the European immigrant farmer. The most common agricultural implement in the country was called in Swahili a panga, a heavy-bladed, single-edged sword, stamped and ground from sheet steel in the English Midlands, able to cut brush, dig holes and kill people under the right conditions. Almost every agricultural worker had one. I am not an anthropologist and what I am describing may be nonsense, but that's how Mau Mau was seen by the European immigrant farmers, their wives and children. Sadly enough, the most people eventually killed and maimed by this bit of applied anthropology were not the European immigrant farming families it was designed to harm but those Kikuyu who resisted oathing and cooperated with the British colonial authorities.

What at the time of this story were known as the White Highlands, a reserve set aside exclusively for European agricultural settlement and which the Kikuyu felt had been stolen from them, lay at higher altitude and were better watered than the traditional lands of the Kamba. Although speaking a Bantu language closely related to Kikuyu, Kamba subsistence farmers needed to hunt and gather more where they lived to supplement their less reliable cultivated fields and were of necessity less site-attached than their Kikuyu neighbors. The cultural differences between the two peoples are subtle and best understood by comparing two nations that live together on the Iberian peninsula, the Spaniards and the Portuguese. Most of us know enough about these two to see why what might work with one would not appeal to the other and so it was with Mau Mau. It did not work in most instances with the Kamba and it is lucky for the Hemingways, both Ernest and Mary, that it didn't, for they would have then stood a good chance of being hacked to death in their beds as they slept by the very servants they so trusted and thought they understood.

By the start of Chapter 6 the threat of an outside attack on the Hemingways' safari camp by a group of oathed Kamba Mau Mau escaped from detention has evaporated like dawn mist under the warmth of the morning sun and the contemporary reader will enjoy what follows without difficulty.

Because of my fortuitous position as number two son, I spent a great deal of time with my father during my later childhood and adolescence, the period of his marriages to Martha Gellhorn and Mary Welsh. I remember one summer when I was thirteen inadvertently walking into Papa's bedroom at the house Marty had found for the two of them in Cuba when they were making love in one of those rather athletic ways recommended in manuals for the pursuit of happiness in married life. I immediately withdrew and I don't believe they saw me, but when editing the story presented here and coming across the passage where Papa describes Marty as a simulator, that scene came back to me very vividly, after fifty-six years of forgetfulness. Some simulator.

Hemingway's untitled manuscript is about two hundred thousand words long and is certainly not a journal. What you will read here is a fiction half that length. I hope Mary will not be too cross with me for making so much of Debba, a sort of dark-matter opposite to what was Mary's real class act as a wife who did end up committing twenty-five-year-long suttee, fueled by gin instead of sandalwood.

Ambiguous counterpoint between fiction and truth lies at the heart of this memoir. Using it the author plays at length in passages that will doubtless please any reader who likes to listen to that music. I spent some time in the safari camp at Kimana and knew every person in it, black, white and read all over, and for a reason I cannot adequately explain it reminds me of some things that happened back in the summer of 1942 on the *Pilar* when my brother Gregory and I, like General Grant's thirteen-year-old son, Fred, at Vicksburg, spent a month as children with its remarkable crew who were in temporary service as naval auxiliaries. The radio operator was a career marine who at one time had been stationed in China. That sub-hunting summer he had an opportunity to read *War and Peace* for the first time, as he was only working for very short periods while on standby duty most of the day and night and the novel was part of the ship's library. I remember him telling us all how much more it meant to him since he had known all those White Russians in Shanghai.

Hemingway was interrupted in his first and only draft of the manuscript by Leland Hayward, then married to the lady who has therefore to live by the long-distance telephone in this story, and the other movie people filming *The Old Man and the Sea* to go and help them fish for a picture marlin in Peru. The Suez Crisis, which closed the canal and ended his plans for another trip to East Africa, could have been one reason he never returned to his unfinished work. We know he was thinking of Paris "in the old days" from what we read in this story and perhaps another reason he left it was he found he could write more felicitously of Paris than East Africa, which for all its photogenic beauty and excitement had lasted but a few months and mauled him badly, the first time with amebic dysentery and the second with the plane crashes.

Were he still alive, I would have asked Ralph Ellison to do this introductory note because of what he wrote in *Shadow and Act*:

"Do you still ask why Hemingway was more important to me than Wright? Not because he was white, or more 'accepted.' But because he appreciated the things of this earth which I love and which Wright was too driven or deprived or inexperienced to know: weather, guns, dogs, horses, love *and* hate and impossible circumstances which to the courageous and dedicated could be turned into benefits and victories. Because he wrote with such precision about the processes and techniques of daily living that I could keep myself and my brother alive during the 1937 Recession by following his descriptions of wing-shooting; because he knew the difference between politics and art and something of their true relationship for the writer. Because all he wrote—and this is very important—was imbued with a spirit beyond the tragic with which I could feel at home, for it is very close to the feeling of the blues, which are, perhaps, as close as Americans can come to expressing the spirit of tragedy."

I am pretty sure Hemingway had read *Invisible Man* and that it helped him pull himself together after the two plane crashes that came so close to killing both Mary and himself, when he started to write again with his African manuscript in the mid-fifties, at least a year after the events that inspired this return to creative work. He may have had Ellison in mind in his remarks in the draft manuscript about writers stealing from each other, for the scene in Ellison's novel of the lunatics from the asylum is very much like that of the vets in the bar in Key West from *To Have and Have Not.*

Ellison wrote his essay piece in the early 1960s, not so long after Hemingway's death in the summer of 1961, and Ellison, of course, had not read the unfinished African manuscript, which I have licked here into what I hope is not the worst of all possible shapes: *True at First Light,* taking what my father wrote in the morning and doing with it what Suetonius describes in his *Lives of Illustrious Men:*

"When Virgil was writing the 'Georgics,' it is said to have been his custom to dictate each day a large number of verses which he composed in the morning, and then to spend the rest of the day in reducing them to a very small number, wittily remarking that he fashioned his poem after the manner of a she-bear, and gradually licked it into shape."

Only Hemingway himself could have licked his unfinished draft into the *Ursus horribilis* it might have been. What I offer in *True at First*

Light is a child's teddy bear. I will take it to bed now always and having laid myself down to sleep and prayed the Lord my soul to keep, if I die before I wake, I will pray the Lord my soul to take and God bless you, Papa.

Patrick Hemingway
Bozeman, Montana
July 16, 1998

1

THINGS WERE not too simple in this safari because things had changed very much in East Africa. The white hunter had been a close friend of mine for many years. I respected him as I had never respected my father and he trusted me, which was more than I deserved. It was, however, something to try to merit. He had taught me by putting me on my own and correcting me when I made mistakes. When I made a mistake he would explain it. Then if I did not make the same mistake again he would explain a little more. But he was nomadic and he was finally leaving us because it was necessary for him to be at his farm, which is what they call a twenty-thousand-acre cattle ranch in Kenya. He was a very complicated man compounded of absolute courage, all the good human weaknesses and a strangely subtle and very critical understanding of people. He was completely dedicated to his family and his home and he loved much more to live away from them. He loved his home and his wife and his children.

"Do you have any problems?"

"I don't want to make a fool of myself with elephants."

"You'll learn."

"Anything else?"

"Know everybody knows more than you but you have to make the decisions and make them stick. Leave the camp and all that to Keiti. Be as good as you can."

There are people who love command and in their eagerness to assume it they are impatient at the formalities of taking over from someone else. I love command since it is the ideal welding of freedom and slavery. You can be happy with your freedom and when it becomes too dangerous you take refuge in your duty. For several years I had exercised no command except over myself and I was bored with this since I knew myself and my defects and strengths too well and they permitted me little freedom and much duty. Lately I had read with distaste various books written about myself by people who knew all about my inner life, aims and motives. Reading them was like reading an account of a battle where you had fought written by someone who had not only not been present but, in some cases, had not even been born when the battle had taken place. All these people who wrote of my life both inner and outer wrote with an absolute assurance that I had never felt.

On this morning I wished that my great friend and teacher Philip Percival did not have to communicate in that odd shorthand of understatement which was our legal tongue. I wished that there were things that I could ask him that it was impossible to ask. I wished more than anything that I could be instructed fully and competently as the British instruct their airmen. But I knew that the customary law which prevailed between Philip Percival and myself was as rigid as the customary law of the Kamba. My ignorance, it had been decided long ago, was to be lessened only through learning by myself. But I knew that from now on I had no one to correct my mistakes and, with all the happiness one has in assuming command, it made the morning a very lonely one.

For a long time we had called each other Pop. At first, more than twenty years before, when I had called him Pop, Mr. Percival had not minded as long as this violation of good manners was not made in public. But after I had reached the age of fifty, which made me an elder or Mzee, he had taken, happily, to calling me Pop, which was in a way a compliment, lightly bestowed and deadly if it were withdrawn. I cannot imagine a situation, or, rather, I would not wish to survive a situation in which I called him, in private, Mr. Percival or he addressed me by my proper name.

So on this morning there were many questions I wished to ask and many things I had wondered about. But we were, by custom, mute on these subjects. I felt very lonely and he knew it of course.

"If you did not have problems it would not be fun," Pop said. "You're not a mechanic and what they call white hunters now are mostly mechanics who speak the language and follow other people's tracks. Your command of the language is limited. But you and your disreputable companions made what tracks there are and you can make a few new ones. If you can't come up with the proper word in your new idiom, Kikamba, just speak Spanish. Everyone loves that. Or let the Memsahib talk. She is slightly more articulate than you."

"Oh go to hell."

"I shall go to prepare a place for thee," Pop said.

"And elephants?"

"Never give them a thought," Pop said. "Enormous silly beasts. Harmless everyone says. Just remember how deadly you are with all other beasts. After all they are not the woolly mastodon. I've never seen one with a tusk that made two curves."

"Who told you about that?"

"Keiti," Pop said. "He told me you bag thousands of them in the off-season. Those and your saber-toothed tiger and your brontosauruses."

"The son of a bitch," I said.

"No. He more than half believes it. He has a copy of the magazine and they look very convincing. I think he believes it some days and some days not. It depends on whether you bring him any guinea fowl and how you're shooting in general."

"It was a pretty well illustrated article on prehistoric animals."

"Yes. Very. Most lovely pictures. And you made a very rapid advance as a white hunter when you told him you had only come to Africa because your mastodon license was filled at home and you had shot over your limit on saber-toothed tiger. I told him it was God's truth and that you were a sort of escaped ivory poacher from Rawlins, Wyoming, which was rather like the Lado Enclave in the old days and that you had come out here to pay reverence to me who had started you in as a boy, barefoot of course, and to try to keep your hand in for when they would let you go home and take out a new mastodon license."

"Pop, please tell me one sound thing about elephants. You know I have to do away with them if they are bad behaving and if they ask me to."

"Just remember your old mastodon technique," Pop said. "Try and get your first barrel in between that second ring of the tusk. On frontals the seventh wrinkle on the nose counting down from the first wrinkle on the high forehead. Extraordinary high foreheads they have. Most abrupt. If you are nervous stick it in his ear. You will find it's simply a pastime."

"Thank you," I said.

"I've never worried ever about you taking care of the Memsahib but take care of yourself a little bit and try to be as good a boy as you can."

"You try too."

"I've tried for many years," he said. Then, in the classic formula he said, "Now it is all yours."

So it was. It was all mine on a windless morning of the last day of the month of the next to the last month of the year. I looked at the dining tent and at our own tent. Then back to the small tents and the men moving around the cooking fire and then at the trucks and the hunting car, the vehicles seeming frosted in the heavy dew. Then I looked through the trees at the Mountain showing very big and near this morning with the new snow shining in the first sunlight.

"Will you be all right in the truck?"

"Quite. It's a good road you know when it's dry."

"You take the hunting car. I won't need it."

"You're not that good," Pop said. "I want to turn this truck in and send you one that is sound. They don't trust this truck."

It was always they. They were the people, the watu. Once they had been the boys. They still were to Pop. But he had either known them all when they were boys in age or had known their fathers when their fathers were children. Twenty years ago I had called them boys too and neither they nor I had any thought that I had no right to. Now no one would have minded if I had used the word. But the way things were now you did not do it. Everyone had his duties and everyone had a name. Not to know a name was both impolite and a sign of sloppiness. There were special names too of all sorts and shortening of names and friendly and unfriendly nicknames. Pop still cursed them in English or in Swahili and they loved it. I had no right to curse them and I never did. We also all, since the Magadi expedition, had certain secrets and certain things privately shared. Now there were many things that were secrets and there were things that went beyond secrets and were understandings. Some of the secrets were not at all gentle and some were so comic that you would see one of the three gun bearers suddenly laughing and look toward him and know what it was and you would both be laughing so hard that trying to hold in the laughter your diaphragm would ache.

It was a clear and beautiful morning as we drove out across the plain with the Mountain and the trees of the camp behind us. There were many Thomson's gazelle ahead on the green plain switching their tails as they fed. There were herds of wildebeests and Grant's gazelle feeding close to the patches of bush. We reached the airstrip we had made in a long open meadow by running the car and the truck up and down through the new short grass and grubbing out the stumps and roots of a patch of brush at one end. The tall pole of a cut sapling drooped from the heavy wind of the night before and the wind sock, homemade from a flour sack, hung limp. We stopped the car and I got out and felt the pole. It was solid although bent and the sock would fly once the breeze rose. There were wind clouds high in the sky and it was beautiful looking across the green meadow at the Mountain looking so huge and wide from here.

"Do you want to shoot any color of it and the airstrip?" I asked my wife.

"We have that even better than it is this morning. Let's go and see the bat-eared foxes and check on the lion."

"He won't be out now. It's too late."

"He might be."

So we drove along our old wheel tracks that led to the salt flat. On the left there was open plain and the broken line of tall green-foliaged yellow-trunked trees that marked the edge of the forest where the buffalo herd might be. There was old dry grass growing high along the edge and there were many fallen trees that had been pulled down by elephants or uprooted by storms. Ahead there was plain with new short green grass and to the right there were broken glades with islands of thick green bush and occasional tall flat-topped thorn trees. Everywhere there was game feeding. They moved away as we came close, moving sometimes in quick bursts of galloping; sometimes at a steady trot; sometimes only feeding off away from the car. But they always stopped and fed again. When we were on this routine patrol or when Miss Mary was photographing they paid no more attention to us than they do to the lion when he is not hunting. They keep out of his way but they are not frightened.

I was leaning out of the car watching for tracks in the road as my gun bearer, Ngui, who sat in the outside position behind me was doing. Mthuka, who was driving, watched all the country ahead and on both sides. He had the best and quickest eyes of any of us. His face was ascetic, thin and intelligent and he had the arrowhead tribal cuts of the Wakamba on both cheeks. He was quite deaf and he was Mkola's son and he was a year older than I was. He was not a Mohammedan as his father was. He loved to hunt and he was a beautiful driver. He would never do a careless or irresponsible thing but he, Ngui and myself were the three principal bads.

We had been very close friends for a long time and one time I asked him when he had gotten the big formal tribal cuts which no one else had. Those who did have them had very lightly traced scars.

He laughed and said, "At a very big Ngoma. You know. To please a girl." Ngui and Charo, Miss Mary's gun bearer, both laughed.

Charo was a truly devout Mohammedan and was also known to be very truthful. He did not know how old he was, of course, but Pop thought he must be over seventy. With his turban on he was about two inches shorter than Miss Mary and watching them standing together looking across the gray flat at the waterbuck that were now going carefully, upwind, into the forest, the big buck with his beautiful horns looking back and to either side as he entered last in line, I thought what a strange pair Miss Mary and Charo must look to the animals. No animals had any visual fear of them. We had seen this proven many times. Rather than fearing them, the small blond one in the forest green coat, and the even smaller black one in the blue jacket, the animals appeared interested in them. It was as though they had been permitted to see a circus or at least something extremely odd and the preda- tory animals seemed to be definitely attracted by them. On this morning we were all relaxed. Something, or something awful or something wonderful was certain to happen on every day in this part of Africa. Every morning when you woke it was as exciting as though you were going to compete in a downhill ski race or drive a bobsled on a fast run. Something, you knew, would happen and usually before eleven o'clock. I never knew of a morning in Africa when I woke that I was not happy. At least until I remembered unfinished business. But on this morning we were relaxed in the momentary irresponsibility of command and I was happy that the buffalo, which were our basic problem, were evidently someplace where we could not reach them. For what we hoped to do it was necessary for them to come to us rather than for us to go to them.

"What are you going to do?"

"Bring the car up and make a quick swing to check for tracks at the big water and then go into that place in the forest where it borders the swamp and check and then get out. We'll be downwind of the elephant and you might see him. Probably not."

"Can we go back through the gerenuk country?"

"Of course. I'm sorry we started late. But with Pop going away and everything."

"I like to go in there in that bad place. I can study what we need for a Christmas tree. Do you think my lion is in there?"

"Probably. But we won't see him in that kind of country."

"He's such a smart bastard lion. Why didn't they let me shoot that easy beautiful lion under the tree that time. That's the way women shoot lions."

"They shoot them that way and the finest black-maned lion ever shot by a woman had maybe forty shots fired into him. Afterwards they have the beautiful pictures and then they have to live with the god-damn lion and lie about him to all their friends and themselves the rest of their lives."

"I'm sorry I missed the wonderful lion at Magadi."

"Don't you be sorry. You be proud."

"I don't know what made me this way. I have to get him and he has to be the real one."

"We overhunted him, honey. He's too smart. I have to let him get confidence now and make a mistake."

"He doesn't make mistakes. He's smarter than you and Pop both."

"Honey, Pop wanted you to get him or lose him straight. If he didn't love you you could have shot any sort of a lion."

"Let's not talk about him," she said. "I want to think about the Christmas tree. We're going to have a wonderful Christmas."

Mthuka had seen Ngui start down the trail for him and brought up the car. We got in and I motioned Mthuka toward the far water at the corner across the swamp. Ngui and I both hung out over the side watching for tracks. There were the old wheel tracks and the game trails to and from the papyrus swamp. There were fresh wildebeest tracks and the tracks of the zebra and Tommy.

Now we were going closer to the forest as the road swung and then we saw the tracks of a man. Then of another man wearing boots. These tracks had been rained on lightly and we stopped the car to check on foot.

"You and me," I said to Ngui.

"Yes," he grinned. "One of them has big feet and walks as though he is tired."

"One is barefooted and walks as though the

rifle were too heavy for him. Stop the car," I said to Mthuka. We got out.

"Look," said Ngui. "One walks as though he were very old and can hardly see. The one with shoes."

"Look," I said. "The barefoot one walks as though he has five wives and twenty cows. He has spent a fortune on beer."

"They will get nowhere," Ngui said. "Look, the one with shoes walks as though he might die at any time. He staggers under the weight of the rifle."

"What do you think they are doing here?"

"How would I know? Look, the one with shoes is stronger now."

"He is thinking about the Shamba," Ngui said.

"Kwenda na Shamba."

"Ndio," Ngui said. "How old would you say the old one with the shoes is?"

"None of your damn business," I said. We motioned for the car and when it got up we got in and I motioned Mthuka toward the entrance to the forest. The driver was laughing and shaking his head.

"What were you two doing tracking yourselves?" Miss Mary said. "I know it's funny because everybody was laughing. But it looked quite silly."

"We were having fun."

I was always depressed by this part of the forest. The elephants had to eat something and it was proper that they should eat trees rather than destroy the native farms. But the destruction was so great in proportion to the amount they ate from the trees they pulled down that it was depressing to see it. Elephants were the only animal that were increasing steadily throughout their present range in Africa. They increased until they became such a problem to the natives that they had to be slaughtered. Then they were killed off indiscriminately. There were men who did this and enjoyed it. They killed old bulls, young bulls, cows and calves and many liked their work. There had to be some sort of elephant control. But seeing this damage to the forest and the way the trees were pulled down and stripped and knowing what they could do in a native Shamba in a night, I started to think about the problems of control. But all the time I was watching for the tracks of the two elephants we had seen leading into this part of the forest. I knew those two elephants and where they would probably go for the day, but until I had seen their tracks and was sure they were past us I must be careful about Miss Mary wandering around looking for a suitable Christmas tree.

We stopped the car and I took the big gun and helped Miss Mary out of the car.

"I don't need any help," she said.

"Look, honey," I started to explain. "I have to stay with you with the big gun."

"I'm just going to pick out a Christmas tree."

"I know. But there could be every kind of stuff in here. There has been too."

"Let Ngui stay with me then and Charo's here."

"Honey, I'm responsible for you."

"You can be an awful bore about it too."

"I know it." Then I said, "Ngui."

"Bwana?"

The joking was all suspended.

"Go and see if the two elephants went into the far forest. Go as far as the rocks."

"Ndio."

He went off across the open space watching ahead for tracks in the grass and carrying my Springfield in his right hand.

"I only want to pick one out," Miss Mary said. "Then we can come out some morning and dig it up and get it back to camp and plant it while it is still cool."

"Go ahead," I said. I was watching Ngui. He had stopped once and listened. Then he went on walking very carefully. I followed Miss Mary who was looking at the different silvery thorn shrubs trying to find one with the best size and shape but I kept looking back at Ngui over my shoulder. He stopped again and listened then waved toward the deep forest with his left arm. He looked around at me and I waved him back to us. He came in fast; as fast as he could walk without running.

"Where are they?" I asked.

"They crossed and went into the forest. I could hear them. The old bull and his askari."

"Good," I said.

"Listen," he whispered. "Faro." He pointed toward the thick forest on the right. I had heard nothing. "Mzuri motocah," he said, meaning, in shorthand, "Better get into the car."

"Get Miss Mary."

I turned toward where Ngui had pointed. I could see only the silvery shrubs, the green grass and the line of tall trees with vines and creepers hanging from them. Then I heard the noise like a sharp deep purr. It was the noise you would make if you held your tongue against the roof of your mouth and blew out strong so your tongue vibrated as a reed. It came from where Ngui had pointed. But I could see nothing. I slipped the safety catch forward on the .577 and turned my head to the left. Miss Mary was coming at an angle to get behind where I stood. Ngui was holding her by the arm to guide her and she was

walking as though she were treading on eggs.
Charo was following her. Then I heard the
sharp rough purr again and I saw Ngui fall back
with the Springfield ready and Charo move forward and take Miss Mary's arm. They were
even with me now and were working toward
where the car must be. I knew the driver,
Mthuka, was deaf and would not hear the
rhino. But when he saw them he would know
what was happening. I did not want to look
around. But I did and saw Charo urging Miss
Mary toward the hunting car. Ngui was moving
fast with them carrying the Springfield and
watching over his shoulder. It was my duty not
to kill the rhino. But I would have to if he or she
charged and there was no way out. I planned to
shoot the first barrel into the ground to turn the
rhino. If it did not turn I would kill it with the
second barrel. Thank you very much I said to
myself. It is easy.

Just then I heard the motor of the hunting car
start and heard the car coming fast in low gear. I
started to fall back figuring a yard was a yard
and feeling better with each yard gained. The
hunting car swung alongside in a tight turn and
I pushed the safety and jumped for the hand-
hold by the front seat as the rhino came smash-
ing out through the vines and creepers. It was
the big cow and she came galloping. From the

car she looked ridiculous with her small calf galloping behind her.

She gained on us for a moment but the car pulled away. There was a good open space ahead and Mthuka swung the car sharply to the left. The rhino went straight on galloping then slowed to a trot and the calf trotted too.

"Did you get any pictures?" I asked Miss Mary.

"I couldn't. She was right behind us."

"Didn't you get her when she came out?"

"No."

"I don't blame you."

"I picked out the Christmas tree though."

"You see why I wanted to cover you," I said unnecessarily and stupidly.

"You didn't know she was in there."

"She lives around here and she goes to the stream at the edge of the swamp for water."

"Everybody was so serious," Miss Mary said. "I never saw all of you joke people get so serious."

"Honey, it would have been awful if I had had to kill her. And I was worried about you."

"Everybody so serious," she said. "And everybody holding on to my arm. I knew how to get back to the car. Nobody had to hold on to my arm."

"Honey," I said, "they were only holding

your arm so that you wouldn't step in a hole or trip on something. They were watching the ground all the time. The rhino was very close and might charge anytime and we're not allowed to kill her."

"How did you know it was a female with a calf?"

"It stood to reason. She's been around here for four months."

"I wish she wasn't right in the place where the Christmas trees grow."

"We'll get the tree all right."

"You always promise things," she said. "But things are much simpler and better when Mr. P. is here."

"They certainly are," I said. "And they are much easier when G.C. is here. But there is nobody here but us now and please let's not fight in Africa. Please not."

"I don't want to fight," she said. "I'm not fighting. I simply don't like to see all you private joke people get so serious and so righteous."

"Have you ever seen anybody killed by a rhino?"

"No," she said. "And neither have you."

"That's right," I said. "And I don't intend to. Pop's never seen it either."

"I didn't like it when you all got so serious."

"It was because I couldn't kill the rhino. If

you can kill it there's no problem. Then I had to think about you."

"Well, stop thinking about me," she said. "Think about us getting the Christmas tree."

I was beginning to feel somewhat righteous and I wished that Pop was with us to make a diversion. But Pop was not with us anymore.

"We are going back through the gerenuk country at least aren't we?"

"Yes," I said. "We turn to the right at those big stones up ahead across the mud flat at the edge of the high tree bush those baboons are crossing into now and we proceed across the flat to the east until we come to that other rhino drop. Then we go southeast to the old Manyatta and we are in the gerenuk country."

"It will be nice to be there," she said. "But I certainly miss Pop."

"So do I," I said.

There are always mystical countries that are a part of one's childhood. Those we remember and visit sometimes when we are asleep and dreaming. They are as lovely at night as they were when we were children. If you ever go back to see them they are not there. But they are as fine in the night as they ever were if you have the luck to dream of them.

In Africa when we lived on the small plain in the shade of the big thorn trees near the river at the edge of the swamp at the foot of the great mountain we had such countries. We were no longer, technically, children although in many ways I am quite sure that we were. Childish has become a term of contempt.

"Don't be childish, darling."

"I hope to Christ I am. Don't be childish yourself."

It is possible to be grateful that no one that you would willingly associate with would say, "Be mature. Be well-balanced, be well-adjusted."

Africa, being as old as it is, makes all people except the professional invaders and spoilers into children. No one says to anyone in Africa, "Why don't you grow up?" All men and animals acquire a year more of age each year and some acquire a year more of knowledge. The animals that die the soonest learn the fastest. A young gazelle is mature, well-balanced and well-adjusted at the age of two years. He is well-balanced and well-adjusted at the age of four weeks. Men know that they are children in relation to the country and, as in armies, seniority and senility ride close together. But to have the heart of a child is not a disgrace. It is an honor. A man must comport himself as a man. He must fight always preferably and soundly with the odds in his favor but on necessity against any sort of odds and with no thought of the outcome. He should follow his tribal laws and customs insofar as he can and accept the tribal discipline when he cannot. But it is never a reproach that he has kept a child's heart, a child's honesty and a child's freshness and nobility.

No one knew why Mary needed to kill a gerenuk. They were a strange long-necked gazelle and the bucks had heavy short curved horns set far forward on their heads. They were excellent to eat in this particular country. But Tommy and impala were better to eat. The boys thought that it had something to do with Mary's religion.

Everyone understood why Mary must kill her lion. It was hard for some of the elders who had been on many hundreds of safaris to understand why she must kill it in the old straight way. But all of the bad element were sure it had something to do with her religion like the necessity to kill the gerenuk at approximately high noon. It evidently meant nothing to Miss Mary to kill the gerenuk in an ordinary and simple way.

At the end of the morning's hunt, or patrol, the gerenuk would be in the thick bush. If we sighted any by unlucky chance Mary and Charo would get out of the car and make their stalk. The gerenuk would sneak, run or bound away.

Ngui and I would follow the two stalkers from duty and our presence would ensure the gerenuk would keep on moving. Finally it would be too hot to keep on moving the gerenuk about and Charo and Mary would come back to the car. As far as I know no shot was ever fired in this type of gerenuk hunting.

"Damn those gerenuk," Mary said. "I saw the buck looking directly at me. But all I could see was his face and his horns. Then he was behind another bush and I couldn't tell he was not a doe. Then he kept moving off out of sight. I could have shot him but I might have wounded him."

"You'll get him another day. I thought you hunted him very well."

"If you and your friend didn't have to come."

"We have to, honey."

"I'm sick of it. Now I suppose you all want to go to the Shamba."

"No. I think we'll cut straight home to camp and have a cool drink."

"I don't know why I like this crazy part of the country," she said. "I don't have anything against the gerenuk either."

"It's sort of an island of desert here. It's like the big desert we have to cross to get here. Any desert is fine."

"I wish I could shoot well and fast and as

quick as I see to shoot. I wish I wasn't short. I couldn't see the lion that time when you could see him and everybody else could see him."

"He was in an awful place."

"I know where he was and it wasn't so far from here either."

"No," I said and to the driver, "Kwenda na campi."

"Thank you for not going to the Shamba," Mary said. "You're good about the Shamba sometimes."

"You're who is good about it."

"No, I'm not. I like you to go there and I like you to learn everything you should learn."

"I'm not going there now until they send for me about something."

"They'll send for you all right," she said. "Don't worry about that."

When we did not go to the Shamba the drive back to camp was very beautiful. There was one long open glade after another. They were linked together like lakes and the green trees and the brush made their shores. There were always the square white rumps of the Grant's gazelle and their brown-and-white bodies as they trotted, the does moving fast and lightly and the bucks with their proud heavy horns swung back. Then we would round a long curve of green bushy trees and there would be the green tents of the camp with the yellow trees and the Mountain behind them.

This was the first day we had been alone in this camp and as I sat under the flap of the dining tent in the shade of a big tree and waited for Mary to come from washing up so we could have our drink together before lunch I hoped that there would be no problems and that it would be an easy day. Bad news came in quickly enough but I had seen no harbingers waiting around the cooking fires. The wood truck was still out. They would be bringing water too and when they came in they would probably bring news of the Shamba. I had washed and changed my shirt and changed into shorts and a pair of moccasins and felt cool and comfortable in the shade.

The rear of the tent was open and a breeze blew through off the Mountain that was cool with the freshness of the snow.

Mary came into the tent and said, "Why, you haven't had a drink. I'll make one for us both."

She was fresh looking in her freshly ironed, faded safari slacks and shirt and beautiful and as she poured the Campari and gin into the tall glasses and looked for a cold siphon in the canvas water bucket she said, "I'm so glad we're alone really. It will be just like Magadi but nicer." She made the drinks and gave me mine and we touched glasses. "I love Mr. Percival so much and I love to have him. But with you and me alone it's wonderful. I won't be bad about you taking care of me and I won't be irascible. I'll do everything but like the Informer."

"You're awfully good," I said. "We always do have the most fun alone together too. But you be patient with me when I'm stupid."

"You're not stupid and we're going to have a lovely time. This is so much nicer a place than Magadi and we live here and have it all to our own. It is going to be lovely. You'll see."

There was a cough outside the tent. I recognized it and thought something that I had better not write down.

"All right," I said. "Come in." It was the Game Department Informer. He was a tall dignified man who wore full-length trousers, a clean dark blue sport shirt with thin white lateral strips, a shawl around his shoulders and a porkpie hat. All of these articles of clothing looked as though they had been gifts. The shawl I had recognized as being made from trade goods sold in one of the Hindu general stores at Laitokitok. His dark brown face was distinguished and must once have been handsome. He spoke accurate English slowly and with a mixture of accents.

"Sir," he said, "I am happy to report that I have captured a murderer."

"What kind of a murderer?"

"A Masai murderer. He is badly wounded and his father and uncle are with him."

"Who did he murder?"

"His cousin. Don't you remember? You dressed his wounds."

"That man's not dead. He's in the hospital."

"Then he is only an attempted murderer. But I captured him. You will mention it in your report, brother, I know. Please, sir, the attempted murderer is feeling very badly and he would like you to dress his wounds."

"OK," I said. "I'll go out and see him. I'm sorry, honey."

"It doesn't matter," Mary said. "It doesn't matter at all."

"May I have a drink, brother?" the Informer asked. "I am tired from the struggle."

"Bullshit," I said. "I'm sorry, honey."

"It's all right," Miss Mary said. "I don't know any better word for it."

"I did not mean an alcoholic drink," the Informer said nobly. "I meant only a sip of water."

"We'll get some," I said.

The attempted murderer, his father and his uncle all looked very depressed. I greeted them and we all shook hands. The attempted murderer was a young moran, or warrior, and he and another moran had been playing together making mock fighting with their spears. It had

not been about anything, his father explained.
They were only playing and he had wounded
the other young man accidentally. His friend
had thrust back at him and he had received a
wound. Then they had lost their heads and
fought but never seriously; never to kill. But
when he saw his friend's wounds he was frightened that he might have killed him and had
gone off into the brush and hidden. Now he had
come back with his father and his uncle and he
wished to surrender. The father explained all
this and the boy nodded his assent.

I told the father through the interpreter that
the other boy was in the hospital and was doing
well and that I had heard neither he nor his
male relatives had made any charges against this
boy. The father said he had heard the same
thing.

The medical chest had been brought from the
dining tent and I dressed the boy's wounds.
They were in the neck, the chest and the upper
arm and back and were all suppurating badly. I
cleaned them out, poured peroxide into them
for the magic bubbling effect and to kill any
grubs, cleaned them again, especially the neck
wound, painted the edges with Mercurochrome,
which gave a much admired and serious color
effect, and then sifted them full of sulfa and put
a gauze dressing and plaster across each wound.

Through the Informer, who was acting as

interpreter, I told the elders that as far as I was concerned it was better for the young men to exercise at the use of their spears than to drink Golden Jeep sherry in Laitokitok. But that I was not the law and the father must take his son and present him to the police in that village. He should also have the wounds checked there and should be given penicillin.

After receiving this message the two elders spoke together and then to me and I grunted knowingly throughout their speech with that peculiar rising inflection grunt that means you are giving the matter your deepest attention.

"They say, sir, that they wish you to give a judgment on the case and they will abide by your judgment. They say all that they say is true and that you have already spoken with the other Mzees."

"Tell them that they must present the warrior to the police. It is possible that the police will do nothing since no complaint has been made. They must go to the Police Boma and the wound must be checked and the boy receive penicillin. It must be done."

I shook hands with the two elders and with the young warrior. He was a good-looking boy, thin and very straight but he was tired and his wounds hurt him although he had never flinched when they were cleaned out.

The Informer followed me to the front of our sleeping tent where I washed up carefully with blue soap. "Listen," I said to him. "I want you to tell the police exactly what I said and what the Mzee said to me. If you try anything fancy you know what will happen."

"How can my brother think I would not be faithful and do my duty? How can my brother doubt me? Will my brother loan me ten shillings? I will pay it back the first of the month."

"Ten shillings will never get you out of the trouble you are in."

"I know it. But it is ten shillings."

"Here is ten."

"Do you not want to send any presents to the Shamba?"

"I will do that myself."

"You are quite right, brother. You are always right and doubly generous."

"Bullshit to you. Go along now and wait with the Masai to go in the truck. I hope you find the Widow and don't get drunk."

I went in the tent and Mary was waiting. She was reading the last *New Yorker* and was sipping at her gin and Campari.

"Was he badly hurt?"

"No. But the wounds were infected. One pretty badly."

"I don't wonder after being in the Manyatta that day. The flies were really something awful."

"They say the fly blows keep a wound clean," I said. "But the maggots always give me the creeps. I think while they keep it clean they enlarge the wound greatly. This kid has one in the neck that can't stand much enlarging."

"The other boy was hurt worse though, wasn't he?"

"Yes. But he had prompt treatment."

"You're getting quite a lot of practice as an amateur doctor. Do you think you can cure yourself?"

"Of what?"

"Of whatever you get sometimes. I don't mean just physical things."

"Like what?"

"I couldn't help hearing you and that Informer talking about the Shamba. I wasn't overhearing. But you were right outside the tent and because he is a little deaf you talk a little loud."

"I'm sorry," I said. "Did I say anything bad?"

"No. Just about presents. Do you send her many presents?"

"No. Mafuta always for the family and sugar and things they need. Medicines and soap. I buy her good chocolate."

"The same as you buy me."

"I don't know. Probably. There's only about three kinds and they are all good."

"Don't you give her any big presents?"

"No. The dress."

"It's a pretty dress."

"Do we have to do this, honey?"

"No," she said. "I'll stop it. But it interests me."

"If you say so I'll never see her."

"I don't want that," she said. "I think it's wonderful that you have a girl that can't read nor write so you can't get letters from her. I think it's wonderful that she doesn't know that you are a writer or even that there are such things as writers. But you don't love her do you?"

"I like her because she has such a lovely impudence."

"I have too," Miss Mary said. "Maybe you like her because she's like me. It could be possible."

"I like you more and I love you."

"What does she think of me?"

"She respects you very much and she is very much afraid of you."

"Why?"

"I asked her. She said because you have a gun."

"So I have," said Miss Mary. "What does she give you for presents?"

"Mealies, mostly. Ceremonial beer. You know everything is based on exchanges of beer."

"What do you have in common, really?"

"Africa, I guess, and a sort of not too simple trust and something else. It's hard to say it."

"You're sort of nice together," she said. "I think I'd better call for lunch. Do you eat better here or there?"

"Here. Much better."

"But you eat better than here up at Mr. Singh's in Laitokitok."

"Much better. But you're never there. You're always busy."

"I have my friends there too. But I like to come into the back room and see you sitting there happily with Mr. Singh eating in the back room and reading the paper and listening to the sawmill."

I loved it at Mr. Singh's too and I was fond of all the Singh children and of Mrs. Singh, who was said to be a Turkana woman. She was beautiful and very kind and understanding and extremely clean and neat. Arap Meina, who was my closest friend and associate after Ngui and Mthuka, was a great admirer of Mrs. Singh. He had reached the age when his principal enjoyment of women was in looking at them and he told me many times that Mrs. Singh was probably the most beautiful woman in the world after Miss Mary. Arap Meina, who for many months I had called Arab Minor by mistake thinking it was an English public school type name, was a Lumbwa, which is a tribe related to the Masai, or perhaps a branch tribe of the Masai, and they are great hunters and poachers. Arap Meina was said to have been a very successful ivory poacher, or at least a widely traveled and little arrested ivory poacher, before he had become a Game Scout. Neither he, nor I, had any idea of his age but it was probably between sixty-five and seventy. He was a very brave and skillful elephant hunter and when G.C. his commanding officer was away he did the elephant control in this district. Everyone loved him very much and when he was sober, or unusually drunk, he had an extremely sharp military bearing. I have rarely been saluted with such violence as Arap Meina could put into a salute when he would announce that he loved both Miss Mary and myself and no one else and too much for him to stand it. But before he had reached this state of alcoholic consumption with its attendant declarations of undying heterosexual devotion he used to like to sit with me in the back room of Mr. Singh's bar and look at Mrs. Singh waiting

on the customers and going about her household duties. He preferred to observe Mrs. Singh
in profile and I was quite happy observing Arap
Meina observing Mrs. Singh and with studying
the oleographs and paintings on the wall of the
original Singh, who was usually depicted in the
act of strangling a lion and a lioness; one in
either hand.

If there was anything we needed to make
absolutely clear with Mr. or Mrs. Singh or if I
had any formal talks with local Masai elders we
would use a Mission-educated boy who would
stand in the doorway to interpret, holding a
bottle of Coca-Cola prominently in his hand.
Usually I tried to use the services of the Mission
boy as little as possible since he was officially
saved and contact with our group could only
corrupt him. Arap Meina was allegedly a
Mohammedan, but I had long ago noticed that
our devout Mohammedans would eat nothing
that he, Arap Meina, halaled; that is, made the
ceremonial throat cut that made the meat legal
to eat if the cut was made by a practicing
Moslem.

Arap Meina, one time when he had drunk
quite a lot, told several people that he and I had
been to Mecca together in the old days. The
devout Mohammedans knew this was not true.
Charo had wished to convert me to Islam some

twenty years before and I had gone all through Ramadan with him observing the fast. He had given me up as a possible convert many years ago. But nobody knew whether I had actually ever been to Mecca except myself. The Informer, who believed the best and worst of everyone, was convinced that I had been to Mecca many times. Willie, a half-caste driver who I had hired on his story that he was the son of a very famous old gun bearer who, I found, had not sired him, told everyone in strictest confidence that we were going to Mecca together.

Finally I had been cornered by Ngui in a theological argument and while he did not ask the question direct I told him for his own information that I had never been to Mecca and had no intention of going. This relieved him greatly.

Mary had gone to take a nap in the tent and I sat in the shade of the dining tent and read and thought about the Shamba and Laitokitok. I knew I mustn't think about the Shamba too much or I would find some excuse to go there. Debba and I never spoke to each other in front of the others except for me to say "Jambo, tu," and she would bow her head very gravely if there were others than Ngui and Mthuka present. If there were just the three of us she would laugh and they would laugh too and then the others would stay in the car or walk in another direction and she and I would walk a little way together. The thing she liked best about public society was to ride in the front seat of the hunting car between Mthuka, who was driving, and me. She would always sit very straight and look at everyone else as though she had never seen them before. Sometimes she would bow politely to her father and her mother but sometimes she would not see them. Her dress, which we had bought in Laitokitok, was pretty well worn out now in the front by sitting so straight and the color was not resisting the daily washing she gave it.

We had agreed about a new dress. This was to be for Christmas or when we got the leopard. There were various leopards but this was one which had a special importance. He, for reasons, was as important to me as the dress was to her.

"With another dress I would not have to wash this one so much," she had explained.

"You wash it so much because you like to play with soap," I told her.

"Perhaps," she said. "But when can we go to Laitokitok together?"

"Soon."

"Soon is no good," she said.

"It's all I have."

"When will you come to drink beer in the evening?"

"Soon."

"I hate soon. You and soon are lying brothers."

"Then neither of us will come."

"You come and bring soon too."

"I will."

When we rode together in the front seat she liked to feel the embossing on the old leather holster of my pistol. It was a flowered design and very old and worn and she would trace the design very carefully with her fingers and then take her hand away and press the pistol and its holster close against her thigh. Then she would sit up straighter than ever. I would stroke one finger very lightly across her lips and she would laugh and Mthuka would say something in Kamba and she would sit very straight and press her thigh hard against the holster. A long time after this had first started I found that what she wanted, then, was to impress the carving of the holster into her thigh.

At first I only spoke to her in Spanish. She learned it very quickly and it is simple if you start with the parts of the body and the things one can do and then food and the different relationships and the names of animals and of birds. I never spoke a word of English to her and we retained some Swahili words but the rest was a new language made up of Spanish and Kamba. Messages were brought by the

Informer. Neither she nor I liked this because the Informer felt it his duty to tell me exactly her feelings in regard to me, which he learned at second hand from her mother the Widow. This third-party communication was difficult, sometimes embarrassing but often interesting and, at times, rewarding.

The Informer would say, "Brother, it is my duty to inform you that your girl loves you very much, truly very much, too much. When can you see her?"

"Tell her not to love an ugly old man and not to confide in you."

"I am serious, brother. You do not know. She wishes you to marry her by your tribe or by hers. There are no costs. There is no wife price. She wishes only one thing, to be a wife if Memsahib, my lady, will accept her. She understands that Memsahib is the principal wife. She is also afraid of Memsahib as you know. You do not know how serious this is. All of it."

"I have a faint idea," I said.

"Since yesterday you cannot conceive how things have been. She asks me only that you will show a certain politeness and formality to her father and her mother. The case has been reduced to that. There is no question of payment. Only of a certain formality. There are certain ceremonial beers."

"She should not care for a man of my age and habits."

"Brother, the case is that she cares. I could tell you many things. This is a serious thing."

"What can she care for?" I said, making a mistake.

"Yesterday there was the matter of you catching the roosters of the village and then putting them to sleep by some form of magic and laying them asleep in front of her family's lodge. [Neither of us could say hut.] This has never been seen and I do not ask you what magic was employed. But she says you sprung at them with a movement that could not be seen almost like a leopard. Since then she has not been the same. Then she has on the walls of the lodge the pictures from *Life* magazine of the great beasts of America and of the washing machine, the cooking machines and miraculous ranges and the stirring machines."

"I am sorry about that. It was a mistake."

"It is because of that she washes her dress so much. She is trying to be like the washing machine to please you. She is afraid that you will become lonely for the washing machine and go away. Brother, sir, there is tragedy. Can you do nothing positive for her?"

"I will do what I can," I said. "But remember that putting the roosters to sleep was not magic. It is a trick. Catching them is only a trick too."

"Brother, she loves you very much."

"Tell her there is no such word as love. Just as there is no word for sorry."

"That is true. But there is the thing although there is no word for it."

"You and I are the same age. It is not necessary to explain so much."

"I tell you this only because it is serious."

"I cannot break the law if we are here to enforce the law."

"Brother, you do not understand. There is no law. This Shamba is here illegally. It is not in Kamba country. For thirty-five years it has been ordered removed and it has never happened. There is not even customary law. There are only variations."

"Go on," I said.

"Thank you, brother. Let me tell you that for the people of this Shamba you and Bwana Game are the law. You are a bigger law than Bwana Game because you are older. Also he is away and his askaris are with him. Here you have your young men and warriors such as Ngui. You have Arap Meina. Everyone knows you are Arap Meina's father."

"I'm not."

"Brother, please try not to misunderstand me.

You know the sense in which I say father. Arap Meina says you are his father. Also you brought him to life after he died in the airplane. You brought him back to life after he lay dead in Bwana Mouse's tent. It is known. Many things are known."

"Too many things are improperly known."

"Brother, may I have a drink?"

"If I do not see you take it."

"Chin chin," the Informer said. He had taken the Canadian gin instead of the Gordon's and my heart went out to him. "You must forgive me," he said. "I have lived all my life with the Bwanas. May I tell you more or are you tired of the subject?"

"I am tired of part of it, but other parts interest me. Tell me more about the history of the Shamba."

"I do not know it exactly because they are Kamba and I am Masai. That shows there is something wrong with the Shamba or I would not be living there. There is something wrong with the men. You have seen them. For some reason they came here originally. This is a long way from Kamba country. Neither true tribal law nor any other law runs here. You have also seen the condition of the Masai."

"We have to talk about that another day."

"Willingly, brother, things are not well. It is a

long story. But let me tell you about the Shamba. Why you went there in the early morning and spoke through me about the all-night Ngoma of the great drunkenness with such severity, the people say afterwards that they could see the gallows in your eyes. The man who was still so drunk that he couldn't understand was taken to the river and washed in the water from the Mountain until he understood and he entered the neighboring province the same day climbing the Mountain on foot. You do not know what serious law you are."

"It is a small Shamba. But very beautiful. Who sold them the sugar for the beer of that Ngoma?"

"I do not know. But I could find out."

"I know," I said and told him. I knew that he knew. But he was an informer and he had lost out in life long ago and it was the Bwanas who had ruined him although he gave full credit for that process to a Somali wife. But it was a Bwana, a great Lord, who was the greatest friend the Masai ever had but who liked, he said, to do things backwards who, if what he said was true, had ruined him. No one knows how much is true that an informer says but his description of this great man had been done with such a mixture of admiration and remorse that it seemed to explain many things that I had never understood. I had never heard of any backward tendency on the part of this great man until I came to know the Informer. I always expressed disbelief at some of these surprising tales.

"You will hear, of course," the Informer said to me now that his zeal for informing had been heightened by the Canadian gin, "that I am an agent of the Mau Mau and you may believe it because I have said such things about this backwardness. But, brother, it is not true. I truly love and believe in the Bwanas. True all but one or two of the great Bwanas are dead and I should have led a far different life," the Informer said. "Thinking of these great dead Bwanas fills me with the resolution to lead a better and finer life. It is permitted?"

"The last one," I said. "And only as a medicine."

At the word medicine, the Informer brightened. He had a very nice and rather noble large face covered with the lines and wrinkles of good temper and uncomplaining dissipation and debauchery. It was not an ascetic face nor was there any depravity in it. It was the face of a dignified man who, being a Masai and ruined by the Bwanas and by a Somali wife, now lived in an outlaw Kamba village with the status of protector of a Widow and earned eighty-six shillings a month betraying anyone betrayable. Yet it was a handsome face, ravaged and cheerful, and I was very fond of the Informer although I disapproved of him completely and had several times told him that it might be my duty to see him hanged.

"Brother," he said. "There must be those medicines. How would the great doctor with the Dutch name have written about them in such a serious review as the *Reader's Digest* if they did not exist?"

"They exist," I said. "But I do not have them. I can send them to you."

"Brother, only one thing more. The girl is a very serious thing."

"If you ever say that again I will know you are a fool. Like all people when they drink you repeat yourself."

"I will excuse myself."

"Go, brother. I will try, truly, to send you the medicine and other good medicines. When I see you next be prepared to bring me more of the history of the Shamba."

"Do you have any messages?"

"No messages."

It always shocked me to realize that the Informer and I were the same age. We were not exactly the same age but were of the same age group, which was near enough and bad enough.

And here I was with a wife that I loved and who loved me and tolerated my errors and referred to this girl as my fiancée, tolerating because I was in some ways a good husband and for other reasons of generosity and kindness and detachment and wanting me to know more about this country than I had any right to know. We were happy at least a good part of each day and nearly always at night and this night, in bed together, under the mosquito netting with the flaps of the tent open so that we could see the long burned-through logs of the big fire and the wonderful darkness that receded jaggedly as the night wind struck the fire and then closed in quickly as the wind dropped, we were very happy.

"We're too lucky," Mary said. "I love Africa so. I don't know how we can ever leave it."

It was a cold night with the breeze off the snows of the Mountain and we were snug under the blankets. The night noises were starting and we had heard the first hyena and then the others. Mary loved to hear them at night. They make a pleasant noise if you love Africa and we laughed together as they moved around the camp and out past the cook's tent where the meat was hung in a tree. They could not reach the meat but they kept talking about it.

"You know if you are ever dead and I'm not

lucky so we die together, if anyone asks me what I remember best about you I'll tell them about how much room you could give your wife in a canvas cot. Where do you put yourself, really?"

"Sort of sideways on the edge. I've lots of room."

"We can sleep comfortably in a bed one person couldn't be comfortable in if it's cold enough."

"That's the thing. It has to be cold."

"Can we stay longer in Africa and not go home until spring?"

"Sure. Let's stay until we're broke."

Then we heard the thud of a lion's cough as he came hunting across the long meadow up from the river.

"Listen," Mary said. "Hold me close and tight and listen.

"He's come back," Mary whispered.

"You can't tell it's him."

"I'm sure it is him," Mary said. "I've heard him enough nights. He's come down from the Manyatta where he killed the two cows. Arap Meina said he would come back."

We could hear his coughing grunt as he moved across the meadow toward where we had made the airstrip for the small plane.

"We'll know if it's him in the morning," I said. "Ngui and I know his tracks."

"So do I."

"OK, you track him."

"No. I only meant that I do know his tracks."

"They're awfully big." I was sleepy and I thought if we are going to hunt lion with Miss Mary in the morning I should get some sleep. For a long time we had known, in some things, what the other one of us was going to say or, often, to think and Mary said, "I'd better get in my own bed so you'll be comfortable and sleep well."

"Go to sleep here. I'm fine."

"No. It wouldn't be good."

"Sleep here."

"No. Before a lion I ought to sleep in my own bed."

"Don't be such a bloody warrior."

"I am a warrior. I'm your wife and your love and your small warrior brother."

"All right," I said. "Good night, warrior brother."

"Kiss your warrior brother."

"You get in your own bed or stay here."

"Maybe I'll do both," she said.

In the night I heard a lion speak several times as he was hunting. Miss Mary was sleeping soundly and breathing softly. I lay awake and thought about too many things but mostly about the lion and my obligation to Pop and to

Bwana Game and to others. I did not think about Miss Mary except about her height, which was five feet two inches, in relation to tall grass and bush and that, no matter how cold the morning was, she must not wear too much clothing as the stock on the 6.5 Mannlicher was too long for her if her shoulder was padded and she might let the rifle off as she raised it to shoot. I lay awake thinking about this and about the lion and the way Pop would handle it and how wrong he had been the last time and how right he had been more times than I had ever seen a lion.

2

BEFORE IT WAS daylight when the coals of the fire were covered by the gray ashes that sifted in the early morning breeze I put on my high soft boots and an old dressing gown and went to wake Ngui in his pup tent.

He woke sullen and not at all my blood brother and I remembered that he never smiled before the sun was up and sometimes it took him longer to get rid of wherever he had been when he was asleep.

We talked at the dead ashes of the cook fire.

"You heard the lion?"

"Ndio, Bwana."

This, a politeness, was also a rudeness as we both knew for we had discussed the phrase, "Ndio, Bwana," which is what the African says always to the White Man to get rid of him through agreement.

"How many lions did you hear?"

"One."

"Mzuri," I said, meaning that was better and he was correct and had heard the lion. He spat and took snuff and then offered it to me and I took some and put it under my upper lip.

"Was it the big lion of Memsahib?" I asked, feeling the lovely quick bite of the snuff against the gums and the pocket of the upper lip.

"Hapana," he said. This was the absolute negative.

Keiti was standing by the cooking fire now with his slashed flat doubting smile. He had wound his turban in the dark and there was an end that should have been tucked in. His eyes were doubting too. There was nothing of the feeling of a serious lion hunt.

"Hapana simba kubwa sana," Keiti said to me, his eyes mocking but apologetic and absolutely confident. He knew it was not the big lion that we had heard so many times. "Nanyake," he said to make an early morning joke. This meant, in Kamba, a lion old enough to be a warrior and marry and have children but not old enough to drink beer. His saying it and making the joke in Kamba was a sign of friend-liness, made at daylight when friendliness has a low boiling point, to show, gently, that he knew I was trying to learn Kamba with the non-Moslem and alleged bad element and that he approved or tolerated.

I had functioned on this lion business almost as long as I could remember anything that had happened. In Africa you could remember around a month at a time if the pace was fast. The pace had been almost excessive and there had been the allegedly criminal lions of Salengai, the lions of Magadi, the lions of here, against whom allegations had now been repeated four times and this new intruding lion who had, as yet, no fiche nor dossier. This was a lion who had coughed a few times and gone about hunting the game that he was entitled to. But it was necessary to prove that to Miss Mary and to prove that he was not the lion she had hunted for so long who was charged with many offenses and whose huge pug marks, the left hind one scarred, we had followed so many times only finally to see him going away into tall grass that led to the heavy timber of the swamp or to the thick bush of the gerenuk country up by the old Manyatta on the way to the Chulu hills. He was so dark with his heavy black mane he looked almost black and he had a huge head that swung low when he moved off into country where it was impossible for Mary to follow him. He had been hunted for many years and he was very definitely not a picture lion.

Now I was dressed drinking tea in the early morning light by the built-up fire and waiting for Ngui. I saw him coming across the field with the spear on his shoulder stepping out smartly through the grass still wet with dew. He saw me and came toward the fire leaving a trail behind him through the wet grass.

"Simba dumi kidogo," he said, telling me he was a small male lion. "Nanyake," he said, making the same joke Keiti had made. "Hapana mzuri for Memsahib."

"Thank you," I said. "I'll let Memsahib sleep."

"Mzuri," he said and went off to the cooking fire.

Arap Meina would be in with the report on the big black-maned lion who had been reported by the Masai from a Manyatta up in the Western Hills to have killed two cows and dragged one away with him. The Masai had suffered under him for a long time. He traveled restlessly and he did not return to his kills as a lion would be expected to. Arap Meina had the theory that this lion had once returned and fed on a kill that had been poisoned by a former Game Ranger and that he had been made terribly sick by it and had learned, or decided, never to return to a kill. That would account for his moving about so much, but not for the haphazard way he visited the various Masai villages or Manyattas. Now the plain, the salt licks and the bush country were heavy with game since the good grass had come with the violent spot rains of November and Arap Meina, Ngui and I all expected the big lion to leave the hills and come down to the plain where he could hunt out of the edge of the swamp. This was his customary way of hunting in this district.

The Masai can be very sarcastic and their cattle are not only their wealth but something much more to them and the Informer had told me that one chief had spoken very badly about the fact that I had two chances to kill this lion and instead had waited to let a woman do it. I had sent word to the chief that if his young men were not women who spent all their time in Laitokitok drinking Golden Jeep sherry he would have no need to ask for me to kill his lion but that I would see he was killed the next time he came into the area where we were. If he cared to bring his young men I would take a spear with them and we would kill him that way. I asked him to come into camp and we would talk it over.

He had turned up at camp one morning with three other elders and I had sent for the Informer to interpret. We had a good talk. The chief explained that the Informer had misquoted him. Bwana Game, G.C., had always killed the lions that it was necessary to kill and was a very brave and skillful man and they had great confidence in him and affection for him. He remembered too that when we had been here last in the time of the dryness Bwana Game had killed a lion and Bwana Game and I had killed a lioness with the young men. This lioness had done much damage.

I answered that these facts were known and that it was the duty of Bwana Game, and for this time myself, to kill any lions that molested cattle, donkeys, sheep, goats or people. This we would always do. It was necessary for the religion of the Memsahib that she kill this particular lion before the Birthday of the Baby Jesus. We came from a far country and were of a tribe of that country and this was necessary. They would be shown the skin of this lion before the Birthday of the Baby Jesus.

As always I was a little appalled by my oratory after it was over and had the usual sinking feeling about commitments made. Miss Mary must, I thought, belong to a fairly warlike tribe if she, a woman, had to kill a longtime marauding lion before the Birthday of the Baby Jesus. But at least I had not said she had to do it every year. Keiti took the Birthday of the Baby Jesus very seriously since he had been on so many safaris with churchgoing and even devout Bwanas. Most of these Bwanas since they were paying so much for their safari and since the time was short did not let the Birthday interfere with their shooting. But there was always a special dinner with wine and, if possible, champagne, and it was always a special occasion. This year it was even more special since we were in a permanent camp and with Miss Mary taking it so seriously and it being so obviously such an important part of her religion and attended by so many ceremonials, especially that of the tree, that Keiti, loving order and ceremony, gave it a great importance. The ceremony of the tree appealed to him since in his old religion, before he had become a Moslem, a grove of trees had been of the highest importance.

The rougher pagan element of the camp thought that Miss Mary's tribal religion was one of the sterner branches of religion since it involved the slaying of a gerenuk under impossible conditions, the slaughter of a bad lion and the worship of a tree which fortunately Miss Mary did not know produced the concoction which excited and maddened the Masai for war and lion hunting. I am not sure that Keiti knew this was one of the properties of the particular Christmas tree that Miss Mary had selected but about five of us knew it and it was a very carefully kept secret.

They did not believe that the lion was a part of Miss Mary's Christmas duty because they had been with her while she had sought a big lion now for several months. But Ngui had put forth a theory that perhaps Miss Mary had to kill a large black-maned lion in the year sometime before Christmas and being too short to see in the high grass she had started early. She had started in September to kill the lion before the end of the year or whenever the Birthday of the Baby Jesus was. Ngui was not sure. But it came before that other great holiday the Birth of the Year which was a payday.

Charo did not believe any of this because he had seen too many Memsahibs shoot too many lions. But he was unsteadied because nobody helped Miss Mary. He had seen me help Miss Pauline years before and he was puzzled by the whole thing. He had been very fond of Miss Pauline but nothing to what he felt for Miss Mary, who was obviously a wife from another tribe. Her tribal scars showed it. They were very fine delicately cut scars across one cheek and horizontal light traces of cuts on the forehead. They were the work of the best plastic surgeon in Cuba after a motor car accident and nobody could see them who did not know how to look for almost invisible tribal scars as Ngui did.

Ngui had asked me one day very brusquely if Miss Mary was from the same tribe that I came from.

"No," I said. "She is from a Northern Frontier tribe in our country. From Minnesota."

"We have seen the tribal marks."

Then afterwards one time when we were talking tribes and religion he asked me if we were going to brew and drink the Baby Jesus birthday tree. I told him I did not think so and he said, "Mzuri."

"Why?"

"Gin for you. Beer for us. Nobody thinks Miss Mary should drink it unless her religion requires it."

"I know if she kills the lion she will not have to drink it."

"Mzuri," he said. "Mzuri sana."

Now on this morning I was waiting for Miss Mary to wake up of her own accord so she would be rested and have a good backlog of normal sleep behind her. I was not worried about the lion but I thought of him quite a lot and always in connection with Miss Mary.

There is as much difference between a wild lion and a marauding lion and the type of lion tourists take pictures of in the National Parks as there is between the old grizzly that will follow your trap line and ruin it and tear the roofs off your cabins and eat the supplies and yet never be seen and the bears that come up alongside the road to be photographed in Yellowstone

Park. True, the bears in the park injure people every year and if the tourists do not stay in their cars they will get in trouble. They even get in trouble in their cars sometimes and some bears get bad and have to be destroyed.

Picture lions that are accustomed to being fed and photographed sometimes wander away from the area where they are protected and having learned not to fear human beings are easily killed by alleged sportsmen and their wives always, of course, backed up by a professional hunter. But our problem was not to criticize how other people had killed lions or would kill lions but to find and have Miss Mary find and kill an intelligent, destructive and much hunted lion in a way that had been defined if not by our religion by certain ethical standards. Miss Mary had hunted by these standards for a long time now. They were very severe standards and Charo, who loved Miss Mary, was impatient of them. He had been mauled twice by leopards when things had gone wrong and he thought I was holding Mary to a standard of ethics which was too rigid and slightly murderous. But I had not invented them. I had learned them from Pop and Pop, on his last lion hunt and taking out his last safari, wanted things to be as they were in the old days before the hunting of dangerous game had been corrupted and made easy by what he always called "these bloody cars."

This lion had beaten us twice and both times I had easy chances at him which I had not taken because he was Mary's. The last time Pop had made a mistake because he was so anxious for Mary to get the lion before he had to leave us that he made an error, as anyone can who is trying too hard.

Afterwards we had sat by the fire in the evening, Pop smoking his pipe while Mary wrote in her diary where she put in all the things she did not wish to say to us and her heartaches and disappointments and her new knowledge that she did not wish to parade in conversation and her triumphs that she did not wish to tarnish by talking of them. She was writing by the gaslight in the dining tent and Pop and I were sitting by the fire in our pajamas, dressing gowns and mosquito boots.

"He's a damned smart lion," Pop said. "We should have had him today if Mary had been a little taller. But it was my fault."

We avoided talking of the error which we both knew about.

"Mary will get him. But keep this in mind. I don't think he's too brave, mind you. He's too smart. But when he's hit he'll be brave enough when the time comes. Don't you let the time come."

"I'm shooting all right now."

Pop ignored that. He was thinking. Then he

said, "Better than all right, actually. Don't get overconfident but stay as confident as you are. He'll make a mistake and you'll get him. If only some lioness would come into heat. Then he'd be money from home. But they're about ready to pup now."

"What sort of a mistake will he make?"

"Oh, he'll make one. You'll know. I wish I didn't have to go before Mary gets him. Take really good care of her. See she gets some sleep. She's been at this now for a long time. Rest her and rest the damn lion. Don't hunt him too hard. Let him get some confidence."

"Anything else?"

"Keep her shooting the meat and get her confident if you can."

"I thought of having her stalk until fifty yards and then maybe to twenty."

"Might work," said Pop. "We've tried everything else."

"I think it will work. Then she can take them longer."

"She makes the damnedest shots," Pop said. "Then for two days who knows where it's going?"

"I think I have it figured out."

"So did I. But don't take her to any twenty yards on lion."

It was more than twenty years before that

Pop and I had first sat together by a fire or the ashes of a fire and talked about the theory and practice of shooting dangerous game. He disliked and distrusted the target range or woodchuck hunter type.

"Hit a golf ball off the caddy's head at a mile," he said. "Wooden or steel caddy of course. Not a live caddy. Never miss until they have to shoot a really great kudu at twenty yards. Then couldn't hit the mountainside. Bloody gun waving around the great shooter shaking until I was shaking myself." He drew on his pipe. "Never trust any man until you've seen him shoot at something dangerous or that he wants really badly at fifty yards or under. Never buy him until you've seen him shoot at twenty. The short distance uncovers what's inside of them. The worthless ones will always miss or gut shoot at the range we get to so we can't miss."

I was thinking about this and happily about the old days and how fine this whole trip had been and how awful it would be if Pop and I would never be out together again when Arap Meina came up to the fire and saluted. He always saluted very solemnly but his smile started to come out as his hand came down.

"Good morning, Meina," I said.

"Jambo, Bwana. The big lion killed as they

said at the Manyatta. He dragged the cow a long way into thick brush. He did not return to the kill after he had eaten but went in the direction of the swamp for water."

"The lion with the scarred paw?"

"Yes, Bwana. He should come down now."

"Good. Is there other news?"

"They say that the Mau Mau who were imprisoned at Machakos have broken out of jail and are coming this way."

"When?"

"Yesterday."

"Who says?"

"A Masai I met on the road. He had ridden in the lorry of a Hindu trader. He did not know which duka."

"Get something to eat. I will need to speak to you later."

"Ndio, Bwana," he said and saluted. His rifle shone in the morning sunlight. He had changed to a fresh uniform at the Shamba and he looked very smart and he looked very pleased. He had two happy pieces of news. He was a hunter and now we would have hunting.

I thought I better go over to the tent and see if Miss Mary was awake. If she was still sleeping, all the better.

Miss Mary was awake but not all the way awake. If she had left a definite call to be wakened at a half past four or five she woke fast and efficiently and impatient with all delay. But this morning she woke slowly.

"What's the matter," she asked sleepily. "Why didn't anybody call me? The sun's up. What's the matter?"

"It wasn't the big lion, honey. So I let you sleep."

"How do you know it wasn't the big lion?"

"Ngui checked."

"What about the big lion?"

"He isn't down yet."

"How do you know that?"

"Arap Meina came in."

"Are you going out to check on the buff?"

"No. I'm going to leave everything alone. We've got a little trouble of some sort."

"Can I help you?"

"No, honey. You sleep some more."

"I think I will for a little while if you don't need me. I've been having the most wonderful dreams."

"See if you can get back into them. You call for chakula when you're ready."

"I'll sleep just a little more," she said. "They're really wonderful dreams."

I reached under my blanket and found my pistol on the belt with the sling strap hanging from the holster. I washed in the bowl, rinsed my eyes with boric acid solution, combed my hair with a towel, it was now clipped so short that neither brush nor comb were needed, and dressed and shoved my right foot through the leg strap on the pistol, pulled it up and buckled the pistol belt. In the old days we never carried pistols but now you put the pistol on as naturally as you buttoned the flap of your trousers. I carried two extra clips in a small plastic bag in the right-hand pocket of my bush jacket and carried the extra ammunition in a screw top, wide-mouth medicine bottle which had held liver capsules. This bottle had held fifty red-and-white capsules and now held sixty-five rounds of hollow points. Ngui carried one and I another.

Everyone loved the pistol because it could hit guinea fowl, lesser bustard, jackals, which carried rabies, and it could kill hyenas. Ngui and Mthuka loved it because it would make little sharp barks like a dog yapping and puffs of dust would appear ahead of the squat-running hyena then there would be the plunk, plunk, plunk, and the hyena would slow his gallop and start to circle. Ngui would hand me a full clip he had taken from my pocket and I would shove it in and then there would be another dust puff, then a plunk, plunk, and the hyena would roll over with his legs in the air.

I walked out to the lines to speak to Keiti

about the developments. I asked him to come where we could speak alone and he stood at ease looking old and wise and cynical and partly doubting and partly amused.

"I do not believe they would come here," he said. "They are Wakamba Mau Mau. They are not so stupid. They will hear that we are here."

"My only problem is if they come here. If they come here where will they go?"

"They will not come here."

"Why not?"

"I think what I would do if I were Mau Mau. I would not come here."

"But you are a Mzee and an intelligent man. These are Mau Mau."

"All Mau Mau are not stupid," he said. "And these are Wakamba."

"I agree," I said. "But these were all caught when they went to the Reserve as missionaries for Mau Mau. Why were they caught?"

"Because they got drunk and bragged how great they were."

"Yes. And if they come here where there is a Kamba Shamba they will want drink. They will need food and they will need more than anything drink if they are the same people who were taken prisoner from drinking."

"They will not be the same now. They have escaped from prison."

"They will go where there is drink."

"Probably. But they will not come here. They are Wakamba."

"I must take measures."

"Yes."

"I will let you know my decision. Is everything in order in the camp? Is there any sickness? Have you any problems?"

"Everything is in order. I have no problems. The camp is happy."

"What about meat?"

"We will need meat tonight."

"Wildebeest?"

He shook his head slowly and smiled the cleft smile.

"Many cannot eat it."

"How many can eat it?"

"Nine."

"What can the others eat?"

"Impala mzuri."

"There are too many impala here and I have two more," I said. "I will have the meat for tonight. But I wish it killed when the sun is going down so it will chill in the cold from the Mountain in the night. I wish the meat wrapped in cheesecloth so that the flies will not spoil it. We are guests here and I am responsible. We must waste nothing. How long would it take them to come from Machakos?"

"Three days. But they will not come here."

"Ask the cook please to make me breakfast."

I walked back to the dining tent and sat at the table and took a book from one of the improvised bookshelves made from empty wooden boxes. It was the year there were so many books about people who had escaped from prison camps in Germany and this book was an escape book. I put it back and drew another one. This was called *The Last Resorts,* and I thought it would be more diverting.

As I opened the book to the chapter on Bar Harbor I heard a motor car coming very fast and then looking out through the open back of the tent I saw it was the police Land Rover coming at full speed through the lines, raising a cloud of dust that blew over everything, including the laundry. The open motor car pulled up to a dirt track racing stop alongside the tent. The young police officer came in, saluted smartly and put out his hand. He was a tall fair boy with an unpromising face.

"Good morning, Bwana," he said and removed his uniform cap.

"Have some breakfast?"

"No time, Bwana."

"What's the matter?"

"The balloon's gone up, Bwana. We're for it now. Fourteen of them, Bwana. Fourteen of the most desperate type."

"Armed?"

"To the teeth, Bwana."

"These the lot that escaped from Machakos?"

"Yes. How did you hear about that?"

"Game Scout brought the word in this morning."

"Governor," he said, this was a fatherly term that he employed and had no relation to the title of one who governs a colony. "We must coordinate our effort again."

"I am at your service."

"How would you go about it, governor? The combined operation?"

"It's your shauri. I'm only acting Game here."

"Be a good chap, governor. Help a bloke out. You and Bwana Game helped me out before. In these times we must all play the game together. Play it up to the hilt."

"Quite," I said. "But I'm not a policeman."

"You're acting bloody Game though. We cooperate. What would you do, governor? I'll cooperate to the hilt."

"I'll make a screen," I said.

"Could I have a glass of beer?" he asked.

"Pour a bottle and I'll split it with you."

"My throat's dry from the dust."

"Next time don't get it all over our fucking laundry," I said.

"Sorry, governor. Couldn't be sorrier. But I was preoccupied with our problem and I thought it had rained."

"Day before yesterday. Dry now."

"Go ahead, governor. So you'll put out a screen."

"Yes," I said. "There's a Kamba Shamba here."

"I had no idea of that. Does the D.C. know?"

"Yes," I said. "There are, in all, four Shambas where beer is made."

"That's illegal."

"Yes, but you'll find they frequently do it in Africa. I propose to put a man in each of these Shambas. If any of these characters show up he'll let me know and I'll close in on the Shamba and we'll take them."

"Dead or alive," he said.

"You're sure about that?"

"Absolutely, governor. These are desperate types."

"We ought to check on it."

"No need, governor. Word of honor. But how will you get word from the Shamba to you here?"

"In anticipation of this type of thing we've organized a form of Women's Auxiliary Corps. They're frightfully efficient."

"Good show. I'm glad you laid that on. Is it widely extended?"

"Quite. Frightfully keen girl at the head of it. True underground type."

"Could I meet her sometime?"

"Be a bit tricky with you in uniform. I'll think about it though."

"Underground," he said. "I always thought it just my dish. The underground."

"Could be," I said. "We can get some old parachutes down and practice after this show is over."

"Can you gen it out just a little more, governor. We have the screen now. The screen sounds like the thing. But there's more."

"I keep the balance of my force here in hand but absolutely mobile to move on any sensitive parts of the screen. You go back to the Boma now and put yourself in a state of defense. Then I suggest that you lay on a roadblock in daylight on the turn of the road at about mile ten from here. Take it off on your speedometer. I suggest you move this roadblock at night down to where the road comes out of the swamp. Do you remember where we went after the baboons?"

"Never forget it, Bwana."

"There, if you have any trouble I will be in touch with you. Be awfully careful about shooting people up at night. There's a lot of traffic comes through there."

"There's supposed to be none."

"There is though. If I were you I would post three signs outside the three dukas that the curfew is to be enforced absolutely on the roads. It could save you some trouble."

"Can you give me any people, Bwana?"

"Not unless the situation deteriorates. Remember I'm screening for you. Tell you what I'll do. I'll send a chit by you that you can telephone through Ngong and I'll get the plane down. I need her for something else anyway."

"Right, Bwana. Would there be any chance I could fly with you?"

"I think not," I said. "You're needed on the ground."

I wrote the chit asking for the plane anytime after lunch tomorrow to bring mail and papers from Nairobi and put in two hours flying here.

"You'd better get along up to the Boma," I said. "And please, kid, never come into camp in that cowboy style. It puts the dust on the food, in the men's tents and on the laundry."

"Couldn't be sorrier, governor. It'll never happen again. And thanks for helping me staff things out."

"Maybe I'll see you in town this afternoon."

"Good show."

He drained his beer, saluted and went out and commenced to shout for his driver.

Mary came into the tent looking morning fresh and shining. "Wasn't that the boy from the police? What kind of trouble is it?"

I told her about the gang breaking out of the jail in Machakos and the rest of it. She was properly unimpressed.

As we ate breakfast she asked, "Don't you think it is awfully expensive to get the plane down now?"

"I have to have that mail from Nairobi and any cables. We need to check on the buff to get those pictures. They're definitely not in the swamp now. We ought to know what's going on toward the Chulus and I can make good use of her on this nonsense."

"I can't go back with her to Nairobi now to get the things for Christmas because I haven't got the lion."

"I've a hunch we are going to get the lion if we take it easy and rest him and rest you. Arap Meina said he was coming down this way."

"I don't need any rest," she said. "That's not fair to say."

"OK. I want to let him get confident and make a mistake."

"I wish he would."

About four o'clock I called for Ngui and when he came told him to get Charo and the rifles and a shotgun and tell Mthuka to bring up the hunting car. Mary was writing letters and I told her I had asked for the car and then Charo and Ngui came and pulled the guns in their full length cases out from under the cots and Ngui assembled the big .577. They were finding shells and counting them and checking on solids for the Springfield and the Mannlicher. It was the first of the fine movements of the hunt.

"What are we going to hunt?"

"We have to get the meat. We'll try an experiment Pop and I were talking about for practice for the lion. I want you to kill a wildebeest at twenty yards. You and Charo stalk him."

"I don't know if we can ever get that close."

"You'll get up. Don't wear your sweater. Take it and put it on if it gets cool coming home. And roll up your sleeves now if you're going to roll them up. Please, honey."

Miss Mary had a habit, just before she was going to shoot, of rolling up the right sleeve of her bush jacket. Maybe it was only turning back the cuff. But it would frighten an animal at a hundred yards and over.

"You know I don't do that anymore."

"Good. The reason I mentioned the sweater is because it might make the rifle stock too long for you."

"All right. But what if it's cold in the morning when we find the lion?"

"I only want to see how you shoot without it. To see what difference it makes."

"Everybody's always experimenting with me. Why can't I just go out and shoot and kill cleanly?"

"You can, honey. You're going to now."

We rode out past the airstrip. Ahead on our right was the broken park country and in one meadow I saw two groups of wildebeest feeding and an old bull lying down not far from a clump of trees. I nodded at him to Mthuka, who had already seen him, and motioned with my hand for us to circle widely to the left and then back where we could not be seen behind the trees.

I signaled to Mthuka to stop the car and Mary got out and Charo after her carrying a pair of field glasses. Mary had her 6.5 Mannlicher and when she was on the ground she lifted the bolt, pulled it back, shoved it forward and saw that the cartridge went into the chamber, turned it down and then moved the safety lever over.

"Now what am I to do?"

"You saw the old bull lying down?"

"Yes. I saw two other bulls in the bunches."

"You and Charo see how close you can get to that old bull. The wind is right and you ought to be able to get up to the trees. Do you see the patch?"

The old bull wildebeest lay there, black and strange looking with his huge head, down-curved, widespread horns and savage-looking mane. Charo and Mary were getting closer to the clump of trees now and the wildebeest stood up. He looked even stranger now and in the light he looked very black. He had not seen Mary and Charo and he stood broadside to them and looking toward us. I thought what a fine and strange-looking animal he was and that we took them too much for granted because we saw them every day. He was not a noble-looking animal but he was a most extraordinary looking beast and I was delighted to watch him and watch the slow, bent double approach of Charo and Mary.

Mary was at the edge of the trees where she could shoot now and we watched Charo kneel and Mary raise her rifle and lower her head. We heard the shot and the sound of the bullet strik-ing bone almost at the same time and saw the black form of the old bull raise up in the air and fall heavily on his side. The other wildebeest burst into a bounding gallop and we roared toward Mary and Charo and the black hump in the meadow. Mary and Charo were standing close to the wildebeest when we all piled out of the hunting car. Charo was very happy and had his knife out. Everyone was saying, "Piga mzuri.

Piga mzuri sana, Memsahib. Mzuri, mzuri, sana."

I put my arm around her and said, "It was a beautiful shot, kitten, and a fine stalk. Now shoot him just at the base of the left ear for kindness."

"Shouldn't I shoot him in the forehead?"

"No, please. Just at the base of the ear."

She waved everyone back, turned the safety bolt over, raised the rifle, checked it properly, took a deep breath, expelled it, put her weight on her left front foot and fired a shot that made a small hole at the exact juncture of the base of the left ear and the skull. The wildebeest's front legs relaxed slowly and his head turned very gently. He had a certain dignity in death and I put my arm around Mary and turned her away so she would not see Charo slip the knife into the sticking place which would make the old bull legal meat for all Mohammedans.

"Aren't you happy I got so close to him and killed him clean and good and just how I was supposed to? Aren't you a little bit proud of your kitten?"

"You were wonderful. You got up to him beautifully and you killed him dead with one shot and he never knew what happened nor suffered at all."

"I must say he looked awfully big and, honey, he even looked fierce."

"Kitten, you go and sit in the car and have a drink from the Jinny flask. I'll help them load him in the back."

"Come and have a drink with me. I've just fed eighteen people with my rifle and I love you and I want to have a drink. Didn't Charo and I get up close?"

"You got up beautifully. You couldn't have done better."

The Jinny flask was in one pocket of the old Spanish double cartridge pouches. It was a pint bottle of Gordon's we had bought at Sultan Hamud and it was named after another old famous silver flask that had finally opened its seams at too many thousand feet during a war and had caused me to believe for a moment that I had been hit in the buttocks. The old Jinny flask had never repaired properly but we had named this squat pint bottle for the old tall hip-fitting flask that bore the name of a girl on its silver screw top and bore no names of the fights where it had been present nor any names of those who had drunk from it and now were dead. The battles and the names would have covered both sides of the old Jinny flask if they had been engraved in modest size. But this new and unspectacular Jinny flask had close to tribal status.

Mary drank from it and I drank from it and Mary said, "You know, Africa is the only place where straight gin doesn't taste any stronger than water."

"A little bit."

"Oh, I meant it figuratively. I'll take another one if I may."

The gin did taste very good and clean and pleasantly warming and happy making and to me, not like water at all. I handed the water bag to Mary and she took a long drink and said, "Water's lovely too. It isn't fair to compare them."

I left her holding the Jinny flask and went to the back of the car where the tailgate was down to help hoist the wildebeest in. We hoisted him in entire to save time and so that those that liked tripe could take their pieces when he would be dressed out at camp. Hoisted and pushed in he had no dignity and lay there glassy eyed and big bellied, his head at an absurd angle, his gray tongue protruding, like a hanged man. Ngui, who with Mthuka had done the heaviest lifting, put his finger in the bullet hole which was just above the shoulder. I nodded and we pushed the tailgate up and made it fast and I borrowed the water bag from Mary to wash my hands.

"Please take a drink, Papa," she said. "What are you looking gloomy about?"

"I'm not gloomy. But let me have a drink. Do you want to shoot next? We have to get a

Tommy or an impala for Keiti, Charo, Mwindi, you and me."

"I'd like to get an impala. But I don't want to shoot anymore today. Please, I'd rather not. I don't want to spoil it. I'm shooting just where I want to now."

"Where did you hold on him, kitten?" I said, hating to ask the question. I was taking a drink while I asked it to make it very easy and not too casual.

"Right on the center of his shoulder. Dead in the center. You saw the hole."

There had been a big drop of blood that had rolled down from the tiny hole high in the spine, that had rolled down to the center of the shoulder and stopped there. I had seen it when the strange, black antelope lay there in the grass with the front part of him still alive, but quiet, and the after part quite dead.

"Good, kitten," I said.

"I'll take the Jinny flask," Mary said. "I don't have to shoot anymore. I'm so happy that I shot him so that it pleased you. I wish Pop had been here too."

But Pop was not here and, at point-blank range, she had shot fourteen inches higher than she had aimed, killing the beast with a perfect high spinal shot. So a certain problem still existed.

We were going up through the park country

now straight into the wind and the sun at our back. Ahead I saw the square white patches on the buttocks of the Grant's gazelles and the flicking tails of the Thomson's gazelles as they grazed ahead of us, bounding off as the car came close. Ngui knew what it was all about and so did Charo. Ngui turned back to Charo and said, "Jinny flask."

Charo handed it over the seat back between the upended big gun and the shotgun in their clamps. Ngui unscrewed the top and handed it to me. I took a drink and it tasted nothing like water. I could never drink when we hunted lion with Mary because of the responsibility but the gin would loosen me up and we had all tightened up after the wildebeest except the porter who was happy and proud. Miss Mary was happy and proud too.

"He wants you to show off," she said. "Show off, Papa. Please show off."

"OK," I said. "One more to show off."

I reached for the Jinny flask and Ngui shook his head. "Hapana," he said. "Mzuri."

Ahead, in the next glade, two Tommy rams were feeding. They both had good heads, exceptionally long and symmetrical and their tails were switching as they fed quickly and eagerly. Mthuka nodded that he had seen them and turned the car so that when he stopped it my approach would be covered. I ejected two shells from the Springfield and put in two solids, lowered the bolt and got down and started to walk toward the heavy clump of bush as though I took no interest in it. I did not stoop over because the bush was sufficient cover and I had come to the conclusion that in stalking, when there was much game around, it was better to walk upright and in a disinterested way. Otherwise, you risked alarming other animals that could see you and they might alarm the animal you were after. Remembering that Miss Mary had asked me to show off I raised my left hand carefully and slapped it against the side of my neck. This was calling the location of the shot I would try for and anything else was worthless. No one can call their shot that way on a small animal like a Tommy when he may run. But if I should hit him there it was good for morale and if it did not, it was an obvious impossibility.

It was pleasant walking through the grass with the white flowers in it and I slouched along with the rifle held behind me close to my right leg, the muzzle pointing down. As I walked forward I did not think about anything at all except that it was a lovely early evening and that I was lucky to be in Africa. Now I was at the far right edge of the clump and I should have crouched and crawled but there was too much grass and too many flowers and I wore glasses and I was too old to crawl. So I pulled the bolt back, holding my finger on the trigger so there was no snick, took my finger off the trigger and lowered it into place silently, checked the aperture in the rear sight and then stepped out past the right end of the clump.

The two Tommy rams broke into full speed as I raised the rifle. The furthest one had his head turned toward me as I came out. They dug in with their small hooves into a bounding gallop. I picked up the second one in the sights, lowered my weight onto my left front foot, held with him and passed him smoothly with the sights and squeezed when the rifle had gone ahead of him. There was the report of the rifle, the dry whunck, and as I shucked in the second shell I could see his four legs stiff in the air and his white belly and then the legs lowered slowly. I walked out to him, hoping I had not shot him in the behind and raked him or given him the high spinal by mistake or hit him in the head and I heard the car coming. Charo dropped out from it with his knife out and ran to the Tommy and then stood there.

I came up and said, "Halal."

"Hapana," Charo said and touched the poor dead eyes with the point of his knife.

"Halal anyway."

"Hapana," Charo said. I had never seen him cry and he was very close to it. This was a religious crisis and he was an old and devout man.

"OK," I said. "Stick him, Ngui."

Everybody had been very quiet on account of Charo. He went back to the hunting car and there were only us unbelievers. Mthuka shook hands with me and bit his lips. He was thinking of his father being deprived of the Tommy meat. Ngui was laughing but trying not to show it. Pop's gun bearer that he had left with us had a face like a round, very brown elf. He put his hand up to his head in sorrow. Then slapped his neck. The porter looked on happy, cheerful and stupid and happy to be out with hunters.

"Where did you hit him?" Mary asked.

"In the neck, I'm afraid."

Ngui showed her the hole and he and Mthuka and the porter picked the ram up and swung him into the back of the car.

"It's a little too much like witchcraft," Mary said. "When I said to show off I didn't mean that far off."

We came into camp, pulling around carefully to drop off Miss Mary and raise no dust.

"It was a lovely afternoon," she said. "Thank you, everybody, so much."

She went toward her tent where Mwindi

would have the hot bathwater ready to pour into the canvas tub and I was happy that she was happy about her shot and I was sure, aided by the Jinny flask, that we would work out all the problems and the hell with a small variation of fourteen inches vertical at twenty-five yards on a lion. Sure the hell with that. The car drove out, gently, to the grounds where we butchered and skinned out. Keiti came out with the others following and I got down and said, "Memsahib shot a wildebeest beautifully."

"Mzuri," Keiti said.

We left the lights of the car on for the game to be dressed out. Ngui had my best knife out and was joining the skinner, who had started work and who was squatting by the wildebeest.

I went over and tapped Ngui on the shoulder and drew him out of the light. He was intent at the butchering but he understood and came fast out of the light.

"Take a good big cut high on the back for the Shamba," I said. I marked it with my finger on his own back.

"Ndio," he said.

"Wrap it in a part of the belly when the belly is clean."

"Good."

"Give them a good piece of ordinary meat."

"Ndio."

I wanted to give away more meat but I knew it was not right to do so and I covered my conscience with the fact that it was necessary for the next two days' operations and remembering this I said to Ngui, "Put in plenty of stew meat too for the Shamba."

Then I walked away from the lights of the car to the tree just beyond the light of the cooking fire to where the Widow, her little boy and Debba were waiting. They wore their bright, now faded, dresses and they leaned against the tree. The little boy came out and bumped his head hard against my belly and I kissed the top of his head.

"How are you, Widow?" I asked. She shook her head.

"Jambo, tu," I said to Debba. I kissed her on the top of the head too and she laughed and I raised my hand up over her neck and her head feeling the close, stiff loveliness and she butted me twice against my heart and I kissed her head again. The Widow was very tense and she said, "Kwenda na shamba," which meant, let's go to the village. Debba said nothing. She had lost her lovely Kamba impudence and I stroked her bowed head, which felt lovely, and touched the secret places behind her ears and she put her hand up, stealthily, and touched my worst scars.

"Mthuka will take you now in the car," I

said. "There is meat for the family. I cannot go. Jambo, tu," I said, which is the roughest and the most loving you can talk and ends things quickest.

"When will you come?" the Widow asked.

"Any day. When it is my duty."

"Will we go to Laitokitok before the Birthday of the Baby Jesus?"

"Surely," I said.

"Kwenda na shamba," Debba said.

"Mthuka will take you."

"You come."

"No hay remedio," I said. It was one of the first things I had taught her to say in Spanish and she said it now very carefully. It was the saddest thing I knew in Spanish and I thought it was probably best for her to learn it early. She thought that it was part of my religion, which she was learning, since I had not explained to her what it meant, but only that it was a phrase that she must know.

"No hay remedio," she said very proudly.

"You have beautiful hard hands," I told her in Spanish. This was one of our first jokes and I had translated it very carefully. "You are the Queen of the Ngomas."

"No hay remedio," she said modestly. Then in the dark she said very fast, "No hay remedio, no hay remedio, no hay remedio."

"No hay remedio, tú," I said. "Get the meat and go."

That night while I woke listening to the hyenas talking and disputing over the refuse from the butchering and watching the firelight through the door of the tent I thought about Mary sleeping soundly now and happy about her good stalk and clean kill on the wildebeest and wondered where the big lion was and what he was doing now in the dark. I figured he would kill again on his way down to the swamp. Then I thought about the Shamba and how there was no remedy nor any solution. I was full of remorse that I had ever become involved with the Shamba but no hay remedio now and maybe there never was a time. I did not start it. It started by itself. Then I thought some more about the lion and about the Kamba Mau Mau and that we would have to expect them from tomorrow afternoon. Then, for a moment, there were no night noises at all. Everyone had stopped and I thought shit this is probably the Kamba Mau Mau and I have been sloppy and I took the Winchester pump that I had loaded with buckshot and listened with my mouth open to hear better while I could feel my heart pounding. Then the night noises started again and I heard a leopard cough down by the stream. It was a noise like the C string on a bass viol being stroked by a farrier's rasp. He coughed again, hunting, and all the night began to speak about him and I put the shotgun under my leg again and started to go to sleep feeling proud of Miss Mary and loving her and being proud of Debba and caring about her very much.

3

I GOT UP AT daylight and went out to the cook tent and the lines. Keiti was always conservative so we inspected the camp in a very military manner and I could see he was not upset about anything. Our meat was hung wrapped in cheesecloth and there was plenty of meat for three days for the men. Some of it was being roasted on sticks by the early risers. We went over the plans for intercepting the Mau Mau if they should come to any of the four Shambas.

"The plan is good but they will not come," he said.

"Did you hear the quiet before the leopard last night?"

"Yes," he said and smiled. "But it was a leopard."

"Didn't you think it might be those people?"

"Yes. But it was not."

"All right," I said. "Please send Mwindi to me at the fire."

At the fire that had been built up by pushing the unburned ends of the logs together and putting a little brush on top of the ashes I sat down and drank my tea. It was cold by now and Mwindi brought another pot of tea with him. He was as formal and as conservative as Keiti and he had the same sense of humor except that his was rougher than Keiti's. Mwindi spoke English and understood it better than he spoke it. He was an old man and looked like a very black, narrow-faced Chinese. He kept all my keys and was in charge of the tent, making the beds, bringing the baths, doing laundry and boots, bringing early morning tea and he also kept my money and all the money I carried to run the safari. This money was locked in the tin trunk and he kept the keys. He liked being trusted as people were trusted in the old days. He was teaching me Kamba but not the same Kamba I was learning from Ngui. He thought Ngui and I were bad influences on each other but he was too old and too cynical to be disturbed by anything except interruptions in the order of his work. He liked to work and he loved responsibility and he had made an orderly and pleasant pattern of safari life.

"Bwana wants something?" he asked, standing looking solemn and dejected.

"We have too many guns and too much ammunition in this camp," I said.

"Nobody knows," he said. "You bring hidden from Nairobi. Nobody sees anything at Kitanga. We always carry hidden. Nobody sees. Nobody knows. You always sleep with pistol by your leg."

"I know. But if I were Mau Mau I would attack this camp at night."

"If you were Mau Mau many things would happen. But you are not Mau Mau."

"Good. But if you are not in the tent, someone must be in the tent armed and responsible."

"Have them stand the watch outside please, Bwana. I do not want anyone in the tent. For the tent, I am responsible."

"They will be outside."

"Bwana, they have to cross an open plain to come to this camp. Everybody would see them."

"Ngui and I came through the camp from end to end three times at Fig Tree and no one saw us."

"I saw you."

"Truly?"

"Twice."

"Why did you not say so?"

"I do not have to say everything I see that you and Ngui do."

"Thank you. Now you know about the guard. If Memsahib and I are gone and you leave the tent call the guard. If Memsahib is here alone and you are not here, call the guard."

"Ndio," he said. "You don't drink the tea? It gets cold."

"Tonight I make some booby traps around the tent and we will leave a lantern on that tree."

"Mzuri. We will make a very big fire too. Keiti is sending out for wood now so the lorry driver can be free. He goes to one of the Shambas. But these people that they say come here will not come here."

"Why do you say that so surely?"

"Because it is stupid to come here into a trap and they are not stupid. These are Wakamba Mau Mau."

I sat by the fire with the new pot of tea and drank it slowly. The Masai were a pastoral and war-making people. They were not hunters. The Wakamba were hunters; the best hunters and trackers that I had ever known. And now their game had been killed off by the white men and by themselves on their Reserve and the only place they could hunt was in the Masai Reserves. Their own Reserve was overcrowded and over-farmed and when the rains failed there was no pasture for the cattle and the crops were lost.

As I sat and drank the tea I thought that the cleavage, a friendly cleavage, in the camp, but a cleavage in spirit and in outlook, was not between the devout and the unbelievers, nor the good and the bad, nor the old and the new but basically between the active hunters and warriors and the others. Keiti had been a fighting man, a soldier, a great hunter and tracker and it was he that held everything together by his great experience, knowledge and authority. But Keiti was a man of considerable and a conservative wealth and property and in the changing times we had now the conservatives had a difficult role. The young men who had been too young for the war and who had never learned to hunt because there was no longer any game in their country and they were too good and inexperienced boys to be poachers and not trained to be cattle thieves looked up to Ngui and the bad boys who had fought their way through Abyssinia and again through Burma. They were on our side in everything but their loyalty to Keiti, to Pop and to their work. We made no attempt to recruit them or to convert them or to corrupt them. They were all volunteers. Ngui had told me the whole thing and trusted me and put it on a straight base of tribal loyalty. I knew we, the hunting Wakamba, had gone a long way together. But sitting there, drinking the tea, and watching the yellow and green trees change in color as the sun hit them I thought about how far we had gone. I finished the tea and walked over to the tent and looked in. Mary had drunk her early cup of tea and the empty cup lay on the saucer where the mosquito netting now hung to the canvas ground sheet by the side of the cot. She was sleeping again and her lightly tanned face and her lovely rumpled blond hair were against the pillow. Her lips were turned toward me and as I watched her sleeping, touched deeply as always by her beautiful face, she smiled lightly in her sleep. I wondered what she was dreaming about. Then I picked up the shotgun from underneath the blankets on my bed and took it outside the tent to take the shell out of the barrel. This morning was another morning that Mary could get her proper sleep.

I went over to the dining tent and told Nguili, who was tidying it up, what I wanted for breakfast. It was an egg sandwich with the egg fried firm with either ham or bacon and sliced raw onion. If there was any fruit I would have some and first I would have a bottle of Tusker beer.

G.C. and I nearly always drank beer for breakfast unless we were hunting lion. Beer before or at breakfast was a fine thing but it slowed you up, possibly a thousandth of a second. On the other hand it made things seem better sometimes when they were not too good and it was very good for you if you had stayed up too late and had gastric remorse.

Nguili opened the bottle of beer and poured a

glass. He loved to pour beer and see that the foam rose just at the very last and topped the glass without spilling. He was very good-looking, almost as good-looking as a girl without being at all effeminate and G.C. used to tease him and ask him if he plucked his eyebrows. He may very well have since one of the great amusements of primitive people is to arrange and rearrange their appearance and it has nothing to do with being homosexual. But G.C. used to tease him too much, I thought, and because he was shy, friendly and very devoted, an excellent mess attendant who worshipped the hunters and fighters, we used to take him hunting with us sometimes. Everyone made fun of him a little for his wonderful surprise at and ignorance of animals. But he learned every time he was out and we all teased him lovingly. We all regarded any form of wound or disaster to one of us which was not crippling nor fatal as extremely comic and this was hard on this boy who was delicate and gentle and loving. He wanted to be a warrior and a hunter but instead he was an apprentice cook and a mess attendant. In the meantime that we lived in and were all so happy in that year, one of his great pleasures, since he was not yet allowed by tribal law to drink, was to pour beer for those who were allowed to drink it.

"Did you hear the leopard?" I asked him.

"No, Bwana, I sleep too hard."

He went off to get the sandwich which he had called out to the cook to make and he hurried back to pour more beer.

Msembi, the other mess attendant, was tall, handsome and rough. He always wore his green mess attendant's gown with the air of participating in a masquerade. He achieved this by the angle he wore his green skullcap and he had ways of manipulating the gown which showed that while he respected it for his service he realized it was a little comic. With Mary and I alone we did not need two men for the mess but the cook was going back to see his family shortly and take allotments to the families of the men and while he was away Msembi would cook. Like everyone but me he hated the Informer and this morning when the Informer appeared outside the mess tent and coughed discreetly he looked at me meaningfully, bowed, closing his eyes slightly, and they both went out.

"Come in, Informer," I said. "What is the word?"

"Jambo, my brother," the Informer said. He was closely muffled in his shawl and he removed his porkpie hat. "There is a man from beyond Laitokitok waiting to see you. He claims that his Shamba was destroyed by elephants."

"Do you know him?"

"No, brother."

"Leave and send him in."

The Shamba owner came in and bowed at the door and said, "Good morning, sir."

I saw he had the town Mau Mau style of haircut, parted on the side with the part cut out with a razor. But that could mean nothing.

"These elephants?" I asked.

"They came last night and destroyed my Shamba," he said. "I believe it is your duty to control them. I would like you to come tonight and kill one to drive them away."

And leave the camp unguarded and this nonsense on, I thought. "Thank you for the report on the elephants," I said. "A plane is arriving here shortly and we will take you with us and make a reconnaissance of the damage done to your Shamba and attempt to locate the elephants. You will show us your Shamba and the exact damage done."

"But I have never flown, sir."

"You'll fly today. And you will find it both interesting and instructive."

"But I have never flown, sir. And I could be ill."

"Sick," I said. "Not ill. One must respect the English language. Sick is the word. But paper containers will be provided. Aren't you interested in seeing your property from the air?"

"Yes, sir."

"It will be most interesting. It will be almost as though you had a map of your domain. You will have a knowledge of its topographical features and its contours impossible to acquire in any other way."

"Yes, sir," he said. I was feeling a little bit ashamed but there was the haircut and the camp had enough stuff in it to be well worth a raid in force and if Arap Meina and Ngui and I were sucked off from it on an elephant and bull story it would be easy to rush.

Then he tried once more not knowing that each time he made it a little worse.

"I do not think that I should fly, sir."

"Look," I said. "Every one of us here has flown or has wished to fly. It is a privilege for you to see your own country from the air. Have you never envied the birds? Have you never wished to be the eagle or even the hawk?"

"No, sir," he said. "But today I will fly."

Then I thought even if he is our enemy or a crook or merely wants an elephant killed for meat he has made the correct and dignified decision. I stepped out and told Arap Meina that this man was under arrest and not to inform him but guard him properly and not allow him to leave the camp nor to look into the tents and that we were taking him up in the ndege.

"He is guarded," Arap Meina said. "Do I fly too?"

"No. You flew enough last time. Ngui flies today."

Ngui grinned too and said, "Mzuri sana."

"Mzuri," Arap Meina said, and grinned. I told him I would send the Shamba owner out and I asked Ngui to go down and check on the wind sock and spook any animals off the home-made landing strip in the meadow.

Mary came out to the mess tent in her fresh bush kit that Mwindi had washed and ironed for her. She looked as new and young as the morning and noticed that I had drunk beer with or before breakfast.

"I thought you only did that when G.C. was here," she said.

"No. Often I drink it in the morning before you're awake. I'm not writing and it's the only time of day it's cold."

"Did you find out anything about the lion from all those people who were here talking?"

"No. There's no news of the lion. He didn't talk in the night."

"You did," she said. "You were talking to some girl that wasn't me. What was it that there was no remedy for?"

"I'm sorry I talked in my sleep."

"You were talking in Spanish," she said. "It was all about there being no remedy."

"Must be no remedy then. I'm sorry I don't remember the dream."

"I never asked you to be faithful to me in dreams. Are we going to hunt the lion?"

"Honey, what's the matter with you? We agreed we wouldn't hunt the lion even if he came down. We were going to lay off him and let him get confident."

"How do you know he won't go away?"

"He's smart, honey. He always moves on after he kills cattle. But he gets confident after he kills game. I'm trying to think in his head."

"Maybe you ought to think in your own head a little."

"Honey," I said. "Would you maybe order breakfast? There's Tommy liver and bacon."

She called Nguili and ordered her breakfast very graciously.

"What were you smiling about in your sleep after you had your tea?"

"Oh, that was my wonderful dream. I met the lion and he was so nice to me and so cultured and polite. He'd been at Oxford, he said, and he spoke with practically a BBC voice. I was sure I had met him before someplace and then suddenly he ate me up."

"We live in very difficult times," I said. "I guess when I saw you smiling was before he ate you up."

"It must have been," she said. "I'm sorry I was cross. He ate me up so suddenly. He never gave any sign that he disliked me. He didn't roar or anything like the Magadi lion."

I kissed her and then Nguili brought in the beautiful small slices of browned liver with upcountry bacon spread across them, fried potatoes and coffee and tinned milk and a dish of stewed apricots.

"Please have one piece of the liver and bacon," Mary said. "Are you going to have a rough day, darling?"

"No. I don't think so."

"Will I be able to fly?"

"It doesn't look like it. But maybe if there's time."

"Is there a lot of work?"

I told her what we had to do and she said, "I'm so sorry I came in cross. It was just the lion eating me up I think. Eat the liver and bacon and finish the beer, honey, and take it easy until the ndege comes. Nothing has reached the no hay remedio stage. Don't ever even think it in your sleep."

"Don't you ever think about the lion eating you up either."

"I never do in the daytime. I'm not that sort of girl."

"I'm not a no hay remedio boy, really."

"Yes. You are a little bit. But you're happier now than when I first knew you, aren't you?"

"I'm truly happy with you."

"And you're happy with everything else too. My, it will be wonderful to see Willie again."

"He's much better than either of us."

"But we can try to be better," Mary said.

We did not know what time the plane would be in nor even if it would surely come. There had been no confirmation of the signal the young police officer had sent but I expected the plane from one o'clock on; although if there was any weather building over the Chulus or on the eastern flank of the Mountain, Willie might come earlier. I got up and looked at the weather. There was some cloud over the Chulus but the Mountain looked good.

"I wish I could fly today," Mary said.

"You'll fly plenty, honey. Today's just a job."

"But will I fly over the Chulus?"

"I promise. We'll fly anywhere you want."

"After I kill the lion I'd like to fly into Nairobi to get the things for Christmas. Then I want to be back in time to get a tree to have it beautiful. We picked out a fine tree before that rhino came. It will be really beautiful but I have to get all the things for it and everybody's presents."

"After we kill the lion Willie can come down with the Cessna and you can see the Chulus and we'll go way up the Mountain if you want and we'll check the property and then you go back to Nairobi with him."

"Do we have enough money for that?"

"Sure."

"I want you to learn and to know about everything so we won't have just wasted the money. Truly I don't care what you do as long as it's good for you. All I want is that you love me the most."

"I love you the most."

"I know it. But please don't do other people harm."

"Everybody does other people harm."

"You shouldn't. I don't care what you do as long as you don't hurt other people or spoil their lives. And don't say no hay remedio. That's too easy. When it is all fantastic and you all make up your lies and live in this strange world you all have, then it is just fantastic and charming sometimes and I laugh at you. I feel superior to such nonsense and to the unrealness. Please try to understand me, because I'm your brother too. That dirty Informer isn't your brother."

"He invented that."

"Then suddenly the nonsense gets so real that it is like having somebody chop your arm off. Chop it off truly. Not like chop it off in a dream. I mean chop it off truly the way Ngui uses a panga. I know Ngui is your true brother." I didn't say anything.

"Then when you speak so harshly to that

girl. When you speak like that it's like watching
Ngui butcher. It's not the lovely life we have
where everyone has fun."

"Haven't you been having fun?"

"I never was as happy in my life, ever, ever.
And now that you have confidence in my shoot-
ing, I'm really happy today and confident except
I only hope it will last."

"It will last."

"But you see what I mean about how it suddenly becomes so different from the lovely
dream way it is? The way it is when it is like
a dream or the loveliest part of when we were
both children? We being here with the Mountain every day more beautiful than anything and
you people with your jokes and everyone happy.
Everyone is so loving to me and I love them too.
And then there is this other thing."

"I know," I said. "It's all a part of the same
thing, kitten. Nothing is as simple as it looks.
I'm not really rude to that girl. That's just being
sort of formal."

"Please never be rude to her in front of me."

"I won't."

"Nor to me in front of her."

"I won't."

"You're not going to take her up to fly in the
aircraft are you?"

"No, honey. I promise you that truly."

"I wish Pop were here or that Willie would come."

"So do I," I said, and went out and looked at the weather again. There was a little more cloud over the Chulus but the shoulder of the Mountain was still clear.

"You're not going to drop that Shamba owner out of the aircraft are you? You and Ngui?"

"Good God, no. Will you believe me that I hadn't thought of it?"

"I'd thought of it when I heard you talking to him this morning."

"Who's getting to have bad thoughts now?"

"It's not that you think things so bad. All of you do things in that sudden awful way as though there were no consequences."

"Honey, I think a lot about consequences."

"But there's that strange suddenness and the inhumanity and the cruel jokes. There's death in every joke. When will it start being nice and lovely again?"

"Right away. This nonsense only goes on for a few days more. We don't think those people are coming down here and they'll be caught wherever they go."

"I want it to be the way it was when every morning we woke and knew something wonderful would happen. I hate this hunting men."

"This isn't hunting men, honey. You've never seen that. That's what goes on up in the North. Here, everybody is our friend."

"Not in Laitokitok."

"Yes, but those people will be picked up. Don't worry about that."

"I only worry about all of you when you are bad. Pop was never bad."

"Do you really think so?"

"I mean bad the way you and G.C. are. Even you and Willie are bad when you're together."

4

I WENT OUTSIDE and checked the weather. There was just the steady building up of cloud over the Chulus and the flank of the Mountain was clear. As I watched I thought I heard the plane. Then I was sure and called out for the hunting car. Mary came out and we scrambled for the car and started out from camp and on the motor car tracks through the new green grass for the landing strip. The game trotted and then galloped out of our way. The aircraft buzzed the camp and then it came down, clean silver and blue, lovely wings shining, with the big flaps down and for a moment we were keeping almost abreast of it before Willie, smiling out through the Plexiglas as the blue of the prop passed us, touched the aircraft down so that she landed strutting gently like a crane and then wheeled around to come fanning up to us.

Willie opened the door and smiled, "Hello, you chaps." He looked for Mary and said, "Get the lion yet, Miss Mary?"

He spoke in a sort of swinging lilting voice

that moved with the rhythm that a great boxer has when he is floating in and out with perfect, unwasting movements. His voice had a sweetness that was true but I knew it could say the most deadly things without a change of tone.

"I couldn't kill him, Willie," Miss Mary called. "He hasn't come down yet."

"Pity," said Willie. "I have to get a few odds and ends out here. Ngui can give me a hand. Pots of mail for you, Miss Mary. Papa has a few bills. Here's the mail."

He tossed the big manila envelope to me and I caught it.

"Good to see you retain some sign of basic reflexes," Willie said. "G.C. sent his love. He's on his way."

I handed the mail to Mary and we commenced to unload the plane and put the packages and boxes into the hunting car.

"Better not do any actual physical labor, Papa," Willie said. "Don't tire yourself. Remember we're saving you for the Main Event."

"I heard it was canceled."

"Still on I believe," Willie said. "Not that I'd pay to see it."

"Even you and Willie," Mary said.

"Come on let's go to campi," she said to Willie.

"Coming, Miss Mary," Willie said. He came

down now in his white shirt with the sleeves rolled up, his blue serge shorts and his low brogues and smiled lovingly at Miss Mary as he took her hand. He was handsome with fine merry eyes and an alive tanned face and dark hair and shy without any awkwardness. He was the most natural and best-mannered person I have ever known. He had all the sureness of a great pilot. He was modest and he was doing what he loved in the country he loved.

We had never asked each other any questions except about aircraft and flying. Everything else was supposed to be understood. I assumed he had been born in Kenya because he spoke such fine Swahili and was gentle and understanding with Africans but it never occurred to me to ask him where he was born and he might have come out to Africa as a boy for all I knew.

We drove slowly into camp in order not to raise dust and got out under the big tree between our tents and the lines. Miss Mary went over to see Mbebia the cook to have him make lunch at once and Willie and I walked over to the mess tent. I opened a bottle of beer that was still cold in the canvas bag that hung against the tree and poured one in each of our glasses.

"What's the true gen, Papa," Willie asked. I told him.

"I saw him," Willie said. "Old Arap Meina

seemed to have him under fairly close arrest. He does look a little bit the type, Papa."

"Well, we'll check his Shamba. Maybe he has a Shamba and maybe they had elephant trouble."

"We'll check the elephants too. That will save time and then we'll drop him off here and then have a general look around on the other thing. I'm taking Ngui. If there are elephant and we have to work it out Meina knows all the country and he and Ngui and I will do it and Ngui and I will have made the recon."

"It all seems sound," Willie said. "You fellows do keep quite busy here for a quiet area. Here comes Miss Mary."

Mary came in delighted with the prospect of the meal.

"We're having Tommy chops, mashed potatoes and a salad. And it will be here right away. And a surprise. Thank you so much for finding the Campari, Willie. I'm going to have one now. Will you?"

"No thank you, Miss Mary. Papa and I are drinking a beer."

"Willie, I wish I could go. But anyway I'll have all the lists made and write the checks and the letters ready and after I kill the lion I'll fly in with you to Nairobi to get the things for Christmas."

"You must be shooting very well, Miss Mary,

from that beautiful meat I saw hanging in the cheesecloth."

"There's a haunch for you and I told them to change it around carefully to be in the shade all day and then wrap it well for you just before you go back."

"How is everything at the Shamba, Papa?" Willie asked.

"My father-in-law has some sort of combination chest and stomach ailment," I said. "I've been treating it with Sloan's liniment. Sloan's came to him as rather a shock the first time I rubbed it in."

"Ngui told him it was part of Papa's religion," Mary said. "They all have the same religion now and it's reached a point where it is basically awful. They all eat kipper snacks and drink beer at eleven o'clock and explain it is part of their religion. I wish you'd stay here Willie and tell me what really goes on. They have horrible slogans and dreadful secrets."

"It's Gitchi Manitou the Mighty versus All Others," I explained to Willie. "We retain the best of various other sects and tribal law and customs. But we weld them into a whole that all can believe. Miss Mary coming from the Northern Frontier Province, Minnesota, and never having been to the Rocky Mountains until we were married is handicapped."

"Papa has everybody but the Mohammedans

believing in the Great Spirit," Mary said. "The Great Spirit is one of the worst characters I've ever known. I know Papa makes up the religion and makes it more complicated every day. He and Ngui and the others. But the Great Spirit frightens even me sometimes."

"I try to hold him down, Willie," I said. "But he gets away from me."

"How does he feel about aircraft?" Willie asked.

"I can't reveal that before Mary," I said. "When we are airborne I'll give you the word."

"Anything I can do to help you, Miss Mary, count on me," Willie said.

"I just wish you could stay around or that G.C. or Mr. P. was here," Mary said. "I've never been present at the birth of a new religion before and it makes me nervous."

"You must be something along the lines of the White Goddess, Miss Mary. There's always a beautiful White Goddess isn't there?"

"I don't think I am. One of the basic points of the faith as I gather it is that neither Papa nor I are white."

"That is timely."

"We tolerate the whites and wish to live in harmony with them as I understand it. But on our own terms. That is on Papa's and Ngui's and Mthuka's terms. It's Papa's religion and it is a frightfully old religion and now he and the others are adapting it to Kamba custom and usage."

"I was never a missionary before, Willie," I said. "It is very inspiring. I've been very fortunate that we have Kibo here that is almost the exact counterpart of one of the foothills of the Wind River range where the religion was first revealed to me and where I had my early visions."

"They teach us so little at school," Willie said. "Could you give me any gen on the Wind Rivers, Papa?"

"We call them the Fathers of the Himalayas," I explained modestly. "The main low range is approximately the height of that mountain Tensing the Sherpa carried that talented New Zealand beekeeper to the top of last year."

"Could that be Everest?" Willie asked. "There was some mention of the incident in the *East African Standard*."

"Everest it was. I was trying to remember the name all day yesterday when we were having evening indoctrination at the Shamba."

"Jolly good show the old beekeeper put up being carried so high so far from home," Willie said. "How did it all come about, Papa?"

"No one knows," I said. "They're all reluctant to talk."

"Always had the greatest respect for mountaineers," Willie said. "No one ever gets a word out of them. They're as tight mouthed a lot as old G.C. or you yourself Papa."

"Nerveless too," I said.

"Like us all," Willie said. "Should we try for that food, Miss Mary? Papa and I have to go out and have a little look around the estate."

"Lete chakula."

"Ndio Memsahib."

When we were airborne and flying along the side of the Mountain watching the forest, the openings, the rolling country and the broken ground of the watersheds, seeing the zebra always fat-looking from the air running foreshortened below us, the plane turning to pick up the road so that our guest who sat beside Willie might orient himself as we spread the road and the village before him, there was the road that came up from the swamp behind us and now leading into the village where he could see the crossroads, the stores, the fuel pump, the trees along the main street and the other trees leading to the white building and high wire fence of the police Boma where we could see the flagpole with the flag in the wind.

"Where is your Shamba?" I said in his ear and as he pointed, Willie turned and we were over the Boma and up and along the flank of the Mountain where there were many clearings and

cone-shaped houses and fields of mealies growing green out of the red brown earth.

"Can you see your Shamba?"

"Yes." He pointed.

Then his Shamba roared up at us and spread
green and tall and well watered ahead and
behind the wing.

"Hapana tembo," Ngui said very low in my
ear.

"Tracks?"

"Hapana."

"Sure that's your Shamba?" Willie said to the
man.

"Yes," he said.

"Looks in pretty good shape to me, Papa,"
Willie called back. "We'll have another dekko."

"Drag her good and slow."

The fields roared by again but slower and
closer as though they might hover next. There
was no damage and no tracks.

"Don't have to stall her."

"I'm flying her, Papa. Want to see the other
side of it?"

"Yes."

This time the fields came up gently and softly
as though they were maybe a green formally
arranged disk being raised gently for our inspec-
tion by a skilled and gentle servant. There was
no damage and no elephant tracks. We rose fast

and turned so I could see the Shamba in relation to all of the others.

"Are you very sure that is your Shamba?" I asked the man.

"Yes," he said and it was impossible not to admire him.

None of us said anything. Ngui's face had no expression on it at all. He looked out of the Plexiglas window and drew the first finger of his right hand carefully across his throat.

"We might as well wash this and go home," I said.

Ngui put his hand on the side of the plane as though grasping the handle of the door and made a motion as though turning it. I shook my head and he laughed.

When we landed at the meadow and taxied up to where the hunting car was waiting by the wind sock on the leaning pole the man got out first. No one spoke to him.

"You watch him, Ngui," I said.

Then I went over to Arap Meina and took him aside.

"Yes," he said.

"He's probably thirsty," I said. "Give him some tea."

Willie and I rode over to the tents of the camp in the hunting car. We were sitting on the front seat. Arap Meina was in the back with our guest. Ngui had stayed behind with my 30-06 to guard the plane.

"Seems a little on the sticky side," Willie said. "When did you make up your mind, Papa?"

"The law of gravity business? Before we went out."

"Very thoughtful of you. Bad for the company. Put me out of business. Do you think Miss Mary would care to fly this afternoon? That would put us all up and we could have an interesting, instructional and educational flight in pursuit of your duties and all of us be airborne until I leave."

"Mary would like to fly."

"We could have a look at the Chulus and check the buff and your other beasts. G.C. might be pleased to know where the elephant really are."

"We'll take Ngui. He's getting to like it."

"Is Ngui very high in the religion?"

"His father once saw me changed into a snake. It was an unknown type of snake never seen before. That has a certain amount of influence in our religious circles."

"It should, Papa. And what were Ngui's father and you drinking when the miracle occurred?"

"Nothing but Tusker beer and a certain amount of Gordon's gin."

"You don't remember what type of snake it was?"

"How could I. It was Ngui's father who had the vision."

"Well, all we can do at the moment is hope Ngui watches the kite," Willie said. "I don't want it changing into a troop of baboons."

Miss Mary wanted to fly very much. She had seen the guest in the back of the hunting car and she was quite relieved.

"Was his Shamba damaged, Papa?" she asked. "Will you have to go up there?"

"No. There was no damage and we don't have to go up."

"How will he get back up there?"

"He's hitchhiking, I think."

We had some tea and I took a Campari and Gordon's with a splash of soda.

"This exotic life is charming," Willie said. "I wish I could join in it. What does that stuff taste like, Miss Mary?"

"It's very good, Willie."

"I'll save it for my old age. Tell me, Miss Mary, have you ever seen Papa turn into a snake?"

"No, Willie. I promise."

"We miss everything," Willie said. "Where would you like to fly, Miss Mary?"

"The Chulus."

So we flew to the Chulus going by Lion Hill and crossing Miss Mary's private desert and then down over the great swampy plain with the marsh birds and the ducks flying and all the treacherous places that made that plain impassable clearly revealed so that Ngui and I could see all of our mistakes and plan a new and different route. Then we were over the herds of eland on the far plain, dove colored, white striped and spiral horned, the bulls heavy with their awkward grace, breaking away from the cows that are the antelope cast in the form of cattle.

"I hope it wasn't too dull, Miss Mary," Willie said. "I was trying not to disturb any of G.C.'s and Papa's stock. Only to see where it was. I didn't want to frighten any creatures away from here or disturb your lion."

"It was lovely, Willie."

Then Willie was gone, first coming down the truck path at us bouncing into a roar as the widespread crane-like legs came joggling closer to clear the grass where we stood and then rising into an angle that creased your heart to take his course as he diminished in the afternoon light.

"Thank you for taking me," Mary said, as we watched Willie until the plane could no longer be seen. "Let's just go now and be good lovers and friends and love Africa because it is. I love it more than anything."

"So do I."

In the night we lay together in the big cot with the fire outside and the lantern I had hung on the tree making it light enough to shoot. Mary was not worried but I was. There were so many trip wires and booby snares around the tent that it was like being in a spiderweb. We lay close together and she said, "Wasn't it lovely in the plane?"

"Yes. Willie flies so gently. He's so thoughtful about the game too."

"But he frightened me when he took off."

"He was just proud of what she can do and remember he didn't have any load."

"We forgot to give him the meat."

"No. Mthuka brought it."

"I hope it will be good this time. He must have a lovely wife because he's so happy and kind. When people have a bad wife it shows in them quicker than anything."

"What about a bad husband?"

"It shows too. But sometimes much slower because women are braver and more loyal. Blessed Big Kitten, will we have a sort of normal day tomorrow and not all these mysterious and bad things?"

"What's a normal day?" I asked watching the

firelight and the unflickering light from the lantern.

"Oh, the lion."

"The good kind normal lion. I wonder where he is tonight."

"Let's go to sleep and hope he's happy the way we are."

"You know he never struck me as the really happy type."

Then she was really asleep and breathing softly and I bent my pillow over to make it hard and double so I could have a better view out of the open door of the tent. The night noises all were normal and I knew there were no people about. After a while Mary would need more room to sleep truly comfortably and would get up without waking and go over to her own cot where the bed was turned down and ready under the mosquito netting and when I knew that she was sleeping well I would go out with a sweater and mosquito boots in a heavy dressing gown and build up the fire and sit by the fire and stay awake.

There were all the technical problems. But the fire and the night and the stars made them seem small. I was worried though about some things and to not think about them I went to the dining tent and poured a quarter of a glass of whisky and put water in it and brought it back to the

fire. Then having a drink by the fire I was lonesome for Pop because we had sat by so many
fires together and I wished we were together and
he could tell me about things. There was enough
stuff in camp to make it well worth a full-scale
raid and G.C. and I were both sure that there
were many Mau Mau in Laitokitok and the
area. He had signaled them more than two
months before only to be informed that it was
nonsense. I believed Ngui that the Wakamba
Mau Mau were not coming our way. But I
thought they were the least of our problems. It
was clear that the Mau Mau had missionaries
among the Masai and were organizing the
Kikuyu that worked in the timber-cutting operations on Kilimanjaro. But whether there was any
fighting organization we would not know. I had
no police authority and was only the acting
Game Ranger and I was quite sure, perhaps
wrongly, that I would have very little backing if
I got into trouble. It was like being deputized to
form a posse in the West in the old days.

G.C. turned up after breakfast, his beret over
one eye, his boy's face gray and red with dust
and his people in the back of the Land Rover
as trim and dangerous looking and cheerful as
ever.

"Good morning, General," he said. "Where
is your cavalry?"

"Sir," I said. "They are screening the main body. This is the main body."

"I suppose the main body is Miss Mary. You haven't strained yourself thinking this all out have you?"

"You look a little battle fatigued yourself."

"I'm damned tired actually. But there's some good news. Our pals in Laitokitok are all going in the bag finally."

"Any orders, Gin Crazed?"

"Just continue the exercise, General. We'll drink a cold one and I must see Miss Mary and be off."

"Did you drive all night?"

"I don't remember. Will Mary be over soon?"

"I'll get her."

"How is she shooting?"

"God knows," I said piously.

"We'd better have a short code," G.C. said. "I'll signal shipment received if they come out the way they should."

"I'll send the same if they show up here."

"If they come this way I imagine I'll hear of it through channels," then as the mosquito bar opened, "Miss Mary. You're looking very lovely."

"My," she said. "I love Chungo. It's absolutely platonic."

"Memsahib Miss Mary, I mean." He bowed

over her hand. "Thank you for inspecting the troops. You're their Honorary Colonel you know. I'm sure they were all most honored. I say, can you ride sidesaddle?"

"Are you drinking too?"

"Yes, Miss Mary," G.C. said gravely. "And may I add no charges of miscegenation will be preferred for your avowed love for Game Ranger Chungo. The D.C. will never hear of it."

"You're both drinking and making fun of me."

"No," I said. "We both love you."

"But you're drinking though," Miss Mary said. "What can I make you to drink?"

"A little Tusker with the lovely breakfast," G.C. said. "Do you agree, General?"

"I'll go out," Miss Mary said. "If you want to talk secrets. Or drink beer without being uncomfortable."

"Honey," I said, "I know that in the war the people in charge of the war used to tell you everything about it before it happened. But there are many things G.C. doesn't tell me about. And I am sure there are people who don't tell G.C. things too long ahead of time. Also when people told you all about everything in the war you weren't camped in the heart of possibly enemy country. Would you want to be wandering around by yourself knowing projects?"

"Nobody ever lets me wander around by

myself and I'm always looked after as though I were helpless and might get lost or hurt. Anyway I'm sick of your speeches and you all playing at mysteries and dangers. You're just an early morning beer drinker and you get G.C. into bad habits and the discipline of your people is disgraceful. I saw four of your men who had obviously been on a drinking bout all night. They were laughing and joking and still half drunk. Sometimes you're preposterous."

There was a heavy cough outside the door of the tent. I went outside and there was the Informer, taller, and more dignified than ever and impressive in his shawl-wrapped, porkpie-hatted drunkenness.

"Brother, your Number One Informer is present," he said. "May I enter and make my compliments to the Lady Miss Mary and place myself at her feet?"

"Bwana Game is talking with Miss Mary. He'll be out directly."

Bwana Game came out of the mess tent and the Informer bowed. G.C.'s usually merry and kind eyes closed like a cat's and peeled the layer of protective drunkenness from the Informer as you might slice the outer layers from an onion or strip the skin from a plantain.

"What's the word from town, Informer?" I asked.

"Everyone was surprised that you did not fly

down the main street nor show Britain's might in the air."

"Spell it 'mite,' " G.C. said.

"To respectfully inform I did not spell it. I enunciated it," the Informer went on. "All of the village knew that the Bwana Mzee was in search of marauding elephants and had no time for aerial display. A Mission-educated owner of a Shamba returned to the village late in the afternoon having flown with the ndege of Bwana and he is being tailed by one of the children of the bar and duka run by the bearded Sikh. The child is intelligent and all contacts are being noted. There are between one hundred and fifty and two hundred and twenty certifiable Mau Mau in the village or within short outlying districts. Arap Meina appeared in the village shortly after the arrival of the airborne owner of the Shamba and devoted himself to his usual drunkenness and neglect of duty. He is voluble in talking about the Bwana Mzee in whose presence I stand. His story, which has wide credence, is that the Bwana occupies a position in America similar to that of the Aga Khan in the Moslem world. He is here in Africa to fulfill a series of vows he and Memsahib Lady Miss Mary have made. One of these vows deals with the need for the Memsahib Lady Miss Mary to kill a certain cattle-killing lion indicated by the Masai before the Birthday of the Baby Jesus. It is known and believed that a great part of the success of all things known depend on this. I have informed certain circles that after this vow has been performed the Bwana and I will make the visit to Mecca in one of his aircraft. It is rumored that a young Hindu girl is dying for the love of Bwana Game. It is rumored—"

"Shut up," said G.C. "Where did you learn the word tailed?"

"I also attend the cinema when my small wages permit. There is much to learn in the cinema for an informer."

"You are almost forgiven," G.C. said. "Tell me. Is the Bwana Mzee regarded as sane in the village?"

"With all respect, Bwanas, he is regarded as mad in the greatest tradition of Holy Men. It is rumored too that if the Honorable Lady Miss Mary does not kill the marauding lion before the Birthday of the Baby Jesus the Memsahib will commit suttee. Permission, it is said, has been obtained for this from the British Raj and special trees have been marked and cut for her funeral pyre. These trees are those from which the Masai make the medicine which both of you Bwanas know. It is said that in the event of this suttee, to which all tribes have been invited, there will be a giant Ngoma lasting a week, after which Bwana Mzee will take a Kamba wife. The girl has been chosen."

"Is there no other news from town?"

"Almost none," the Informer said modestly. "Some talk about the ritual killing of a leopard."

"You are dismissed," G.C. said to the Informer. The Informer bowed and retired to the shade of a tree.

"Well, Ernie," G.C. said. "Miss Mary had better bloody well kill this lion."

"Yes," I said. "I've thought so for some time."

"No wonder she is a little irascible."

"No wonder."

"It's not the Empire nor white prestige since you seem to have rather withdrawn from us palefaces for the moment. It's become rather personal. We have those five hundred rounds on nonexistent arms licenses that your outfitter sent out rather than hang if they were found on him. I think they might be impressive in a suttee in the very center of the pyre. I don't know the drill unfortunately."

"I'll get it from Mr. Singh."

"It puts a little heat on Miss Mary," G.C. said.

"I understand suttee always does."

"She'll kill the lion but make good peace with her and handle it sweetly and well and try to make him confident."

"That was the plan."

I spoke to G.C.'s people and I made a few jokes and they were off driving wide around the camp to keep from raising dust. Keiti and I talked about the camp and the way things were going and he was very cheerful so I knew everything was all right. He had walked down to the river and across to the road while the dew was still fresh and had seen no tracks of people. He had sent Ngui on a wide circle up past the meadow where the airstrip was and he had seen nothing. No one had come to any of the Shambas.

"They will think I am a careless fool that the men go twice in a row to drink at night," he said. "But I told them to say that I had fever. Bwana, you must sleep today."

"I will. But I must go now and see what Memsahib wishes to do."

At the camp I found Mary sitting in her chair under the biggest tree writing in her diary. She looked up at me and then smiled and I was very glad.

"I'm sorry I was cross," she said. "G.C. told me a little about your problems. I'm just sorry they come at Christmastime."

"I am too. You've put up with so much and I want you to have fun."

"I'm having fun. It's such a wonderful morning and I'm enjoying it and watching the birds and identifying them. Have you seen that wonderful roller? I'd be happy just watching the birds."

It was quiet around camp and everyone had settled into normal life. I felt badly about Mary having the feeling she was never allowed to hunt alone and I had realized long before why white hunters were paid as well as they were and I understood why they shifted camp to hunt their clients where they could protect them accurately. Pop would never have hunted Miss Mary here, I knew, and would have taken no nonsense. But I remembered how women almost always fell in love with their white hunters and I hoped something spectacular would come up where I could be my client's hero and thus become beloved as a hunter by my lawful wedded wife instead of her unpaid and annoying bodyguard. Such situations do not come by too often in real life and when they do they are over so quickly, since you do not permit them to develop, that the client thinks they were extremely facile. It seemed natural I should be reprimanded and it was certainly not the way a white hunter, that iron-nerved panderer to what a woman expects, should behave.

I went to sleep in the big chair under the big shade tree and when I woke the clouds had come down from the Chulus and were black across the flank of the Mountain. The sun was still out but you could feel the wind coming and the rain behind it. I shouted to Mwindi and to Keiti and by the time the rain hit, coming across the plain and through the trees in a solid white, then torn curtain everyone was pounding stakes, loosening and tightening guy ropes and then ditching. It was a heavy rain and the wind was wild. For a moment it looked as though the main sleeping tent might go but it held when we pegged the windward end heavily. Then the roar of the wind was gone and the rain held steadily. It rained all that night and nearly all of the next day.

During the rain of the first evening a native policeman came in with a message from G.C., "Shipment passed through." The askari was wet and had walked from where a truck was stranded up the road. The river was too deep to cross.

I wondered how G.C. had the word so quickly and had been able to send it back. He must have run into a scout who was bringing it to him and sent it back by one of the Hindu lorries. There was no more problem so I went out in my raincoat through the driving rain walking in the heavy mud and around the running

streams and lakes of water to the lines and told
Keiti. He was surprised that there had been a
signal so soon but happy that the alert was over.
It would have been a difficult problem as conditions were to continue the exercise in the rain. I
left work with Keiti to tell Arap Meina he could
sleep in the mess tent if he showed up and Keiti
said Arap Meina was too intelligent to show up
to keep watch by a fire in this rain.

As it turned out Arap Meina turned up, really
wet, having walked all the way from the
Shamba in the worst of the storm. I gave him a
drink and asked him if he did not want to stay
and put on dry clothes and sleep in the mess
tent. But he said that he would rather go back to
the Shamba where he had dry clothes and that it
was better for him to be there because this rain
would last another day and maybe two days. I
asked him if he had seen it coming and he said
that he had not and neither had anyone else and
that if they said they had they were liars. For a
week it had looked as though it would rain and
then it had come with no warning. I gave him
an old cardigan of mine to wear next to his skin
and a short waterproof skiing jacket and put
two bottles of beer in the back pocket and he
took a small drink and set off. He was a fine
man and I wished that I had known him all my
life and that we had spent our lives together. I

thought for a moment about how odd our lives would have been in certain places and that made me happy.

We were all spoiled by too much perfect weather and the older men were more uncomfortable and intolerant of the rain than the young outfit. Also they did not drink, being Mohammedans, and so you could not give them a shot to warm them when they were soaked through.

There had been much discussion as to whether this rain could also have fallen in their own tribal lands in the Machakos area and the general opinion was that it had not. But as it kept up and rained steadily all night everyone was cheered that it was probably falling in the north as well. It was pleasant in the mess tent with the heavy beating of the rain and I read and drank a little and did not worry at all about anything. Everything had been taken out of my control and I welcomed, as always, the lack of responsibility and the splendid inactivity with no obligation to kill, pursue, protect, intrigue, defend or participate and I welcomed the chance to read. We were getting a little far down into the book bag but there were still some hidden values mixed in with the required reading and there were twenty volumes of Simenon in French that I had not read. If you are to be rained in while camped in Africa there is nothing better than Simenon and with him I did not care how long it rained. You draw perhaps three good Simenons out of each five but an addict can read the bad ones when it rains and I would start them, mark them bad, or good; there is no intermediate grade with Simenon and then having classified a half dozen and cut the pages, I would read happily, transferring all my problems to Maigret, bearing with him in his encounters with idiocy and the Quai des Orfieves, and very happy in his sagacious and true understanding of the French, a thing only a man of his nationality could achieve, since Frenchmen are barred by some obscure law from understanding themselves *sous peine des travaux forcés à la perpétuité.*

Miss Mary seemed resigned to the rain, which was steadier now and no less heavy, and she had given up writing letters and was reading something that interested her. It was *The Prince* by Machiavelli. I wondered what it would be like if it should rain three days or four. With Simenon in the quantities that I possessed of him I was good for a month if I stopped reading and thought between books, pages or chapters. Driven by continuing rain I could think between paragraphs, not thinking of Simenon but of other things, and I thought I could last a month quite easily and profitably even if there should be nothing to drink and I should be driven to using Arap Meina's snuff or trying out the different brews from the medicinal trees and plants we had come to know. Watching Miss Mary, her attitude exemplary, her face beautiful in repose as she read, I wondered what would happen to a person who since little past her adolescence had been nurtured on the disasters of daily journalism, the problems of Chicago social life, the destruction of European civilization, the bombing of large cities, the confidences of those who bombed other large cities in retaliation, and the large- and small-scaled disasters, problems and incalculable casualties of marriage which are only relieved by some painkilling unguent, a primitive remedy against the pox, the paste compounded of newer and finer violences, changes of scene, extensions of knowledge, exploration of the different arts, the places, the people, the beasts, the sensations; I wondered what a six-week rain would be to her. But then I remembered how good and fine and brave she was and how much she had put up with through many years and I thought she would be better at it than I would. Thinking this I saw her put down her book, go and unhook her raincoat, put it on, put on her floppy hat and start out in the straight up and down rain to see how her troops were.

I'd seen them in the morning and they were

uncomfortable but fairly cheerful. The men all had tents and there were picks and shovels for ditching and they had seen and felt rain before. It seemed to me that if I were trying to keep dry under a pup tent and live through a rain I would want as few people in waterproof clothing, high boots and hats inspecting my living conditions as possible, especially since they could do nothing to better them except see that some local grog was served. But then I realized this was no way to think and that the way to get along on a trip was not to be critical of your partner and, after all, visiting the troops was the only positive action there was to offer her.

When she came back and flapped the rain from her hat, hung her Burberry on the tent pole and changed her boots for dry slippers I asked how the troops were.

"They're fine," she said. "It is wonderful how they keep the cooking fire sheltered."

"Did they come to attention in the rain?"

"Don't be bad," she said. "I just wanted to see how they cooked in this rain."

"Did you see?"

"Please don't be bad and let's be happy and have a good time since we have the rain."

"I was having a good time. Let's think about how wonderful it will be after the rain."

"I don't have to," she said. "I'm happy with

being forced to do nothing. We have such a wonderful exciting life every day that it is good to be forced to stop and appreciate it. When it is over we are going to wish we'd had time to appreciate it more."

"We'll have your diary. Do you remember how we used to read it in bed and remember that wonderful trip through the snow country out around Montpelier and the east end of Wyoming after the blizzard and the tracks in the snow and how we would see the eagles and racing with the streamliner that was the Yellow Peril and all the way along the border in Texas and when you used to drive? You kept a lovely diary then. Do you remember when the eagle caught the possum and he was so heavy he had to drop him?"

"This time I'm always tired and sleepy. Then we'd stop early and be in a motel with a light to write by. It's harder now when you've been up since daylight and you can't write in bed and have to write it outside and so many unknown bugs and insects come to the light. If I knew the names of the insects that interfere with me it would be simpler."

"We have to think about poor people like Thurber and how Joyce was finally when they get so they can't even see what they write."

"I can hardly read mine sometimes and thank

God no one else can read it with the things I put down."

"We put in rough jokes because this has been a rough-joking outfit."

"You and G.C. joke so very rough and Pop jokes quite rough too. I joke rough too I know. But not as bad as all of you."

"Some jokes are all right in Africa but they don't travel because people don't realize what the country and the animals are like where it is all the world of the animals and they have predators. People who have never known predators don't know what you are talking about. Nor people that never had to kill their meat nor if they don't know the tribes and what is natural and normal. I put it very badly I know, kittner, but I'll try and write it so it can be understood. But you have to say so many things that most people will not understand nor conceive of doing."

"I know," Mary said. "And the liars write the books and how can you compete with a liar? How can you compete with a man who writes how he shot and killed a lion and then they carried him to camp in a lorry and suddenly the lion came alive? How can you compete with the truth against a man who says the Great Ruaha was maggoty with crocodiles? But you don't have to."

"No," I said. "And I won't. But you can't blame the liars because all a writer of fiction is really is a congenital liar who invents from his own knowledge or that of other men. I am a writer of fiction and so I am a liar too and invent from what I know and that I've heard. I'm a liar."

"But you would not lie to G.C., or Pop, or me on what a lion did, or a leopard did, or what a buff did."

"No. But that is private. My excuse is that I make the truth as I invent it truer than it would be. That is what makes good writers or bad. If I write in the first person, stating it is fiction, critics now will still try to prove these things never happened to me. It is as silly as trying to prove Defoe was not Robinson Crusoe so therefore it is a bad book. I'm sorry if I sound like speeches. But we can make speeches together on a rainy day."

"I love to talk about writing and what you believe and know and care about. But it's only on a rainy day that we can talk."

"I know it, kittner. That's because we're here in a strange time."

"I wish I'd known it in the old days with you and Pop."

"I was never here in the old days. They just seem old now. Actually now is much more interesting. We couldn't have been friends and brothers the way we are now in the old days. Pop never would have let me. When Mkola and I got to be brothers it wasn't respectable. It was just condoned. Now Pop tells you all sorts of things he never would have told me in the old days."

"I know. I'm very honored that he tells me."

"Honey, are you bored? I'm perfectly happy reading and not being wet in the rain. You have to write letters too."

"No. I love for us to talk together. It's the thing I miss when there is so much excitement and work and we're never alone except in bed. We have a wonderful time in bed and you say lovely things to me. I remember them and the fun. But this is a different kind of talking."

The rain was still a steady, heavy beating on the canvas. It had replaced all other things and it fell without varying its beat or its rhythm.

"Lawrence tried to tell about it," I said. "But I could not follow him because there was so much cerebral mysticism. I never believed he had slept with an Indian girl. Nor even touched one. He was a sensitive journalist sightseeing in Indian country and he had hatreds and theories and prejudices. Also he could write beautifully. But it was necessary for him, after a time, to become angry to write. He had done some

things perfectly and he was at the point of discovering something most people do not know
when he began to have so many theories."

"I follow it pretty well," Miss Mary said,
"but what does it have to do with the Shamba?
I like your fiancée very much because she is a lot
like me and I think she'd be a valuable extra
wife if you need one. But you don't have to justify her by some writer. Which Lawrence were
you talking about, D.H. or T.E.?"

"OK," I said. "I think you make very good
sense and I'll read Simenon."

"Why don't you go to the Shamba and try
living there in the rain?"

"I like it here," I said.

"She's a nice girl," Miss Mary said. "And she
may think it's not very genteel of you to not turn
up when it rains."

"Want to make peace?"

"Yes," she said.

"Good. I won't talk balls about Lawrence
and dark mysteries and we'll stay here in the
rain and the hell with the Shamba. I don't think
Lawrence would like the Shamba too much anyway."

"Did he like to hunt?"

"No. But that's nothing against him, thank
God."

"Your girl wouldn't like him then."

"I don't think she would. But thank God that's nothing against him either."

"Did you ever know him?"

"No. I saw him and his wife once in the rain outside of Sylvia Beach's book shop in the Rue de l'Odéon. They were looking in the window and talking but they didn't go in. His wife was a big woman in tweeds and he was small in a big overcoat with a beard and very bright eyes. He didn't look well and I did not like to see him getting wet. It was warm and pleasant inside Sylvia's."

"I wonder why they didn't go in?"

"I don't know. That was before people spoke to people they did not know and long before people asked people for autographs."

"How did you recognize him?"

"There was a picture of him in the shop behind the stove. I admired a book of stories he wrote called *The Prussian Officer* very much and a novel called *Sons and Lovers*. He used to write beautifully about Italy too."

"Anybody who can write ought to be able to write about Italy."

"They should. But it's difficult even for Italians. More difficult for them than for anyone. If an Italian writes at all well about Italy he is a phenomenon. Stendhal wrote the best about Milan."

"The other day you said all writers were crazies and today you say they're all liars."

"Did I say they were all crazies?"

"Yes, you and G.C. both said it."

"Was Pop here?"

"Yes. He said all Game Wardens were crazy and so were all White Hunters and the White Hunters had been driven crazy by the Game Wardens and the writers and by motor vehicles."

"Pop is always right."

"He told me never to mind about you and G.C. because you were both crazy."

"We are," I said. "But you mustn't tell outsiders."

"But you don't really mean all writers are crazy?"

"Only the good ones."

"But you got angry when that man wrote a book about how you were crazy."

"Yes, because he did not know about it nor how it worked. Just as he knew nothing about writing."

"It's awfully complicated," Miss Mary said.

"I won't try to explain it. I'll try to write something to show you how it works."

So I sat for a while and reread *La Maison du Canal* and thought about the animals getting wet. The hippos would be having a good time today. But it was no day for the other animals and especially for the cats. The game had so many things that bothered them that the rain would only be bad for those that never had known it and those would only be the beasts born since the last rain. I wondered if the big cats killed in the rain when it was as heavy as this. They must have to, to live. The game would be much easier to approach but the lion and leopard and cheetah must hate to get so wet when they hunted. Maybe the cheetah not so much because they seemed part dog and their coats were made for wet weather. The snake holes would be full of water and the snakes would be out and this rain would bring the flying ants too.

I thought how lucky we were this time in Africa to be living long enough in one place so that we knew the individual animals and knew the snake holes and the snakes that lived in them. When I had first been in Africa we were always in a hurry to move from one place to another to hunt beasts for trophies. If you saw a cobra it was an accident as it would be to find a rattler on the road in Wyoming. Now we knew many places where cobras lived. We still discovered them by accident but they were in the area where we lived and we could return to them afterwards and when, by accident, we killed a snake he was the snake who lived in a particular place and hunted his area as we lived in ours and moved out from it. It was G.C. who had given us this great privilege of getting to know and live in a wonderful part of the country and have some work to do that justified our presence there and I always felt deeply grateful to him.

The time of shooting beasts for trophies was long past with me. I still loved to shoot and to kill cleanly. But I was shooting for the meat we needed to eat and to back up Miss Mary and against beasts that had been outlawed for cause and for what is known as control of marauding animals, predators and vermin. I had shot one impala for a trophy and an oryx for meat at Magadi which turned out to have fine enough horns to make it a trophy and I had shot a single buffalo in an emergency which served for meat at Magadi when we were very short and which had a pair of horns worth keeping to recall the manner of the small emergency Mary and I had shared. I remembered it now with happiness and I knew I would always remember it with happiness. It was one of those small things that you can go to sleep with, that you can wake with in the night and that you could recall if necessary if you were ever tortured.

"Do you remember the morning with the buff, kittner?" I asked.

She looked across the mess table and said, "Don't ask me things like that. I'm thinking about the lion."

That night after cold supper we went to bed early, since Mary had written her diary in the late afternoon, and lay in bed listening to the heaviness of the rain on that taut canvas.

But in spite of the steady noise of the rain I did not sleep well and I woke twice sweating with nightmares. The last one was a very bad one and I reached out under the mosquito net and felt for the water bottle and the square flask of gin. I brought it into the bed with me and then tucked the netting back under the blanket and the air mattress of the cot. In the dark I rolled my pillow up so I could lay back with my head against it and found the small balsam-needle pillow and put it under my neck. Then I felt for my pistol alongside my leg and for the electric torch and then unscrewed the top of the flask of gin.

In the dark with the heavy noise of the rain I took a swallow of the gin. It tasted clean and friendly and made me brave against the night-mare. The nightmare had been about as bad as they come and I have had some bad ones in my time. I knew I could not drink while we were hunting Miss Mary's lion; but we would not be hunting him tomorrow in the wet. Tonight was a bad night for some reason. I had been spoiled by too many good nights and I had come to think that I did not have nightmares anymore. Well I knew now. Perhaps it was because the tent was so battened down against the rain that there was no proper ventilation. Perhaps it was because I had had no exercise all day.

I took another swallow of the gin and it tasted even better and more like the old Giant Killer. It had not been such an exceptional nightmare, I thought. I've had much worse than that. But what I knew was that I had been through with nightmares, the real ones that could drench you in sweat, for a long time and I had only had good or bad dreams and most of the night they were good dreams. Then I heard Mary say, "Papa are you drinking?"

"Yes. Why?"

"Could I have some too?"

I reached the flask over from under the net and she put her hand out and took it.

"Do you have the water?"

"Yes," I said and reached it over too. "You have yours too by your bed."

"But you told me to be careful about things and I did not want to wake you with the light."

"Poor kitten. Haven't you slept?"

"Yes. But I had the most awful dreams. Too bad to tell before breakfast."

"I had some bad ones too."

"Here's the Jinny flask back," she said. "In case you need it. Hold my hand tight, please. You aren't dead and G.C. isn't dead and Pop isn't dead."

"No. We're all fine."

"Thank you so much. And you sleep too. You don't love anybody else do you? White I mean?"

"No. Not white nor black nor red all over."

"Sleep well, my blessed," she said. "Thank you for the lovely midnight drink."

"Thank you for killing the nightmares."

"That's one of the things I'm for," she said.

I lay and thought about that for a long time remembering many places and really bad times and I thought how wonderful it would be now after the rain and what were nightmares anyway and then I went to sleep and woke sweating again with the horrors but I listened carefully and heard Mary breathing softly and regularly and then I went back to sleep to try it once more.

5

IN THE MORNING it was cold with heavy cloud over all the Mountain. There was a heavy wind again and the rain came in patches but the heavy solid rain was over. I went out to the lines to talk with Keiti and found him very cheerful. He was wearing a raincoat and an old felt hat. He said the weather would probably be good by the next day and I told him we would wait until Memsahib woke before driving in the tent pegs and loosening the wet ropes. He was pleased that the ditching had turned out so well and that neither the sleeping tent nor the mess tent had been wet. He had already sent for a fire to be built and everything was looking better. I told him I had a dream that it had rained heavily up in the Reserve. This was a lie but I thought it was good to weigh in with a good heavy lie in case we had good news from Pop. If you are going to prophesy it is good to prophesy with the odds in your favor.

Keiti heard my dream through with attention and with simulated respect. Then he told me that he had dreamed that it had rained heavily all the way to the Tana River, which was on the edge of the desert, and that six safaris were cut off and would not be able to move for weeks. This, as it was calculated to do, made a very small thing of my dream. I knew that my dream had been registered and would be checked on but I thought I ought to back it up. So I told him, quite truly, that I dreamed that we had hanged the Informer. Recounting this I gave him the exact procedure: where, how, why, how he had taken it and how we had taken him out, afterwards, in the hunting car to be eaten by the hyenas.

Keiti hated the Informer and had for many years and he loved this dream but was careful that I should know that he himself had not dreamed of the Informer at all. This was important, I knew, but I gave him some more details of the execution. He was delighted with them and he said wistfully, but in full judgment, "You must not do."

"I cannot do. But maybe my dream will do."

"You must not make uchawi."

"I do not make uchawi. Have you ever seen me harm a man or a woman?"

"I did not say you were a mchawi. I said you must not be one and that it cannot be to hang the Informer."

"If you wish to save him I can forget the dream."

"Good dream," Keiti said. "But make too much trouble."

The day after a heavy rain is a splendid day for the propagation of religion while the time of the rain itself seems to turn men's minds from the beauty of their faith. All rain had stopped now and I was sitting by the fire drinking tea and looking out over the sodden country. Miss Mary was still sleeping soundly because there was no sun to wake her. Mwindi came to the table by the fire with a fresh pot of hot tea and poured me a cup.

"Plenty rain," he said. "Now finished."

"Mwindi," I said. "You know what the Mahdi said. 'We see plainly in the laws of nature that rain comes down from the heavens in the time of need. The greenness and verdure of the earth depend upon heavenly rain. If it ceases for a time the water in the upper strata of the earth gradually dries up. Thus we see that there is an attraction between the heavenly and the earthly waters. Revelation stands in the same relation to human reason as heavenly water does to the earthly water.' "

"Too much rain for campi. Plenty good for Shamba," Mwindi announced.

" 'As with the cessation of heavenly water earthly water begins gradually to dry up; so also is the case of the human reason which without the heavenly revelation loses its purity and strength.' "

"How I know that is Mahdi?" Mwindi said.

"Ask Charo."

Mwindi grunted. He knew Charo was very devout but not a theologian.

"If hang Informer let police hang too," Mwindi said. "Keiti ask me to say it."

"That was only a dream."

"Dream can be very strong. Can kill like bunduki."

"I'll tell Informer dream. Then it has no power."

"Uchawi," Mwindi said. "Uchawi kubwa sana."

"Hapana uchawi."

Mwindi broke it off and asked almost brusquely if I wanted more tea. He was looking away at the lines with his old Chinese profile and I saw what it was he wanted me to see. It was the Informer.

He had come wet and not happy. His style and his gallantry were not gone but they had been dampened. He coughed his cough at once so there would be no doubt of it and it was a legitimate cough.

"Good morning, brother. How have you and my lady endured the weather?"

"It rained a little here."

"Brother, I am a sick man."

"Do you have fever?"

"Yes."

He was not lying. His pulse was one hundred and twenty.

"Sit down and have a drink and take an aspirin and I'll give you medicine. Go home and go to bed. Can the hunting car get through the road?"

"Yes. It is sandy to the Shamba and the car can go around the pools."

"How is the Shamba?"

"It did not need the rain because it is irrigated. It is a sad Shamba with the cold from the Mountain. Even the chickens are sad. A girl came with me whose father needs medicine for his chest. You know her."

"I will send medicine."

"She is unhappy that you do not come."

"I have my duties. Is she well?"

"She is well but sad."

"Tell her I will come to Shamba when it is my duty."

"Brother, what is this of the dream that I am hanged?"

"It is a dream that I had but I should not tell it to you before I have eaten breakfast."

"But others have heard it before."

"It is better that you do not hear it. It was not an official dream."

"I could not bear to be hanged," the Informer said.

"I will never hang you."

"But others could misunderstand my activities."

"No one will hang you unless you deal with the other people."

"But I must constantly deal with the other people."

"You understood the sense in which I speak. Now go to the campfire and get warm and I will make up the medicine."

"You are my brother."

"No," I said. "I am your friend."

He went off to the fire and I opened the medicine chest and got out Atabrine and aspirin and liniment and some sulfa and some cough lozenges and hoped I had made a small blow against uchawi. But I could remember all the details of the execution of the Informer in about the third of the nightmares and I was ashamed of having such a nocturnal imagination. I told him what medicines to take and what to give to the father of the girl. Then we walked out to the lines together and I gave the girl two tins of kipper snacks and a glass jar of hard candies and asked Mthuka to drive them to the Shamba and then come straight back. She had brought me four ears of corn and never looked up when I

spoke to her. She put her head against my chest
as a child does and when she got into the car on
the off side where no one could see her she
dropped her arm and with her whole hand
gripped the muscles of my thigh. I did the same
thing when she was in the car and she did not
look up. Then I thought the hell with it all and
kissed her on the top of the head and she
laughed as impudently as ever and Mthuka
smiled and they drove off. The tract was sandy
with a little standing water but the bottom was
firm and the hunting car went off through the
trees and nobody looked back.

I told Ngui and Charo that we would go
north on a routine look around as far as it was
possible to go as soon as Miss Mary had wakened and had breakfast. They could get the guns
now and clean them after the rain. I told them
to be sure and wipe the bores dry of all oil. It
was cold and the wind was blowing. The sun
was overcast. But the rain was over except for
possible showers. Everybody was very busi-
nesslike and there was no nonsense.

Mary was very happy at breakfast. She had
slept well after she had wakened in the night
and her dreams had been happy. Her bad dream
had been that Pop, G.C. and I had all been
killed. She did not remember the details. Someone had brought the news. She thought it was in

an ambush of some kind. I wanted to ask her if she had dreamed about the hanging of the Informer but I thought that would be interference and the important thing was that she had waked happily and looked forward to the day. I thought that I was rough enough and worthless enough to become involved in the things that I did not understand in Africa but I did not want to involve her. She involved herself enough by going out to the lines and learning the music and the drum rhythms and the songs, treating everyone so well and so kindly that they fell in love with her. In the old days I know Pop would never have permitted this. But the old days were gone. No one knew that better than Pop did.

When breakfast was over and the hunting car was back from the Shamba Mary and I made a trip out as far as the ground was possible to drive over. The earth was drying fast but it was still treacherous and the wheels spun and dug in where tomorrow the car could go with security. This was so even on the hard ground and where the track had been firmed and hardened. To the north where the slippery clay was it was impassable.

You could see the new grass coming bright green across the flats and the game was scattered and paid little attention to us. There had been no great movement of game in yet but we saw the tracks of elephants that had crossed the track early in the morning after the rain stopped going toward the swamp. They were the lot we had seen from the plane and the bull had a very big track even allowing for the spreading by the wetness of the mud.

It was gray and cold and blowing and all over the flats and in and beside the tracks were the plover running and feeding busily and then calling sharply and wildly as they flew. There were three different kinds only one of which was really good to eat. But the men would not eat them and thought I wasted a cartridge to shoot them. I knew there might be curlew up on the flat but we could try for them another day.

"We can go on a little further," I said. "There is a pretty good ridge of fairly high ground where we can turn," I said to Mary.

"Let's go on then."

Then it began to rain and I thought we had better get turned around where we could and back to camp before we were stuck in some of the soft places.

Close to camp, which showed happily against the trees and the gray mist, the smoke of the fires rising and the white-and-green tents looking comfortable and home-like, there were sand grouse drinking at the small pools of water on the open prairie. I got out with Ngui to get some for us to eat while Mary went on to camp. They were hunched low beside the little pools and scattered about in the short grass where the sand burrs grew. They clattered up and they were not hard to hit if you took them quickly on the rise. These were the medium-sized sand grouse and they were like plump little desert pigeons masquerading as partridges. I loved their strange flight, which was like a pigeon or a kestrel, and the wonderful way they used their long back-swept wings once they were in full flight. Walking them up this way was nothing like shooting them when they came in great strings and packs to the water in the morning in the dry season when G.C. and I would take only the highest-crossing birds and high incomers and paid a shilling penalty any time we took more than one bird to a shot fired. Walking them up you missed the guttural chuckling noise the pack made as they talked across the sky. I did not like to shoot so close to camp either so I took only four brace, which would make at least two meals for the two of us or a good meal if anyone dropped in.

The safari crew did not like to eat them. I did not like them as well as lesser bustard, teal or snipe or the spur-winged plover. But they were very good eating and would be good for supper. The small rain had stopped again but the mist and the clouds came down to the foot of the Mountain.

Mary was sitting in the dining tent with a Campari and soda.

"Did you get many?"

"Eight. They were a little like shooting pigeons at the Club de Cazadores del Cerro."

"They break away much faster than pigeons."

"I think it just seems that way because of the clatter and because they are smaller. Nothing breaks faster than a really strong racing pigeon."

"My, I'm glad we're here instead of shooting at the Club."

"I am too. I wonder if I can go back there."

"You will."

"I don't know," I said. "I think maybe not."

"There are an awful lot of things I'm not sure I can go back to."

"I wish we didn't have to go back at all. I wish we didn't have any property nor any possessions nor any responsibilities. I wish we only owned a safari outfit and a good hunting car and two good trucks."

"I'd be the most popular hostess under canvas in the world. I know just how it would be. People would turn up in their private planes and the pilot would get out and open the door for the man and then the man would say, 'Bet you can't tell me who I am. I'll bet you don't remember me. Who am I?' Sometime somebody is going to say that and I'm going to ask Charo for my bunduki and shoot the man right straight between the eyes."

"And Charo can halal him."

"They don't eat men."

"The Wakamba used to. In what you and Pop always refer to as the good old days."

"You're part Kamba. Would you eat a man?"

"No."

"Do you know I've never killed a man in my life? Remember when I wanted to share everything with you and I felt so terribly because I had never killed a Kraut and how worried everyone became?"

"I remember very well."

"Should I make the speech about when I kill the woman who steals your affection?"

"If you'll make me a Campari and soda too."

"I will and I'll make you the speech."

She poured the red Campari bitters and put in some Gordon's and then squirted the siphon.

"The gin is a reward for listening to the speech. I know you've heard the speech many times. But I like to make it. It's good for me to make it and it's good for you to hear it."

"OK. Start it."

"Ah hah," Miss Mary said. "So you think

you can make my husband a better wife than I can. Ah hah. So you think you are ideally and perfectly suited to one another and that you will be better for him than I am. Ah hah. So you think that you and he would lead a perfect existence together and at least he would have the love of a woman who understands communism, psychoanalysis and the true meaning of the word love? What do you know about love you bedraggled hag? What do you know about my husband and the things we have shared and have in common?"

"Hear. Hear."

"Let me go on. Listen, you bedraggled specimen, thin where you should be robust, bursting with fat where you should show some signs of race and breeding. Listen, you woman. I have killed an innocent buck deer at a distance of three hundred and forty estimated yards and have eaten him with no remorse. I have shot the kongoni and the wildebeest which you resemble. I have shot and killed a great and beautiful oryx and that is more beautiful than any woman and has horns more decorative than any man. I have killed more things than you have made passes at and I tell you cease and desist in your mealymouthed mouthings to my husband and leave this country or I will kill you dead."

"It's a wonderful speech. You wouldn't ever make it in Swahili would you?"

"There's no need to make it in Swahili," Miss Mary said. She always felt a little like Napoleon at Austerlitz after the speech. "The speech is for white women only. It certainly does not apply to your fiancée. Since when does a good loving husband not have a right to a fiancée if she only wishes to be a supplementary wife? That is an honorable position. The speech is directed against any filthy white woman who thinks that she can make you happier than I can. The upstarts."

"It's a lovely speech and you make it more clear and forcible each time."

"It's a true speech," Miss Mary said. "I mean every word of it. But I've tried to keep all bitterness and any sort of vulgarity out of it. I hope you didn't think mealymouthed had anything to do with mealies."

"I didn't think so."

"That's good. Those were really nice mealies she brought you too. Do you think one time we could have them roasted in the ashes of the fire? I love them that way."

"Of course we can."

"Is there anything special about her bringing you four?"

"No. Two for you and two for me."

"I wish someone were in love with me and brought me presents."

"Everybody brings you presents every day

and you know it. Half the camp cuts toothbrushes for you."

"That's true. I have lots of toothbrushes. I
still have plenty from Magadi even. I'm glad
you have such a nice fiancée though. I wish
everything was as simple always as things are
here at the foot of the Mountain."

"They're not really simple at all. We're just
lucky."

"I know. And we must be good and kind to
each other to deserve all our luck. Oh I hope my
lion will come and I'll be tall enough to see him
clearly when the time comes. Do you know how
much he means to me?"

"I think so. Everybody does."

"Some people think I'm crazy I know. But in
the old days people went to search for the Holy
Grail and for the Golden Fleece and they
weren't supposed to be silly. A great lion is better and more serious than any cups or sheep-
skins. I don't care how Holy or Golden they
were. Everybody has something that they want
truly and my lion means everything to me. I
know how patient you've been about him and
how patient everyone has been. But now I'm
sure after this rain I'll meet him. I can't wait
until the first night that I hear him roar."

"He has a wonderful roar and you'll see him
soon."

"Outside people will never understand. But he will make up for everything."

"I know. You don't hate him do you?"

"No. I love him. He's wonderful and he is intelligent and I don't have to tell you why I have to kill him."

"No. Certainly not."

"Pop knows. And he explained to me. He told me about that terrible woman too that everyone shot her lion forty-two times. I better not talk about it because no one can ever understand."

We did understand because together one time we had seen the tracks of the first great lion. They were twice the size a lion's tracks should be and they were in light dust that had just been rained on only enough to dampen it so that they were a true print. I had been working up on some kongoni to kill meat for camp and when Ngui and I saw the tracks we pointed with grass stems and I could see the sweat come on his forehead. We waited for Mary without moving and when she saw the tracks she drew a deep breath. She had seen many lion tracks by then and several lions killed but these tracks were unbelievable. Ngui kept shaking his head and I could feel the sweat under my armpits and in my crotch. We followed the tracks like hounds and saw where he had drunk at a muddy spring

and then gone up the draw to the escarpment. I
had never seen such tracks, ever, and by the mud
of the spring they were even clearer.

I had not known whether to go back and find
the kongoni and run the risk of shooting and
perhaps having him leave that country with the
sound of the rifle shot. But we needed meat and
this was a country where there was not much
meat and all the game was wild because there
were so many predators. You never killed a
zebra that did not have black, riven lion claw
scars on his hide and the zebra were as shy and
unapproachable as desert oryx. It was a buffalo,
rhino, lion and leopard country and nobody
liked to hunt it except G.C. and Pop and it
made Pop nervous. G.C. had so many nerves
that he had ended by having no nerves and he
never admitted the presence of danger until he
had shot his way out of it. But Pop had said that
he never had hunted this country without having trouble and he had hunted it, making the
trek across the deadly flats at night to avoid the
heat, which could be one hundred and twenty
degrees Fahrenheit in the shade, many years
before G.C. had been here or motor cars had
been brought to East Africa.

I was thinking of this when we saw the tracks
of the lion and afterwards, when we started to
maneuver the kongoni, I thought only of that.

But the lion track was in my mind as though it had been branded there and I knew that Mary, from having seen other lions, had imagined him as he must have looked coming along that trail. We had killed the highly edible, horse-faced, awkward, tawny kongoni, which was as innocent or more innocent than anything could be and Mary had finished it with a shot where the neck joins the head. She had done this to perfect her shooting and because it was necessary and someone must do it.

Sitting there in the tent I thought how abhorrent this would be to real vegetarians but everyone who has ever eaten meat must know that someone has killed it and since Mary, having engaged in killing, wanted to kill without inflicting suffering, it was necessary for her to learn and to practice. Those who never catch fish, not even a tin of sardines, and who will stop their cars if there are locusts on the road, and have never eaten even meat broth should not condemn those who kill to eat and to whom the meat belonged to before the white men stole their country. Who knows what the carrot feels, or the small young radish, or the used electric light bulb, or the worn phonograph disc, or the apple tree in winter. Who knows the feelings of the overaged aircraft, the chewed gum, the cigarette butt or the discarded book riddled by

woodworms? In my copy of the regulations of
the Game Department not one of these cases
was treated nor was there any regulation about
the treatment of yaws and of venereal disease
which was one of my daily duties. There were
no regulations regarding the fallen limbs of trees
nor dust nor biting flies, other than Tsetse; see
Fly Areas. The hunters who took out licenses to
hunt and were allowed by valid permits to hunt
for a limited time in certain of the Masai countries which had formerly been reserves and were
now controlled areas kept a schedule of what
beasts they were permitted to kill and then paid
a very nominal fee which was later paid to the
Masai. But the Wakamba, who used to hunt at
great risk to themselves in the Masai country for
meat, were not permitted now to do so. They
were hunted down as poachers by Game Scouts,
who were also, mostly, Wakamba, and G.C. and
Mary thought Game Scouts were better loved
than they were.

Game Scouts were nearly all of them a very
high type of soldier who had come from the
hunting Wakamba. But things were getting very
difficult Ukambani. They had farmed their land
in their own and their old fashion but shortening the fallow that should last a generation as
the Wakamba grew and their land did not, it
had eroded along with all the rest of Africa.

186 • ERNEST HEMINGWAY

Their warriors had always fought in all of
Britain's wars and the Masai had never fought
in any. The Masai had been coddled, preserved,
treated with a fear that they should never have
inspired and been adored by all the homosexuals like Thessinger who had worked for the
Empire in Kenya or Tanganyika because the
men were so beautiful. The men were very beautiful, extremely rich, were professional warriors
who, now for a long time, would never fight.
They had always been drug addicts and now
they were becoming alcoholics.

The Masai never killed game but only cared
about their cattle. Trouble between the Masai
and the Wakamba was always over cattle stealing, never over the killing of game.

The Wakamba hated the Masai as rich show-
offs protected by the government. They despised
them as men whose women were completely
faithless and nearly always syphilitic and as men
who could not track because their eyes were
destroyed by filth diseases carried by flies;
because their spears bent after they had been
used a single time and finally, and most of all,
because they were only brave when under the
influence of drugs.

The Wakamba, who liked to fight, really
fight, not Masai fight, which is, usually, a mass
hysteria which cannot come off except under

the influence of drugs, lived at lower than subsistence level. They had always had their
hunters and now there was no place for them to
hunt. They loved to drink and drinking was
strictly controlled by tribal law. They were not
drunkards and drunkenness was severely punished. Meat was a staple of their diet and it was
gone now and they were forbidden to hunt it.
Their illegal hunters were as popular as smug-
glers in England in the old days or as those people were who brought good liquor into the
United States in Prohibition.

It had not been this bad when I had been
there many years before. But it had not been
good. The Wakamba were completely loyal to
the British. Even the young men and the bad
boys were loyal. But the young men were upset
and things were not simple at all. The Mau Mau
were suspect because it was a Kikuyu organization and the oaths were repulsive to the
Wakamba. But there had been some infiltration.
There was nothing about this in the Wild Animal Protection Ordinance. I had been told by
G.C. to use my common sense, if any, and that
only shits got in trouble. Since I knew that I
could qualify for that class at times I tried to use
my common sense as carefully as possible and
avoid shithood so far as I could. For a long time
I had identified myself with the Wakamba and

now had passed over the last important barrier so that the identification was complete. There is no other way of making this identification. Any alliance between tribes is only made valid in one way.

Now, with the rain, I knew that everyone would be less worried about their families and if we got some meat everyone would be happy. Meat made men strong; even the old men believed that. Of the old men in camp I thought Charo was the only one who might possibly be impotent and I was not sure about him. I could have asked Ngui and he would have told me. But it was not a proper thing to ask and Charo and I were very old friends. Kamba men, if they have meat to eat, retain their ability to make love well after they are seventy. But there are some sorts of meat that are better for a man than others. I do not know why I had started to think about this. It had started with the killing of the kongoni the day we had first seen the track of the huge Rift Valley escarpment lion and then it had wandered around like an old man's tale.

"What about going out and getting a piece of meat, Miss Mary?"

"We do need some don't we?"

"Yes."

"What have you been thinking about?"

"Kamba problems and meat."

"Bad Kamba problems?"

"No. In general."

"That's good. What did you decide?"

"That we needed meat."

"Well, should we go for the meat?"

"It's a good time to start. If you'd like to walk."

"I'd love to walk. When we come home we'll have a bath and change and there will be the fire."

We had found the herd of impala that were usually close to the road where it crossed the river and Mary had killed an old buck that had one horn. He was very fat and in good shape and my conscience was clear about taking him for meat, as he would never have provided the Game Department with a trophy to dispose of and, since he had been driven out of the herd, he was no use anymore for breeding. Mary had made a beautiful shot on him hitting him in the shoulder exactly where she had aimed. Charo was very proud of her and he had been able to butcher absolutely legally by perhaps a hundredth of a second. Mary's shooting, by now, was regarded as completely in the hands of God and since we had different Gods, Charo took complete credit for the shot. Pop, G.C. and I had all seen Miss Mary come into perfect form shooting and make astounding and lovely shots. Now it was Charo's turn.

"Memsahib piga mzuri sana," Charo said.

"Mzuri. Mzuri," Ngui told her.

"Thank you," Mary said. "That's three now," she said to me. "I'm happy and confident now. It's strange about shooting, isn't it?"

I was thinking how strange it was and forgot to answer.

"It's wicked to kill things. But it's wonderful to have good meat in camp. When did meat get so important to everybody?"

"It always has been. It's one of the oldest and most important things. Africa's starved for it. But if they killed the game the way the Dutch did in South Africa there wouldn't be any."

"But do we keep the game for the natives? Who are we taking care of the game for, really?"

"For itself and to make money for the Game Department and keep the white hunting racket going and to make extra money for the Masai."

"I love our protecting the game for the game itself," Mary said. "But the rest of it is sort of shoddy."

"It's very mixed up," I said. "But did you ever see a more mixed-up country?"

"No. But you and your mob are all mixed up too."

"I know it."

"But do you have it straight in your head yourself, really?"

"Not yet. We're on a day-by-day basis now."

"Well I like it anyway," Mary said. "And after all we didn't come out here to bring order into Africa."

"No. We came out to take some pictures and write some captions for them and then to have fun and learn what we could."

"But we certainly got mixed up in it."

"I know. But are you having fun?"

"I've never been happier."

Ngui had stopped and was pointing at the right-hand side of the road. "Simba."

There was the big track, too big to believe.

The left hind foot clearly showed the old scar. He had crossed the road quietly more or less at the time Mary had shot the buck. He had gone on into the broken bush country.

"Him," Ngui said. There was no doubt of it at all. With luck we could have met him on the road. But he would have been careful and let us pass. He was a very intelligent and unhurried lion. The sun was almost down and with the clouds there would be no light to shoot in another five minutes.

"Now things aren't so complicated," Mary said very happily.

"Go to camp for the motor car," I told Ngui.

"We'll go back to wait with Charo with the meat."

That night when we had gone to our own beds but were not yet asleep we heard the lion roar. He was north of the camp and the roar came low and mounting in heaviness and then ended in a sigh.

"I'm coming in with you," Mary said.

We lay close together in the dark under the mosquito bar, my arm around her, and listened to him roar again.

"There's no mistaking when it's him," Mary said. "I'm glad we're in bed together when we hear him."

He was moving to the north and west, grunting deeply and then roaring.

"Is he calling up the lionesses or is he angry? What is he really doing?"

"I don't know, honey. I think he's angry because it's wet."

"But he roared too when it was dry and we tracked him in the bush."

"I was just joking, honey. I only hear him roar. I can see him when he sets himself and tomorrow you'll see where he tears the ground up."

"He's too great to joke about."

"I have to joke about him if I'm going to back you up. You wouldn't want me to start worrying about him would you?"

"Listen to him," Mary said.

We lay together and listened to him. You cannot describe a wild lion's roar. You can only say that you listened and the lion roared. It is not at all like the noise the lion makes at the start of Metro Goldwyn Mayer pictures. When you hear it you first feel it in your scrotum and it runs all the way up through your body.

"He makes me feel hollow inside," Mary said. "He really is the king of the night."

We listened and he roared again still moving to the northwest. This time the roar ended with a cough.

"Just hope he kills," I said to her. "Don't think about him too much and sleep well."

"I have to think about him and I want to think about him. He's my lion and I love him and respect him and I have to kill him. He means more to me than anything except you and our people. You know what he means."

"Too bloody well," I said. "But you ought to sleep, honey. Maybe he is roaring to keep you awake."

"Well then let him keep me awake," Mary said. "If I'm going to kill him he has a right to keep me awake. I love everything he does and everything about him."

"But you ought to sleep a little bit, honey. He wouldn't like you not to sleep."

"He doesn't care about me at all. I care about

him and that's why I kill him. You ought to understand."

"I understand. But you ought to sleep good now, my kitten. Because tomorrow in the morning it starts."

"I'll sleep. But I want to hear him speak once more."

She was very sleepy and I thought that this girl who had lived all her life never wishing to kill anything until she had fallen in with bad characters in the war had been hunting lions too long on a perfectly straight basis, which, without a professional to back her up, was not a sound trade or occupation and could be very bad for one and obviously was being that at this moment. Then the lion roared again and coughed three times. The coughs came from the earth where he was direct into the tent.

"I'll go to sleep now," Miss Mary said. "I hope he didn't cough because he had to. Can he catch cold?"

"I don't know, honey. Will you sleep well and good now?"

"I'm asleep already. But you must wake me long before first light no matter how asleep I am. Do you promise?"

"I promise." Then she was asleep and I lay far against the wall of the tent and felt her sleeping softly and when my left arm began to ache I took it from under her head and felt her to be comfortable and then I occupied a small part of the big cot and then listened to the lion. He was silent until about three o'clock when he killed. After that the hyenas all started to speak and the lion fed and from time to time spoke gruffly. There was no talk from the lionesses. One I knew was about to have cubs and would have nothing to do with him and the other was her girlfriend. I thought it was still too wet to find him when it was light. But there was always a chance.

6

LONG BEFORE IT was light in the morning Mwindi woke us with the tea. He said "Hodi" and left the tea outside the door of the tent on the table. I took a cup in to Mary and dressed outside. It was overcast and you could not see the stars.

Charo and Ngui came in the dark to get the guns and the cartridges and I took my tea out to the table where one of the boys who served the mess tent was building up the fire. Mary was washing and getting dressed, still between sleeping and waking. I walked out on the open ground beyond the elephant skull and the three big bushes and found the ground was still quite damp underfoot. It had dried during the night and it would be much drier than the day before. But I still doubted if we could take the car much past where I figured the lion had killed and I was sure it would be too wet beyond there and between there and the swamp.

The swamp was really misnamed. There was an actual papyrus swamp with much flowing

water in it that was a mile and a half across and
perhaps four miles long. But the locality that we
referred to as the swamp also consisted of the
area of big trees that surrounded it. Many of
these were on comparatively high ground and
some were very beautiful. They made a band of
forest around the true swamp but there were
parts of this timber that had been so pulled
down by feeding elephants that it was almost
impassable. There were several rhino that lived
in this forest; there were nearly always some elephant now and sometimes there was a great
herd of elephant. Two herds of buffalo used it.
Leopards lived in the deep part of this forest and
hunted out of it and it was the refuge of the particular lion when he came down to feed on the
game of the plains.

This forest of great, tall and fallen trees
was the western boundary of the open and
wooded plain and the beautiful glades that were
bounded on the north by the flat salt flats and
the broken lava rock country that led to the
other great marsh that lay between our country
and the Chulu hills. On the east was the minia-
ture desert that was the gerenuk country and
further to the east was a country of bushy broken hills that later rose in height toward the
flanks of Mt. Kilimanjaro. It was not as simple
as that but that was how it seemed from a map

or from the center of the plain and the glades country.

The lion's habit was to kill on the plain or in the broken glades during the night and then, having eaten, retire to the belt of forest. Our plan was to locate him on his kill and stalk him there, or to have the luck to intercept him on his way to the forest. If he got enough confidence so that he would not go all the way to the forest we could track him up from the kill to wherever he might lie up after he had gone for water.

While Mary was dressing and then making her way on the track across the meadow to the belt of trees where the green canvas latrine tent was hidden, I was thinking about the lion. We must take him on if there was any chance of success. Mary had shot well and was confident. But if there was only a chance of frightening him or of spooking him into high grass or diffi- cult country where she could not see him because of her height, we should leave him alone to become confident. I hoped we would find that he had gone off after he had fed, drunk at some of the surface water that still lay in the mud holes of the plain, and then gone to sleep in one of the brush islands of the plain or the patches of trees in the glades.

The car was ready with Mthuka at the wheel and I had checked all the guns when Mary came back. It was light now but not light enough to shoot. The clouds were still well down the slopes of the Mountain and there was no sign of the sun except that the light was strengthening. I looked through the sights of my rifle at the elephant skull but it was still too dark to shoot. Charo and Ngui were both very serious and formal.

"How do you feel, kitten?" I said to Mary.

"Wonderful. How did you think I'd feel?"

"Did you use the Eygene?"

"Of course," she said. "Did you?"

"Yes. We're just waiting for it to get a little lighter."

"It's light enough for me."

"It isn't for me."

"You ought to do something about your eyes."

"I told them we'd be back for breakfast."

"That will give me a headache."

"We brought some stuff. It's in a box back there."

"Does Charo have plenty of ammo for me?"

"Ask him."

Mary spoke to Charo, who said he had "Mingi risasi."

"Want to roll your right sleeve up?" I asked.

"You asked me to remind you."

"I didn't ask you to remind me in an evil bad temper."

"Why don't you get angry at the lion instead of me?"

"I'm not angry at the lion in any way. Do you think there is enough light for you to see now?"

"Kwenda na Simba," I said to Mthuka. Then to Ngui, "Stand up in back to watch."

We started off; the tires taking hold very well on the drying track; me leaning out with both boots outside the cutout door; the morning air cold off the Mountain; the rifle feeling good. I put it to my shoulder and aimed a few times. Even with the big yellow light concentrating glasses I saw that there was not enough light yet to shoot safely. But it was twenty minutes to where we were going and the light was strengthening every minute.

"Light's going to be fine," I said.

"I thought it would," Mary said. I looked around. She was sitting with great dignity and she was chewing gum.

We went up the track past the improvised airstrip. There was game everywhere and the new grass seemed to have grown an inch since the morning of the day before. There were white flowers coming up too, solid in the spread of the grass and making the whole field white. There was still some water in the low parts of the tracks and I motioned to Mthuka to turn off the track to the left to avoid some standing water.

The flowered grass was slippery. The light was getting better all the time.

Mthuka saw the birds perched heavily in the two trees off the right beyond the next two glades and pointed. If they were still up it should mean the lion was on the kill. Ngui slapped on the top of the car with the palm of his hand and we stopped. I remember thinking that it was strange that Mthuka should have seen the birds before Ngui when Ngui was much higher. Ngui dropped to the ground and came alongside of the car crouching so his body would not break its outline. He grabbed my foot and pointed to the left toward the belt of forest.

The great black-maned lion, his body looking almost black and his large head and shoulders swinging, was trotting into the tall grass.

"You see him?" I asked Mary softly.

"I see him."

He was into the grass now and only his head and shoulders showed; then only his head; the grass swaying and closing behind him. He had evidently heard the car or else he had started for the forest early and seen us coming up the road.

"There's no sense you going in here," I said to Mary.

"I know all that," she said. "If we'd have been out earlier we would have found him."

"It wasn't light enough to shoot. If you had wounded him I'd have had to follow him in there."

"We'd have had to follow him."

"The hell with the we stuff."

"How do you propose to get him then?" She was angry but only angry with the prospect of action and a termination gone and not stupid in her anger so that she could expect to demand to be allowed to go into grass taller than her head after a wounded lion.

"I expect him to get confident when he sees us drive on now without even going over to his kill." Then I interrupted to say, "Get in, Ngui. Go ahead poli poli Mthuka." Then feeling Ngui beside me and the car proceeding slowly along the track with my two friends and brothers watching the vultures perched in the trees, I said to Mary, "What do you think Pop would have done? Chased him into the grass and the down timber and taken you in where you're not tall enough to see? What are we supposed to do? Get you killed or kill the lion?"

"Don't embarrass Charo with your shouting."

"I wasn't shouting."

"You ought to hear yourself sometime."

"Listen," I whispered.

"Don't say listen and don't whisper. And don't say on your own two feet and when the chips are down."

"You certainly make lion hunting lovely sometimes. How many people have betrayed you in it so far?"

"Pop and you and I don't remember who else. G.C. probably will too. If you know so much you lion-hunting general who knows everything why haven't the birds come down if the lion's left the kill?"

"Because either one or both of the lionesses are still on it or laying up close to it?"

"Aren't we going to see?"

"From further up the road and so as not to spook anything. I want them all to be confident."

"Now I'm getting a little tired of the phrase, 'I want them to be confident.' If you can't vary your thinking you could try to vary your language."

"How long have you been hunting this lion, honey?"

"It seems like forever and I could have killed him three months ago if you and G.C. would have let me. I had an easy chance and you wouldn't let me take him."

"Because we didn't know he was this lion. He might have been a lion that had come from Amboseli with the drought. G.C. has a conscience."

"Both of you have the consciences of bushwacky delinquents," Miss Mary said. "When will we see the lionesses?"

"To your right bearing forty-five degrees about three hundred more yards up this track."

"And what Force is the wind?"

"About Force Two," I said. "Honey, you are a little lion-wacky."

"Who has more right to be? Of course I am. But I take lions seriously."

"I do too, really. And I think I care as much about them as you do even if I don't talk about it."

"You talk about it plenty. Don't worry. But you and G.C. are just a pair of conscience-ridden murderers. Condemning things to death and carrying out the sentence. And G.C. has a much better conscience than you too and his people are properly disciplined."

I touched Mthuka on the thigh so that he would stop the car. "Look, honey. There is what's left of the zebra kill and there are the two lionesses. Can we be friends?"

"I've always been friends," she said. "You just misinterpret things. May I have the bini please?"

I handed her the good binoculars and she watched the two lionesses. The one was so big with cubs that she looked to be a maneless lion. The other was possibly her grown daughter; perhaps only a devoted friend. They each lay under the shelter of an island of brush; the one calm, dignified and pre-matronly, her tawny jaws dark with blood; the other young and lithe and equally dark about the jowls. There was not much of the zebra left but they were protecting their property. I could not have told from the sounds I had heard in the night whether they had killed for the lion or whether he had killed and they had joined him.

The birds perched heavily in both of the small trees and in the biggest tree in one of the green islands of bush there must have been a hundred more. The vultures were heavy, hump shouldered and ready to drop but the lionesses were too close to the striped quarter and neck of the zebra that lay on the ground. I saw a jackal, looking neat and handsome as a fox, at the edge of one of the patches of bush and then another one. There were no hyenas in sight.

"We shouldn't spook them," I said. "I favor not going near it at all."

Mary was friends now. Seeing any lions always excited and pleased her and she said, "Do you think they killed or he killed?"

"I think he killed and ate what he wanted and they came much later."

"Would the birds come in the night?"

"No."

"There are an awful lot of them. Look at the ones stretching their wings to dry like the buzzards do at home."

"They're awfully ugly to be Royal Game and when they have rinderpest or other cattle diseases they must spread it terribly with their droppings. There are certainly too many of them for this area. The insects and the hyenas and the jackals could clean up after any kills made here and the hyenas can kill what is sick or too old and eat on the spot and not spread it all over the countryside."

Seeing the lionesses in their shelter and the truly horrible vultures clumped in such numbers in the trees had made me talk too much; that and that we were friends again and that I would not have to pit my truly loved Miss Mary with the lion until another day. Then too I hated vultures and I believed their true utility as scavengers was greatly overrated. Someone had decided that they were the great garbage disposers of Africa and they had been made Royal Game and could not be held down in numbers and their role as spreaders of disease was heresy against that magic word Royal Game. The Wakamba thought it was very funny and we always called them King's birds.

They did not look funny now though perched obscenely above the remains of the zebra and when the big lioness rose and yawned and went out to feed again two big vultures dropped as soon as she was on the meat. The young lioness flicked her tail once and charged them and they rose running and heavy winged as she slapped at them as a kitten slaps. She then lay down by the big lioness and started to feed and the birds stayed in the trees but the closest ones were almost overbalanced with hunger.

It would not take the lionesses long to finish off what was left of the zebra and I told Mary it was probably better to leave them feeding and drive on up the road as though we had not seen them. Ahead of us there was a small bunch of zebra and beyond were wildebeest and many more zebra.

"I love to watch them," Mary said. "But if you think it's better we can go on up and see how the salt flats are and maybe see the buff."

So we went up as far as the edge of the salt flat and saw no tracks of buffalo and no buffalo. The flats were still too wet and slippery for a car and so was the ground to the east. We found the tracks of the two lionesses at the edge of the salt flats headed in the direction of the kill. They were fresh tracks and it was impossible to tell when they had hit the kill. But I thought it must have been the lion who killed and Ngui and Charo agreed. "Perhaps if we just drive back the way we've come he'll get used to seeing the car," Mary said. "I don't have a headache but it would be fun to have breakfast."

208 • ERNEST HEMINGWAY

It was what I had been hoping she would suggest.

"If we don't shoot at all." I stopped because I would have said that it would give him confidence.

"Maybe he will think it is a car that just goes up and down," Mary finished for me. "We'll have a lovely breakfast and I will do all the letters I should write and we'll be patient and good kittens."

"You're a good kitten."

"We'll drive back to camp like tourists and see the new wonderful green fields and breakfast feels so good in advance."

But when we got to camp for breakfast there was the young policeman in his mud-spatted Land Rover waiting for us. The car was under a tree and his two askaris were back at the lines. He got out of the car as we came up and his young face was lined with his great cares and responsibilities.

"Good morning, Bwana," he said. "Good morning, Memsahib. Been making an early patrol I see."

"Will you have some breakfast?" I asked.

"If I'm not in the way. Turn up anything interesting, governor?"

"Just checking on the stock. What's the word from the Boma?"

"They nailed them, governor. They got them over on the other side. North of Namanga. You can call in your people."

"Much of a show?"

"No details yet."

"Pity we couldn't have fought here."

Miss Mary looked at me warningly. She was not happy at having the young policeman for breakfast but she knew he was a lonesome boy and while she was intolerant with fools she was feeling kindly until we had seen the policeman exhausted in his mud-covered vehicle.

"It would have meant a lot to me. Governor, we had almost the perfect plan. Perhaps it was the perfect plan. The only aspect I worried about was the little Memsahib here. If you'll pardon my saying it, ma'am, this is no work for a woman."

"I wasn't in it at all," Mary said. "Would you have some kidneys and bacon?"

"You were in it," he said. "You were a part of The Screen. I'm mentioning you in my report. It's perhaps not the same as a Mention in Dispatches. But it's all part of one's record. Someday those who fought in Kenya will be very proud."

"After wars I've found that the people are usually just crashing bores," Miss Mary said.

"Only to those who did not fight," the

policeman said. "Fighting men, and with your permission fighting women, have a code."

"Try some beer," I said. "Have any gen on when we'll fight again?"

"You'll have the word, governor, before anyone else has it."

"You're too kind to us," I said. "But I suppose there is glory enough for all."

"Too true," the young policeman said. "In a way, governor, we're the last of the Empire builders. In a way we're like Rhodes and Dr. Livingstone."

"In a way," I said.

That afternoon I went to the Shamba. It was cold since the sun was under the cloud of the Mountain and a heavy wind was blowing from the heights where all the rain that had fallen on us must now be snow. The Shamba was at about six thousand feet and the Mountain was over nineteen thousand feet high. Its sudden cold winds, when heavy snow had fallen, were punishing to those who lived on the upland plain. Higher in the foothills, the houses, we did not call them huts, were built in the folds of hills to have a lee against the wind. But this Shamba had the full force of the wind and on this afternoon it was very cold and bitter with the smell of not quite frozen dung and all birds and beasts were out of the wind.

The man who Miss Mary referred to as my father-in-law had a chest cold too and bad rheumatic pains in his back. I gave him medicine and then rubbed him and applied Sloan's liniment. None of us Kamba regarded him as the father of his daughter but since he was technically such by tribal law and custom, I was bound to respect him. We treated him in the lee of the house with his daughter watching. She was carrying her sister's child on her hip and was wearing my last good woolly sweater and a fishing cap which had been given me by a friend. My friend had ordered my initials embroidered on the front of the cap and this had some significance with all of us. Until she had decided that she wanted it, the initials had always been an embarrassment. Under the woolly sweater she wore the last and too many times washed dress from Laitokitok. It was not correct etiquette for me to speak to her while she was carrying the child of her sister and, technically, she should have not watched the treatment of her father. She handled this by keeping her eyes downcast at all times.

The man who was known by a name which means potential father-in-law was not particularly brave under the ordeal of Sloan's liniment. Ngui, who knew Sloan's well, and had no regard for the men of this Shamba, wanted me to rub it in and signaled once that I let a few drops fall where they should not go. Mthuka with his beautiful tribal scars on both cheeks was completely happy in his deafness watching what he considered to be a worthless Kamba suffer in a good cause. I was completely ethical with the Sloan's to the disappointment of everyone including the daughter and all lost interest.

"Jambo, tu," I said to the daughter when we left and she said with her eyes down and her chest up, "No hay remedio."

We got into the car, no one waving to anyone, the cold closing in with the formality. There was too much of both and we all felt badly to see a Shamba so miserable.

"Ngui," I asked. "How can they have such miserable men and such wonderful women in this Shamba?"

"Great men have passed through this Shamba," Ngui said. "Formerly this was the route to the south until the new route." He was angry with the men of the Shamba because they were worthless Kamba.

"Do you think we ought to take this Shamba?"

"Yes," he said. "You and I and Mthuka and the young men."

We were going into the African world of unreality that is defended and fortified by reality past any reality there is. It was not an escape world or a daydreaming world. It was a ruthless real world made of the unreality of the real. If there were still rhino, and we saw them every day while it was obviously impossible for there to be such an animal, then anything was possible. If Ngui and I could talk to a rhinoceros, who was incredible to start with, in his own tongue well enough for him to answer back and I could curse and insult him in Spanish so that he would be humiliated and go off, then unreality was sensible and logical beside reality. Spanish was regarded as Mary's and my tribal language and it was considered to be the all-purpose language of Cuba where we came from. They knew we also had an inner or secret tribal language. We were not supposed to have anything in common with the British except the color of our skin and a mutual tolerance. While Mayito Menocal was with us he was greatly admired because of his very deep voice, the way he smelled, his courtesy and because he had arrived in Africa speaking both Spanish and Swahili. They also revered his scars and as he spoke Swahili with a strong Camagüey accent and looked like a bull he was, truly, almost revered.

I had explained that he was the son of the King of his own country, in the time when it had great kings, and had described the thousands of acres of land that he owned and its quality, the number of cattle I had known that he owned and the quantities of sugar that he produced. Since sugar was the universally sought food by the Wakamba after meat and since Pop had backed me up to Keiti that these things were true and since Mayito was obviously a sound cattleman who knew exactly what he spoke of and, when he spoke of it, spoke in a voice very similar to that of a lion and had never been unjust, rude, contemptuous or boastful, he was really loved. In all the time he was in Africa I only told one lie about Mayito. This was in respect to his wives.

Mwindi, who was a true admirer of Mayito, asked me, flat out, how many wives Mayito had. Everyone had wondered and it was not the sort of statistic they could get from Pop. Mwindi was in one of his gloomy days and there had evidently been a discussion. I did not know which side he had taken but it was evidently a question that he had been asked to settle.

I thought the question and the aspects of the strangeness over and said, "In his own country no one would wish to count them."

"Ndio," Mwindi said. This was the proper language of Mzees.

Mayito had one actually. She was very beautiful. Mwindi went out as gloomy as ever.

Now today, coming back from the Shamba, Ngui and I were engaged in that characteristic occupation of men, planning the operation which will never take place.

"All right," I said. "We take it."

"Good."

"Who takes Debba?"

"She is yours. She is your fiancée."

"Good. After we take it how do we hold it when they send a company of K.A.R.?"

"You get troops from Mayito."

"Mayito is in Hong Kong now. In China."

"We have aircraft."

"Not that kind. What do we do without Mayito?"

"We go up into the Mountain."

"Very cold. Too damn cold right now. Also we lose the Shamba."

"War is shit," Ngui said.

"I'll sign that," I said. We were both happy now. "No. We take the Shamba day by day. The day is our unit. Now we have what the old men believe they will have when they die. Now we hunt good; eat good meat; drink well once Memsahib kills her lion; and make the happy hunting grounds while we are alive."

Mthuka was too deaf to hear anything we said. He was like a motor which is functioning perfectly but the gauges have cut out. This usually only happens in dreams but Mthuka had

216 • Ernest Hemingway

the finest sight of any of us and was the best wild driver, and he had, if such a thing exists, complete extrasensory perception. As we drove up to the camp and stopped the car Ngui and I knew he had not heard a word we had said but he said, "It is better, much, much better."

He had pity and kindness in his eyes and I knew he was a better and kinder man than I could ever be. He offered me his snuffbox. It was semi-normal snuff with none of the strange additions of Arap Meina but it tasted very good and I put a big three-fingered pinch of it under my upper lip.

None of us had been drinking at all. Mthuka always carried himself rather like a crane in cold weather with his shoulders hunched. The sky was overcast and the cloud was down to the plain and as I handed him back the snuffbox he said, "Wakamba tu."

We both knew it and there was nothing to do about it and he covered the car and I walked over to the tent.

"Was the Shamba in good shape?" Miss Mary asked.

"It's fine. It's a little cold and rough."

"Is there anything I can do for anyone there?"

You good lovely kind kitten, I thought and I said, "No. I think everything is fine. I'm going to get a medicine chest for the Widow and teach her to use it. It's awful for the kids' eyes not to be cared for when they're Wakamba."

"If they are anybody," Miss Mary said.

"I'm going out to talk to Arap Meina. Would you please ask Mwindi to call me when the bath is ready?"

Arap Meina did not think that the lion would kill that night. I told him he had looked very heavy when he had gone off into the forest that morning. He doubted if the lionesses would kill that night either although they might and the lion might join them. I asked him if I should have made a kill and tied it up or covered it with brush to try to hold the lion. He said the lion was much too intelligent.

A large part of time in Africa is spent in talk. Where people are illiterate this is always true. Once you start the hunt hardly a word is spoken. You all understand each other and in hot weather your tongue is stuck dry in your mouth. But in planning a hunt in the evening there is usually much talking and it is quite rare that things come off as they are planned; especially if the planning is too complicated.

Later, when we were both in bed that night the lion proved us all to be wrong. We heard him roar to the north of the field where we had made the airstrip. Then he moved off roaring from time to time. Then another and less impressive lion roared several times. Then it was quiet for a long time. After that we heard the hyenas and from the way they called and from the high quavering laughing noise they made I was sure some lion had killed. After that there was the noise of lions fighting. This quieted down and the hyenas started to howl and laugh.

"You and Arap Meina said it was going to be a quiet night," Mary said very sleepily.

"Somebody killed something," I said.

"You and Arap Meina tell each other about it in the morning. I have to go to sleep now to get up early. I want to sleep well so I won't be cross."

7

I SAT DOWN to the eggs and bacon, the toast, coffee and jam. Mary was on her second cup of coffee and seemed quite happy. "Are we really getting anywhere?"

"Yes."

"But he outsmarts us every morning and he can keep it up forever."

"No he can't. We're going to start to move him a little too far out and he'll make a mistake and you'll kill him."

That afternoon after lunch we did baboon control. We were supposed to keep the population of baboons down to protect the Shambas but we had been doing it in a rather stupid way trying to catch the bands in the open and fire on them as they made for the shelter of the forest. In order neither to sadden nor enrage baboon lovers I will give no details. We were not charged by the ferocious beasts and their formidable canine teeth by the time I reached them were stilled in death. When we got back to camp with the four disgusting corpses G.C. had already arrived.

He was muddy and he looked tired but happy.

"Good afternoon, General," he said. He looked into the back of the hunting car and smiled. "Babooning I see. Two brace. A splendid bag. Going to have them set up by Roland Ward?"

"I'd thought of a group mounting, G.C., with you and me in the center."

"How are you, Papa, and how is Miss Mary?"

"Isn't she here?"

"No. They said she'd gone for a walk with Charo."

"She's fine. The lion's been a little on her mind. But her morale is good."

"Mine's low," G.C. said. "Should we have a drink?"

"I love a drink after babooning."

"We're going in for big-time babooning on a large scale," G.C. said. He took off his beret and then reached into his tunic pocket and brought out a buff envelope. "Read this and memorize our role."

He called to Nguili to bring drinks and I read the operation orders.

"This makes good sense," I said. I read it on skipping, temporarily, the parts that had nothing to do with us and that I would have to check on the map, looking for where we came in.

"It does make sense," G.C. said. "My morale's not low because of it. It's what's holding my morale up."

"What's the matter with your morale? Moral problems?"

"No. Problems of conduct."

"You must have been a wonderful problem child. You have more damned problems than a character in Henry James."

"Make it Hamlet," G.C. said. "And I wasn't a problem child. I was a very happy and attractive child, only slightly too fat."

"Mary was wishing you were back only this noon."

"Sensible girl," G.C. said.

We saw them then coming across the new bright green grass of the meadow; the same size, Charo as black as a man could be, wearing his old soiled turban and a blue coat, Mary bright blond in the sun, her green shooting clothes dark against the bright green of the grass. They were talking happily and Charo was carrying Mary's rifle and her big bird book. Together they always looked like a numero from the old Cirque Médrano.

G.C. came out from washing up without a shirt on. His whiteness contrasted with the rose brown of his face and neck.

"Look at them," he said. "What a lovely pair."

"Imagine running into them if you'd never seen them before."

"The grass will be over their heads in a week's time. It's nearly to their knees now."

"Don't criticize the grass. It's only three days old."

"Hi, Miss Mary," G.C. called. "What have you two been up to?"

Mary drew herself up very proudly.

"I killed a wildebeest."

"And who gave you permission to do that?"

"Charo. Charo said to kill him. He had a broken leg. Really badly broken."

Charo shifted the big book to his other hand and flopped his arm to show how the leg had been.

"We thought you would want a bait," Mary said. "You did, didn't you? He's close to the road. We heard you come by afterwards, G.C. But we couldn't see you."

"You did quite right to kill him and we did need a bait. But what were you doing hunting alone?"

"I wasn't. I was identifying birds and I have my list. Charo wouldn't take me where there were any bad beasts. Then I saw the wildebeest and he was standing looking so sad and his leg looked awful with the bone sticking out. Charo said to kill him and I did."

"Memsahib piga. Kufa!"

"Shot him right behind the ear."

"Piga! Kufa!" Charo said and he and Miss Mary looked at each other proudly.

"It's the first time I ever had the responsibility of killing without you or Papa or Pop along."

"May I kiss you, Miss Mary?" G.C. asked.

"You certainly may. But I'm awfully sweaty."

They kissed and then we kissed and Mary said, "I'd like to kiss Charo too but I know I shouldn't. Do you know the impala barked at me just as though they were dogs. Nothing is afraid of Charo and me."

She shook hands with Charo and he took her book and her rifle over to our tent. "I'd better go and wash too. Thank you for being so nice about my shooting the beast."

"We'll send the truck for him and then put him out where he should be."

I went over to our tent and G.C. went to his tent to dress. Mary was washing with the safari soap and changing her shirt and smelling her fresh shirt that had been washed with a different soap and dried in the sun. We each liked to watch the other bathe but I never watched her when G.C. was around because it could be sort of hard on him. I was sitting on a chair in front of the tent reading and she came over and put her arms around my neck.

"Are you all right, honey?"

"No," she said. "I was so proud and Charo was so proud and it was one shot whack like the pelota ball hitting the wall of the fronton. He couldn't have heard the shot even and Charo and I were shaking hands. You know what it's like to do something yourself for the first time with all the responsibility. You and G.C. know and that's why he kissed me."

"Anybody'd kiss you anytime."

"Maybe if I wanted them to. Or made them. But this wasn't like that."

"Why do you feel bad, honey?"

"You know. Don't pretend you don't know."

"No, I don't," I lied.

"I held straight on the center of his shoulder. It was big and black and shiny and I was about twenty yards from him. He was half toward me and looking toward us. I could see his eyes and they looked so sad. He looked as though he would cry. He looked sadder than anything I've ever seen and his leg looked awful. Honey, he had such a long sad face. I don't have to tell G.C. do I?"

"No."

"I didn't have to tell you. But we're going after the lion together and now my god-damn confidence is gone again."

"You'll shoot beautifully. I'm proud to be with you with the lion."

"The awful thing is that I can shoot properly too. You know it."

"I remember all the beauty shots you made. And all the wonderful times you shot better than anyone at Escondido."

"You just help me get back my confidence. But there's such a short time."

"You'll get it back and we won't tell G.C."

We sent the lorry for the wildebeest. When they came back with him G.C. and I climbed up to have a look at him. They are never a handsome animal when dead. He lay big paunched and dusty, all his bluff gone and his horns gray and undistinguished. "Mary took an awfully fancy shot at him," G.C. said. The wildebeest's eyes were glazed and his tongue out. His tongue was dusty too and he had been drilled behind the ear just at the base of the skull.

"Now where do you suppose she actually held?"

"She shot him from only twenty yards. She had a right to hold up there if she wanted to."

"I'd have thought she'd have taken him through the shoulder," G.C. said.

I didn't say anything. There was no use trying to fool him and if I lied to G.C. he would not forgive me.

"What about that leg?" I asked.

"Someone chasing at night with a car. Could be something else."

"How old would you say it was?"

"Two days. It's maggoty."

"Somebody up the hill then. We've heard no cars at night. He'd come downhill with the leg anyway. He certainly wouldn't climb with it."

"He's not you and me," G.C. said. "He's a wildebeest."

We had stopped under the hitching post tree and were all getting out. G.C. and I went over to the truck which still held the wildebeest and he explained to his Chief Game Scout and the other scouts who had come up where we wanted the bait tied up. It was only to be dragged up to the tree from the road and then hung up out of reach of hyenas. The lions would pull it down if they came to it. It was to be dragged past where last night's kill had been. They were to go up and get it up as quickly as possible and return to camp. My people had all the baboon baits hung up and I told Mthuka to wash the car out well. He said he had stopped at the stream and washed it.

We all took our baths. Mary took hers first and I helped dry her with a big towel and held her mosquito boots for her. She put a bathrobe on over her pajamas and went out by the fire to have a drink with G.C. before they started their cooking. I stayed with them until Mwindi came out from the tent and said "Bathi Bwana," and then I took my drink into the tent and undressed and lay back in the canvas tub and soaped myself and relaxed in the hot water.

"What do the old men say the lion will do tonight?" I asked Mwindi, who was folding my clothes and laying out pajamas, dressing gown and my mosquito boots.

"Keiti says Memsahib's lion maybe eats on bait maybe not. What does Bwana say?"

"The same as Keiti."

"Keiti says you mganga with the lion."

"No. Only a little good medicine to find out when he dies."

"When he die?"

"In three days. I could not find out which day."

"Mzuri. Maybe he dies tomorrow."

"I don't think so. But he may."

"Keiti don't think so either."

"When does he think?"

"In three days."

"Mzuri. Please bring me the towel."

"Towel right by your hand. Bring him if you like."

"I'm sorry," I said. There is no word for I'm sorry in Swahili.

"Hapana sorry. I just say where it was. You want me rub back?"

"No thank you."

"You feel good?"

"Yes. Why?"

"Hapana why. I ask to know."

"Feel very good." I stood up and got out of the tub and started to dry myself. I wanted to say that I felt good and very relaxed and a little sleepy and did not feel much like talking and would have preferred fresh meat to spaghetti but had not wished to kill anything and that I was worried about all three of my children for different causes and that I was worried about the Shamba and I was a little worried about G.C. and quite worried about Mary and that I was a fake as a good witch doctor, but no more a fake than the others were, and that I wished Mr. Singh would keep out of trouble and that I hoped the operation we were committed in as from Christmas Day would go well and that I had some more 220 grain solids and that Simenon would write fewer and better books. I did not know all the things Pop would discuss with Keiti when he had his bath but I knew Mwindi wanted to be friendly and so did I. But I was tired tonight for no reason and he knew it and was worried.

"You ask me for Wakamba words," he said.

So I asked him for Wakamba words and tried to memorize them and then I thanked him and went out to the fire to sit by the fire in an old pair of pajamas from Idaho, tucked into a pair of warm mosquito boots made in Hong Kong and wearing a warm wool robe from Pendleton, Oregon, and drank a whisky and soda made from a bottle of whisky Mr. Singh had given me as a Christmas present and boiled water from the stream that ran down from the Mountain animated by a siphon cartridge made in Nairobi.

I'm a stranger here, I thought. But the whisky said no and it was the time of day for the whisky to be right. Whisky can be as right as it can be wrong and it said I was not a stranger and I knew it was correct at this time of night. Anyway my boots had come home because they were made of ostrich hide and I remembered the place where I had found the leather in the bootmaker's in Hong Kong. No, it was not me who found the leather. It was someone else and then I thought about who had found the leather and about those days and then I thought about different women and how they would be in Africa and how lucky I had been to have known fine women that loved Africa. I had known some really terrible ones who had only gone there to have been there and I had known some true bitches and several alcoholics to whom Africa had just been another place for more ample bitchery or fuller drunkenness.

230 • ERNEST HEMINGWAY

Africa took them and changed them all in some ways. If they could not change they hated it.

So I was very happy to have G.C. back in camp and so was Mary. He was happy to be back too because we had become a family and we always missed each other when we were apart. He loved his job and believed in it and its importance almost fanatically. He loved the game and wanted to care for it and protect it and that was about all he believed in, I think, except a very stern and complicated system of ethics.

He was a little younger than my oldest son and if I had gone to Addis Ababa to spend a year and write back in the middle thirties as I had planned I would have known him when he was twelve since his best friend then had been the son of the people I was going out to stay with. But I had not gone because Mussolini's armies had gone instead and my friend that I had been going out to stay with had been moved to another diplomatic post and so I had missed the chance to know G.C. when he was twelve. By the time I met him he had a long, very difficult and unrewarding war behind him plus the abandonment of a British Protectorate where he had made the start of a fine career. He had commanded irregular troops, which is, if you are honest, the least rewarding way there is to make a war. If an action is fought perfectly so that you have almost no casualties and inflict large losses on the enemy it is regarded at Headquarters as an unjustified and reprehensible massacre. If you are forced to fight under unfavorable conditions and at too great odds and win but have a large butcher bill the comment is, "He gets too many men killed."

There is no way for an honest man commanding irregulars to get into anything but trouble. There is some doubt as to whether any truly honest and talented soldier can ever hope for anything except to be destroyed.

By the time I met G.C., he was well started in another career in another British Colony. He was never bitter and he did not look back at all. Over the spaghetti and the wine he told us of how he had been reproved by some newly arrived expatriate civil servant for using a bad word which might be overheard by this young man's wife. I hated for G.C. to have to be bored by these people. The old Pukka Sahibs have been often described and caricatured. But no one has dealt much with these new types except Waugh a little bit at the end of *Black Mischief* and Orwell completely in *Burmese Days*. I wished Orwell were still alive and I told G.C. about the last time I had seen him in Paris in 1945 after the Bulge fight and how he had come in what looked something like civilian clothes to Room 117 of the Ritz where there was still a small arsenal to borrow a pistol because "They" were after him. He wanted a small pistol easily concealed and I found one but warned him that if he shot someone with it they probably would die eventually but that there might be a long interval. But a pistol was a pistol and he needed this one more as a talisman than a weapon, I thought.

He was very gaunt and looked in bad shape and I asked him if he would not stay and eat. But he had to go. I told him I could give him a couple of people who would look after him if "They" were after him. That my characters were familiar with the local "They" who would never bother him nor intrude on him. He said no, that the pistol was all he needed. We asked about a few mutual friends and he left. I sent two characters to pick him up at the door and tail him and check if anybody was after him. The next day their report was "Papa nobody is after him. He is a very chic type and he knows Paris very well. We checked with so and so's brother and he says no one pursues him. He is in touch with the British Embassy but he is not an operative. This is only hearsay. Do you want the timetable of his movements?"

"No. Did he amuse himself?"

"Yes, Papa."

"I'm happy. We will not worry about him. He has the pistol."

"That worthless pistol," one of the characters said. "But you warned him against it, Papa?"

"Yes. He could have had any pistol he wished."

"Perhaps he would have been happier with a stinger."

"No," the other character said. "A stinger is too compromising. He was happy with that pistol."

We let it go at that.

G.C. did not sleep well and often would lie awake most of the night reading. He had a very good library at his house in Kajiado and I had a big duffel bag full of books that we had arranged in empty boxes in the mess tent as a library. There was an excellent bookstore in the New Stanley Hotel in Nairobi and another good one down the road and whenever I had been in town I bought most of the new books that looked worth reading. Reading was the best palliative for G.C.'s insomnia. But it was no cure and I would often see his light on all night in his tent. Because he had a career as well as because he had been brought up properly he could have nothing to do with African women.

He did not think they were beautiful either nor attractive and the ones I knew and liked the best did not care for him either. But there was an Ismaili Indian girl who was one of the nicest people I have ever known and she was completely and hopelessly in love with G.C. She had convinced him that it was her sister, who was in strictest purdah, who loved him and she sent him gifts and messages from this sister. It was a sad but also clean and happy story and we all liked it. G.C. had nothing to do with the girl at all except to speak pleasantly to her when he was in her family's shop. He had his own white Nairobi girls that he was fond of and I never talked with him about them. Mary probably did. But we had no personal gossip among the three of us on serious personal things.

In the Shamba it was different. There and in the lines there were no books to read, no radio, and we talked. I asked the Widow and the girl who had decided she wished to be my wife about why they did not like G.C. and at first they would not tell me. Finally the Widow explained that it was not polite to say. It turned out that it was a question of smell. All people with the color of skin I had smelled very badly usually.

We were sitting under a tree by the bank of a river and I was waiting for some baboons that, by their talking, were working down toward us.

"Bwana Game smells good," I said. "I smell him all the time. He has a good smell."

"Hapana," the Widow said. "You smell like Shamba. You smell like smoked hide. You smell like pombe." I did not like the smell of pombe and I was not sure I liked smelling like it.

The girl put her head against the back of my bush shirt, which I knew was salty with dried sweat. She rubbed her head against the back of my shoulders and then the back of my neck and then came around for me to kiss her head.

"You see?" the Widow asked. "You smell the same as Ngui."

"Ngui, do we smell the same?"

"I don't know how I smell. No man knows. But you smell the same as Mthuka."

Ngui was sitting against the opposite side of the tree looking downstream. He had his legs drawn up and was resting his head against the tree. He had my new spear beside him.

"Widow, you talk to Ngui."

"No," she said. "I look after girl."

The girl had laid her head in my lap and was fingering the pistol holster. I knew she wanted me to trace the outline of her nose and her lips with my fingers and then touch the line of her chin very lightly and feel the line where she had her hair cut back to make a square line on the forehead and the sides and feel around her ears and over the top of her head. This was a great delicacy of courtship and all I could do if the Widow was there. But she could explore too, gently if she wished.

"You hard-handed beauty."

"Be good wife."

"You tell Widow go away."

"No."

"Why?"

She told me and I kissed her on top of the head again. She explored very delicately with her hands and then picked my right hand up and put it where she wished it. I held her very close and put the other hand where it should be.

"No," the Widow said.

"Hapana tu," the girl said. She turned over and put her head facedown where it had been and said something in Kamba that I could not understand. Ngui looked down the stream and I looked up it and the Widow had moved behind the tree and lay there with our fused, implacable sorrow and I reached up to the tree and got the rifle and laid it by my right leg.

"Go to sleep, tu," I said.

"No. I sleep tonight."

"Sleep now."

"No. Can I touch?"

"Yes."

"As a last wife."

"As my hard-handed wife."

She said something else in Kamba that I did not understand and Ngui said, "Kwenda na campi."

"I have to stay," the Widow said. But as Ngui went off walking with his careless walk and casting a long shadow through the trees she walked a little way with him and spoke in Kamba. Then she took up her post about four trees back and looking downstream.

"Are they gone?" the girl asked.

I said yes and she moved up so we lay tight and close together and she put her mouth against mine and we kissed very carefully. She liked to play and explore and be delighted at the reactions and at the scars and she held my ear-lobes between her thumb and forefinger where she wanted them pierced. Hers had never been pierced and she wished me to feel where they would be pierced for me and I felt them carefully and kissed them and then bit them a little very gently.

"Really bite them with the dog teeth."

"No."

She bit mine a little bit to show me the place and it was a very nice feeling.

"Why did you never do it before?"

"I don't know. In our tribe we do not do it."

"It is better to do it. It is better and more honest."

238 • ERNEST HEMINGWAY

"We will do many good things."

"We have already. But I want to be a useful wife. Not a play wife or a wife to leave."

"Who would leave you?"

"You," she said.

There is, as I said, no word for love and no word for I am sorry in Kikamba. But I told her in Spanish that I loved her very much and that I loved everything about her from her feet to her head and we counted all the things that were loved and she was truly very happy and I was happy too and I did not think I lied about any one of them nor about all of them.

We lay under the tree and I listened to the baboons coming down toward the river and we slept for a while and then the Widow had come back to our tree and she whispered in my ear, "Nyanyi."

The wind was blowing down the stream toward us and a troop of baboons were crossing the stream on the rocks of the ford coming out of the bush toward the fence of the mealie Shamba where the maize (our field corn) was twelve and fourteen feet high. The baboons could not smell us and they did not see us lying in the broken shade under the tree. The baboons came out of the bush quietly and started to cross the stream like a raiding party. There were three very big old man baboons at the head, one big-

ger than the others, walking carefully, their flattened heads and long muzzles and huge heavy
jaws swinging and turning. I could see their big
muscles, heavy shoulders and thick rumps and
the arched and drooping tails and the big heavy
bodies and behind them was the tribe, the
females and the young ones still coming out of
the bush.

The girl rolled away very slowly so I was free
to shoot and I raised the rifle carefully and
slowly and still lying down stretched it out
across my leg and pulled the bolt back, holding
it by the knurl with my finger on the trigger and
then letting it forward to the cocked position so
there was no click.

Still lying down I held on the shoulder of the
biggest old dog baboon and squeezed very gently. I heard the thump but did not look to see
what had happened to him as I rolled over and
got to my feet and started to shoot at the other
two big baboons. They were both going back
over the rocks toward the bush and I hit the
third and then the second as he jumped over
him. I looked back at the first baboon and he
was lying facedown in the water. The last one I
had shot was screaming and I shot and finished
him. The others were out of sight. I reloaded in
the brush and Debba asked if she could hold the
rifle. She stood at attention with it, imitating

Arap Meina. "It was so cold," she said. "Now it is so hot."

At the shots people had come down from the Shamba. The Informer was with them and Ngui came up with the spear. He had not gone to camp but to the Shamba and I knew how he smelt. He smelt of pombe.

"Three dead," he said. "All important generals. General Burma. General Korea. General Malaya. Buona notte."

He had learned "Buona notte" in Abyssinia with the K.A.R. He took the rifle from Debba, who was now holding it very demurely and looking out at the baboons on the rocks and in the water. They were not a handsome sight and I told the Informer to tell the men and boys to haul them out from the stream and sit them up against the fence of the mealie plantation with their hands crossed in their laps. Afterwards I would send some rope and we would hang them from the fence to frighten away the others or place them as baits.

The Informer gave the order and Debba, very demure, formal and detached, watched the big baboons with their long arms, obscene bellies and really bad faces and dangerous jaws being pulled out of the water and up the bank and then being composed in death against the wall. One of the heads was tipped back in contemplation. The other two were sunk forward in the appearance of deep thought. We walked away from this scene toward the Shamba where the car was parked. Ngui and I walked together; I was carrying the rifle again; the Informer walked to one side and Debba and the Widow walked behind.

"Great generals. Important generals," Ngui said. "Kwenda na campi?"

"How are you feeling, Informer old-timer?" I asked.

"Brother, I have no feelings. My heart is broken."

"What is it?"

"The Widow."

"She is a very good woman."

"Yes. But now she wants you to be her protector and she does not treat me with dignity. She wishes to go with you and the small boy that I have cared for as a father to the Land of Mayito. She wishes to care for the Debba who wishes to be the assistant wife to the Lady Miss Mary. Everyone's thought is bent in this direction and she talks of it to me all night."

"That's bad."

"The Debba should never have carried your gun." I saw Ngui look at him.

"She did not carry it. She held it."

"She should not hold it."

"You say this?"

"No. Of course not, brother. The village says it."

"Let the village shut up or I will withdraw my protection."

This was the sort of statement which was valueless. But the Informer was moderately valueless too.

"Also you had no time to hear anything from the village because it happened a half an hour ago. Don't start to be an intriguer." Or finish as one I thought.

We had come to the Shamba with the red earth and the great sacred tree and the well-built huts. The Widow's son butted me in the stomach and stood there for me to kiss the top of his head. I patted the top of his head instead and gave him a shilling. Then I remembered the Informer only made sixty-eight shillings a month and that a shilling was close to half a day's wages to give to a little boy so I called the Informer to come away from the car and I felt in the pocket of my bush-shirt and found some ten-shilling notes that were sweated together.

I unfolded two and gave them to the Informer.

"Don't talk balls about who holds my gun. There isn't a man in this Shamba that could hold a shit-pot."

"Did I ever say there was, brother?"

"Buy the Widow a present and let me know what goes on in town."

"It is late to go tonight."

"Go down to the road and wait for the lorry of the Anglo-Masai."

"If it does not come, brother?"

Ordinarily he would have said, "Yes, brother." And the next day, "It did not come, brother." So I appreciated his attitude and his effort.

"Go at daylight."

"Yes, brother."

I felt badly about the Shamba and about the Informer, and the Widow and everyone's hopes and plans and we drove off and did not look back.

That had been several days ago before the rain and before the lion came back and there was no reason to think of it now except that tonight I was sorry for G.C., who because of custom, law and choice too perhaps had to live alone on safari and had to read all night.

One of the books we had brought with us was Alan Paton's *Too Late the Phalarope*. I had found it almost unreadable due to the super-biblical style and the amount of piety in it. The piety seems to be mixed in a cement mixer and then carried in hods to the building of the book

244 • ERNEST HEMINGWAY

and it was not that there was an odor of piety; piety was like the oil on the sea after a tanker had been sunk. But G.C. said it was a good book and so I would read on in it until my brain would feel that it was not worth it to spend time with such stupid, bigoted, awful people as Paton made with their horrible sense of sin because of an act passed in 1927. But when I finally finished it I knew G.C. was right because Paton had been trying to make just such people; but being more than a little pious himself he had bent backwards trying to understand them or, at least, could not condemn them except by more scripture. Until finally in his greatness of soul he approved of them; I saw what G.C. meant about the book though, but it was a sad thing to think of.

G.C. and Mary were talking happily about a city called London that I knew of largely by hearsay and knew concretely only under the most abnormal conditions, so I could listen to them talk and think about Paris. That was a city that I knew under almost all circumstances. I knew it and loved it so well that I never liked to talk about it except with people from the old days. In the old days we all had our own cafés where we went alone and knew no one except the waiters. These cafés were secret places and in the old days everyone who loved Paris had

his own café. They were better than clubs and
you received the mail there that you did not
wish have come to your flat. Usually you had
two or three secret cafés. There would be one
where you went to work and read the papers.
You never gave the address of this café to anyone and you went there in the morning and had
a café crême and brioche on the terrace and
then, when they had cleaned the corner where
your table was, inside and next to the window,
you worked while the rest of the café was being
cleaned and scrubbed and polished. It was nice
to have other people working and it helped
you to work. By the time the clients started to
come to the café you would pay for your half
bottle of Vichy and go out and walk down the
quay to where you would have an aperitif and
then have lunch. There were secret places to
have lunch and also restaurants where people
went that you knew.

The best secret places were always discovered
by Mike Ward. He knew Paris and loved her
better than anyone I knew. As soon as a French-
man discovered a secret place he would give a
huge party there to celebrate the secret. Mike
and I hunted secret places that had one or two
good small wines and had a good cook, usually
a rummy, and were making a last effort to make
things go before having to sell out or go into

bankruptcy. We did not want any secret places that were becoming successful or going up in the world. That was what always happened with Charley Sweeny's secret places. By the time he took you there the secret had been so revealed that you had to stand in line to get a table.

But Charley was very good about secret cafés and he had a wonderful security consciousness about his own and yours. These were of course our secondary or afternoon and early evening cafés. This was a time of day when you might want to talk to someone and sometimes I would go to his secondary café and sometimes he would come to mine. He might say he wished to bring a girl he wanted me to meet or I might tell him I would bring a girl. The girls always worked. Otherwise they were not serious. No one, except fools, kept a girl. You did not want her around in the daytime and you did not want the problems she brought. If she wanted to be your girl and worked then she was serious and then she owned the nights when you wanted her and you fed her evenings and gave her things when she needed them. I never brought many girls to show them off to Charley, who always had beautiful and docile girls, all of whom worked and all of whom were under perfect discipline, because at that time my concierge was my girl. I had never known a young concierge before and it was an inspiring experience. Her greatest asset was that she could never go out, not only in society, but at all. When I first knew her, as a locataire, she was in love with a trooper in the Garde Républicaine. He was the horse tail–plumed, medaled, mustached type and his barracks were not very far away in the quarter. He had regular hours for his duty and he was a fine figure of a man and we always addressed each other formally as "Monsieur."

I was not in love with my concierge but I was very lonely at night at that time and the first time she came up the stairs and through the door, which had the key in it, and then up the ladder that led to the sort of loft where the bed was beside the window that gave such a lovely view over the Cemetery Montparnasse and took off her felt-soled shoes and lay on the bed and asked me if I loved her I answered, loyally, "Naturally."

"I knew it," she said. "I've known it too long."

She undressed very quickly and I looked out at the moonlight on the cemetery. Unlike the Shamba she did not smell the same but she was clean and fragile out of sturdy but insufficient nourishment and we paid honor to the view which neither saw. I had it in my mind however and then she said that the last tenant had entered and we lay and she told me that she could never love a member of the Garde Républicaine truly. I said that I thought Monsieur was a nice man, I said *un brave homme et très gentil,* and that he must look very well on a horse. But she said that she was not a horse and also there were inconveniences.

So I was thinking this about Paris while they were talking of London and I thought that we were all brought up differently and it was good luck we got on so well and I wished G.C. was not lonely nights and that I was too damned lucky to be married to somebody as lovely as Mary and I would straighten things out at the Shamba and try to be a really good husband.

"You're being awfully silent, General," G.C. said. "Are we boring you?"

"Young people never bore me. I love their careless chatter. It keeps me from feeling old and unwanted."

"Balls to you," G.C. said. "What were you thinking about with the semi-profound look? Not brooding are you or worrying about what the morrow will bring?"

"When I start worrying about what the morrow will bring you'll see a light burning in my tent late at night."

"Balls to you again, General," G.C. said.

"Don't use rough words G.C.," Mary said. "My husband is a delicate and sensitive man and they repugn him."

"I'm glad something repugns him," G.C. said. "I love to see the good side of his character."

"He hides it carefully. What were you thinking about darling?"

"A trooper in the Garde Républicaine."

"You see?" G.C. said. "I always said he had a delicate side. It comes out completely unexpectedly. It's his Proustian side. Tell me, was he very attractive? I try to be broad-minded."

"Papa and Proust used to live in the same hotel," Miss Mary said. "But Papa always claims it was at different times."

"God knows what really went on," G.C. said. He was very happy and not at all taut tonight and Mary with her wonderful memory for forgetting was happy too and without any problems. She could forget in the loveliest and most complete way of anyone I ever knew. She could carry a fight overnight but at the end of a week she could forget it completely and truly. She had a built-in selective memory and it was not built entirely in her favor. She forgave herself in her memory and she forgave you too. She was a very strange girl and I loved her very much. She had, at the moment, only two

defects. She was very short for honest lion hunting and she had too good a heart to be a killer
and that, I had finally decided, made her either
flinch or squeeze off a little when shooting at an
animal. I found this attractive and was never
exasperated by it. But she was exasperated by it
because, in her head, she understood why we
killed and the necessity for it and she had come
to take pleasure in it, after thinking that she
never would kill an animal as beautiful as an
impala and would only kill ugly and dangerous
beasts. In six months of daily hunting she had
learned to love it, shameful though it is basically
and unshameful as it is if done cleanly, but there
was something too good in her that worked
subconsciously and made her pull off the target.
I loved her for it in the same way that I could
not love a woman who could work in the stock-
yards or put dogs or cats out of their suffering
or destroy horses who had broken their legs at a
race course.

"What was the trooper's name," G.C. asked.
"Albertine?"

"No. Monsieur."

"He's baffling us, Miss Mary," G.C. said.

They went on talking about London. So I
started to think about London too and it was
not unpleasant although much too noisy and
not normal. I realized I knew nothing about

London and so I started to think about Paris and in greater detail than before. Actually I was worried about Mary's lion and so was G.C. and we were just handling it in different ways. It was always easy enough when it really happened. But Mary's lion had been going on for a long time and I wanted to get him the hell over with.

Finally, when the different dudus, which was the generic name for all bugs, beetles and insects, were thick enough on the dining tent floor so that they made a light crunching when you walked we went to bed.

"Don't worry about the morrow," I said to G.C. as he went off to his tent.

"Come here a moment," he said. We were standing halfway to his tent and Mary had gone into ours. "Where did she aim at that unfortunate wildebeest?"

"Didn't she tell you?"

"No."

"Go to sleep," I said. "We don't come in until the second act anyway."

"You couldn't do the old husband and wife thing?"

"No. Charo's been begging me to do that for a month."

"She's awfully admirable," G.C. said. "You're even faintly admirable."

"Just a lot of admirals."

"Good night, Admiral."

"Put a telescope to my blind eye and kiss my ass, Hardy."

"You're confusing the line of battle."

Just then the lion roared. G.C. and I shook hands.

"He probably heard you misquoting Nelson," G.C. said.

"He got tired of hearing you and Mary talk about London."

"He is in good voice," G.C. said. "Go to bed, Admiral, and get some sleep."

In the night I heard the lion roar several more times. Then I went to sleep and Mwindi was pulling on the blanket at the foot of the cot.

"Chai, Bwana."

It was very dark outside but someone was building up the fire. I woke Mary with her tea but she did not feel well. She felt ill and had bad cramps.

"Do you want to cancel it, honey?"

"No. I just feel awful. After the tea maybe I'll be better."

"We can wash it. It might be better to give him another day's rest."

"No. I want to go. But just let me try and feel better if I can."

I went out and washed in the cold water in the basin and washed my eyes with boric, dressed and went out to the fire. I could see G.C. shaving in front of his tent. He finished, dressed and came over.

"Mary feels rocky," I told him.

"Poor child."

"She wants to go anyway."

"Naturally."

"How'd you sleep?"

"Well. You?"

"Very well. What do you think he was doing last night?"

"I think he was just going walkabout. And sounding off."

"He talks a lot. Want to split a bottle of beer?"

"It won't hurt us."

I went and got the beer and two glasses and waited for Mary. She came out of the tent and walked down the path to the latrine tent. She came back and walked down again.

"How do you feel, honey?" I asked when she came over to the table by the fire with her tea. Charo and Ngui were getting the guns and the binoculars and shell bags out from under the tents and taking them to the hunting car.

"I don't feel good at all. Do we have anything for it?"

"Yes. But it makes you feel dopey. We've got Terramycin too. It's supposed to be good for both kinds but it can make you feel funny too."

"Why did I have to get something when my lion's here?"

"Don't you worry, Miss Mary," G.C. said. "We'll get you fit and the lion will get confident."

"But I want to go out after him."

She was in obvious pain and I could see it coming back on her again.

"Honey, we'll lay off him this morning and rest him. It's the best thing to do anyway. You take it easy and take care of yourself. G.C. can stay a couple of more days anyway."

G.C. shook his hand, palm down, in negation. But Mary did not see him.

"He's your lion and you take your time and be in shape to shoot him and all the time we let him alone he will be getting more confident. If we don't go out at all this morning it's much better."

I went over to the car and said we were not going out. Then I went and found Keiti by the fire. He seemed to know all about it but he was very delicate and polite.

"Memsahib is sick."

"I know."

"Maybe spaghetti. Maybe dysentery."

"Yes," Keiti said. "I think spaghetti."

"Meat too old."

"Yes. Maybe little piece. Made in the dark."

"We leave lion alone take care of Memsahib. The lion gets confident."

"Mzuri," Keiti said. "Poli poli. You shoot kwali or kanga. Mbebia make Memsahib broth."

After we were sure that the lion would have left the bait if he had been on it G.C. and I went out to have a look at the country in his Land Rover.

I asked Ngui for a bottle. It was wrapped in a wet sack and was still cold from the night and we sat in the Land Rover in the shade of the tree and drank it out of the bottle and looked off across the dried mud flat and watched the small Tommies and the black movement of the wildebeest and the zebra that looked a gray white in this light as they moved out across the flat to the grass on the far side and at the end toward the Chulu hills. The hills were a dark blue this morning and looked very far away. When we turned to look back at the great Mountain it looked very close. It seemed to be just behind camp and the snow was heavy and bright in the sun.

"We could hunt Miss Mary on stilts," I said. "Then she could see him in the tall grass."

"There's nothing in the Game Laws against it."

"Or Charo could carry a stepladder such as they have in libraries for the higher stacks."

"That's brilliant," G.C. said. "We'd pad the rungs and she could take a rest with the rifle on the rung above where she stood."

"You don't think it would be too immobile?"

"It'd be up to Charo to make it mobile."

"It would be a beautiful sight," I said. "We could mount an electric fan on it."

"We could build it in the form of an electric fan," G.C. said happily. "But that would probably be considered a vehicle and illegal."

"If we rolled it forward and had Miss Mary keep climbing in it like a squirrel would it be illegal?"

"Anything that rolls is a vehicle," G.C. said judicially.

"I roll slightly when I walk."

"Then you're a vehicle. I'll run you and you'll get six months and be shipped out of the Colony."

"We have to be careful, G.C."

"Care and moderation have been our watchwords haven't they?"

"Any more in that bottle?"

"We can share the dregs."

8

THE DAY THAT Miss Mary shot her lion was a very beautiful day. That was about all that was beautiful about it. White flowers had blossomed in the night so that with the first daylight before the sun had risen all the meadows looked as though a full moon was shining on new snow through a mist. Mary was up and dressed long before first light. The right sleeve of her bush jacket was rolled up and she had checked all the rounds in her Mannlicher .256. She said she did not feel well and I believed her. She acknowledged G.C.'s and my greetings briefly and we were careful not to make any jokes. I did not know what she had against G.C. except his tendency to lightheartedness in the face of undeniably serious work. Her being angry at me was a sound reaction, I thought. If she were in a bad mood I thought she might feel mean and shoot as deadly as I knew she knew how to shoot. This agreed with my last and greatest theory that she had too kind a heart to kill animals. Some people shoot easily and loosely; others

shoot with a dreadful speed that is still so controlled that they have all the time they need to
place the bullet as carefully as a surgeon would
make his first incision; others are mechanical
shots who are very deadly unless something
happens to interfere with the mechanics of the
shooting. This morning it looked as though
Miss Mary was going out to shoot with grim
resolution, contemptuous of all those who did
not take things with appropriate seriousness,
armored in her bad physical condition, which
provided an excuse if she missed, and full of
rigid, concentrated do-or-die deadliness. It
seemed fine to me. It was a new approach.

We waited by the hunting car for it to be light
enough to start and we were all solemn and
deadly. Ngui nearly always had an evil temper
in the very early morning so he was solemn,
deadly and sullen. Charo was solemn, deadly
but faintly cheerful. He was like a man going to
a funeral who did not really feel too deeply
about the deceased. Mthuka was happy as
always in his deafness watching with his wonderful eyes for the start of the lightening of the
darkness.

We were all hunters and it was the start of
that wonderful thing, the hunt. There is much
mystic nonsense written about hunting but it is
something that is probably much older than

religion. Some are hunters and some are not. Miss Mary was a hunter and a brave and lovely one but she had come to it late instead of as a child and many of the things that had happened to her in hunting came as unexpectedly as being in heat for the first time to the kitten when she becomes a cat. She grouped all these new knowledges and changes as things we know and other people don't.

The four of us who had seen her go through these changes and had seen her now, for months, hunting something grimly and seriously against every possible sort of odds were like the cuadrilla of a very young matador. If the matador was serious the cuadrilla would be serious. They knew all the matador's defects and they were all well paid in different ways. All had lost completely any faith in the matador and all had regained it many times. As we sat in the car or moved around it waiting for it to be light enough to set out I was reminded very much of how it is before a bullfight. Our matador was solemn; so we were solemn, since as is unusual, we loved our matador. Our matador was not well. This made it even more necessary that he be protected and given even a better chance in everything he chose to do. But as we sat and leaned and felt sleep drain from us we were as happy as hunters. Probably no one is as happy as hunters with the always new, fresh, unknowing day ahead and Mary was a hunter too. But she had set herself this task and being guided and trained and indoctrinated into absolute purity and virtue of killing a lion by Pop who had made her his last pupil and given her ethics he had never been able to impose on other women so that her killing of her lion must not be the way such things are done but the way such things should ideally be done; Pop finding finally in Mary the spirit of a fighting cock embodied in a woman; a loving and belated killer with the only defect that no one could say where the shot would go. Pop had given her the ethics and then it was necessary that he go away. She had the ethics now but she only had G.C. and me and neither of us was to be really trusted as Pop was. So now she was going out again to her corrida that always was postponed.

Mthuka nodded to me that the light was beginning to be possible and we started off through the fields of white flowers where yesterday all the meadows had been green. As we came even with the trees of the forest with the high dead yellow grass on our left Mthuka slid the car to a quiet stop. He turned his head and I saw the arrow-shaped scar on his cheek and the slashes. He said nothing and I followed his eyes. The great black-maned lion, his head huge above the yellow grass, was coming out toward us. Only his head showed above the stiff tall yellow grass.

"What do you say we circle easy back to camp?" I whispered to G.C.

"I quite agree," he whispered.

As we spoke the lion turned and moved back toward the forest. All you could see of him was the movements of the high grass.

When we got back to camp and had breakfast Mary understood why we had done what we did and agreed that it was right and necessary. But the corrida had been called off again when she was all set and tense for it and we were not popular. I felt so sorry that she felt ill and I wanted her to let down in tension if she could. There was no use going on talking about how the lion had made a mistake finally. Both G.C. and I were sure we had him now. He had not fed during the night and had come out to look for the bait in the morning. He had gone back into the forest again. He would lie up hungry and, if he were not disturbed, he should be out early in the evening; that is he should be. If he was not G.C. had to leave the next day no matter what happened and he would revert back to Mary and me on our own. But the lion had broken his pattern of behavior and made a very grave mistake and I did not worry anymore about our getting him. I might have been happier to hunt him with Mary without G.C. but I loved to hunt with G.C. too and I was not so stupid as to want any sort of bad show to happen with me alone with Mary. G.C. had pointed out too well how it could be. I always had the great illusion of Mary hitting the lion exactly where she should and the lion rolling over like anything else I had seen them do so many times and be as dead as only a lion can be. I was going to drive two into him if he rolled over alive and that was that. Miss Mary would have killed her lion and been happy about it always and I would only have given him the puntilla and she would know it and love me very much forever world without end amen. It was now the sixth month that we had looked forward to this. Just then a new Land Rover, one of the new, larger and faster models we had never seen before, drove into camp through the wonderful field of white flowers that had been dust a month ago and mud one week before. This car was driven by a red-faced man of middle height who wore a faded khaki uniform of an officer in the Kenya police. He was dusty from the road and there were white smile wrinkles at the corners of his eyes that cracked the dust.

"Anybody home?" he asked coming into the mess tent and taking off his cap. Through the open, muslin-screened end that faced toward the Mountain I had seen the car come up.

"Everybody home," I said. "How are you, Mr. Harry?"

"I'm quite well."

"Sit down and let me make you something. You can stay the night can't you?"

He sat down and stretched his legs and moved his shoulders as pleasantly as a cat does.

"Couldn't drink anything. No proper people drink at this hour."

"What do you want?"

"Would you share a beer?"

I opened the beer and poured it out and watched him relax and smile with his dead tired eyes as we raised the glasses.

"Have them put your gear in young Pat's tent. It's that green one that's empty."

Harry Dunn was shy, overworked, kind and ruthless. He was fond of Africans and understood them and he was paid to enforce the law and carry out orders. He was as gentle as he was tough and he was not revengeful nor a hater nor was he ever stupid nor sentimental. He did not hold grudges in a grudge-holding country and I never saw him be petty about anything. He was administering the law in a time of corruption, hatreds, sadism and considerable hysteria and he worked himself, each day, past the limit that a man can possibly go, never working to seek promotion or advancement because he knew his worth at what he was doing. Miss Mary one time said that he was a portable fortress of a man.

"Are you having fun here?"

"Very much."

"I've heard a little. What's this about having to kill the leopard before the Birthday of the Baby Jesus?"

"That's for that picture story for that magazine we were making the pictures for in September. Before we met. We had a photographer and he took thousands of pictures and I've written a short article and captions for the pictures they use. They have a beautiful picture of a leopard and I shot him but he isn't mine."

"How does that work?"

"We were after a big lion that was very smart. It was over on the other side of the Ewaso Ngiro beyond Magadi under the escarpment."

"Well off my beat."

"We were trying to work up on this lion and this friend of mine climbed up a little rock kopje with his gun bearer to look ahead to see if the lion had showed. The lion was for Mary because he and I had both killed lions. So we didn't know what the hell had happened when we heard him shoot and then something was down in the dust roaring. It was a leopard and the dust was so deep that it rose solid in a cloud and the leopard kept on roaring and nobody knew which direction he was coming out of the dust. This friend of mine, Mayito, had hit him twice from up above and I had shot into the moving center of the dust and ducked and moved to the right where it was natural he would break out. Then he showed his head up just once out of the dusk, still talking bad and I hit him in the neck and the dust started to settle. It was sort of like a gunfight in the dust outside of an old-time saloon out West. Except the leopard didn't have any gun but he was close enough to have mauled anyone and he was awfully worked up. The photographer took pictures of Mayito and him and of all of us and him and of me and him. He was Mayito's because Mayito hit him first and hit him again. So the best picture of him was the one with me and the magazine wanted to use it and I said they couldn't unless I killed a good leopard alone by myself. And so far I've failed three times."

"I didn't know the ethics were so rigid."

"Unfortunately they are. It's the law too. First blood and continuous pursuit."

Arap Meina and the Chief Game Scout had

brought back the word that the two lionesses and the young lion had killed far up on the edge of the salt flat. The bait had not been uncovered except where hyenas had pulled at it and the two scouts recovered it carefully. There were birds in the trees around it that would surely draw the lion but the birds could not get at the remains of the zebra, which were high enough to draw the lion surely. He had not fed nor killed in the night, and since he was not hungry and had not been disturbed we might, almost surely, find him in the open in the evening.

We had lunch, finally, and Mary was very cheerful and gracious with all of us. I believe she even asked me if I wanted any more of the cold meat. When I said no thank you, that I had enough, she said it would be good for me, that any man who drinks a great deal needs to eat. This was not only a very old truth but had been the basis of an article in the *Reader's Digest* that we had all read. That number of the *Digest* was down in the latrine now. I said that I had decided to run on a platform of true rummy-hood and deceive none of my constituents. Churchill drank twice what I did if you could believe the accounts and he had just been awarded the Nobel Prize for Literature. I was simply trying to step up my drinking to a reasonable amount when I might win the Prize myself; who knows?

G.C. said that the Prize was as good as mine and that I ought to win it for bragging alone since Churchill had been awarded it, at least partially, for oratory. G.C. said that he had not followed the Prize awards as closely as he should but that he felt I might well be awarded it for my work in the religious field and for my care of the natives. Miss Mary suggested that if I would try to write something, occasionally, I might win it for writing. This moved me very deeply and I said that once she had the lion I would do nothing but write just to please her. She said that if I wrote even a little it would certainly please her. G.C. asked me if I planned to write something about how mysterious Africa was and that if I planned to write in Swahili he could get me a book on up-country Swahili that might be invaluable to me. Miss Mary said that we already had the book and that she thought even with the book it would be better if I tried to write in English. I suggested that I might copy sections of the book to help me get an up-country style. Miss Mary said I could not write one correct sentence in Swahili nor speak one either and I agreed with her very sadly that this was true.

"Pop speaks it so beautifully and so does G.C. and you are a disgrace. I don't know how anyone can speak a language as badly as you do."

I wanted to say that at one time, years before, it had looked as though I were going to speak it quite well. But that I had been a fool not to have stayed on in Africa and instead had gone back to America where I had killed my homesickness for Africa in different ways. Then before I could get back came the Spanish war and I became involved in what was happening to the world and I had stayed with that for better and for worse until I had finally come back. It had not been easy to get back nor to break the chains of responsibility that are built up, seemingly, as lightly as spiderwebs but that hold like steel cables.

They were all having a good time now joking and making fun of one another and I joked a little but was careful to be very modest and contrite hoping to win back Miss Mary's favor and hoping to keep her in a good humor in case the lion would show. I had been drinking Bulmer's Dry Cider, which I had found to be a marvelous drink. G.C. had brought some in from Kajiado from the Stores. It was very light and refreshing and did not slow you down at all shooting. It came in full quarts and had screw-in tops and I used to drink it in the night when I woke instead of water. Mary's extremely nice cousin had given us two small square sacking-covered pillows filled with balsam needles. I always slept with mine under my neck or, if I slept on my side, with my ear on it. It was the smell of Michigan when I was a boy and I wished I could have had a sweet-grass basket to keep it in when we traveled and to have under the mosquito net in the bed at night. The cider tasted like Michigan too and I always remembered the cider mill and the door which was never locked but only fitted with a hasp and wooden pin and the smell of the sacks used in the pressing and later spread to dry and then spread over the deep tubs where the men who came to grind their wagon loads of apples left the mill's share. Below the dam of the cider mill there was a deep pool where the eddy from the falling water turned out back in under the dam. You could always catch trout if you fished there patiently and whenever I caught one I would kill him and lay him in the big wicker creel that was in the shade and put a layer of fern leaves over him and then go into the cider mill and take the tin cup off the nail on the wall over the tubs and pull up the heavy sacking from one of the tubs and dip out a cup of cider and drink it. This cider that we had now reminded me of Michigan, especially with the pillow.

Sitting now at the table I was pleased Mary seemed to be feeling better and I hoped the lion would show in the late afternoon and that she would kill him dead as snake shit and be happy forever after. We finished lunch and everybody was very cheerful and we all said we would take a nap and I would call Miss Mary when it was time to go to look for the lion.

Mary went to sleep almost as soon as she lay down on her cot. The back of the tent was propped open and a good cool breeze blew down from the Mountain and through the tent. We ordinarily slept facing the open door of the tent but I took the pillows and placed them at opposite ends of the cot and doubling them over and with the balsam pillow under my neck lay on the cot with my boots and trousers off and read with the good light behind me. I was reading a very good book by Gerald Hanley, who had written another good book called *The Consul at Sunset*. This book was about a lion who made much trouble and killed practically all the characters in the book. G.C. and I used to read this book in the mornings on the latrine to inspire us. There were a few characters the lion did not kill but they were all headed for some other sort of bad fate so we did not really mind. Hanley wrote very well and it was an excellent book and very inspiring when you were in the lion-hunting business. I had seen a lion come, at speed, once and I had been very impressed and am still impressed. On this afternoon I was reading the book very slowly because it was such a good book and I did not want to finish it. I was hoping the lion would kill the hero or the Old Major because they were both very noble and nice characters and I had gotten very fond of the lion and wanted him to kill some upper-bracket character. The lion was doing very well though and he had just killed another very sympathetic and important character when I decided it would be better to save the rest and got up and pulled on my trousers and put my boots on without zipping them up and went over to see if G.C. was awake. I coughed outside his tent the way the Informer always did outside the mess tent.

"Come in, General," G.C. said.

"No," I said. "A man's home is his castle. Are you feeling up to facing the deadly beasts?"

"It's too early yet. Did Mary sleep?"

"She's still sleeping. What are you reading?"

"Lindbergh. It's damned good. What were you reading?"

"*The Year of the Lion.* I'm sweating out the lion."

"You've been reading that for a month."

"Six weeks. How are you coming with the mysticism of the air?"

That year we were both, belatedly, full of the mysticism of the air. I had given up on the mysticism of the air finally in 1945 when flying home in an overaged unreconditioned flight-weary B-17.

When it was time I got Mary up while the gun bearers got her rifle and my big gun from under the beds and checked the solids and the soft-nosed.

"He's there, honey. He's there and you'll get him."

"It's late."

"Don't think about anything. Just get out in the car."

"I have to put my boots on, you know that."

I was helping her on with them.

"Where's my damned hat?"

"Here's your damned hat. Walk, don't run, to the nearest Land Rover. Don't think about anything but hitting him."

"Don't talk to me so much. Leave me alone."

Mary and G.C. were in the front seats with Mthuka driving. Ngui, Charo and I were in the open back with the Game Scout. I was checking the cartridges in the barrel and the magazine of the 30-06, checking those in my pockets and checking and cleaning the rear sight aperture of any dust with a toothpick. Mary was holding her rifle straight up and I had a fine view of the new wiped dark barrel and the Scotch tape that held her rear sight leaves down, of the back of her head and her disreputable hat. The sun was just above the hills now and we were out of the flowers and going north on the old track that ran parallel to the woods. Somewhere on the right was the lion. The car stopped and everyone got out except Mthuka, who stayed at the wheel. The lion's tracks went off to the right toward a clump of trees and brush on our side of the lone tree where the bait was covered by a pile of brush. He was not on the bait and there were no birds on it either. They were all up in the trees. I looked back at the sun and it did not have more than ten minutes before it would be behind the far hills to the west. Ngui had climbed the anthill and looked carefully over the top. He pointed with his hand held close by his face so that you could hardly see it move and then came fast down from the mound.

"Hiko huko," he said. "He's out there. Mzuri motocah."

G.C. and I both looked at the sun again and G.C. waved his arm for Mthuka to come up. We climbed into the car and G.C. told Mthuka how he wanted him to go.

"But where is he?" Mary asked G.C.

G.C. put his hand on Mthuka's arm and he stopped the car.

"We leave the car back here," G.C. told Mary. "He must be in that far clump of trees and brush. Papa will take the left flank and block him off from breaking back to the forest. You and I will move straight in on him."

The sun was still above the hills as we moved up toward where the lion must be. Ngui was behind me and on our right Mary was walking a little ahead of G.C. Charo was behind G.C. They were walking straight toward the trees with the thin brush at their base. I could see the lion now and I kept working to the left, walking sideways and forward. He was watching us and I thought what a bad place he had gotten himself into now. Every step I made I was blocking him worse from his safety that he had retreated into so many times. He had no choice now except to break toward me, to come out toward Mary and G.C., which he did not figure to do unless he were wounded, or to try for the next island of heavy cover, trees and thick brush, that was four hundred and fifty yards away to the north. To reach there he would have to cross open flat plain.

Now I figured that I was far enough to the left and began moving in toward the lion. He stood there thigh deep in brush and I saw his head turn once to look toward me; then it swung back to watch Mary and G.C. His head was huge and dark but when he moved it the head did not look too big for his body. His body was heavy, great and long. I did not know how close G.C. would try to work Mary toward the lion. I did not watch them. I watched the lion and waited to hear the shot. I was as close as I needed to be now and have room to take him if he came and I was sure that if he were wounded he would break toward me as his natural cover was behind me. Mary must take him soon, I thought. She can't get any closer. But maybe G.C. wants her closer. I looked at them from the corner of my eyes, my head down, not looking away from the lion. I could see Mary wanted to shoot and that G.C. was preventing her. They were not trying to work closer so I figured that from where they were, there were some limbs of brush between Mary and the lion. I watched the lion and felt the change in his coloring as the first peak of the hills took the sun. It was good light to shoot now but it would go fast. I watched the lion and he moved very slightly to his right and then looked at Mary and G.C. I could see his eyes. Still Mary did not shoot. Then the lion moved very slightly again and I heard Mary's rifle go and the dry whack of the bullet. She had hit him. The lion made a bound into the brush and then came out of the far side headed for the patch of heavy cover to the north. Mary was firing at him and I was sure she hit him. He was moving in long bounds his great head swinging. I shot and raised a puff of dirt behind him. I swung with him and squeezed off as I passed him and was behind him again. G.C.'s big double was firing and I saw the blossomings of dirt from it. I fired again picking the lion up in the sights and swung ahead of him and a bunch of dirt rose ahead of him. He was running now heavy and desperate but beginning to look small in the sights and almost certain to make the far cover when I had him in the sights again, small now and going away fast, and swung gently ahead and lifting over him and squeezed as I passed him and no dirt rose and I saw him slide forward, his front feet plowing, and his great head was down before we heard the thunk of the bullet. Ngui banged me on the back and put his arm around me. The lion was trying to get up now and G.C. hit him and he rolled onto his side.

I went over to Mary and kissed her. She was happy but something was wrong.

"You shot before I did," she said.

"Don't say that, honey. You shot and hit him. How could I shoot before you when we'd waited all that time?"

"Ndio. Memsahib piga," Charo said. He had been right behind Mary.

"Of course you hit him. You hit him the first time in the foot I think. You hit him again too."

"But you killed him."

"We all had to keep him from getting into the thick stuff after he was hit."

"But you shot first. You know you did."

"I did not. Ask G.C."

We were all walking up to where the lion lay. It was a long walk and the lion grew larger and deader as we walked. With the sun going it was getting dark fast. The shooting light was gone already. I felt wrung out inside and very tired. G.C. and I were both wet with sweat.

"Of course you hit him, Mary," G.C. told her. "Papa didn't shoot until he went into the open. You hit him twice."

"Why couldn't I have shot him when I wanted to when he was just standing there and looking at me?"

"There were branches that could have deflected the bullet or broken it up. That was why I made you wait."

"Then he moved."

"He had to move for you to shoot him."

"But did I really hit him first?"

"Of course you did. Nobody would have shot at him before you did."

"You're not just lying to make me happy?"

This was a scene that Charo had seen before.

"Piga!" he said violently. "Piga, Memsahib. PIGA!"

I slapped Ngui on the hip with the side of my

hand and looked toward Charo and he went over.

"Piga," he said harshly. "Piga Memsahib. Piga bili."

G.C. came over to walk by me and I said, "What are you sweating for?"

"How far did you hold over him you son of a bitch?"

"A foot and a half. Two feet. It was bow and arrow shooting."

"We'll pace it when we walk back."

"Nobody would ever believe it."

"We will. That's all that matters."

"Go over and make her realize she hit him."

"She believes the boys. You broke his back."

"I know."

"Did you hear how long it took for the sound of the bullet hitting to come back?"

"I did. Go over and talk to her."

The Land Rover pulled up behind us.

Now we were there with the lion and he was Mary's and she knew it now and she saw how wonderful and long and dark and beautiful he was. The camel flies were crawling on him and his yellow eyes were not dull yet. I moved my hand through the heavy black of his mane. Mthuka had stopped the Land Rover and come over and shaken Mary's hand. She was kneeling by him.

Then we saw the lorry coming out across the plain from camp. They had heard the shooting and Keiti had come out with everyone except two guards that they had left in camp. They were singing the lion song and when they piled out of the lorry Mary had no more doubt about whose lion it was. I have seen many lions killed and many celebrations. But not one like this. I wanted Mary to have all of it. I was sure it was all right with Mary now and I walked on to the island of trees and thick brush the lion had been making for. He had nearly made it and I thought of what it would have been like if G.C. and I had to go in there to dig him out. I wanted a look at it before the light was gone. He would have made it there in sixty more yards and it would have been dark when we got up to it. I thought about what could have happened and went back to the celebration and the picture taking. The headlights of the lorry and the Land Rover were centered on Mary and the lion and G.C. was making the photographs. Ngui brought me the Jinny flask from the shell bag in the Land Rover and I took a small swallow and handed it to Ngui. He took a small drink and shook his head and handed it to me.

"Piga," he said and we both laughed. I took a long drink and felt it warm and felt the strain slip off me like a snake shedding his skin. Until that moment I had not realized that we had the lion finally. I knew it technically when the unbelievable long bow and arrow shot had hit and broken him down and Ngui had hit me across the back. But then there had been Mary's worry and being upset and walking up to him we had been as unemotional and as detached as though it were the end of an attack. Now with the drink and the celebrating going on and the photography, the hated and necessary photography, too late at night, no flash, no professionals to do it properly to make Miss Mary's lion immortal now on film, seeing her shining happy face in the glare of the headlights and the lion's great head that was too heavy for her to lift, proud of her and loving the lion, me feeling as empty inside as an empty room, seeing Keiti's gashed slant of a smile as he bent over Mary to touch the lion's unbelievable black mane, everyone cooing in Kikamba like birds and each man individually proud of this our lion, ours and belonging to all of us and Mary's because she had hunted him for months and had hit him in that barred phrase standing on her own two feet and when the chips were down, and now happy and shining in the headlights looking like a small, not quite deadly, bright angel and everyone loving her and this our lion, I began to relax and to have fun.

Charo and Ngui had told Keiti how it was and he came over to me and we shook hands and he said, "Mzuri sana Bwana. Uchawi tu."

"It was lucky," I said which God knows it had to be.

"Not lucky," Keiti said. "Mzuri. Mzuri. Uchawi kubwa sana."

Then I remembered that I had given this afternoon for the lion's death and that it was all over now and that Mary had won and I talked with Ngui and Mthuka and Pop's gun bearer and the others of our religion and we shook our heads and laughed and Ngui wanted me to take another drink from the Jinny flask. They wanted to wait until we would get to camp for beer but they wanted me to drink now with them. They only touched the bottle with their lips. Mary stood up now after the photography and saw us drinking and she asked for the flask and drank from it and passed it to G.C. They passed it back and I drank and then lay down by the lion and talked to him very softly in Spanish and begged his pardon for us having killed him and while I lay beside him I felt for the wounds. There were four. Mary had hit him in the foot and in one haunch. While I stroked his back I found where I had hit him in the spine and the larger hole G.C.'s bullet had made well forward in his flank behind the shoulder. All the

time I was stroking him and talking to him in
Spanish but many of the flat hard camel flies
were shifting from him to me so I drew a fish in
front of him with my forefinger in the dirt and
then rubbed it out with the palm of my hand.

On the way into camp Ngui and Charo and I
did not talk. I heard Mary once ask G.C. if I had
not really shot before she did and heard him tell
her that she had gotten her lion. That she had
hit him first and that these things did not always
go off ideally and that when an animal was
wounded he had to be killed and that we were
damned lucky and she should be happy. But
I knew that her happiness came and went
because it had not been as she had hoped and
dreamed and feared and waited for all of six
months. I felt terribly about how she felt and I
knew it made no difference to anyone else and it
made all the difference in the world to her. But if
we had to do it over again there was no way we
could have done it differently. G.C. had taken
her up closer than anyone but a great shot had a
right to take her. If the lion had charged when
she hit him G.C. would have had time for only
one shot before the lion would have been on
them. His big gun was as deadly and efficient if
the lion came as it was a handicap if he had to
shoot it at two and three hundred yards. We
both knew that and had not even joked about it.

Taking the lion at the range she did Mary had been in great danger and both G.C. and I knew that at the distance he had brought her to she had, recently, a possible error of eighteen inches on live game. This was not the time to talk about that but Ngui and Charo knew it too and I had slept with it for a long time. The lion, by deciding to make his fight in the thick cover, where he was heavy odds on to get someone, had made his choice and had very nearly won. He was not a stupid lion and he was not cowardly. He wanted to make his fight where the odds were in his favor.

We came into camp and sat in chairs by the fire and stretched our legs out and drank tall drinks. Who we needed was Pop and Pop was not there. I had told Keiti to break out some beer for the lines and then I waited for it to come. It came as suddenly as a dry streambed filling with the high, foam-crested roar of water from a cloudburst. It had only taken time enough for them to decide who was to carry Miss Mary and then the wild, stooped dancing rush of Wakamba poured in from behind the tents all singing the lion song. The big mess boy and the truck driver had the chair and they put it down and Keiti dancing and clapping his hands led Miss Mary to it and they hoisted her up and started dancing around the fire with her and then out toward the lines and around the lion where he had been laid on the ground and then through the lines and around the cook fire and the men's fire and around the cars and the wood truck and in and out. The Game Scouts were all stripped to their shorts and so was everyone else except the old men. I watched Mary's bright head and the black strong fine bodies that were carrying her and crouching and stamping in the dance and then moving forward to reach up and touch her. It was a fine wild lion dance and at the end they put Mary down in the chair by her camp chair at the fire and everyone shook hands with her and it was over. She was happy and we had a fine happy meal and went to bed.

In the night I woke and could not get back to sleep. I woke very suddenly and it was absolutely quiet. Then I heard Mary's regular, smooth breathing and I had a feeling of relief that we would not have to pit her against the lion every morning. Then I began to feel sorrow that the lion's death had not been as she hoped it would be and as she planned it. With the celebration and the really wild dance and the love of all her friends and their allegiance to her the disappointment that she felt had been anesthetized. But I was sure that after the more than a hundred mornings that she had gone out after a

great lion the disappointment would return. She
did not know the danger she had been in.
Maybe she did and I did not know. Neither
G.C. nor I wanted to tell her because we had
both cut it too fine and we had not soaked in
sweat that way in the cool of the evening for
nothing. I remembered how the lion's eyes had
looked when he had looked toward me and
turned them down and then looked toward
Mary and G.C. and how his eyes had never left
them. I lay in the bed and thought how a lion
can come one hundred yards from a standing
start in just over three seconds. He comes low
down to the ground and faster than a grey-
hound and he does not spring until he is on his
prey. Mary's lion would weigh well over four
hundred pounds and he was strong enough to
have leaped out over a high thorn Boma carrying a cow. He had been hunted for many years
and he was very intelligent. But we had lulled
him into making a mistake. I was happy that
before he died he had lain on the high yellow
rounded mound with his tail down and his great
paws comfortable before him and looked off
across his country to the blue forest and the
high white snows of the big Mountain. Both
G.C. and I wanted him to be killed by Mary's
first shot or, wounded, charge. But he had
played it his own way. The first shot could not

have felt more than a sharp, slapping sting to him. The second that passed high through a leg muscle while he was bounding toward the heavy cover where he would make us fight would, at most, have felt like a hard slap. I did not like to think what my long-thrown running shot that was thrown at all of him, hoping to rake him and bring him down, must have felt like when it by chance took him in the spine. It was a two-hundred-and-twenty-grain solid bullet and I did not have to think how it would have felt. I had never yet broken my back and I did not know. I was glad G.C.'s wonderful distance shot had killed him instantly. He was dead now and we would miss hunting him too.

I tried to go to sleep but I started to think about the lion and what the moves would have been if he had reached the heavy cover, remembering other people's experiences under the same circumstances and then I thought the hell with all that. That's stuff for G.C. and I to talk over together and to talk with Pop. I wished Mary would wake and say, "I'm so glad I got my lion." But that was too much to expect and it was three o'clock in the morning. I remembered how Scott Fitzgerald had written that in the something something of the soul something something it is always three o'clock in the morning. For many months three o'clock in the morning had been two hours, or an hour and a half, before you would get up and get dressed and put your boots on to hunt Miss Mary's lion. I untucked the mosquito net and reached for and found the cider bottle. It was cool with the night and I built up the two pillows by doubling them over and then leaned back against them with the rough square balsam pillow under my neck and thought about the soul. First I must verify the Fitzgerald quotation in my mind. It had occurred in a series of articles in which he had abandoned this world and his former extremely shoddy ideals and had first referred to himself as a cracked plate. Turning my memory back I remembered the quotation. It went like this. "In a real dark night of the soul it is always three o'clock in the morning."

And I thought sitting up awake in the African night that I knew nothing about the soul at all. People were always talking of it and writing of it but who knew about it? I did not know anyone who knew anything of it nor whether there was such a thing. It seemed a very strange belief and I knew I would have a very difficult time trying to explain it to Ngui and Mthuka and the others even if I knew anything about it. Before I woke I had been dreaming and in the dream I had a horse's body but a man's head and shoulders and I had wondered why no one had

known this before. It was a very logical dream
and it dealt with the precise moment at which
the change came about in the body so that they
were human bodies. It seemed a very sound and
good dream and I wondered what the others
would think of it when I told it to them. I was
awake now and the cider was cool and fresh but
I could still feel the muscles I had in the dream
when my body had been a horse's body. This
was not helping me with the soul and I tried to
think what it must be in the terms that I
believed. Probably a spring of clear fresh water
that never diminished in the drought and never
froze in the winter was closest to what we had
instead of the soul they all talked about. I
remembered how when I was a boy the Chicago
White Sox had a third baseman named Harry
Lord who could foul off pitches down the third-
base line until the opposing pitcher was worn
out or it would get dark and the game be called.
I was very young then and everything was exag-
gerated but I can remember it beginning to get
dark, this was before there were lights in ball-
parks, and Harry still fouling them off and the
crowd shouting, "Lord, Lord Save Your Soul."
This was the closest I had ever come to the soul.
Once I had thought my own soul had been
blown out of me when I was a boy and then that
it had come back in again. But in those days I

was very egotistical and I had heard so much talk about the soul and read so much about it that I had assumed that I had one. Then I began to think if Miss Mary or G.C. or Ngui or Charo or I had been killed by the lion would our souls have flown off somewhere? I could not believe it and I thought that we would all just have been dead, deader than the lion perhaps, and no one was worrying about his soul. The worst part would have been the trip to Nairobi and the inquiry. But all I really knew was that it would have been very bad for G.C.'s career if Mary or I had been killed. It would have been bad luck for G.C. if he had been killed. It would have certainly been very bad for my writing if I had been killed. Neither Charo nor Ngui would have liked to be killed and if she had been killed it would have come as a great surprise to Miss Mary. It was something to be avoided and it was a relief to not have to put yourself in a position where it could happen day after day.

But what did this have to do with "In a real dark night of the soul it is always three o'clock in the morning"? Did Miss Mary and G.C. have souls? They had no religious beliefs as far as I knew. But if people had souls they must have them. Charo was a very devout Mohammedan so we must credit him with a soul. That left only Ngui and me and the lion.

Now here it was three o'clock in the morning and I stretched my recent horse's legs and thought I would get up and go outside and sit by the coals of the fire and enjoy the rest of the night and the first light. I pulled on my mosquito boots and put on my bathrobe and buckled the pistol belt over it and went out to the remains of the fire. G.C. was sitting by it in his chair.

"What are we awake about?" he said very softly.

"I had a dream I was a horse. It was very vivid."

I told G.C. about Scott Fitzgerald and the quotation and asked him what he thought of it.

"Any hour can be a bad hour when you wake," he said. "I don't see why he picked three especially. It sounds quite good though."

"I think it is just fear and worry and remorse."

"We've both had enough of those haven't we?"

"Sure; to peddle. But I think what he meant was his conscience and despair."

"You don't ever have despair do you, Ernie?"

"Not yet."

"You'd probably have had it by now if you were going to have it."

"I've seen it close enough to touch it but I always turned it down."

"Speaking of turning things down should we share a beer?"

"I'll get it."

The big bottle of Tusker was cold too in the canvas water bag and I poured beer into two glasses and set the bottle on the table.

"I'm sorry I have to go, Ernie," G.C. said. "Do you think she'll take it really badly?"

"Yes."

"You ride it out. She may take it perfectly all right."

9

I WENT IN TO the tent to see if Mary was awake, but she was still sleeping heavily. She had awakened and drunk some of her tea and then gone back to sleep again.

"We'll let her sleep," I said to G.C. "It doesn't make any difference if we don't skin out until half past nine even. She should get all the sleep she can."

G.C. was reading the Lindbergh book but I had no stomach for *The Year of the Lion* this morning and so I read the bird book. It was a good new book by Praed and Grant and I knew that by hunting one beast too hard and concentrating on him I had missed much in not observing the birds properly. If there had been no animals we could have been quite happy observing the birds but I knew that I had neglected them terribly. Mary had been much better. She was always seeing birds that I did not notice or watching them in detail while I sat in my camp chair and just looked out across the country. Reading the bird book I felt how stupid I had been and how much time I had wasted.

At home sitting in the shade at the head of the pool I was happy to see the kingbirds dip down to take insects off the water and to watch the gray white of their breasts show green from the reflection of the pool. I loved to watch the doves nesting in the alamo trees and to watch the mockingbirds as they sang. Seeing the migratory birds come through in the fall and the spring was an excitement and it made an afternoon happy to see the small bittern come to drink at the pool and watch him search the gutters for tree frogs. Now here in Africa there were beautiful birds around the camp all of the time. They were in the trees and in the thorn bushes and walking about on the ground and I only half saw them as moving bits of color while Mary loved and knew them all. I could not think how I had become so stupid and calloused about the birds and I was very ashamed.

For a long time I realized I had only paid attention to the predators, the scavengers and the birds that were good to eat and the birds that had to do with hunting. Then as I thought of which birds I did notice there came such a great long list of them that I did not feel quite as bad but I resolved to watch the birds around our camp more and to ask Mary about all the ones I did not know, and most of all, to really see them and not look past them.

This looking and not seeing things was a

great sin, I thought, and one that was easy to fall into. It was always the beginning of something bad and I thought that we did not deserve to live in the world if we did not see it. I tried to think how I had gotten into not seeing the small birds around camp and I thought some of it was reading too much to take my mind off the concentration of the serious hunting and some was certainly drinking in camp to relax when we came in from hunting. I admired Mayito, who drank almost nothing because he wanted to remember everything in Africa. But G.C. and I were drinkers and I knew it was not just a habit nor a way of escaping. It was a purposeful dulling of a receptivity that was so highly sensitized, as film can be, that if your receptiveness were always kept at the same level it would become unbearable. You make out quite a noble case for yourself, I thought, and you know too that you and G.C. drink because you love it too and Mary loves it the same way and we have such good fun drinking. You better go in and see if she is awake now, I thought.

So I went in and she was still asleep. She always looked beautiful asleep. Her face, when she slept, was neither happy nor unhappy. It simply existed. But today the line of it was too finely drawn. I wished that I could make her happy but the only thing I knew to do for this was to let her keep on sleeping.

I went out again with the bird book and identified a shrike, a starling and a bee eater, and then I heard movement in the tent and went in and found Mary sitting on the edge of her cot putting her moccasins on.

"How do you feel, honey?"

"Awful. And you shot at my lion first and I'd rather not see you."

"I'll just keep out of the way for a while."

Out at the lines Keiti told me that the Game Scouts were planning a really big Ngoma; everyone in the camp would be dancing and the whole Shamba was coming. Keiti said that we were short of beer and of Coca-Cola and I said I would go up to Laitokitok in the hunting car with Mthuka and Arap Meina and anybody who wanted to buy anything in the village. Keiti wanted some more posho too and I would try to get a sack or a couple of sacks as well as some sugar. The Wakamba liked the corn meal that was brought in by way of Kajiado and sold by the Indian duka whose owner was a follower of the Aga Khan. They did not like the other type that was sold in the other Indian general stores. I had learned to tell the kind they liked by color, texture and taste but I could always make a mistake and Mthuka would check. The Coca-Cola was for the Mohammedans who could not drink beer and for the girls and the women who would come to the Ngoma. I would drop Arap

Meina off at the first Masai Manyatta and he would tell the Masai to come and see the lion so they would know, surely, that he had been killed. They were not invited to the Ngoma, which was to be strictly for Wakamba.

We stopped in front of the gasoline pumps and the duka where we traded and Keiti got down. I passed my rifle back to Mwengi, Pop's gun bearer, who locked it in the rack that was built against the back of the front seat. I told Keiti I would go down to Mr. Singh's to order the beer and soft drinks and told Mthuka to get the car filled with petrol and then drive it down to Mr. Singh's and put it in the shade. I did not go into the big general store with Keiti but walked down under the shade of the trees to Mr. Singh's.

It was cool inside and smelled of cooking from the kitchen in the living quarters and of sawdust from the sawmill. Mr. Singh had only three cases of beer but thought he could get two more at a place across the street. Three Masai elders came in from the disreputable drinking place next door. We were friends and greeted each other with dignity and I could smell they had already been drinking Golden Jeep sherry, which accounted for the affection that was mixed with their dignity. Mr. Singh had only six bottles of beer cold so I bought two for the three of them and one for myself and told them Miss Mary had killed the big lion. We drank to each other and to Miss Mary and the lion and then I excused myself because I had business with Mr. Singh in the back room.

There was no real business. Mr. Singh wanted me to eat something with him and drink a whisky and water with him. He had something to tell me that I couldn't understand and went out and got the Mission-educated boy to translate for him. The young man wore trousers and a white shirt tucked in and big, heavy black square-toed boots which were the badge of his education and civilization.

"Sir," he said. "Mr. Singh here requests me to tell you that these Masai chiefs take a constant advantage of you in respect to beer. They congregate at the beer hall next door which calls itself a tea room and when they see you arrive they come over solely to take an advantage of you."

"I know those three elders and they are not chiefs."

"I used the designation chiefs as one speaks to a European," the Mission-educated boy said. "But the observation of Mr. Singh here is exact. They abuse your friendship in respect to beer."

Mr. Singh nodded his head solemnly and handed me the bottle of White Heather. He had understood two words of the Mission English: friendship and beer.

"One thing must always be clear. I am not a European. We are Americans."

"But there is no such distinction. You are classified as Europeans."

"It is a classification that will be remedied. I am not a European. Mr. Singh and I are brothers."

I poured water in my glass as did Mr. Singh. We toasted each other and then embraced. We then stood and looked at the oleograph of the original Singh strangling two lions one in each hand. We were both deeply moved.

"You are a follower of the Baby Jesus, I presume?" I asked the Mission-educated Chagga.

"I am a Christian," he said with dignity.

Mr. Singh and I looked at each other sadly and shook our heads. Then Mr. Singh spoke to the Interpreter.

"Mr. Singh here says he is saving the three cold bottles for you and your people. When the Masai Mzees return he will serve them wine."

"Excellent," I said. "Will you see if my people have arrived in my shooting brake?"

He went out and Mr. Singh tapped his head with his forefinger and offered me the White Heather in the square squat bottle. He said he was sorry we had no time to eat together. I told him to keep off the god-damn roads at night. He asked me how I liked the Interpreter. I said he was marvelous and had strong black shoes to prove his Christianity.

"Two of your people are outside with the shooting lorry," the Interpreter said as he came in.

"Shooting brake," I said and went out to motion Mthuka in. He came in his check shirt; tall and stooped and long-lipped with the beautiful Kamba arrow scars on his cheeks. He saluted Mrs. Singh behind the counter where the bolts of cloth, beads, medicines and novelty goods were and looked at her appreciatively. His grandfather had been a cannibal and his father was Keiti and he was fifty-five at least. Mr. Singh gave him one of the cold quarts of beer and handed me mine, which had been corked up. He drank a third of his and said, "I'll take it out to Mwengi."

"No. We have a cold one for him too."

"I'll take this out now and we will keep watch."

"There are two left," Mr. Singh said. Mthuka nodded.

"Give the Interpreter an Orange Crush," I said.

Holding his soft drink the Interpreter said, "Before your friends the Masai return may I ask a few questions, sir?"

"What are the questions?"

"Sir, how many aircraft do you have?"

"Eight."

"You must be one of the richest men in the world."

"I am," I said modestly.

"Why then, sir, do you come here to do the work of a Game Ranger?"

"Why do some go to Mecca? Why does any man go anywhere? Why would you go to Rome?"

"I am not of the Catholic faith. I would not go to Rome."

"I thought you were not of that faith from the shoes."

"We have many things in common with the Catholic faith but we do not worship images."

"Too bad. There are many great images."

"I would like to be a Game Scout and have employment with you, sir, or with the Bwana Game."

Just then the Masai elders returned bringing with them two new comrades. I had never met them but my oldest friend among the elders told me that they had many problems with lions who not only carried cattle out of the Bomas but donkeys, morani, totos, women and goats. They would like for Miss Mary and me to come and liberate them from this terror. All these Masai were quite drunk by now and one was a little inclined to be rude.

We had known many fine Masai and great ones and unspoiled Masai but drinking was foreign to Masai as it was natural to Wakamba and they disintegrated under it and some of the elders could remember when they were a great ruling tribe of warriors and raiders instead of a syphilis-ridden, anthropological, cattle-worshipping curiosity. This new comrade elder was drunk at eleven o'clock in the morning and rude drunk. That was apparent from his first question and I decided to use the Interpreter to make a formal distance between us and also, since the five elders were carrying spears of Morani length, which showed bad tribal discipline, it was almost certain that the Interpreter would be speared first since it was he who would utter the provoking words if there should be such words uttered. If there was an argument with five drunken, spear-carrying Masai in the small front room of a general store one was certain oneself of being speared. But the presence of the Interpreter meant that you had a chance to get three of your drunken friends with the pistol instead of one or possibly two. I moved the holster around so it lay on the front of the leg, was pleased that it was buckled down and tripped the buckle on the strap with my little finger.

"Interpret, Big Shoes," I said. "Interpret accurately."

"He here says, sir, that he has heard that one

302 • ERNEST HEMINGWAY

of your wives, he said women, has killed a lion and that he wonders if in your tribe the killing of lions is left to the women."

"Tell the great chief whom I have never met that in my tribe we sometimes leave the killing of lions to women as in his tribe he leaves to the young warriors the drinking of Golden Jeep sherry. There are young warriors who spend their time drinking and have never killed a lion."

The Interpreter was sweating hard at this moment and things were not getting better. The Masai, who was a good-looking old man of possibly my own age or possibly older, spoke and the Interpreter said, "He here says, sir, that if you had wished to be polite and to talk as one chief to another you would have learned his language so that you and he could talk together as man to man."

It was over now and cheap enough so I said, "Say to this chief who I have not known until now that I am ashamed not to have learned his language properly. It has been my duty to hunt lions. The wife I have brought here has the duty to hunt lions. She has killed yesterday and there are two more bottles of cold beer here which I was reserving for my people but I will drink one of them with this chief and with him only and Mr. Singh will provide wine for all other chiefs."

The Interpreter said this and the Masai came

forward and shook hands. I buttoned the strap on the holster and patted the gun back against my thigh where it belonged.

"An Orange Crush for the Interpreter," I said to Mr. Singh.

The Interpreter took it but the Masai who had wanted trouble spoke to him earnestly and confidentially. The Interpreter took one swallow of his soft drink to clear his throat and said to me, "This chief here asks in absolute confidence how much you paid for this wife who kills lions. He says that such a wife for breeding could be as valuable as a great bull."

"Tell the chief, who I see is a man of great intelligence, that I paid two small airplanes and one larger airplane and one hundred head of cattle for this wife."

The Masai elder and I drank together and then he spoke to me again rapidly and seriously. "He says that is a great price to pay for any wife and no woman could be worth that. He said you spoke of cattle. Were they cows or were there bulls too?"

I explained that the ndege were not new aircraft but had been used in war. The cattle I said were all cows.

The old Masai said this was more understandable but no woman could be worth that much money.

I agreed that it was a high price but that the wife had been worth it. Now, I said, it was necessary for me to return to the camp. I ordered another round of the wine and left the big beer bottle with the elder. We had drunk from glasses and I set my glass top down on the counter. He urged me to take another glass and I poured one half full and drained it. We shook hands and I smelled the leather and smoke and dried dung and sweat smell that is not unpleasant and I went out into the sharp light of the road with the hunting car half shaded by the leaves. Mr. Singh had five cases of beer in the back of the car and his boy brought out the last cold bottle wrapped in a newspaper. He had figured the beer and the bottle of wine for the Masai on a pad of paper and I paid him and gave the Interpreter a five-shilling note.

"I would prefer employment, sir."

"I cannot give you employment except as an interpreter. This has been given and paid for."

"I would like to come with you as an interpreter."

"Would you interpret between me and the animals?"

"I could learn, sir. I speak Swahili, Masai, Chagga and of course English as you see."

"Do you speak Kamba?"

"No, sir."

"We speak Kamba."

"I could learn it easily, sir. I could tutor you to speak proper Swahili and you could teach me hunting and the language of animals. Do not be prejudiced against me because I am a Christian. It was my parents who sent me to the Mission School."

"Did you not like the Mission School? Remember God is listening. He hears your every word."

"No, sir. I hated the Mission School. I am a Christian through instruction and ignorance."

"We will take you out hunting sometime. But you will have to come barefoot and in shorts."

"I hate my shoes, sir. I must wear them because of Bwana McCrea. If it were reported to him that I was without my shoes or that I had been with you in Mr. Singh's I would be punished. Even if I had only drunk Coca-Cola. Coca-Cola is the first step Bwana McCrea says."

"We will take you to hunt sometime. But you are not from a hunting tribe. What good will it do? You will be frightened and you will be unhappy."

"Sir, if you keep me in your mind I will prove myself to you. With this five shillings I will make a down payment on a spear at Benji's store. I will walk at night without the shoes to toughen my feet as those of a hunter's are. If you ask me for a proof I will make a proof."

"You are a good boy but I do not wish to interfere with your religion and I have nothing to offer you."

"I will make you a proof," he said.

"Kwisha," I said. Then to Mthuka, "Kwenda na duka."

In the duka it was very crowded with Masai shopping and watching others who were buying. The women stared at you boldly from head to foot and the young warriors with their heavy ochered pigtails and bangs were insolent and cheerful. Masai smell good and the women have cold hands and when their hand is in yours they never remove it but delight in the warmth of your palm and explore it happily without movement. Benji's was a cheerful busy place like an Indian trading post at home on a Saturday afternoon or a monthly payoff day. Keiti had found good posho and all the Coca-Cola and soft drinks that were needed for the Ngoma and he was ordering a few unnecessary items from high shelves so that he could watch the lovely and intelligent Indian girl, who was in love with G.C. from a great distance and who we all admired and would have been in love with if it were not useless, reaching them down and bringing them to him. This was the first time

that I had seen how Keiti loved to watch this girl
and I was happy that it gave us a faint advantage
over him. She spoke to me in her lovely voice
and asked about Miss Mary and said how
happy she was about the lion and while I took
great pleasure in seeing her and hearing her
voice and in our shaking hands I could not help
seeing how far gone Keiti was. It was only then I
noticed how smart and fresh and well pressed
his clothes were and that he was wearing his
best safari uniform and his good turban.

The people from the duka aided by Mthuka
started taking the sacks of meal and the cases of
soft drinks out and I paid the bill and bought a
half dozen whistles for the Ngoma. Then, since
the duka was shorthanded, I went out to guard
the rifle while Keiti helped with the cases. I
would have been glad to help with the loading
but it was not considered seemly. When we were
alone hunting we always worked together but in
town and in public it would have been misun-
derstood so I sat in the front seat with the rifle
between my legs and heard the petitions of the
Masai who wanted to ride down the Mountain
with us. The Chevrolet truck chassis on which
the hunting car body had been built had good
brakes but with the load we had we could not
carry more than about six extra people. I had
seen days of a dozen or more. But it was too

dangerous on the curves, which sometimes made the Masai women sick. We never carried warriors down the Mountain road although we often picked them up coming up. At first there had been some bitterness about this but now it was an accepted practice and men we had carried up would explain it to the others.

Finally we had everything stowed and four women with their bags, bundles, gourds and mixed loads were in the back, three more sat on the second seat with Keiti at the right of them, and myself, Mwengi and Mthuka in front. We started off with the Masai waving and I opened the cold bottle of beer still wrapped in the newspapers and offered it to Mwengi. He motioned for me to drink and sank lower in the seat to be out of sight of Keiti. I drank and handed it to him and he drank deep using the side of his mouth to not tip the big quart bottle into sight. He handed it back to me and I offered it to Mthuka.

"Later," he said.

"When a woman is sick," Mwengi said.

Mthuka was driving very carefully getting the feel of his load on the steep dropping turns. Usually there would have been a Masai woman between Mthuka and me; one we knew was proof against roadsickness and two more being tested out between Ngui and Mwengi in the second seat. Now we all felt three women were being wasted on Keiti. One of them was a famous beauty who was as tall as I was, built wonderfully, and with the coldest and most insistent hands I had ever known. She usually sat between Mthuka and me on the front seat and she held my hand and courted Mthuka lightly and purposefully with her other hand while she looked at us both and laughed when there were reactions to her courtship. She was very classically beautiful with a lovely skin and she was quite shameless. I knew that both Ngui and Mthuka gave her their favors. She was curious about me and loved to provoke visible reactions and when we dropped her off to go to her Manyatta someone almost always dropped off with her too and made their way to camp later by foot.

But today we were riding down the road looking out on all our own country and Mthuka could not even have any beer because of Keiti his father sitting directly behind him and I was thinking about morality and drinking beer with Mwengi; we having torn a mark in the paper covering the bottle to mark the place below which the beer all belonged to Mthuka. According to basic morality it was perfectly all right for two of my best friends to go with this Masai woman but if I did so while I was on probation as a mkamba and while Debba and I felt seriously about each other it would have proved me to be irresponsible and profligate and not a serious man. On the other hand if I had not responded, visibly, when in unsought contact or when incited it would have been very bad all around. These simple studies in our tribal moeurs always made the trips to Laitokitok pleasant and instructive but sometimes, until you understood them, they could have been frustrating and puzzling except that you knew that if you wished to be a good mkamba it was necessary never to be frustrated and to never admit that you were puzzled.

Finally they called out from the back of the car that a woman was sick and I signaled to Mthuka to stop the car. We knew Keiti would take advantage of this halt to go into the brush and urinate so when he did with great dignity and casualness I passed the quart of beer to Mthuka and he drank his share rapidly leaving the rest for Mwengi and me.

"Drink it before it gets hot."

The car loaded up again and with three unloadings we were relieved of our passengers and across the stream and going through the park country toward camp. We saw a herd of impala crossing through the woods and I got out of the car with Keiti to head them off. They looked red against the heavy green and a young buck looked back as I whistled almost silently. I held my breath, squeezed the trigger softly, and broke his neck and Keiti ran toward him to halal as the others leaped and jumped floatingly into the cover.

I did not go up with Keiti to see him halal so it was a question of his own conscience and I knew his conscience was not as rigid as Charo's. But I did not want to lose the buck for the Mohammedans any more than I had wanted to shoot the meat up so I walked forward slowly over the springy grass and when I came up he had cut the impala's throat and was smiling.

"Piga mzuri," he said.

"Why not?" I said. "Uchawi."

"Hapana uchawi. Piga mzuri sana."

10

THERE WERE PEOPLE all under the trees and out behind the lines, the women with their lovely brown heads and faces in their bright cloth top covers and beautiful wide bead collars and bracelets. The big drum had been brought down from the Shamba and the Game Scouts had three other drums. It was early yet but the Ngoma was starting to take shape. We rode past the people and the preparations and stopped in the shade and the women got out and children came running to see the animals unloaded. I handed the rifle to Ngui to clean and walked over to the mess tent. The wind was blowing quite hard from the Mountain now and the mess tent was cool and pleasant.

"You took all our cold beer," Miss Mary said. She looked much better and more rested.

"I brought one bottle back. It's coming in the bag. How are you, honey?"

"G.C. and I are much better. We didn't find your bullet. Only G.C.'s. My lion looks so noble and beautiful when he is white and naked. He's dignified again as when he was alive. Did you have fun at Laitokitok?"

"Yes. We did all the errands."

"Make him welcome, Miss Mary," G.C. said. "Show him around and see that he's comfortable. You've seen an Ngoma before haven't you my good man?"

"Yes, sir," I said. "And we have them in my own country too. We are all very fond of them."

"Is that what they call baseball in America? I always thought that was a form of rounders."

"At home, sir, our Ngomas are a sort of Harvest Festival with folk dancing. It's rather like your cricket I believe."

"Quite," said G.C. "But this Ngoma is something new. It's going to be danced entirely by natives."

"What fun, sir," I said. "May I accompany Miss Mary as you call this charming young lady to the Ngoma?"

"I've been spoken for," Miss Mary said. "I'm going to the Ngoma with Mr. Chungo of the Game Scouts Department."

"The hell you are Miss Mary," G.C. said.

"Is Mr. Chungo that very well built young man with the mustache and shorts on who was fixing ostrich plumes onto his head, sir?"

"He looked a very good sort, sir. Is he one of your colleagues in the Game Scouts Department? I must say, sir, you have a magnificent body of men."

"I am in love with Mr. Chungo and he is my hero," Miss Mary said. "He told me that you were a liar and had never hit the lion at all. He said all the boys know you are a liar and Ngui and some of the others only pretend to be friends of yours because you give them presents all the time and have no discipline. He said look how Ngui had broken your best knife that you paid so much money for in Paris that day when you came home drunk."

"Yes. Yes," I said. "I do remember seeing old Chungo in Paris. Yes. Yes. I remember. Yes. Yes."

"No. No," G.C. said absentmindedly. "No. No. Not Mr. Chungo. He's not a member."

"Yes. Yes," I said. "I'm afraid he is, sir."

"Mr. Chungo told me another interesting thing too. He told me that you had been using Kamba arrow poisoning on your solids and that Ngui makes it for you and that all this risasi moja business of one shot kills is the effect of the arrow poisoning. He offered to show me how fast the arrow poisoning would run up a stream of blood dripping from his own leg."

"Dear, dear. Do you think she had best go to the Ngoma with your colleague Mr. Chungo, sir? It may all be absolutely tickety-boo but she still is a Memsahib, sir. She still comes under the White Man's Burden Act."

"She'll go to the Ngoma with me," G.C. said. "Make us a drink, Miss Mary; or no, I will."

"I can make drinks still," Miss Mary said. "Don't you both look so sinister. I made it all up about Mr. Chungo. Someone has to make jokes here sometimes beside Papa and his pagans and you and Papa and your night wildness and wickedness. What time did you all get up this morning?"

"Not too early. Is it still the same day?"

"The days run into each other and into each other and into each other," Miss Mary said. "That's in my poem about Africa."

Miss Mary was writing a great poem about Africa but the trouble was that she made it up in her head sometimes and forgot to write it down and then it would be gone like dreams. She wrote some of it down but she would not show it to anybody. We all had great faith in her poem about Africa and I still have but I would like it better if she would actually write it. We were all reading the *Georgics* then in the C. Day Lewis translation. We had two copies but they were always being lost or mislaid and I have never known a book to be more mis-layable. The only fault I could ever find with the Mantovan was that he made all normally intelligent people feel as though they too could write great poetry. Dante only made crazy people feel they could write great poetry. That was not true of course but then almost nothing was true and especially not in Africa. In Africa a thing is true at first light and a lie by noon and you have no more respect for it than for the lovely, perfect weed-fringed lake you see across the sun-baked salt plain. You have walked across that plain in the morning and you know that no such lake is there. But now it is there absolutely true, beautiful and believable.

"Is that really in the poem?" I asked Miss Mary.

"Yes, of course."

"Then write it down before it gets to sound like a traffic accident."

"You don't have to spoil people's poems as well as shoot their lions."

G.C. looked up at me like a weary schoolboy and I said, "I found my *Georgics* if you want it. It is the one that hasn't got the introduction by Louis Bromfield in it. That's how you can tell it."

"You can tell mine because it has my name in it."

"And an introduction by Louis Bromfield."

"Who's the man Bromfield?" G.C. asked. "Is it a fighting word?"

"He's a man who writes who has a very well known farm in America, in Ohio. Because he is

well-known about the farm Oxford University
had him write an introduction. Turning the
pages he can see Virgil's farm and Virgil's animals and Virgil's people and even his own stern
and rugged features or figures I forget which. It
must be rugged figures if he is a farmer. Anyway
Louis can see him and he says it forms a great
and eternal poem or poems for every kind of
reader."

"It must be the edition I have without Bromfield," G.C. said. "I think you left it in Kajiado."

"Mine has my name in it," Miss Mary said.

"Good," I said. "And your *Up-Country
Swahili* has your name in it too and right now
it's in my hip pocket and sweated through and
stuck together. I'll get you mine and you can
write your name in it."

"I don't want yours. I want my own and why
did you have to sweat it solidly together and
ruin it?"

"I don't know. It was probably part of my
plot to ruin Africa. But here it is. I'd advise you
to take the clean one."

"This one has words that I'd written in
myself that aren't in the original and it has nota-
tions."

"I'm sorry. I must have put it in my pocket
some morning in the dark by mistake."

"You never make a mistake," Miss Mary
said. "We all know that. And you'd be much

better off if you studied your Swahili instead of trying to speak all the time in Unknown Tongue and reading nothing but French books. We all know you read French. Was it necessary to come all the way to Africa to read French?"

"Maybe. I don't know. This was the first time I ever had a complete set of Simenon and the girl at the book shop in the long passageway at the Ritz was so nice to send and then get them all."

"And then you left them down in Tanganyika at Patrick's. All except a few. Do you think they'll read them?"

"I don't know. Pat's sort of mysterious some ways like me. He might read them and he might not. But he has a neighbor who has a wife who is a Frenchwoman and they'd be good to have for her. No. Pat would read them."

"Did you ever study French and learn to speak it grammatically?"

"No."

"You're hopeless."

G.C. frowned at me.

"No," I said. "I'm not hopeless because I still have hope. The day I haven't you'll know it bloody quick."

"What do you have hope about? Mental slovenliness? Taking other people's books? Lying about a lion?"

"That's sort of alliterative. Just say lying.

"Now I lie me down to sleep.
Conjugate the verb lie *and who with*
And how lovely it can be.

"Conjugate me every morning and every
*   night*
And fire, no sleet, no candlelight
The Mountain cold and close when you're
*   asleep*

"The dark belts of trees are not yews
But the snow's still snow.
Conjugate me once the snow

"And why the Mountain comes closer
And goes farther away.

"Conjugate me conjugable love.
What kind of mealies do you bring?"

It was not a nice way to talk especially to anyone with Virgil on their mind but lunch came then and lunch was always an armistice in any misunderstandings and the partakers of it and its excellence were as safe as malefactors once were said to be in churches with the law after them although I had never had much faith in that sanctuary. So we cleaned it up and rubbed it all off the slate and Miss Mary went to take a nap after lunch and I went to the Ngoma.

It was very much like other Ngomas except extraordinarily pleasant and nice and the Game Scouts had made a huge effort. They were dancing in shorts and they all had four ostrich plumes on their heads, at least at the beginning. Two of the plumes were white and two dyed pink and they kept them on with all sorts of devices from leather straps and thongs to binding them or wiring them into the hair. They wore bell anklets to dance with and they danced well and with beautiful contained discipline. There were three drums and some drumming on tins and empty petrol drums. There were four classic dances and three or four that were improvised. The young women and the young girls and the children did not get to dance until the later dances. They all danced but they did not enter into the figures and dance in the double line until late in the afternoon. You could see from the way the children and the young girls danced that they were used to much rougher Ngomas at the Shamba.

Miss Mary and G.C. came out and took color pictures and Miss Mary was congratulated by everyone and shook hands with everybody. The Game Scouts did feats of agility. One was to start to turn a cartwheel over a coin that was half buried in the earth edge up and then stop the cartwheel when the feet were straight up in the air and to lower the head to the ground, sinking down on the arms, get the coin in the teeth and then come up and spin over to the feet in a single roll. It was very difficult and Denge, who was the strongest of the Game Scouts and the most agile, the kindest and the gentlest, did it beautifully.

Most of the time I sat in the shade and filled in on one of the basic beat empty petrol drums working the end with the base of the hand and watched the dancing. The Informer came over and squatted down by me wearing his imitation paisley shawl and his porkpie hat.

"Why are you sad, brother?" he asked.

"I am not sad."

"Everyone knows you are sad. You must be cheerful. Look at your fiancée. She is the Queen of the Ngoma."

"Don't put your hand on my drum. You deaden it."

"You are drumming very well, brother."

"The hell I am. I can't drum at all. I'm just not doing any harm. What are you sad about?"

"The Bwana Game has spoken to me very roughly and he sends me away. After all our magnificent work he says I do nothing here and he sends me to a place where I may easily be killed."

"You may be killed anywhere."

"Yes. But here I am useful to you and I die happy."

The dance was getting wilder now. I liked to see Debba dance and I didn't. It was as simple as that and, I thought, it must have happened to all followers of this type of ballet. I knew she was showing off to me because she danced down at the end by the petrol drum bongo.

"She is a very beautiful young girl," the Informer said. "And the Queen of the Ngoma."

I went on playing until the end of the dance and then got up and found Nguili, who had his green robe on, and asked him to see the girls had Coca-Cola.

"Come on to the tent," I said to the Informer. "You are sick aren't you?"

"Brother, I have a fever truly. You can take the temperature and see."

"I'll get you some Atabrine."

Mary was still taking pictures and the girls were standing stiff and straight with their breasts standing out against the scarves that looked like tablecloths. Mthuka was grouping some of the girls together and I knew he was trying to get a good picture of Debba. I watched them and saw how shy and downcast Debba's eyes were standing before Miss Mary and how straight she stood. She had none of the impudence she had with me and she stood at attention like a soldier.

The Informer had a tongue as white as though it were sprouting chalk and when I depressed his tongue with a spoon handle I could see he had a bad yellow patch and a yellow and whitish patch in the back of his throat. I put the thermometer under his tongue and he had a temperature of a hundred and one and three tenths.

"You're sick, Informer Old Timer," I said. "I'll give you some penicillin and some penicillin lozenges and send you home in the hunting car."

"I said I was sick, brother. But nobody cares. Can I have one drink, brother?"

"It's never hurt me with penicillin. It might do your throat good."

"I am sure it would, brother. Do you think Bwana Game will let me stay here and serve under you now that you can certify that I am sick?"

"You won't be any ball of fire while you're sick. Maybe I ought to send you in to the hospital in Kajiado."

"No, please, brother. You can cure me here and I will be available for all emergencies and I can be your eyes and your ears and your right hand in battle."

God help us all, I thought, but he is having these ideas with no liquor in him and no bang and none of the stuff and with a septic sore

324 • ERNEST HEMINGWAY

throat and possibly quinsy. It is pretty good morale even if it is just from the mouth.

I was making a half tumbler of half and half Rose's Lime Juice and whisky that would ease the throat and afterwards I would give him the penicillin and the lozenges and drive him home myself.

The mixture made his throat feel better and with the liquor his morale blossomed.

"Brother, I am a Masai. I have no fear of death. I despise death. I was ruined by the Bwanas and by a Somali woman. She took everything; my property, my children and my honor."

"You told me."

"Yes, but now since you bought me the spear I am starting again in life. You have sent for the medicine that brings youth?"

"It is coming. But it can only bring back youth if youth is there."

"It is there. I promise, brother. I feel it flooding into me now."

"That's the stuff."

"Perhaps. But I can feel youth too."

"I'll give you the medicine now and then I'll drive you home."

"No. Please, brother. I came with the Widow and she must go home with me. It is too early for her to go yet. I lost her for three days at the last Ngoma. I will wait and go with her when the truck leaves."

"You ought to be in bed."

"It is better that I wait for the Widow. Brother, you do not know the danger that an Ngoma is for a woman."

I had a sort of an idea of this danger and I did not want the Informer to talk with his throat so bad but he asked, "Could I have just one last drink before the medicine?"

"All right. I think it's OK, medically."

This time I put sugar with the Rose's Lime Juice and made a good big drink. If he was going to wait for the Widow it might be a long time and soon the sun would go down and it would be cold.

"We will do great deeds together, brother," the Informer said.

"I don't know. Don't you think we ought to do a few great deeds separately to sharpen up?"

"Name a great deed and I will do it."

"I'll think up a great deed as soon as your throat is well. I have many small deeds I must do myself now."

"Can I help in a small deed, brother?"

"Not in these. These I must do alone."

"Brother, if we do great deeds together will you take me to Mecca with you?"

"I may not be going to Mecca this year."

"But next year?"

"If it be the wish of Allah."

"Brother, do you remember Bwana Blixen?"

"Too well."

"Brother, many say it is not true that Bwana Blix is dead. They say that he has disappeared until the death of his creditors and that then he will come again to earth like the Baby Jesus. In the theory of the Baby Jesus. Not that he will appear as the actual Baby Jesus. Can there be truth in this?"

"I think there can be no truth in this. The Bwana Blix is truly dead. Friends of mine have seen him dead in the snow with his head broken."

"Too many great men are dead. Few of us remain. Tell me, brother, of your faith that I have heard spoken of. Who is this great Lord who heads your faith?"

"We call him Gitchi Manitou the Mighty. That is not his true name."

"I see. Has he too been to Mecca?"

"He goes to Mecca as you or I might go to the bazaar or enter a duka."

"Do you represent him directly as I have heard?"

"In so far as I am worthy."

"But you hold his authority?"

"It is not for you to ask that."

"Pardon me, brother, in my ignorance. But does he speak through you?"

"He speaks through me if he chooses."

"Can men who are not . . ."

"Do not ask."

"Can . . ."

"I will administer the penicillin and you can go," I said. "It is not fitting to speak of religion in a mess tent."

The Informer did not have the confidence in the oral penicillin that I hoped for from a potential doer of great deeds but it may have been disappointment at not being able to show his bravery under the big needle. He liked the pleasant taste though and took two tablespoonsful with enjoyment. I joined him in a couple of tablespoons just in case he might be poisoned and also because one never knew what might happen at an Ngoma.

"It tastes so good that do you think it can be powerful, brother?"

"The Great Manitou uses it himself," I said.

"Allah's will be done," the Informer said. "When do I take the rest of the flask?"

"In the morning when you wake up. If you are awake in the night suck on these tablets."

"Already I am better, brother."

"Go now and look after the Widow."

"I go."

All this time we had been hearing the beating of the drums and the thin shaking of the ankle bells and the blowing of the traffic whistles. I still did not feel festive nor like dancing so, when the Informer was gone, I mixed a Gordon's gin and Campari and put some soda in it from the siphon. If this mixed well with the double dose of oral, something would have been established even though not perhaps in the realm of pure science. They seemed to blend harmoniously and, if anything, to sharpen the beat of the drums. I listened carefully to see if the police whistles were any shriller but they seemed unaltered. Taking this to be an excellent sign I found a cool quart of beer in the dripping canvas water bag and made my way back to the Ngoma. Someone was playing the head of my metal drum and so I found a good tree to sit against where I was joined by my friend Tony.

Tony was a fine man and one of my best friends. He was a Masai and had been a sergeant in the Tank Corps and had been a very brave and able soldier. If not the only Masai in the British Army he was at least the only Masai sergeant. He worked for G.C. in the Game Department and I always envied G.C. having him because he was a good mechanic, loyal, devoted and always cheerful and he spoke good English, perfect Masai, naturally, Swahili, some

Chagga and some Kamba. He had a very un-Masai build, having short, rather bandied legs and a heavy, powerful chest, arms and neck. I had taught him to box and we sparred together quite often and were very good friends and companions.

"It is a very fine Ngoma, sar," Tony said.

"Yes," I said. "Won't you dance, Tony?"

"No, sar. It is a Kamba Ngoma."

They were dancing a very complicated dance now and the young girls were dancing too in a very intense copulative figure.

"There are some very pretty girls. Who do you like the best, Tony."

"Who do you like, sar?"

"I cannot decide. There are four really beautiful girls."

"There is one who is the best. You see who I mean, sar?"

"She's lovely, Tony. Where is she from?"

"From the Kamba Shamba, sar."

She was the best all right and better than the best. We both watched her.

"Have you seen Miss Mary and the Captain Game Ranger?"

"Yes, sar. They were here a short time ago. I am truly happy that Miss Mary has killed her lion. Do you remember from the early days and the lion spearing with the bubblegum Masai, sar? Do you remember from Fig Tree camp? That was a long time, sar, for her to hunt lion. This morning I told her a Masai proverb. Did she tell you?"

"No, Tony. I don't think she did."

"I told her this saying, 'It is always very quiet when a great bull dies.'"

"That is very true. It is quiet now even with the noise of the Ngoma."

"Did you notice it too, sar?"

"Yes. I have been quiet inside all day. Do you want any beer?"

"No thank you, sar. Will there be boxing tonight?"

"Do you feel like it?"

"If you do, sar. But there are many new boys to try. We can do it better tomorrow without Ngoma."

"Tonight if you like."

"Perhaps it would be better tomorrow. One boy is not a very nice boy. Not bad. But not nice. You know the kind."

"Town boy?"

"A little bit, sar."

"Can he box?"

"Not really, sar. But fast."

"Hit?"

"Yes, sar."

"What is that dance now?"

"The new boxing dance. You see? They make infighting now and left hooks the way you teach."

"Better than I teach."

"Tomorrow is best, sar."

"But you'll be gone tomorrow."

"I forgot, sar. Please excuse me. I am forgetful since the great bull died. We'll make it when we come back. I go now to check the lorry."

I went off to look for Keiti and found him on the outskirts of the dancing. He looked very cheerful and possessive.

"Please send them home in the truck when it gets dark," I said. "Mthuka can take several loads in the hunting car too. Memsahib is tired and we should have dinner early and go to bed."

"Ndio," he agreed.

I found Ngui and he said, "Jambo, Bwana," sarcastically in the dusk.

"Jambo, tu," I answered. "Why didn't you dance?"

"Too much law," he said. "It is not my day to dance."

"Nor mine."

That night we had a cheerful dinner. Mbebia, the cook, had made breaded cutlets of the lion tenderloin and they were excellent. In September, when we had eaten the first lion cutlets, it had been a matter for discussion and was

regarded as an eccentricity or something bar-
baric. Now everyone ate them and they were
regarded as a great delicacy. The meat was
white as veal and tender and delicious. It had no
gamy flavor at all.

"I don't think anyone could tell it from a cos-
toletta Milanesa at a really good Italian restau-
rant except that the meat is better," Mary said.

I had been sure it would be good meat the
first time I had ever seen a lion skinned. Mkola,
who was my gun bearer in those days, told me
that the tenderloin was the best meat there was
to eat. But we had been very disciplined then by
Pop, who was trying to make at least a semi-
pukka Sahib of me and I had never had the
nerve to cut a tenderloin and ask the cook to
prepare it. This year, though, when we killed the
first lion and I asked Ngui to take the two ten-
derloins it had been different. Pop said it was
barbarous and that no one ever ate lion. But this
was almost surely the last safari we would ever
make together and we had come to the point
where we both regretted things we had not done
rather than those we had and so he made only
perfunctory opposition and when Mary showed
Mbebia how to prepare the cutlets and when we
smelled their fine savor and when he saw how
the meat cut exactly like veal and how much we
enjoyed it, he tried some too and liked it.

"You ate bear in America hunting in the Rockies. It's like pork but too rich. You eat pork and a hog will feed fouler than a bear or a lion."

"Don't badger me," Pop had said. "I'm eating the damned stuff."

"Isn't it good?"

"Yes. Damn it. It's good. But don't badger me."

"Have some more, Mr. P. Please have some more," Mary said.

"All right. I'll have some more," making his voice into a high complaining falsetto. "But don't keep staring at me while I eat it."

It was pleasant talking about Pop whom Mary and I both loved and whom I was fonder of than any man that I had ever known. Mary told some of the things Pop had told her on the long drive they had made together through Tanganyika when we had gone down to hunt the Great Ruaha river country and the Bohoro flats. Hearing these stories and imagining the things he had not told it was like having Pop there and I thought that even in his absence he could make things all right when they were difficult.

Then too it was wonderful to be eating the lion and have him in such close and final company and tasting so good.

That night Mary said she was very tired and she went to sleep in her own bed. I lay awake for a while and then went out to sit by the fire. In the chair watching the fire and thinking of Pop and how sad it was he was not immortal and how happy I was that he had been able to be with us so much and that we had been lucky to have three or four things together that were like the old days along with just the happiness of being together and talking and joking, I went to sleep.

11

WALKING IN THE early morning watching Ngui striding lightly through the grass thinking how we were brothers it seemed to me stupid to be white in Africa and I remembered how twenty years before I had been taken to hear the Moslem missionary who had explained to us, his audience, the advantages of a dark skin and the disadvantages of the white man's pigmentation. I was burned dark enough to pass as a half-caste.

"Observe the White Man," the Missionary had said. "He walks in the sun and the sun kills him. If he exposes his body to the sun it is burned until it blisters and rots. The poor fellow must stay in the shade and destroy himself with alcohol and stinghas and chutta pegs because he cannot face the horror of the sun rising on the next day. Observe the White Man and his mwanamuki; his memsahib. The woman is covered with brown spots if she goes into the sun; brown spots like the forerunners of leprosy. If she continues the sun strips the skin as from a person who has passed through fire."

On this lovely morning I did not try to remember further about the Sermon against the White Man. It had been long ago and I had forgotten many of the more lively parts but one thing I had not forgotten was the White Man's heaven and how this had been shown to be another of his horrifying beliefs which caused him to hit small white balls with sticks along the ground or other larger balls back and forth across nets, such as are used on the big lakes for catching fish, until the sun overcame him and he retired into the Club to destroy himself with alcohol and curse the Baby Jesus unless his wanawaki were present.

Together Ngui and I passed another brush patch where a cobra had his hole. The cobra was either still out or had gone visiting leaving no address. Neither of us were great snake hunters. That was a White Man's obsession and a necessary one since snakes, when trodden on, bit the cattle and the horses and there was a standing reward of shillings for them on Pop's farm; both cobras and puff adders. Snake hunting, for pay, was as low as a man could fall. We knew cobras as quick, lithe-moving creatures who sought their holes which were so small that it seemed impossible for them to enter them and we had jokes about this. There were tales of ferocious mambas that rose high on their tails and pursued the helpless colonists or intrepid Game Rangers while they were mounted on horses but these tales left us indifferent since they came from the south, where hippos with personal names were alleged to wander across hundreds of miles of dry country seeking water and snakes performed biblical feats. I knew these things must be true since they had been written by honorable men but they were not like our snakes and in Africa it is only your own snakes that matter.

Our snakes were shy or stupid or mysterious and powerful. I made a great show of snake-hunting fervor which deceived nobody except, possibly, Miss Mary, and we were all against the spitting cobra since he had spat at G.C. This morning when we found that the cobra was absent and had not returned to his hole I said to Ngui that he was probably the grandfather of Tony anyway and that we should respect him.

Ngui was pleased at this since the snakes are the ancestors of all the Masai. I said the snake might well have been the ancestor of his girl at the Masai Manyatta. She was a tall, lovely girl and had a certain amount of snake about her. Ngui being cheered up and slightly horrified at the possible ancestry of his illegal love I asked him if he thought the coldness of the Masai women's hands and the stranger occasional coldness of other parts of their bodies could be due to snake blood. First he said that it was impossible; that Masai had always been like that. Then, we were walking side by side now and heading for the high trees of camp that showed etched in yellow and green against the brown wrinkled base and the high snow of the Mountain; camp not visible but only the high trees marking it; he said that it might be true. Italian women, he said, had cold and hot hands. The hand could be cold and then become warm as a hot spring and in other ways they were as scalding as a hot spring if one could remember it. They had no more bubo, the penalty for relations, than the Masai. Perhaps the Masai did have snake blood. I said that the next time we killed a snake we would all feel the blood and see. I had never felt the outrush of snake blood since they were antipathetic to me and I knew they were to Ngui too. But we agreed to feel the blood and have others, if they could control their repugnance, feel it too. This was all in the interests of our anthropological studies which we pursued each day and we kept on walking and thinking of these problems and of our own small problems which we tried to integrate with the greater interests of anthropology until the tents of camp showed under the yellow and green trees which the first light of the sun was now turning to bright dark green and shining gold and we could see the gray smoke of the fires at the lines and the camp breaking of the Game Scouts and, seated by the fire before our own tents now deep under the trees and the sunlight of the new day, the figure of G.C. seated in a camp chair by a wooden table reading with a bottle of beer in his hand.

Ngui took the rifle and shouldered it with the old shotgun and I walked over to the fire.

"Good morning, General," G.C. said. "You were up early."

"We hunters have it rugged," I said. "We hunt on our own two feet and the chips are always down."

"Somebody ought to pick the damned chips up sometime. You'll tread on them with your own two feet. Have some beer."

He poured a glass very carefully from the bottle bringing the head up to the point of running over and then delicately holding it bubble by bubble until the glass was full.

"Satan will find work for idle hands to do," I said and lifted the glass which had been filled so that a swell of the amber beer seemed to hang like the lip of an avalanche and conveyed it gently and unspilling to my lips taking in the first sip with the upper lip.

"Not bad for an unsuccessful hunter," G.C.

said. "Such steady hands and red-rimmed, blood-shot eyes have made our England's greatness."

" 'Neath twisted shards and iron sands we drink it down as God commands," I said. "Are you across the Atlantic yet?"

"I passed over Ireland," G.C. said. "Fright-fully green. I can all but see the lights of Le Bourget. I'm going to learn to fly, General."

"Many have said it before. The question is how are you going to fly?"

"I'm going to straighten up and fly right," G.C. said.

"On your own two feet and when the chips are down?"

"No. In the aircraft."

"Probably sounder in the aircraft. And will you carry these principles into Life, son?"

"Drink your beer, Billy Graham," G.C. said. "What will you do when I am gone, General? No nervous breakdowns, I hope? No trauma? You're up to it, I hope? It's not too late to refuse the flank."

"Which flank?"

"Any flank. It's one of the few military terms that I retained. I always wanted to refuse them a flank. In actual life you're always putting out a defensive flank and anchoring it somewhere. Until I refuse a flank I've been thwarted."

"Mon flanc gauche est protégé par une

colline," I said remembering too well. "J'ai les mittrailleuses bien placés. Je me trouve très bien ici et je reste."

"You're taking refuge in a foreign tongue," G.C. said. "Pour one and we'll go out and get that measuring over while my well-peppered ruffians do whatever it is they do this morning before they are for the town's end to beg during life."

"Did you ever read *Sergeant Shakespeare*?"

"No."

"I'll get it for you. Duff Cooper gave it to me. He wrote it."

"It isn't reminiscences?"

"No."

We had been reading the *Reminiscences* serialized in one of the thin paper airmail editions that came out to Nairobi on the Comets that landed at Entebbe. I had not liked them very much in the newspaper installments. But I had liked *Sergeant Shakespeare* very much and I had liked Duff Cooper without his wife. But there was so much of her in the *Reminiscences* that both G.C. and I had been put off.

"When are you going to write your reminiscences, G.C.?" I asked. "Don't you know old men forget?"

"I hadn't really thought much of writing them."

"You'll have to. There's not many of the really old timers left. You could start on the early phases now. Get in the early volumes. *Far Away and Long Ago in Abyssinia* would be a good one to start with. Skip the university and bohemian times in London and the Continent and cut to *A Youngster with the Fuzzy Wuzzies* then move into your early days as a Game Ranger while you can still recall them."

"Could I use that inimitable style you carved out of a walnut stick in *An Unwed Mother on the Italian Front*?" G.C. asked. "I always liked that the best of your books except for *Under Two Flags*. That was yours wasn't it?"

"No. Mine was *The Death of a Guardsman*."

"Good book too," G.C. said. "I never told you but I modeled my life on that book. Mummy gave it to me when I went away to school."

"You don't really want to go out on this measurement nonsense do you?" I said hopefully.

"I do."

"Should we take neutral witnesses?"

"There are none. We'll walk it ourselves."

"Let's get out then. I'll see if Miss Mary's still sleeping."

She was sleeping and she had drunk her tea and looked as though she might well sleep for another two hours. Her lips were closed and her face was smooth as ivory against the pillow. She was breathing easily but as she moved her head I could tell that she was dreaming.

I picked up the rifle where Ngui had hung it on a tree and climbed into the Land Rover beside G.C. We went and finally picked up the old tracks and found where Miss Mary had shot the lion. Many things were changed as they always are on any old battlefield but we found her empty cartridges and G.C.'s and off to the left we found mine. I put one in my pocket.

"Now I'll drive to where he was killed and then you pace it on a straight line."

I watched him go off in the car, his brown hair shining in the early morning sun; the big dog looking back at me and then turning to look straight ahead. When the Land Rover made a circle and stopped this side of the heavy clump of trees and bush I put my toe a pace to the left of the most westerly of the ejected shells and started to pace toward the vehicle counting as I paced. I carried the rifle over my shoulder holding it by the barrel with my right hand and when I started the Land Rover looked very small and foreshortened. The big dog was out and G.C. was walking around. They looked very small too and sometimes I could only see the dog's head and neck. When I got to the Land

Rover I stopped where the grass was bent where the lion had first lain.

"How many?" G.C. asked and I told him. He shook his head and asked, "Did you bring the Jinny flask?"

"Yes."

We each took a drink.

"We never, never tell anybody how long a shot it was," G.C. said. "Drunk or sober with shits or decent people."

"Never."

"Now we'll set the speedometer and you drive it back in a straight line and I'll pace it."

There was a couple of paces' difference in our tallies and a slight discrepancy between the speedometer reading and the paces so we cut four paces off the whole thing. Then we drove back to camp watching the Mountain and feeling sad because we would not hunt together again until Christmas.

After G.C. and his people were gone I was alone with Miss Mary's sorrow. I was not really alone because there was also Miss Mary and the camp and our own people and the big mountain of Kilimanjaro that everyone called Kibo and all the animals and the birds and the new fields of flowers and the worms that hatched out of the ground to eat the flowers. There were the brown eagles that came to feed on the worms so that eagles were as common as chickens and eagles wearing long brown trousers of feathers and other white headed eagles walked together with the guinea fowl busily eating the worms. The worms made an armistice among all the birds and they all walked together. Then great flocks of European storks came to eat the worms and there would be acres of storks moving on a single stretch of plain grown high with the white flowers. Miss Mary's sorrow resisted the eagles because eagles did not mean as much to her as they did to me.

She had never lain under juniper bush up above timberline at the top of a pass in our own mountains with a .22 rifle waiting for eagles to come to a dead horse that had been a bear bait until the bear was killed. Now he was an eagle bait and then afterwards he would be a bear bait again. The eagles were sailing very high when you first saw them. You had crawled under the bush when it was still dark and you had seen the eagles come out of the sun when it had cleared the opposite peak of the pass. This peak was just a rise of grassy hill with a rock outcropping at the top and scattered juniper bushes on the slope. The country was all high there and very easy traveling once you had come this high and the eagles had come from far away

toward the snow mountains you could have
seen if you had been standing instead of lying
under the bush. There were three eagles and
they wheeled and soared and rode the currents
and you watched them until the sun spotted
your eyes. Then you closed them and through
the red the sun was still there. You opened them
and looked to the side limit of the blind of the
sun and you could see the spread pinions and
the wide fanned tails and feel the eyes in the big
heads watching. It had been cold in the early
morning and you looked out at the horse and
his too old and too exposed now teeth that you
had always had to lift his lip to see. He had a
kind and rubbery lip and when you had led him
to this place to die and dropped the halter he
had stood as he had always been taught to stand
and when you had stroked him on the blaze
on his black head where the gray hairs showed
he had reached down to nip you on the neck
with his lips. He had looked down to see the
saddled horse you had left in the last edge of the
timber as though he were wondering what
he was doing here and what was the new game.
You had remembered how wonderfully he had
always seen in the dark and how you had hung
on to his tail with a bear hide packed across the
saddle to come down trails when you could not
see at all and when the trail led along the rim-

rock in the dark down through the timber. He was always right and he understood all new games.

So you had brought him up here five days before because someone had to do it and you could do it if not gently without suffering and what difference did it make what happened afterwards. The trouble was, at the end, he thought it was a new game and he was learning it. He gave me a nice rubber-lipped kiss and then he checked the position of the other horse. He knew you could not ride him the way the hoof had split but this was new and he wanted to learn it.

"Good-bye, Old Kite," I said and held his right ear and stroked its base with my fingers. "I know you'd do the same for me."

He did not understand, of course, and he wanted to give me another kiss to show that everything was all right when he saw the gun come up. I thought I could keep him from seeing it but he saw it and his eyes knew what it was and he stood very still trembling and I shot him at the intersection between the cross lines that run from opposite eye to opposite ear and his feet went straight down under him and all of him dropped together and he was a bear bait.

Now lying under the juniper I was not finished with my sorrow. I would always feel the same way about Old Kite all of my life, or so I told myself then, but I looked at his lips which were not there because the eagles had eaten them and at his eyes which were also gone and at where the bear had opened him so that he was sunken now and the patch the bear had eaten before I had interrupted him and I waited for the eagles to come down.

One came, finally, dropping like the sound of an incoming shell and breaking, with doubled-forward pinions and feathered legs and talons thrust forward to hit Old Kite as though he were killing him. He then walked pompously around and started working in the cavity. The others came in more gently and heavy winged but with the same long feathered wings and the same thick necks, big heads and dipped beaks and golden eyes.

I lay there watching them eat at the body of my friend and partner that I had killed and thought that they were lovelier in the air. Since they were condemned I let them eat a while and quarrel and go pacing and mincing with their selections from the interior. I wished that I had a shotgun but I hadn't. So I took the .22 Winchester finally and shot one carefully in the head and another twice in the body. He started to fly but could not make it and came down wings spread and I had to chase him up the high slope. Nearly every other bird or beast goes downhill when it is wounded. But an eagle goes uphill and when I ran this one down and caught his legs above the killing and holding claws and, with my moccasined foot on his neck, folded his wings together and held him with his eyes full of hatred and defiance, I had never seen any animal or bird look at me as the eagle looked. He was a golden eagle and full grown and big enough to take bighorn sheep lambs and he was a big thing to hold and as I watched the eagles walking with the guinea fowl and remembered that these birds walk with no one I felt badly about Miss Mary's sorrow but I could not tell her what the eagles meant to me nor why I had killed these two, the last one by smacking his head against a tree down in the timber, nor what their skins had bought at Lame Deer on the Reservation.

We were out riding in the hunting car when we saw the eagles and the guinea together and it was in the open glades of the forest that had been so damaged when the great herd of more than two hundred elephants had come through early that year and pulled and butted the trees down. We had gone there to check on the buffalo herd and perhaps to run onto a leopard that I knew lived there in the big unharmed trees close to the papyrus swamp. But we had seen nothing except the overrunning of the caterpillars and the strange armistice between the birds. Mary had located a few more possible Christmas trees and I had been thinking too much about eagles and about the old days. The old days were supposed to have been simpler but they were not; they were only rougher. The Reservation was rougher than the Shamba. Maybe not. I did not really know but I did know that the white people always took the other people's lands away from them and put them on a reservation where they could go to hell and be destroyed as though they were in a concentration camp. Here they called the Reservations the Reserves and there was much do-gooding about how the natives, now called the Africans, were administered. But the hunters were not allowed to hunt and the warriors were not allowed to make war. G.C. hated poachers because he had to have something to believe in so he had taken to believing in his job. He would, of course, insist that if he did not believe in his job he would never have taken it and he would be right in that too. Even Pop in one of the greatest rackets of all, the safari swindle, had very strict ethics; the strictest. The customer must be taken for every possible cent but he must be given results. All Great White Hunters were touching about how they loved the game and hated to kill anything but usually what they were thinking about was preserving the game for the next client that would come along. They did not want to frighten it by unnecessary shooting and they wanted a country to be left so that they might take another client and his wife or another pair of clients into it and it seem like unspoiled, never shot-over, primitive Africa that they could rush their clients through giving them the best results.

Pop had explained all this to me one time many years before and said when we were up the coast fishing at the end of the safari, "You know no one's conscience would ever let them do this to anyone twice. If they like them I mean. The next time you come out and get some transport, better bring it, and I'll find you the boys and you can hunt anywhere you've been and you'll work out new places and it will cost you no more than to hunt at home."

But it had turned out that rich people liked how much it cost and they came back again and again and it always cost more and was something that others could not do so that it was increasingly attractive. Old rich people died and there were always new ones and the animals decreased as the stock market rose. It was a big revenue-producing industry for the Colony too and because of this the Game Department, which had control over those who practiced the industry, had, with its development, produced new ethics that handled, or nearly handled, everything.

It was no good thinking about ethics now and less good to think about Lame Deer where you sat on a mule deer hide in front of a teepee with your two eagle tails spread out with the under sides up so that the lovely white ends and the soft plumes showed and said nothing while they were looked at and held your tongue in the bargaining. The Cheyenne who wanted them the most cared nothing anymore except for tail plumes. He was beyond all other things or all other things had been removed. To him eagles on the land of the Reservation were as they circled high in the sky and unapproachable when they settled on a pile of gray rock to watch the country. Sometimes they could be found and killed in blizzards when they sat against a rock back against the driving snow. But this man was no good in blizzards anymore. Only the young men were and they were gone.

You sat and did not talk and did not talk and sometimes reached out and touched the tails and stroked the plumes very lightly. You thought about your horse and about the second bear that had come through the pass to the horse after the killing of the eagles while the horse was still a bear bait and how when you had shot him a little too low in the bad light, taking him from the edge of the timber where the wind was right, he had rolled over once and then stood and bawled and slapped both his great arms as though to kill something that was biting him and then come down on all fours and came bouncing like a lorry off a highway and you had shot him twice as he came down the hill and the last time so close you smelled the fur burn. You thought of him and of the first bear. The hide had slipped on him and you took the long cured grizzly claws out of your shirt pocket and laid them out behind the eagle tails. Then you did not talk at all and the trading started. There had been no grizzly claws for many, many years and you made a good trade.

There were not any good trades this morning but the best thing was the storks. Mary had only seen them twice in Spain. The first time was in a small town in Castile on our way across the high country to Segovia. This town had a very fine square and we had stopped there in the heat of the day and gone out of the blinding light into the cool darkness of the inn to get our wine skins filled. It was very cool and pleasant in the inn and they had very cold beer and in this town they had a free bullfight one day each year in the lovely square in which everyone who wished could fight the three different bulls that were turned loose from their boxes. People were nearly always wounded or killed and it was the big social event of the year.

On this particularly hot day in Castile Miss Mary had discovered the storks nested on top of the tower of the church which had looked down on so many tauric incidents. The wife of the innkeeper had taken her up to a high room of the house where she might photograph them and I was talking at the bar with the owner of the local transport and trucking company. We talked about the different Castilian towns which had always had storks' nests on the churches and from all I could learn from the trucking man these were as plentiful as ever. No one had ever molested storks in Spain. They are one of the few birds that are truly respected and, naturally, were the luck of the village.

The innkeeper told me about a compatriot of mine, an inglés of some sort; they believed him to be a Canadian who had been in the town for some time with a broken down motorcycle and no money. He undoubtedly would eventually receive money and he had sent for the part that he needed for his motorcycle to Madrid but it had not come. Everyone liked him in the town and they wished that he were there so I might meet a compatriot who might even be a fellow

townsman. He had gone off somewhere painting but they said someone could go off and find
him and bring him in. The interesting thing
the innkeeper said was that this compatriot of
mine spoke absolutely no Spanish at all except
one word, joder. He was known as Mr. Joder
and if I wished to leave any message for him I
could leave it with the innkeeper. I wondered
what message I should leave for this compatriot
with such a decisive name and finally decided to
leave a fifty peseta folded in a certain way that
old travelers in Spain may be familiar with.
Everyone was delighted at that and they all
promised that Mr. Joder would surely spend the
ten duros that night without leaving the bar but
that he and his wife would be sure to get him to
eat something.

I asked them how Mr. Joder painted and the
transport man said, "Hombre he is neither
Velázquez nor Goya nor Martínez de León.
That I promise you. But times are changing and
who are we to criticize?" Miss Mary came
down from the high room where she had been
photographing and said that she had taken
good and clear pictures of the storks but that
they would be worthless because she had no tel-
escopic lens. We paid up and drank cold beer on
the house and all said good-bye and drove out
of the square and the blinding light on the steep

climb above the town to the high country toward Segovia. I stopped above the town and looked back and saw the male stork come in with his lovely flight to the nest on the top of the church tower. He had been down by the river where the women beat the clothes and later on we had seen a covey of partridges cross the road and later in the same lonely high bracken country we had seen a wolf.

That was this same year when we had been in Spain on the way to Africa and now we were in a yellow green forest that had been destroyed by elephants about the same time that we were riding across the high country to Segovia. In a world where this could happen I had small time for sorrow. I had been sure that I would never see Spain again and I had returned only to show Mary the Prado. Since I remembered all the pictures that I loved truly and so owned them as though I possessed them there was no need for me to see them again before I died. But it was very important that I should see them with Mary if that were possible and could be done without compromise or indignity. Also I wanted her to see Navarre and the two Castiles and I wanted her to see a wolf in high country and storks nesting in a village. I had wanted to show her the paw of a bear nailed onto the door of the church in Barco de Avila but it was too much to expect that would still be there. But we had found the storks quite easily and would find more and we had seen the wolf and had looked down on Segovia from a near and pleasant height, coming onto it naturally on a road that tourists did not take but that travelers would come by naturally. There are no such roads anymore around Toledo but you can still see Segovia as you would see it if you walked over the high country and we studied the city as though it were being seen for the first time by people who had never known it was there but had always lived to see it.

There is a virginity that you, in theory only, bring once to a beautiful city or a great painting. This is only a theory and I think it is untrue. All the things that I have loved I bring this to each time but it is lovely to bring someone else to it and it helps the loneliness. Mary had loved Spain and Africa and had learned the secret things naturally and hardly without knowing she had learned them. I never explained the secret things to her; only the technical things or the comic things and my own greatest pleasure came from her own discovering. It is stupid to expect or hope that a woman that you love should love all the things that you do. But Mary had loved the sea and living on a small boat and she loved fishing. She loved pictures and she had loved the West of the United States when we had first gone there together. She never simulated anything and this was a great gift to be given as I had been associated with a great simulator of everything and life with a true simulator gives a man a very unattractive view of many things and he can begin to cherish loneliness rather than to wish to share anything.

Now this morning with the day becoming hot and the cool wind from the Mountain not having risen we were working out a new trail out of the forest that the elephants had destroyed. After we came out into the open prairie land after having to cut our way through a couple of bad places we saw the first great flock of storks feeding. They were true European storks black and white and red-legged and they were working on the caterpillars as though they were German storks and under orders. Miss Mary liked them and they meant much to her since we had both been worried about the article that said that storks were becoming extinct and now we found that they had merely had good sense enough to come to Africa as we had done ourselves; but they did not take away her sorrow and we went on toward camp. I did not know what to do about Miss Mary's sorrow. It was proofed against eagles and proofed against storks, against neither of which I had any defense at all, and I began to know how great a sorrow it really was.

"What have you been thinking of all morning when you've been so uncommonly silent?"

"About birds and places and how nice you are."

"That was nice of you."

"I didn't do it as a spiritual exercise."

"I'll be all right. People don't just jump in and out of bottomless pits."

"They're going to make it an event in the next Olympic Games."

"You'll probably win it."

"I have my backers."

"Your backers are all dead like my lion. You probably shot all your backers one day when you were feeling especially wonderful."

"Look there's another field of storks."

Africa is a dangerous place for a great sorrow to live very long when there are only two people in a camp and when it gets dark shortly after six o'clock in the evening. We did not talk about lions nor think about them anymore and the emptiness where Mary's sorrow had lived was filling again with the routine and the strange fine life and the coming of the night. When the fire burned down I pulled a long heavy dead tree from the pile of deadwood the lorry had brought in the afternoon onto the coals and we sat in our chairs and watched the night breeze blow the coals up and watched the wood catch fire. This night breeze was a small wind that came off the snows of the Mountain. It was so light that you only felt its coolness but you could see it in the fire. You can see the wind in many ways but the loveliest is at night in the brightening and the lowering and raising of the flame in your fire.

"We're never alone with our fire," Mary said. "I'm glad now there is only us and our fire. Will that log burn until morning?"

"I think so," I said. "If the wind doesn't rise."

"It's strange now without the lion to look forward to in the morning and you haven't any problems or worries now, have you?"

"No. Everything is quiet now," I lied.

"Do you miss all the problems you and G.C. had?"

"No."

"Maybe now we can get some really beautiful pictures of the buffalo and other fine color pictures. Where do you think the buffalo have gone?"

"I think they are over toward the Chulus. We'll find out when Willie brings the Cessna."

"Isn't it strange how the Mountain throwing all those stones hundreds and hundreds of years ago can make a place impossible to get to so that it is absolutely shut off from everyone and no one can reach it since men started to go on wheels."

"They're helpless now without their wheels. Natives won't go as porters anymore and the fly kills pack animals. The only parts of Africa that are left are those that are protected by deserts and by the fly. The tsetse fly is the animal's best friend. He only kills the alien animals and the intruders."

"Isn't it strange how we truly love the animals and still have to kill almost every day for meat?"

"It's no worse than caring about your chickens and still having eggs for breakfast and eating spring chicken when you want it."

"It is different."

"Of course it is. But the principle is the same. So much game has come now with the new grass that we may not have any trouble lions for a long time. There is no reason for them to bother the Masai when we have so much game now."

"The Masai have too many cattle anyway."

"Sure."

"Sometimes I feel as though we were fools protecting their stock for them."

"If you don't feel like a fool in Africa a big

part of the time you are a bloody fool," I said rather pompously, I thought. But it was getting late enough at night for generalizations to appear the way some stars showed reluctant in their distance and disinterest and others always seemed brazen in their clarity.

"Do you think we should go to bed?" I asked.

"Let's go," she said. "And be good kittens and forget anything that's been wrong. And when we're in bed we can listen to the night."

So we went to bed and were happy and loved each other with no sorrow and listened to the night noises. A hyena came close to the tent after we had left the fire and I had crawled in under the mosquito net and between the sheets and the blankets and lay with my back against the canvas wall of the tent with Mary comfortable in the main part of the cot. He cried out a few times in the strange rising pitch and another answered him and they moved through the camp and out beyond the lines. We could see the glow of the fire brightening when the wind came and Mary said, "Us kittens in Africa with our faithful good fire and the beasts having their night life. You really love me don't you?"

"What do you think?"

"I think you do."

"Don't you know?"

"Yes, I know."

After a while we heard two lions coughing as they hunted and the hyenas were quiet. Then a long way away to the north toward the edge of the stony forest beyond the gerenuk country we heard a lion roar. It was the heavy vibrating roar of a big lion and I held Mary close while the lion coughed and grunted afterwards.

"That's a new lion," she whispered.

"Yes," I said. "And we don't know anything against him. I'll be very damned careful about any Masai that talk against him."

"We'll take good care of him, won't we? Then he'll be our lion the way our fire is our fire."

"We'll let him be his own lion. That's what he really cares about."

She was asleep now and after a while I was asleep and when I woke and heard the lion again she was gone and I could hear her breathing softly in her bed.

12

"Memsahib sick?" Mwindi asked as he fixed the pillows so that Mary could lie with her head toward the wide-open end of the tent and tested the air mattress on the cot with the palm of his hand before drawing the sheets smooth over the mattress and folding them tightly under.

"Yes. A little."

"Maybe from eat the lion."

"No. She was sick before kill the lion."

"Lion run very far very fast. Was very angry and sad when he die. Maybe make poison."

"Bullshit," I said.

"Hapana bullshit," Mwindi said gravely. "Bwana Captain Game Ranger eat lion too. He sick too."

"Bwana Captain Game Ranger sick with same sickness long back Salengai."

"Eat lion Salengai too."

"Mingi bullshit," I said. "He sick before I kill lion. Hapana eat lion in Salengai. Eat lion here after safari from Salengai. When lion skinned Salengai all chop boxes packed. Nobody eat that morning. You think back bad."

Mwindi shrugged his shoulders under the long green gown. "Eat lion Bwana Captain Game Ranger sick. Memsahib sick."

"Who eat lion feel fine? Me."

"Shaitani," Mwindi said. "I see you sick to die before. Many years ago when you young man you sick to die after you kill lion. Everybody know you die. Ndege know. Bwana know. Memsahib know. Everybody remember when you die."

"Did I eat the lion?"

"No."

"Was I sick before I kill that lion?"

"Ndio," Mwindi said reluctantly. "Very sick."

"You and me talk too much."

"We are Mzees. All right talk if you wish talk."

"Kwisha talk," I said. I was tired of the pidgin English and I did not think much of the idea that was building up.

"Memsahib goes to Nairobi in the ndege tomorrow. Doctor in Nairobi cures her sickness. Come back from Nairobi well and strong. Kwisha," I said, meaning it is finished.

"Mzuri sana," Mwindi said. "I pack everything."

I went out of the tent and Ngui was waiting under the big tree. He had my shotgun.

"I know where there are two kwali. Shoot them for Miss Mary."

Mary was not back yet and we found the two francolin dusting in a patch of dried dirt at the edge of the big fever trees. They were small and compact and quite beautiful. I waved at them and they started to run crouching for the brush so I shot one on the ground and the other as it rose.

"Any more?" I asked Ngui.

"Only the pair."

I handed the gun to him and we started back for camp, me holding the two plump birds, warm and clear-eyed with their soft feathers blowing in the breeze. I would have Mary look them up in the bird book. I was quite sure I had never seen them before and that they might be a local Kilimanjaro variety. One would make a good broth and the other would be good for her if she wanted solid food. I would give her some Terramycin and some Chlorodyne to tie things up. I was uncertain about the Terramycin but she seemed to get no bad reactions from it.

I was sitting in a comfortable chair in the cool mess tent when I saw Mary come up to our tent. She washed and then came over and into the door of the tent and sat down.

"Oh my," she said. "Should we not mention it?"

"I could drive you back and forth in the hunting car."

"No. It's as big as a hearse."

"Take this stuff now if you can hold it down."

"Would it be terrible to have a gimlet for my morale?"

"You're not supposed to drink but I always did and I'm still here."

"I'm not quite sure whether I'm here or not. It would be nice to find out."

"We'll find out."

I made the gimlet and then said that there was no hurry to take the medicine and for her to go in and lie down on the bed and rest and read if she felt like it or I would read to her if she would like.

"What did you shoot?"

"A couple of very small francolin. They're like small partridges. I'll bring them in after a while and you can look at them. They'll make you supper."

"What about lunch?"

"We'll have some good Tommy broth and mashed potato. You're going to knock this thing right away and it's not so bad that you shouldn't eat. They say that Terramycin kills it better than Yatren in the old days. But I'd feel better if we had Yatren. I was sure we had it in the medical chest."

"I'm thirsty all the time."

"I remember. I'll show Mbebia how to make rice water and we'll keep it cool in a bottle in the water bag and you drink all of that you want. It's good for the thirst and it keeps your strength up."

"I don't know why I had to get ill with something. We lead such a wonderful healthy life."

"Kitten, you could just as well have got fever."

"But I take my antimalarial medicine every night and I always make you take yours when you forget it and we always wear our mosquito boots in the evening by the fire."

"Sure. But in the swamp after the buffalo we were bitten hundreds of times."

"No, dozens."

"Hundreds for me."

"You're bigger. Put your arms around my shoulders and hold me tight."

"We're lucky kittens," I said. "Everybody gets fever if they go in country where there is a lot of it and we were in two bad fever countries."

"But I took my medicine and I made you remember yours."

"So we didn't get fever. But we were in bad sleeping sickness country too and you know how many tsetse flies there were."

"Weren't they bad though by the Ewaso Ngiro. I remember coming home in the evenings and they would bite like red-hot eyebrow tweezers."

"I've never even seen red-hot eyebrow tweezers."

"Neither have I but that's what they bite like in that deep woods where the rhino lived. The one that chased G.C. and his dog Kibo into the river. That was a lovely camp though and we had so much fun when we first started hunting by ourselves. It was twenty times more fun than having somebody with us and I was so good and obedient, remember?"

"And we got so close to everything in the big green woods and it was like we were the first people that were ever there."

"Do you remember where the moss was and the trees so high there was almost no sunlight ever and we walked softer than Indians and you took me so close to the impala that he never saw us and when we found the herd of buffalo just across the little river from the camp? That was a wonderful camp. Do you remember how the leopard came through the camp every night just like having Boise or Mr. Willie moving around the Finca at night at home?"

"Yes, my good kitten, and you're not going to be sick really now because the Terramycin will have taken hold of that by tonight or in the morning."

"I think it's taking hold now."

"Cucu couldn't have said it was better than Yatren and Carbsone if it wasn't really good. Miracle drugs make you feel spooky while you are waiting for them to take hold. But I remember when Yatren was a miracle drug and it really was then too."

"I have a wonderful idea."

"What would it be, honey my good kitten?"

"I just thought we could have Harry come with the Cessna and you and he could check on all your beasts and your problems and then I'd go back with him to Nairobi and see a good doctor about this dysentery or whatever it is and I could buy Christmas presents for everyone and all the things we should have for Christmas."

"We call it the Birthday of the Baby Jesus."

"I still call it Christmas," she said. "And there are an awful lot of things we need. It wouldn't be too extravagant do you think?"

"I think it would be wonderful. We'll send a signal through Ngong. When would you want the plane?"

"How would day after tomorrow be?"

"Day after tomorrow is the most wonderful day there is after tomorrow."

"I'm going to just lie quiet and feel the breeze from the snow on our Mountain. You go and make yourself a drink and read and be comfortable."

"I'll go out to show Mbebia how to make the rice water."

Mary felt much better at noon and in the afternoon she slept again and in the evening felt quite well and was hungry. I was delighted with how the Terramycin had acted and that she had no bad reactions from it and told Mwindi, touching the wood of my gun butt, that I had cured Miss Mary with a powerful and secret dawa but that I was sending her into Nairobi tomorrow in the ndege in order that a European doctor might confirm my cure.

"Mzuri," Mwindi said.

So we ate lightly but well and happily that night and it was a happy camp again and the disease and misfortune through the eating-of-lion-meat party, which had made a strong bid for power in the morning, dissolved as though the subject never had been raised. There were always these theories that came to explain any misfortune and the first and most important thing was someone or something that was guilty. Miss Mary was supposed to have extraordinary and unexplainable bad luck herself, which she was in the process of expiating, but she was also supposed to bring great good luck to other people. She was also well loved. Arap Meina actually worshipped her and Chungo, G.C.'s chief Game Scout, was in love with her. Arap Meina worshipped very few things as his religion had become hopelessly confused but he had moved into a worshipping of Miss Mary that, occasionally, reached peaks of ecstasy that were little short of violence. He loved G.C. but this was a sort of schoolboy fascination combined with devotion. He came to care greatly for me, carrying this affection to the point where I had to explain to him that it was women that I cared for rather than men though I was capable of deep and lasting friendship. But all his love and devotion which he had scattered over one whole slope of Kilimanjaro with complete sincerity and almost always with returned devotion, giving it alike to men, women, children, boys and girls and to all types of alcohol and the available heroic herbs, and they were many, he now concentrated this great talent for affection on Miss Mary.

Arap Meina was not supremely beautiful although he had great elegance and soldierliness in uniform with his ear-laps always coiled neatly over the tops of his ears so that they formed a knot of the sort Greek Goddesses wore their hair in a sort of modified Psyche knot. But he had to offer the sincerity of an old elephant poacher gone straight and into a straightness so unimpeachable that he could offer it to Miss Mary almost as though it were a virginity. The

Wakamba are not homosexual. I do not know about the Lumbwa because Arap Meina was the only Lumbwa I have ever known intimately but I would say that Arap Meina was strongly attracted by both sexes and that the fact that Miss Mary, with the shortest of African haircuts, provided the pure Hamitic face of a boy with a body that was as womanly as a good Masai young wife was one of the factors that channeled Arap Meina's devotion until it became worship. He called her not Mama, which is the ordinary way an African speaks of any married white woman when he does not feel up to saying Memsahib, but always Mummy. Miss Mary had never been called Mummy by anyone and told Arap Meina not to address her in that way. But it was the highest title he had salvaged from his contact with the English language and so he called her Mummy Miss Mary or Miss Mary Mummy, depending on whether he had been using the heroic herbs and barks or had simply made contact with his old friend, alcohol.

We were sitting by the fire after dinner talking of Arap Meina's devotion to Miss Mary and I was worrying about why I had not seen him that day when Mary said, "It isn't bad for everybody to be in love with everybody else the way it is in Africa, is it?"

"No."

"Are you sure something awful won't come out of it suddenly?"

"Awful things come out of it all the time with the Europeans. They drink too much and get all mixed up with each other and then blame it on the altitude."

"There is something about the altitude or it being altitude on the equator. It's the first place I've ever known where a drink of pure gin tastes like water. That's really true and so there must be something about the altitude or something."

"Sure there is something. But we who work hard and hunt on foot and sweat our liquor out and climb the damned escarpment and climb around this Mountain don't have to worry about liquor. It goes out through the pores. Honey, you walk more going back and forth to the latrine than most of the women who come out here on safari walk in the whole of Africa."

"Let's not mention the latrine. It has a wonderful path to it now and it's always stocked with the best reading matter. Have you ever finished that lion book yet?"

"No. I'm saving it for when you're gone."

"Don't save too many things for when I'm gone."

"That's all I saved."

"I hope it teaches you to be cautious and good."

"I am anyway."

"No you're not. You and G.C. are fiends sometimes and you know it. When I think of you a good writer and a valuable man and my husband doing what you and G.C. do on those terrible night things."

"We have to study the animals at night."

"You don't either. You just do devilish things to show off to each other."

"I don't think so really, kitten. We do things for fun. When you stop doing things for fun you might as well be dead."

"But you don't have to do things that will kill you and pretend that the Land Rover is a horse and that you're riding in the Grand National. Neither of you can ride well enough to ride at Aintree on that course."

"That's quite true and that's why we're reduced to the Land Rover. G.C. and I have the simple sports of the honest countryman."

"You're two of the most dishonest and dangerous countrymen I've ever known. I don't even try to discipline you anymore because I know it's hopeless."

"Don't talk bad about us just because you're leaving us."

"I wasn't doing that. I was just horrified for a minute thinking about you two and what your ideas of fun are. Anyway, thank God G.C. isn't here so you'd be alone together."

"You just have a good time in Nairobi and

get checked by the doctor and buy whatever you want and don't worry about this Manyatta. It will be well run and orderly and nobody will take any unnecessary risks. I'll run a nice clean joint while you're gone and you'll be proud."

"Why don't you write something so I'll be really proud?"

"Maybe I'll write something too. Who knows?"

"I don't mind about your fiancée as long as you love me more. You do love me more don't you?"

"I love you more and I'll love you more still when you come back from town."

"I wish you could come too."

"I don't. I hate Nairobi."

"It's all new to me and I like to learn about it and there are nice people too."

"You go to it and have fun and come back."

"Now I wish I didn't have to go. But it will be fun flying with Willie and then I'll have the fun of flying back and coming back to my big kitten and the fun of the presents. You'll remember to get a leopard won't you? You know you promised Bill you'd have a leopard before Christmas."

"I won't forget but I'd rather do it and not worry about it."

"I just wanted to be sure you hadn't forgotten."

"I hadn't forgotten. Also I'll brush my teeth and remember to turn off the stars at night and put the hyena out."

"Don't make fun. I'm going away."

"I know it and it isn't funny at all."

"But I'll be back and I'll have big surprises."

"The biggest and best surprise is always when I see my kitten."

"It's even better when it's in our own airplane. And I'll have a wonderful and special surprise but it's a secret."

"I think you ought to go to bed, kitten, because even though we are winning now with the stuff you ought to rest well."

"Carry me in to my bed the way I thought you would have to carry me when I thought I might start dying this morning."

So I carried her in and she weighed just what a woman that you loved should weigh when you lifted her in your arms and she was neither too long nor too short and did not have the long dangling crane legs of the tall American beauties. She carried easily and well and she slid into the bed as smoothly as a well-launched ship comes down the ways.

"Isn't bed a lovely place?"

"Bed is our Fatherland."

"Who said that?"

"Me," I said rather proudly. "It's more impressive in German."

"Isn't it nice we don't have to talk German?"

"Yes," I said. "Especially since we can't."

"You were very impressive in German in Tanganyika and at Cortina."

"I fake it. That's why it sounds impressive."

"I love you very much in English."

"I love you too and you sleep well and you'll have a good trip tomorrow. We'll both sleep like good kittens and be so happy that you're going to be all right."

When Willie buzzed the camp we went out fast to where the wind sock hung dead against the skinned tree pole and watched his short delicate landing on the crushed flowers the lorry had flattened for him. We unloaded and loaded the hunting car and I ran through the mail and the cables while Mary and Willie talked in the front seat. I sorted Mary's letters and mine and put the Mr. and Mrs. in Mary's lot and opened the cables. There was nothing really bad and two were encouraging.

In the mess tent Mary had her mail at the table and Willie and I shared a bottle of beer while I opened the worst-looking letters. There was nothing that non-answering would not help.

"How's the war, Willie?"

"We still hold Government House, I believe."

"Torr's?"

"Definitely in our hands."

"The New Stanley?"

"The dark and bloody ground? I heard G.C. put a patrol of airline hostesses as far as the Grill. Chap named Jack Block seems to be holding it. Very gallant effort."

"Who has the Game Department?"

"I shouldn't like to say really. From the last gen I had it was rather nip and tuck."

"I know Nip," I said. "But who is this Tuck?"

"A new man I presume. I hear Miss Mary shot a beautiful great lion. Will we be taking him back, Miss Mary?"

"Of course, Willie."

In the afternoon it stopped raining just as Willie said it would and after they had gone in the plane I was very lonesome. I had not wanted to go into the town and I knew how happy I would be alone with the people and the problems and with the country that I loved but I was lonely for Mary.

It was always lonely after rain but I was lucky to have the letters which had meant nothing when they came and I arranged them in an orderly manner again and put all the papers in order too. There were the *East African Standard*, the airmail editions of the *Times* and the

Telegraph on their paper that was like thin onion skin, a *Times Literary Supplement* and an air-edition of *Time*. The letters opened fairly dull and made me glad I was in Africa.

One letter carefully forwarded by my publishers via airmail at considerable cost was from a woman in Iowa:

> Guthrie Center, Iowa
> July 27, 1953

Mr. Ernest Hemingway
Havana, Cuba

Several years ago, I read your "Across the River and Into the Trees," when it was serialized in the *Cosmopolitan*. After the beautiful opening description of Venice, I expected the book to go on, and have considerable stature, but was vastly disappointed. Certainly there was opportunity to disclose the rottenness that MAKES wars, as well as to point out hypocrisy of the military organization itself. Instead, your officer was mainly disgruntled because HE had the PERSONAL MISFORTUNE to lose two companies of men, and as a result, received no promotion. Little or NO grief was shown for the young men themselves. Largely it seemed the ineffectual efforts of an old man to try

to convince himself and other old men that
young, beautiful and even rich young
women would love an old man for himself
alone, not because he could give her
wealth and a position of prominence.

Later, *"Old Man of the Sea"* was published, and I asked my brother, who is
mature, and spent four and a half years in
the Army during War LL. if this book were
any more emotionally mature than *River
and Trees,* and he grimaced and said it
wasn't.

It is amazing to me that a group of people could award you the Pulitzer Prize. At
least everyone does not agree.

This clipping was taken from Harlan
Miller's column of "Over the Coffee,"
from *The Des Moines Register and Tri-
bune,* and I have been meaning for some
time to send it. Just add that Hemingway
is EMOTIONALLY IMMATURE AND
AN AWFUL BORE, and the review is
complete. You have had four "wives," and
if you haven't achieved morality, you
should at least be getting a little common
sense from your past mistakes. Why not
write SOMETHING that is worthwhile,
before you die?

Mrs. G. S. Held

This woman did not like the book in any way and that was her perfect right. If I had been in Iowa I would have refunded her the money she had spent on it as a reward for her eloquence and the reference to War LL. I took to mean two rather than Long and Lousy and I read where a clipping had been inserted:

> *Maybe I've been slightly stuffy about Hemingway: the most over-rated writer of our time, but still a fine writer. His main faults: (1) scant sense of humor, (2) a juvenile brand of realism, (3) meager idealism, or none, (4) hairy chested bombast*

It was enjoyable to sit in the empty mess tent alone with my correspondence and imagine the emotionally mature brother grimacing perhaps in the kitchen over a snack from the Frigidaire, or seated in front of the TV set watching Mary Martin as Peter Pan and I thought how kind it was for this lady from Iowa to write me and how pleasant it would be to have her emotionally mature grimacing brother shaking his head here now at this moment.

You cannot have everything, writer old man, I said to myself philosophically. What you win on the swings you lose on the roundabouts. You simply have to give up this emotionally mature brother. Give him up, I tell you. You must go it alone, boy. So I gave him up and continued to read Our Lady of Iowa. In Spanish I thought of her as Nuestra Senora de los Apple Knockers and at the surge of such a splendid name I felt a rush of piety and Whitman-like warmth. But keep it directed toward her, I cautioned myself. Don't let it lead you toward the grimacer.

It was exciting as well to read the tribute of the brilliant young columnist. It had that simple but instant catharsis that Edmund Wilson has called "The Shock of Recognition," and recognizing the quality of this young columnist who indeed would have had a brilliant future on the *East African Standard* had he been born in the Empire and hence been able to secure a work permit I thought again, as one approaches the edge of a precipice, of the well-loved face of the grimacing brother of my correspondent but my feelings toward the grimacer had changed now and I was no longer attracted to him as I had been but, rather, saw him seated among the corn stalks, his hands uncontrollable in the night as he heard the growth of the stems of the mealies. In the Shamba we had mealies that grew as tall as corn grows in the Middle West. But nobody heard it grow in the night because the nights were cool and the corn grew in the afternoon and at night; even if it had grown at night, you could not have heard it for the talking of the hyenas and the jackals and the lions when they were hunting and the noise the leopards made.

I thought the hell with this stupid Iowa bitch writing letters to people she does not know about things she knows nothing about and I wished her the grace of a happy death as soon as possible, but I remembered her last sentence: "Why not write SOMETHING that is worthwhile, before you die?" and I thought, you ignorant Iowa bitch, I have already done this and I will do it again many times.

Berenson was well, which made me happy, and was in Sicily, which worried me unnecessarily since he knew much more about what he was doing than I did. Marlene had problems but had been triumphant in Las Vegas and enclosed the clippings. Both the letter and clippings were very moving. The place in Cuba was OK but there were many expenses. All the beasts were well. There was still money in the N.Y. bank. Ditto the Paris bank but on the feeble side. Everyone in Venice was well except those who had been confined to nursing homes or were dying of various incurable diseases. One of my friends had been badly injured in a motor accident and I remembered the sudden dips into fog no lights could pierce when driving down the coast in the early mornings. From the description of the various fractures I doubted if he, who had loved shooting better than anything, would ever be able to shoot again. A woman I knew, admired and loved had cancer and was not given three months to live. Another girl I had known for eighteen years, knowing her first when she was eighteen, and loving her and being friends with her and loving her while she had married two husbands and made four fortunes from her own intelligence and kept them, I hoped, and gained all the tangible and countable and wearable and storable and pawnable things in life and lost all the others wrote a letter full of news, gossip and heartbreak. It had genuine news and the heartbreak was not feigned and it had the complaints that all women are entitled to. It made me the saddest of all the letters because she could not come out to Africa now where she would have had a good life even if it were only for two weeks. I knew now since she was not coming that I would never see her anymore ever unless her husband sent her on a business mission to me. She would go to all the places that I had always promised to take her but I would not go. She could go with the husband and they could be nervous together. He would always have the long-distance telephone which was as necessary to him as seeing the sunrise was to me or seeing the stars at night was to

386 • ERNEST HEMINGWAY

Mary. She would be able to spend money and buy things and accumulate possessions and eat in very expensive restaurants and Conrad Hilton was opening, or finishing or planning hotels for her and her husband in all the cities we had once planned to see together. She had no problem now. She could with the aid of Conrad Hilton take her lost looks to be comfortably bedded, never an arm's reach away from the long-distance telephone, and when she woke in the night she could truly know what nothing was and what it's worth tonight and practice counting her money to put herself to sleep so she would wake late and not meet another day too soon. Maybe Conrad Hilton would open a hotel in Laitokitok, I thought. Then she would be able to come out here and see the Mountain and there would be guides from the hotel to take her to meet Mr. Singh and Brown and Benji and there would be a plaque, perhaps, to mark the site of the Old Police Boma and they could buy souvenir spears from the Anglo-Masai Stores Ltd. There would be hot and cold running White Hunters with every room all wearing leopard-skin bands around their hats and instead of Gideon Bibles by every bedside along with the long-distance telephone there would be copies of *White Hunter, Black Heart* and *Something of Value* autographed by their authors and printed on a special all-purpose paper with portraits of their authors done on the back of the dust jackets so that they glowed in the dark.

Thinking of this hotel and the project of how it might be decorated and run featuring the twenty-four-hour safari, all beasts guaranteed, you sleep in your own room each night with piped in coaxial TV, and the menus and the desk staff all anti–Mau Mau commandos and the better White Hunters, and the little courtesies to guests such as each guest finding by his plate the first night at dinner his commission as an Honorary Game Warden and on his second, and for most the last night, his Honorary Membership in the East African Professional Hunters Association delighted me but I did not want to work it out too completely until we should have Mary and G.C. and Willie together. Miss Mary, having been a journalist, had splendid powers of invention. I had never heard her tell a story in the same way twice and always had the feeling she was remolding it for the later editions. We needed Pop too because I wanted his permission to have him mounted full length and placed in the lobby in the event that he should ever die. There might be some opposition from his family but we would have to talk the entire project over and reach the soundest decision. Pop had never expressed any great love for Laitokitok which he regarded more or less as a sin trap and I believe he wanted to be buried up in the high hills of his own country. But we could, at least, discuss it.

Now, realizing that loneliness is best taken away by jokes, derision and contempt for the worst possible outcome of anything and that gallows humor is the most valid if not the most durable since it is of necessity momentary and often ill reported, I laughed reading the sad letter and thinking about the new Laitokitok Hilton. The sun was almost down and I knew Mary would be in the New Stanley by now and probably in her bath. I liked to think of her in her bath and I hoped she would have fun in the town tonight. She did not like the bad dives I frequented and I thought she would probably be at the Travelers Club or some such place and I was glad that it was she who was having that sort of fun and not me.

I stopped thinking about her and thought about Debba and that we had promised to take her and the Widow to buy cloth for dresses that they would have for the celebration of the Birthday of the Baby Jesus. This official buying of dresses with my fiancée present and choosing the cloth which I would pay for while forty to sixty Masai women and warriors watched was as formal and definitive an occasion as Laitokitok would offer in this social season or probably any other. Being a writer which is a disgrace but also sometimes a comfort I wondered, being unable to sleep, how Henry James would have handled this situation. I remembered him standing on the balcony of his hotel in Venice smoking a good cigar and wondering what must go on in that town where it is so much harder to keep out of trouble than to get into it and when, in the nights I could not sleep, I always had great comfort thinking of Henry James standing on the balcony of his hotel looking down at the town and people passing, all of them with their needs and their duties and their problems, their small economies and village happinesses and the sound well-organized life of the canal, and think of James, who knew not one of the places to go, and stayed on his balcony with his cigar. Happy now in the night where I could sleep or not as I wished I liked to think of both Debba and James and I wondered how it would be if I plucked the consolatory cigar from James's lips and handed it to Debba who might put it behind her ear or perhaps hand it to Ngui, who had learned to smoke cigars in Abyssinia where as a rifleman in the K.A.R. opposing, sometimes, white troops and their camp followers and overcoming them he had learned many other things. Then I stopped thinking about Henry James and his consolatory cigar and about the lovely canal which I had been imagining with a fair wind coming to help all my friends and brothers who had to work against the tide and I no longer cared to think of the thick, squat figure with the bald head and the ambulatory dignity and line of departure problems and I thought of Debba and the big skin-covered, smoky, clean-smelling, hand-rubbed wood bed of the big house and the four bottles of sacramental beer I had paid for the use of it, my intentions being honorable, and the beer having its proper tribal custom name; I think it was, among the many ritual beers, known as The Beer For Sleeping In The Bed Of The Mother-in-Law and it was equivalent to the possession of a Cadillac in John O'Hara circles if there be any such circles left. I hoped piously that there were such circles left and I thought of O'Hara, fat as a boa constrictor that had swallowed an entire shipment of a magazine called *Collier's* and surly as a mule that had been bitten by tsetse flies plodding along dead without recognizing it, and I wished him luck and all happiness remembering fairly joyously the white-edged evening tie he had worn at his coming out party in New York and his hostess's nervousness at presenting him and her gallant hope that he would not disintegrate. No matter how bad things go any human being can be cheered remembering O'Hara at his most brilliant epoch.

I thought about our plans for Christmas which I always loved and could remember in so many countries. I knew this Christmas was going to be either wonderful or truly awful since we had decided to invite all of the Masai and all of the Wakamba and this was the sort of Ngoma which could end Ngomas if it were not carried out properly. There would be the magic tree of Miss Mary which the Masai would recognize for what it truly was if Miss Mary did not. I did not know whether we should tell Miss Mary that her tree was really an extra-potent type of marijuana-effect tree because there were so many angles to the problem. First, Miss Mary was absolutely determined to have this particular type of tree and it had been accepted by the Wakamba as a part of her unknown or Thief River Falls tribal customs along with her necessity to have killed the lion. Arap Meina had confided to me that he and I could be drunk on this tree for months and that if an elephant ate this tree that Miss Mary had selected he, the elephant, would be drunk for a matter of days.

I knew that Miss Mary must have had a good evening in Nairobi since she was not a fool and it was the only town we had and there was fresh smoked salmon at the New Stanley and an understanding although conniving headwaiter. But the fish from the great lakes, the non-named fish, would be as good as ever and there would be curries but she should not eat them so soon after dysentery. But I was sure she had dined well and I hoped she was in some good night-club now and I thought about Debba and how we would be going up to buy the material for the two lovely hills that she carried so proudly and modestly and how the cloth would empha-size them as she well knew and how we would look at the different prints and how the Masai women with their long skirts and the flies and their insane, pretending, beauty parlor hus-bands would watch us in their unsatisfied bold-ness and syphilitic, cold-handed beauty and how we, Kamba, neither one with our ears even pierced but proud and worse than insolent because of too many things that Masai could not ever know, would feel the stuffs and look at the patterns and buy other things to give us importance in the store.

13

WHEN MWINDI brought the tea in the morning I was up and dressed sitting by the ashes of the fire with two sweaters and a wool jacket on. It had turned very cold in the night and I wondered what that meant about the weather for today.

"Want fire?" Mwindi asked.

"Small fire for one man."

"I send," Mwindi said. "You better eat. Memsahib go you forget to eat."

"I don't want to eat before I hunt."

"Maybe hunt be very long. You eat now."

"Mbebia isn't awake."

"All old men awake. Only young men asleep. Keiti says for you to eat."

"OK. I'll eat."

"What you want to eat?"

"Codfish balls and hash-browned potatoes."

"You eat Tommy liver and bacon. Keiti says Memsahib says to tell you to take fever pills."

"Where are the fever pills?"

"Here," he brought the bottle out. "Keiti says I watch you eat them."

"Good," I said. "I ate them."

"What you wear?" Mwindi asked.

"Short boots and warm jacket to start and the skin shirt with the solids for when it gets hot."

"I get the other people ready. Today very good day."

"Yeah?"

"Everybody thinks so. Even Charo."

"Good. I feel it is a good day too."

"You don't have any dream?"

"No," I said. "Truly no."

"Mzuri," Mwindi said. "I tell Keiti."

After breakfast we headed straight for the Chulus by the good trail that went north through the gerenuk country. The trail from the Old Manyatta to the hills where the buffalo should be now as they returned to the swamp was gray with mud and treacherous. But we went on it as far as we could and then we left Mthuka with the car, knowing the mud would be drying in the sun. The sun was now baking the plain and we left it and started up into the steep, small, broken hills covered with lava boulders with the new grass thick and wet from the rain. We did not wish to kill any buffalo but it was necessary to have the two guns as there were rhino in these hills and we had seen three of them the day before from the Cessna.

The buffalo should be making their way to the rich new feed at the edge of the papyrus swamp. I wanted to count them and to photograph them if it were possible and to locate the huge old bull with the wonderful horns that we had not seen for more than three months. We did not wish to frighten them or let them know we followed them, but only to check on them so that we might photograph them properly and well when Mary came back.

We had intercepted the buffalo and the big herd was moving along below us. There were the proud herd bulls, the big old cows, the young bulls, and the young cows and the calves. I could see the curve of the horns and the heavy corrugations, the dried mud and the worn patches of hide, the heavy moving blackness and the huge grayness and the birds, small and sharp billed and busy as starlings on a lawn. The buffalo moved slowly, feeding as they moved, and behind them the grass was gone and the heavy cattle smell came to us and then we had the flies. I had pulled the shirt over my head and I counted one hundred and twenty-four buffalo. The wind was right so that the buffalo did not get our scent. The birds did not see us because we were higher than they were and only the flies found us, but evidently they did not bear tales.

* * *

It was almost noon and very hot and we did not know it but all our luck lay ahead of us. We rode along through the park country and all of us watched every likely tree. The leopard we were hunting was a trouble leopard that I had been asked to kill by the people of the Shamba where he had killed sixteen goats and I was hunting him for the Game Department so it was permissible to use the car in his pursuit. The leopard, once officially vermin and now Royal Game, had never heard of his promotion and reclassification or he would never have killed the sixteen goats that made him a criminal and put him back in the category where he started. Sixteen goats were too many goats to kill in one night when one goat was all he could eat. Then, too, eight of the goats had belonged to Debba's family.

We came into a very beautiful glade and on our left there was a tall tree with one of its high branches extending on a straight parallel line to the left and another, more shaded branch extending on a straight line to the right. It was a green tree and its top was heavily foliaged.

"There's an ideal tree for leopard," I said to Ngui.

"Ndio," he said very quietly. "And there is a leopard in that tree."

Mthuka had seen us look and though he could not hear us and could not see the leopard from his side he stopped the car. I got out of the car with the old Springfield I had been carrying across my lap and when I was firmly planted on my feet I saw the leopard stretched long and heavy on the high right limb of the tree. His long spotted length was dappled by the shadows of the leaves that moved in the wind. He was sixty feet up in an ideal place to be on this lovely day and he had made a greater mistake than when he killed the sixteen unnecessary goats.

I raised the rifle breathing in once and letting it out and shot very carefully for the point where his neck bulged behind his ear. It was high and an absolute miss and he flattened, long and heavy along the branch, as I shucked the cartridge case out and shot for his shoulder. There was a heavy thunk and he fell in a half circle. His tail was up, his head was up, his back down. His body was curved like a new moon as he fell and he hit the ground with a heavy thump.

Ngui and Mthuka were whacking me on the back and Charo was shaking hands. Pop's gun bearer was shaking hands and crying because the fall of the leopard had been an emotional thing. He was also giving me the secret Kamba hand grip again and again. In a moment I was reloading with my free hand and Ngui, in excitement, had the .577 instead of the shotgun when we advanced carefully to view the body of the sixteen-goat-killing scourge of my father-in-law. The body of the leopard was not there.

There was a depression in the ground where he had hit and the blood spoor, bright and in chunks, led toward a thick island of bush to the left of the tree. It was as thick as the roots of a mangrove swamp and no one was giving me any secret Kamba hand grips now.

"Gentlemen," I said in Spanish. "The situation has radically changed." It had indeed. I knew the drill now having learned it from Pop but every wounded leopard in thick bush is a new wounded leopard. No two will ever act the same except that they will always come and they will come for keeps. That was why I had shot for the base of the head and neck first. But it was too late for postmortems on missed shots now.

The first problem was Charo. He had been mauled by leopards twice and was an old man, nobody knew how old, but certainly old enough to be my father. He was as excited as a hunting dog to go in.

"You keep the fucking hell out of this and get up on top of the car."

"Hapana, Bwana," he said.

"Ndio too bloody ndio," I said.

"Ndio," he said not saying, "Ndio Bwana," which with us was an insult. Ngui had been loading the Winchester 12-gauge pump with SSG, which is buckshot in English. We had never shot anything with SSG and I did not want any jams so I tripped the ejector and filled it with No. 8 birdshot cartridges fresh out of the box and filled my pockets with the rest of the cartridges. At close range a charge of fine shot from a full-choked shotgun is as solid as a ball and I remembered seeing the effect on a human body with the small hole blue black around the edge on the back of the leather jacket and all the load inside the chest.

"Kwenda," I said to Ngui and we started off on the blood spoor, me with the shotgun covering Ngui, who tracked, and Pop's gun bearer back in the car with the .577. Charo had not gotten onto the roof but sat in the rear seat of the car with the best one of the three spears. Ngui and I were on foot and following the blood spoor.

Out of a clot of blood he picked up a sharp bone fragment and passed it to me. It was a piece of shoulder blade and I put it in my mouth. There is no explanation of that. I did it without thinking. But it linked us closer to the leopard and I bit on it and tasted the new blood which tasted about like my own, and knew that the leopard had not just lost his balance. Ngui and I followed the blood spoor until it went into the mangrove root patch of bush. The leaves of this bush were very green and shiny and the trail of the leopard, which had been made with bounds of irregular length, went into it and there was blood low on the leaves, shoulder high where he had crouched as he went in.

Ngui shrugged his shoulders and shook his head. We were both very serious now and there was no White Man to speak softly and knowingly from his great knowledge, nor any White Man to give violent orders astonished at the stupidity of his "boys" and cursing them on like reluctant hounds. There was only one wounded leopard with terrible odds against him who had been shot from the high branch of a tree, suffered a fall no human being could survive and taken his stand in a place where, if he retained his lovely and unbelievable cat vitality he could maim or grievously injure any human being who came in after him. I wished he had never killed the goats and that I had never signed any contracts to kill and be photographed for any national circulation magazines and I bit with satisfaction on the piece of shoulder bone and waved up the car. The sharp end of the splintered bone had cut the inside of my cheek and I could taste the familiarity of my own blood now mixed with the blood of the leopard and I said, "Twendi kwa chui," the statesman's plural imperative, "Let us go to the leopard."

It was not very easy for us to go to the leopard. Ngui had the Springfield 30-06 and he had also the good eyes. Pop's gun bearer had the .577 which would knock him on his ass if he shot it and he had as good eyes as Ngui. I had the old, well-loved, once burnt-up, three times restocked, worn-smooth old Winchester model 12-pump gun that was faster than a snake and was, from thirty-five years of us being together, almost as close a friend and companion with secrets shared and triumphs and disasters not revealed as the other friend a man has all his life. We covered the enlaced and crossed roots of the thicket from the blood spoor entry to the left, or west end where we could see the car around the corner but we could not see the leopard. Then we went back crawling along and looking into the darkness of the roots until we reached the other end. We had not seen the leopard and we crawled back to where the blood was still fresh on the dark green leaves.

Pop's gun bearer was standing up behind us with the big gun ready and I, sitting down now, started to shoot loads of No. 8 shot into the cross-tangled roots traversing from left to right.

At the fifth shot the leopard roared hugely. The roar came from well into the thick bush and a little to the left of the blood on the leaves.

"Can you see him?" I asked Ngui.

"Hapana."

I reloaded the long magazine tube and shot twice fast toward where I had heard the roar. The leopard roared again and then coughed twice.

"Piga tu," I said to Ngui and he shot toward where the roar had come from.

The leopard roared again and Ngui said, "Piga tu."

I shot twice at the roar and Pop's gun bearer said, "I can see him."

We stood up and Ngui could see him but I could not. "Piga tu," I told him.

He said, "Hapana. Twendi kwa chui."

So we went in again but this time Ngui knew where we were going. We could only go in a yard or so but there was a rise in the ground the roots grew out of. Ngui was directing me by tapping my legs on one side or the other as we crawled. Then I saw the leopard's ear and the small spots on the top of the bulge of his neck and his shoulder. I shot where his neck joined his shoulder and shot again and there was no roar and we crawled back out and I reloaded and we three went around the west end of the island of rush to where the car was on the far side.

"Kufa," Charo said. "Mzuri kubwa sana."

"Kufa," Mthuka said. They could both see the leopard but I could not.

They got out of the car and we all moved in and I told Charo to keep back with his spear. But he said, "No. He's dead, Bwana. I saw him die."

I covered Ngui with the shotgun while he cut his way in with a panga slamming at the roots and brush as though they were our enemy or all our enemies and then he and Pop's gun bearer hauled the leopard out and we swung him up into the back of the car. He was a good leopard and we had hunted him well and cheerfully and like brothers with no White Hunters nor Game Rangers and no Game Scouts and he was a Kamba leopard condemned for useless killing on an illegal Kamba Shamba and we were all Wakamba and all thirsty.

Charo was the only one who examined the leopard closely because he had been mauled twice by leopards and he had shown me where the charge of shot at close range had entered almost alongside the first bullet wound in the shoulder. I knew it must have as I knew the roots and the bank had deflected the other shots, but I was only happy and proud of us all

404 • ERNEST HEMINGWAY

and how we had been all day and happy that we would get to camp and to the shade and to cold beer.

We came into camp with the klaxon of the car going and everyone turned out and Keiti was happy and I think he was proud. We all got out of the car and Charo was the only one who stayed to look at the leopard. Keiti stayed with Charo and the skinner took charge of the leopard. We took no photographs of him. Keiti had asked me, "Piga picha?" and I said, "Piga shit."

Ngui and Pop's gun bearer brought the guns to the tent and laid them on Miss Mary's bed and I carried the cameras and hung them up. I told Msembi to put the table out under the tree and bring chairs and to bring all the cold beer and Coca-Cola for Charo. I told Ngui not to bother about cleaning the guns now but to go and get Mthuka; that we would drink formal beer.

Mwindi said that I should take a bath. He would have the water in no time. I said that I would bathe in the washbasin and to please find me my clean shirt.

"You should take big bath," he said.

"I'll take big bath later. I'm too hot."

"How you get all the blood? From chui?"

This was ironic but carefully concealed.

"From tree branches."

"You wash off good with blue soap. I put on the red stuff."

We always used Mercurochrome instead of iodine if we could get it although some Africans preferred iodine since it hurt and so was considered a stronger medicine. I washed and scrubbed the scratches open and clean and Mwindi painted them carefully.

I put on my clean clothes and I knew Mthuka, Ngui, Pop's gun bearer and Charo were putting on their clean clothes.

"Did chui come?"

"No."

"Why everybody make so happy then?"

"Very funny shauri. Very funny hunt all morning."

"Why you want to be African?"

"I'm going to be Kamba."

"Maybe," said Mwindi.

"Fuck maybe."

"Here come your friends."

"Brothers."

"Brothers maybe. Charo not your brother."

"Charo my good friend."

"Yes," Mwindi said sadly, handing me a pair of slippers that he knew were a little tight and watching to see how much they hurt when I put them on. "Charo good friend. Have plenty bad luck?"

"How?"

"Every way. And is a lucky man."

I went out to join the others, who were standing at the table with Msembi in his green robe and green skullcap standing ready with the beer in the faded green canvas bucket. The clouds were very high in the sky and the sky was the highest sky in the world and I looked back over the tent and could see the Mountain high and white above the trees.

"Gentlemen," I said and bowed and we all sat down in the chairs of the Bwanas and Msembi poured the four tall beers and the Coca-Cola of Charo. Charo was the oldest so I ceded to him and Mwindi poured the Coca-Cola first. Charo had changed his turban to one slightly less gray and he wore a blue coat with brass buttons fastened together at the throat with a blanket pin I had given him twenty years before and a natty pair of well-repaired shorts.

When the drinks had been poured I stood up and proposed the toast, "To the Queen." We all drank and then I said, "To Mr. Chui, gentlemen. He is Royal Game." We drank again with propriety and protocol but with enthusiasm. Msembi refilled the glasses this time starting with me and ending with Charo. He had great respect for an elder but it was hard to respect the carbonated beverage against Tusker beer.

"A noi," I said bowing to Ngui who had learned his Italian in the captured brothels of Addis Ababa and from the hurriedly discarded mistresses of an army in flight. I added, "Wakamba rosa e la liberta, Wakamba rosa triomfera."

We drank it off to the bottom of the glasses and Mwindi refilled.

The next toast was a little rough but with the tendency of the times and the need to give our new religion some form of actionable program which could later be channeled toward the highest and noblest end, I proposed, "Tunaua."

We drank this solemnly although I noticed reservations in Charo and when we sat down I said, "Na jehaad tu," trying to win the Moslem vote. But it is a hard vote to win and we all knew he was with us only in the formal beer drinking and the brotherhood and could never be with us in the new religion or the politics.

Msembi came to the table and poured again and said the beer was now quisha and I said this was the hell of a kind of management and that we would saddle up and leave at once for Laitokitok for more beer. We would take some cold meat to eat on the way up and a few tins of kipper snacks. Mthuka said, "Kwenda na Shamba." So we agreed to go to the Shamba and pick up a few bottles of beer if they had any to hold the group until we could reach another brewing Shamba or Laitokitok. Ngui said I should pick up my fiancée and the Widow and that he and Mthuka both were OK with the third Masai Shamba up the road. Pop's gun bearer said he was OK and would be the protector of the Widow. We wanted to take Msembi but we were four and the Widow and my fiancée made six and we did not know what Masai we would run into. There were always plenty of Masai in Laitokitok.

I went over to the tent and Mwindi had the tin trunk open and my old Hong Kong tweed jacket out with the money buttoned in the flapped-down inner pockets.

"How much money you want?" he asked.

"Four hundred shillingi."

"Plenty money," he said. "What you do? Buy a wife?"

"Buy beer, posho maybe, medicine for Shamba, Christmas presents, buy new spear, fill up car with petrol, buy whisky for mtoto of police, buy kippah snacks."

He laughed at the kippah snacks. "Take five hundred," he said. "You want hard shillingi too?"

Hard shillingi were kept in a leather pouch. He counted me out thirty and asked, "You wear good coat?"

The coat he liked me to wear best was a sort of hacking coat which had also come from Hong Kong.

"No. Wear leather coat. Take leather zip-up."

"Take woollie too. Cold come down from Mountain."

"Dress me as you wish," I said. "But put the boots on very easy."

He had clean washed cotton socks and I put them on and he worked the feet into the boots and left them open without pulling up the zippers at the sides. Ngui came into the tent. He was wearing his clean shorts and a new sport shirt that I had never seen. I told him that we would only take the 30-06 and he said he had ammo. He wiped the big gun clean and put it under the cot. It had not been fired and the Springfield had been shooting with non-corrosive primers and could be cleaned at night.

"Pistol," he said severely and I poked my right leg through the loop at the end of the holster and he buckled the big belt around my waist.

"Jinny flask," Mwindi said and handed the heavy Spanish leather shell pannier to Ngui.

"Money?" Ngui asked.

"Hapana," I said. "Money kwisha."

"Too much money," Mwindi said. He had

the key with which he had locked the tin trunk
where he kept the money.

We went out to the car. Keiti was still benev-
olent and I asked him formally what was needed
for the outfit. He said to bring a sack of posho if
there was any of the good kind that came on the
stage from Kajiado. He looked sad when we left
and his head hung a little forward and to one
side although he was smiling the slit smile.

I felt sad and wrong that I had not asked him
if he wanted to go and then we were on the road
to the Shamba. It was a well-worn road by now
and it would be worn more before this is over, I
thought.

14

MTHUKA HAD no finery except a clean shirt with a checked pattern and his washed trousers with the patches. Pop's gun bearer had a yellow sport shirt with no figured pattern and it went very well with Ngui's, which was muleta-colored red. I was sorry that I was dressed so conservatively but since I had shaved my head the day before after the plane had left and then forgotten all about it I felt that I must have a certain baroque appearance if I removed my cap. When shaved, or even clipped closely enough, my head, unfortunately, has much the appearance of some plastic history of a very lost tribe. It is in no way as spectacular as the Great Rift Valley but there are historical features of terrain which could interest both archaeologist and anthropologist. I did not know how Debba would take it but I had an old fishing cap on with long slanted visor and I was not worried about nor concerned with my appearance when we drove into the Shamba and stopped in the shade of the big tree.

Mthuka, I found later, had sent Nguili, the young boy who wanted to be a hunter but was working as second mess attendant, ahead to warn the Widow and my fiancée that we would be coming by to take them to Laitokitok to buy the dresses for the Birthday of the Baby Jesus. This boy was still a nanake in Kamba and so could not drink beer legally but he had made the trip very fast to show that he could run and he was sweating happily against the trunk of the big tree and trying not to breathe hard.

I got out of the car to stretch my legs and to thank the nanake.

"You run better than a Masai," I said.

"I am Kamba," he said, trying hard to breathe without strain and I could imagine how the pennies tasted in his mouth.

"Do you want to go up the Mountain?"

"Yes. But it would not be proper and I have my duty."

Just then the Informer joined us. He was wearing the paisley and he walked with great dignity, balanced on his heels.

"Good afternoon, brother," he said and I saw Ngui turn away and spit at the word brother.

"Good afternoon, Informer," I said. "How is your health?"

"Better," said the Informer. "Can I go with you up the Mountain?"

"You cannot."

"I can serve as interpreter."

"I have an interpreter on the Mountain."

The child of the Widow came up and bumped his head hard against my belly. I kissed the top of his head and he put his hand in mine and stood up very straight.

"Informer," I said. "I cannot ask beer from my father-in-law. Please bring us beer."

"I will see what beer there is."

If you liked Shamba beer it was all right, tasting like home brew in Arkansas in the time of Prohibition. There was a man who was a shoemaker and who had fought very well in the First World War who brewed a very similar beer that we used to drink in the front parlor of his house. My fiancée and the Widow came out and my fiancée got into the car and sat beside Mthuka. She kept her eyes down except for short triumphant looks at the other women of the village and wore a dress that had been washed too many times and a very beautiful trade goods scarf over her head. The Widow seated herself between Ngui and Pop's gun bearer. We sent the Informer for six more bottles of beer but there were only four in the village. I gave these four bottles to my father-in-law. Debba looked at no one but sat very straight with her breasts pointing at the same angle as her chin.

Mthuka started the car and we were off leaving the village, all people who were jealous or disapproved, many children, the goats, the nursing mothers, the chickens, the dogs and my father-in-law.

"Que tal, tu?" I asked Debba.

"En la puta gloria."

This was the second phrase that she liked best in Spanish. It is a strange phrase and no two people would translate it alike.

"Did the chui hurt you?"

"No. There was nothing."

"Was he big?"

"Not very."

"Did he roar?"

"Many times."

"Did he not hurt anyone?"

"No one. Not even you."

She was pressing the carved leather pistol holster hard against her thigh and then she placed her left hand where she wanted it to be.

"Mimi bili chui," she said. Neither of us were Swahili scholars but I remembered the two leopards of England and someone must have known about leopards a long time ago.

"Bwana," Ngui said and his voice had the same harshness that came from love or anger or tenderness.

"Wakamba, tu," I said. He laughed and broke the rough bad thing.

"We have three bottles of Tuskah that Msembi stole for us."

"Thank you. When we make the big rise we'll turn off and eat the kippah snack."

"Good cold meat," Ngui said.

"Mzuri," I said.

There is no homosexuality among Wakamba people. In the old days homosexuals after the trial of King-ole, which Mwindi had explained to me meant when you gathered together formally to kill a man, were condemned, tied in the river or any water hole for a few days to make them more tender and then killed and eaten. This would be a sad fate for many playwrights, I thought. But, on the other hand and if you have another hand you are lucky in Africa, it was considered very bad luck to eat any part of a homosexual even though he had been tenderized in the Athi in a clean and nearly clear pool and according to some of my older friends a homosexual tasted worse than a water buck and could bring out sores on any part of the body but especially in the groin or in the armpits. Intercourse with animals was also punishable by death although it was not regarded as so fouling a practice as homosexuality and Mkola, who was Ngui's father, since I had proved mathematically that I could not be, had told me that a man who had rogered his sheep or his goats was as tasty as a wildebeest. Keiti and Mwindi would not eat wildebeest but that was a part of anthropology that I had not yet penetrated. And as I was thinking of these facts and confidences and caring greatly for Debba who was a straight Kamba girl replete with modesty and true basic insolence, Mthuka stopped the car under a tree where we could see the great gap and break in the country and the small tin-roofed shine of Laitokitok against the blue of the forest on the Mountain which rose white-sloped and square-topped to give us our religion and our long and lasting hope while behind was all our country spread out as though we were in the aircraft but without the movement, the stress and the expense.

"Jambo, tu," I said to Debba and she said, "La puta gloria."

We let her and the Widow, who had been very happy between Ngui and Pop's gun bearer in the red-and-yellow shirts and with the black arms and the delicate legs, open the tins of kipper snacks and the two tins of false salmon from Holland. They could not open them properly and one key was broken but Mthuka used a pliers to bend the tin back exposing the false smoked salmon that was Holland's glory in Africa and we all ate, exchanging knives, and drinking from the same bottles. Debba wiped the neck of the bottle and its lips the first time she drank using her head cloth but I told her that one man's chancre was every man's chancre and after that we drank without ceremony. The beer was warmer than it was cool but at eight thousand feet and with the country we looked back over and the places we could see now as though we were eagles, it was lovely beer and we finished it with the cold meat. We kept the bottles to trade in and piled the tins together, removing the keys, and left them under a heather bush close to the trunk of the tree.

There were no Game Scouts along so there were no people who had sold their Wakamba heritage to denounce their brothers and no worship of Miss Mary and the hangman or the puppies of the police so that we were free in a way and we looked back at the country where no white woman had ever been, including Miss Mary, unless it counted when we had taken her, unwillingly but with the excitement of children, onto the deck where she had never belonged nor known how its penalties equalized its small glories.

So we looked back at our country and at the Chulu hills which were as blue and strange as ever and we were all happy that Miss Mary had never been there and then we went back into the car and I said to Debba, stupidly, "You will be an intelligent wife," and she, intelligently, took hold of my place and of the well-loved holster and said, "I am as good a wife now as I will ever be."

I kissed her on the crinkly head and we went on up the beautiful road that swung strangely and curved up the Mountain. The tin-roofed town was still glistening in the sun and as we came closer we could see the eucalyptus trees and the formal road that, heavily shaded and with Britannic might, ran up to the small fort and jail and the rest houses where the people who participate in the administration of British justice and paperwork come to take their rest when they are too poor to return to their home country. We were not going up to disturb their rest even though it meant missing the sight of the rock gardens and the tumbling stream that, much later, became the river.

It had been a long hunt for Miss Mary's lion and all except fanatics, converts and true believers in Miss Mary had been tired of it for a long time. Charo, who was none of these, had said to me, "Shoot the lion when she shoots and get it over with." I had shaken my head because I was not a believer but a follower and had made the pilgrimage to Campostella and it had been worth it. But Charo shook his head in disgust. He was a Moslem and there were no Moslems with us today. We needed no one to cut the throats of anything and we were all looking for our new religion which had its first station of whatever cross there was to be outside of Benji's General Store. This station was a gas pump and it was inside the store that Debba and the Widow would select the cloth to make their dresses for the Birthday of the Baby Jesus.

It was not proper for me to go in with her although I loved the different cloths and the smells of the place and the Masai that we knew, the wanawaki, eager and unbuying with their cuckolded husbands up the street drinking Golden Jeep sherry from South Africa with a spear in one hand and the bottle of Golden Jeep in the other. They were cuckolded standing on one leg or on two and I knew where they would be and walked down the right side of the narrow tree-shaded street that was still wider than our wingtips as everyone who lived on it or walked it knew and I walked hurt footed and, I hoped, not insolent nor pistol proud down to the Masai drinking place where I said, "Sopa," and shook a few cold hands and went out without drinking. Eight paces to the right, I turned into Mr. Singh's. Mr. Singh and I embraced and Mrs. Singh and I shook hands and then I kissed her hand, which always pleased her since she was a Turkana and I had learned to kiss hands quite well and it was like a voyage to Paris which she had never heard of but would have ornamented on the clearest day Paris ever had. Then I sent for the Mission-trained Interpreter.

"How are you Singh?" I asked with the Interpreter.

"Not bad. Here. Doing business."

"And beautiful Madame Singh?"

"Four months until the baby."

"Felicidades," I said and kissed Madame Singh's hand again using the style of Alvarito Caro then Marques of Villamayor, a town we had once entered but been forced out of.

"All young Singhs are well I hope?"

"All are well except the third boy, who has a cut on the hand from the sawmill."

"You want me to look at it?"

"They treated him at the Mission. With sulfa."

"Excellent for children. But it destroys the kidneys of old men like you and me."

Mrs. Singh laughed her honest Turkana laugh and Mr. Singh said, "I hope your Memsahib is well. That your children are well and all the aircraft are well."

The Interpreter said, in good condition, in the reference to aircraft and I asked him not to be pedantic.

"The Memsahib, Miss Mary, is in Nairobi. She has gone in the aircraft and will return with the aircraft. All of my children are well. God permitting all aircraft are well."

"We have heard the news," Mr. Singh said. "The lion and the leopard."

"Anyone can kill a lion and a leopard."

"But the lion was from Miss Mary."

"Naturally," I said; pride rising in me of beautifully sculptured, compact, irascible and lovely Miss Mary with the head like an Egyptian coin, the breasts from Rubens and the heart from Bemidji, or Walker or Thief River Falls, any town where it was forty-five below zero in the winter. It was a temperature to make warm hearts that also could be cold.

"With Miss Mary there is no problem with a lion."

"But it was a difficult lion. Many have suffered from this lion."

"The Great Singh strangled them with either hand," I said. "Miss Mary was using a 6.5 Mannlicher."

"That is a small gun for such a lion," said Mr. Singh and I knew then he had done his military service. So I waited for him to lead.

He was too smart to lead and Madame Singh said, "And the leopard?"

"Any man should be able to kill a leopard before breakfast."

"You will eat something?"

"With Madame's permission."

"Please eat," she said. "It is nothing."

"We will go in the back room. You have drunk nothing."

"We can drink together now if you wish."

The Interpreter came in the back room and Mr. Singh brought a bottle of White Heather and a jug of water. The Interpreter took off his Mission shoes to show me his feet.

"I have only worn the shoes when we were in sight of the informers of religion," he explained. "I have never spoken of the Baby Jesus except with contempt. I have not said my morning prayers nor my evening prayers."

"What else?"

"Nothing."

"You rank as a negative convert," I said. He pushed his head hard against my belly as the Widow's son did.

"Think of the Mountain and of the Happy Hunting Grounds. We may need the Baby Jesus. Never speak of him with disrespect. What tribe are you?"

"The same as you."

"No. What are you written as?"

"Masai-Chagga. We are the border."

"There have been good men from the borders."

"Yes, sir."

"Never say sir in our religion or our tribe."

"No."

"How were you when you were circumcised?"

"Not the best, but good."

"Why did you become a Christian?"

"Through ignorance."

"You could be worse."

"I would never be a Moslem," and started to add sir but I checked him.

"It is a long strange road and maybe you had better throw the shoes away. I will give you a good old pair and you can mold them to your feet."

"Thank you. Can I fly in the aircraft?"

"Of course. But it is not for children nor Mission boys."

Then I would have said I am sorry but there is no such word in Swahili nor in Kamba and it is a just way of conducting a language since you are warned not to make errors.

The Interpreter asked me about the scratches and I said that they were from thorn trees and Mr. Singh nodded and showed the Interpreter where his thumb had been cut by the saw in September. It was an impressive cut and I remembered when it had happened.

"But you also fought with a leopard today," the Interpreter said.

"There was no fight. It was a medium-sized

leopard who had killed sixteen goats at the Kamba Shamba. He died without making a fight."

"Everyone said you had fought him with your hands and killed him with the pistol."

"Everyone is a liar. We killed the leopard first with a rifle and then with a shotgun."

"But a shotgun is for birds."

Mr. Singh laughed at this and I wondered some more about him.

"You are a very good Mission boy," I said to the Interpreter. "But shotguns are not always for birds."

"But in principle. That is why you say gun instead of rifle."

"And what would a fucking babu say?" I asked Mr. Singh in English.

"A babu would be in a tree," Mr. Singh said, speaking English for the first time.

"I am very fond of you Mr. Singh," I said. "And I respect your great ancestor."

"I respect all of your great ancestors although you have not named them."

"They were nothing."

"I shall hear of them at the proper time," Mr. Singh said. "Should we drink? The woman, the Turkana, brings more food."

The Interpreter now was avid for knowledge and the scent of it was breast high and he was half Chagga and had a low but strong chest.

"In the library at the Mission there is a book which says the great Carl Akeley killed a leopard with his bare hands. Can I believe that?"

"If you like."

"I ask truly as a boy who wishes to know."

"It was before my time. Many men have asked the same question."

"But I need to know the truth."

"There is very little of it in books. But the great Carl Akeley was a great man."

You could not break him away from scent of knowledge since you had sought it all your life and had to be content with facts, coordinates and statements vouchsafed in drunkenness or taken under duress. This boy, who had removed his shoes and rubbed his feet on the wooden floor of Mr. Singh's back parlor and was so intent on knowledge that he did not know that Mr. Singh and I were embarrassed by his public foot hardening, moved in, as unshod as a hunting dog, from plane geometry to something far beyond calculus.

"Can you justify a European taking an African as his mistress?"

"We don't justify. That is the function of the judiciary. Steps are taken by the police."

"Please do not quibble," he said. "Excuse me, sir."

"Sir is a nicer word than Bwana. At one time it had a certain meaning."

426 • ERNEST HEMINGWAY

"Can you then condone, sir, such a relation-ship?"

"If a girl loves the man and there is no coer-cion, to me it is not a sin if adequate provision is made for the issue per stirpes and not per capita."

This came like an unexpected block and I was as pleased as Mr. Singh that I could throw it with no change of pace. He fell back on the basic that he had been crammed on.

"It is a sin in the Eyes of God."

"Do you carry Him with you and what type of drops do you use to ensure His clearest vision?"

"Please do not make fun of me, sir. I left every-thing behind me when I entered your service."

"I have no service. We are the last free indi-viduals in a country slightly larger than Con-necticut and we believe in a very abused slogan."

"May I hear the slogan?"

"Slogans are a bore, Mission boy. . . . Life, liberty and the pursuit of happiness." Then to take the curse off having offered a slogan and because Mr. Singh was becoming solemn and ready to reenlist I said, "Harden your feet well as you are doing. Keep your bowels open and remember that there is some corner of a foreign field that shall be forever England."

He could not quit which might have been his Chagga blood or might have been the Masai strain and he said, "But you are an officer of the Crown."

"Technically and temporarily. What do you want? The Queen's shilling?"

"I would like to take it, sir."

It was a little bit rough to do but knowledge is rougher and more poorly compensated. I took the hard shillingi out of my pocket and put it in the boy's hand. Our Queen looked very beautiful and shining in silver and I said, "Now you are an informer; no that is wrong," because I saw Mr. Singh had been hurt by the dirty word. "Now you are commissioned as a temporary interpreter for the Game Department and will be remunerated at the stipend of seventy shillings per month in so long as I hold the tenure of acting temporary Game Ranger. On the cessation of my tenure your appointment shall cease and you will receive a gratuity of seventy shillings from the date of ceasing of tenure. This gratuity will be paid from my own private funds and you hereby avow that you have no claims of any sort nor any possible future claims against the Game Department nor any other, etc., and may God have mercy on your soul. The gratuity shall be made in a single payment. What is your name, young man?"

"Nathaniel."

"You will be known in the Game Department as Peter."

"It is an honorable name, sir."

"No one asked for your comments and your duties are strictly confined to accurate and complete interpretation when as and if you are called on. Your contact will be with Arap Meina, who will give you any further instructions. Do you wish to draw any advance?"

"No, sir."

"Then you might go now and toughen your feet in the hills behind town."

"Are you angry with me, sir?"

"Not at all. But when you grow up you may discover that the Socratic method of acquiring knowledge is overrated and if you ask people no questions they will tell you no lies."

"Good day, Mr. Singh," the former convert said, donning his shoes in case there was a spy from the Mission about. "Good day, sir."

Mr. Singh nodded and I said, "Good day."

When the young man had gone out of the back door and Mr. Singh had drifted toward the door almost absentmindedly and then returned to pour another drink of White Heather and pass me the water in the cooling jug, he settled himself comfortably and said, "Another bloody babu."

"But not a shit."

"No," Mr. Singh said. "But you waste your time on him."

"Why did we never speak English together before?"

"From respect," Mr. Singh said.

"Did the original Singh, your ancestor, speak English?"

"I would not know," Mr. Singh said. "That was before my time."

"What was your rank, Mr. Singh?"

"Do you wish my serial number as well?"

"I'm sorry," I said. "And it is your whisky. But you put up with Unknown Tongue for a long time."

"It was a pleasure," Mr. Singh said. "I learned much Unknown Tongue. If you like, I would be very happy to enter your service as an unpaid volunteer," Mr. Singh said. "At present I am informing for three government services none of whom coordinate their information nor have any proper liaison."

"Things are not always exactly as they seem and it is an Empire which has been functioning for a long time."

"Do you admire the way it functions now?"

"I am a foreigner and a guest and I do not criticize."

"Would you like me to inform for you?"

"With carbons furnished of all other information delivered."

"There are no carbons or oral information unless you have a tape recorder. Do you have a tape recorder?"

"Not with me."

"You could hang half Laitokitok with four tape recorders."

"I have no desire to hang half Laitokitok."

"Neither do I. And who would buy at the duka?"

"Mr. Singh, if we did things properly we would perpetrate an economic disaster but now I must go up to where we left the car."

"I will walk with you if you don't mind. Three paces to the rear and on your left."

"Please don't trouble yourself."

"It is no trouble."

I said good-bye to Mrs. Singh and told her we would be by with the car to pick up three cases of Tusker and a case of Coca-Cola and walked out into the lovely main and only street of Laitokitok.

Towns with only one street make the same feeling as a small boat, a narrow channel, the headwaters of a river or the trail up over a pass. Sometimes Laitokitok, after the swamp and the different broken countries and the desert and the forbidden Chulu hills, seemed an important

Capital and on other days it seemed like the Rue Royale. Today it was straight Laitokitok with overtones of Cody, Wyoming, or Sheridan, Wyoming, in the old days. With Mr. Singh, it was a relaxed and pleasant walk which we both enjoyed and in front of Benji's with the gas pump, the wide steps like a Western general store and the many Masai standing around the hunting break. I stopped by it and told Mwengi I would stay with the rifle while he went to shop or drink. He said no that he would rather stay with the rifle. So I went up the steps and into the crowded store. Debba and the Widow were there still looking at cloth, Mthuka helping them, and turning down pattern after pattern. I hated shopping and the rejection of materials and I went to the far end of the long L-shaped counter and began to buy medicines and soaps. When these were stacked into a box I began to buy tinned goods; mostly kipper snacks, sardines, silts, tinned shrimp and various types of false salmon along with a number of tins of local tinned meat which were intended as a gift for my father-in-law and then I bought two tins each of every type of fish exported from South Africa including one variety labeled simply FISH. Then I bought half a dozen tins of Cape Spiny Lobster and, remembering we were short of Sloan's liniment, bought a bottle of that and one half dozen cakes of Lifebuoy soap. By this time there was a crowd of Masai watching this purchasing. Debba looked down and smiled proudly. She and the Widow could still not make up their minds and there were not more than a half a dozen rolls of cloth to be inspected.

Mthuka came down the counter and told me the car had been filled up and that he had found the good posho that Keiti wanted. I gave him a hundred-shilling note and told him to pay for the girls' purchases.

"Tell them to buy two dresses," I said. "One for the cambia and one for the Birthday of the Baby Jesus." Mthuka knew that no woman needed two new dresses. She needed her old one and the new one. But he went down and told the girls in Kikamba and Debba and the Widow looked down, all impudence replaced by a shining reverence as though I had just invented electricity and the lights had gone on over all of Africa. I did not meet their look but continued purchasing, now moving into the field of hard candies, bottled, and the various types of chocolate bars both nutted and plain.

By this time I did not know how the money was standing up but we did have the gas in the car and the posho and I told the relative of the owner who was serving behind the counter to load everything and box it carefully and I would

return to pick it up with the bill. This gave
Debba and the Widow more time to select and I
would drive the hunting car down to Mr.
Singh's and pick up the bottled products.

Ngui had gone to Mr. Singh's. He had found
the dye powder we wanted to dye my shirts and
hunting vests Masai color and he and I drank a
bottle of Tusker and took one out to Mwengi in
the car. Mwengi had the duty but next time it
would be different.

In the presence of Ngui Mr. Singh and I again
conversed in Unknown Tongue and non–flying
pigeon Swahili.

Ngui asked me in Kamba how I would like to
bang Mrs. Singh and I was delighted to see that
either Mr. Singh was a very great actor or that
he had not had the time or opportunity to learn
Kamba.

"Kwisha maru," I said to Ngui, which
seemed sound double talk.

"Buona notte," he said and we clinked bottles.

"Piga tu."

"Piga tu."

"Piga chui, tu," Ngui explained just a little
beerily, I thought, to Mr. Singh, who bowed in
congratulations and indicated that these three
bottles were on the house.

"Never," I said in Hungarian. "Nem, nem,
soha."

Mr. Singh said something in Unknown Tongue and I made signs that he give me the bill, which he proceeded to write out, and I said to Ngui, in Spanish, "Vámonos. Ya es tarde."

"Avanti Savoia," he said. "Nunaua."

"You are a bastard," I said.

"Hapana," he said. "Blood brother."

So we loaded up with the help of Mr. Singh and several of his sons. It was understandable that the Interpreter could not help since no Mission boy could be seen carrying a case of beer. But he looked so sad and he was so obviously troubled by the word nunaua that I asked him to carry the case of Coca-Cola.

"May I ride with you when you drive?"

"Why not?"

"I could have stayed and watched the rifle."

"You don't start on your first day watching the rifle."

"I am sorry. I meant only that I could have relieved your Kamba brother."

"How do you know he is my brother?"

"You addressed him as brother."

"He's my brother."

"I have much to learn."

"Never let it get you down," I said laying the car alongside of Benji's front steps where the Masai who wanted to ride down the Mountain were waiting.

"Fuck 'em all," said Ngui. This was the only English phrase he knew or at least the only one he used, since for some time English had been considered the language of the hangman, government officials, civil servants and Bwanas in general. It was a beautiful language but it was becoming a dead language in Africa and it was tolerated but not approved. Since Ngui, who was my brother, had used it I used it in return and said, "the long and the short and the tall."

He looked at the importuning Masai that had he been born in the older times which were still within the span of my life, he would have enjoyed dining on, and said in Kamba, "All tall."

"Interpreter," I said and corrected to say, "Peter, will you be so good as to go into the duka and tell my brother Mthuka that we are ready to load?"

"How will I know your brother?"

"He is Kamba tu."

Ngui did not approve of the Interpreter nor of his shoes and he was already moving with the compact insolence of an unarmed Kamba through the spear-carrying Masai who had gathered hopeful of a ride, their positive Wassermanns not flying like banners from the spear shafts.

Finally everyone came out and the purchases

were loaded. I stepped out to let Mthuka take the wheel and to let Debba and the Widow in and to pay the bill. I made the bill with ten shillings to spare and I could see Mwindi's face when I came home with no money. He was not only the Secretary of the Treasury but also my self-appointed conscience.

"How many Masai can we take?" I asked Mthuka.

"Kamba only and six others."

"Too many."

"Four others."

So we loaded with Ngui and Mwengi choosing and Debba very excited and stiffly proud and unlooking. We were three in the front seat and five in the back with Kamba only and the Widow riding with Ngui and Mwengi and four second favorites seated on the sacks of posho and the purchases in the rear. We might have taken two more but there were two bad places in the road where the Masai always became seasick.

We came down the hill which was the term we used for the lower slope of the big Mountain and Ngui was opening the beer bottles which are as important in Wakamba life as any other sacrament. I asked Debba how she was. It had been a long and, in some ways, a hard day, and with the shopping and the change of altitude and the curves she had more than a full right to feel any way she was. The plain was laid out before us now and all the features of the terrain and she took hold of the carved holster of the pistol and said, "En la puta gloria."

"Yo también," I said and asked Mthuka for snuff. He passed it to me and I passed it to Debba who passed it back to me, not taking any. It was very good snuff; not as powerful as that of Arap Meina but enough snuff to let you know you had snuff when you tucked it under your upper lip. Debba could not take snuff but she passed the box, in her pride and in our descent of the hill, to the Widow. It was excellent Kajiado snuff and the Widow took it and passed it back to Debba who gave it to me and I returned it to Mthuka.

"You don't take snuff?" I asked Debba. I knew the answer and it was stupid of me and the first undelighting thing that we had done all day.

"I cannot take snuff," she said. "I am unmarried to you and I cannot take snuff."

There was nothing to say about this so we did not say anything and she put her hand back on the holster which she truly loved, it having been carved better in Denver than anyone had ever been carved or tattooed, by Heiser & Company, in a beautiful flowered design which had been worn smooth with saddle soap and lightened and destroyed by sweat, still faintly incrusted from the morning of this day, and she said, "I have all of you in the pistol."

And I said something very rude. Between Kamba there is always impudence by the woman carried into insolence and far past it if there is no love. Love is a terrible thing that you would not wish on your neighbor and as, in all countries, it is a moveable feast. Fidelity does not exist nor ever is implied except at the first marriage. Fidelity by the husband that is. This was the first marriage and I had little to offer except what I had. This was little but not unimportant and neither of us lived with any doubts at all.

15

IT TURNED OUT to be rather a quiet evening. In the tent Debba did not wish to bathe and neither did the Widow. They were afraid of Mwindi, who had to bring the hot water, and they were afraid of the large green canvas tub on its six legs. This was understandable and understood.

We had dropped some people off at the Masai Manyattas and we were past the bravado stage and things, in the dark and in a definite place, were a little bit rough and there was no repeal nor any thought of any. I had told the Widow to leave but since I was protecting her I did not know whether, under Kamba law, she had the right to be there. Any rights she had under Kamba law I was prepared to grant her and she was a very nice and delicate woman with good manners.

The Informer had turned up during the period of unquietness and both Debba and I had seen him steal the bottle of lion fat. It was in an empty bottle of the Grand MacNish and both Debba and I knew that it had been adulterated with eland fat by Ngui before he and I had decided to be brothers. It was like eighty-six proof whisky instead of one hundred proof and we came awake to see him steal it and she laughed very happily, she always laughed happily, and said, "Chui tu," and I said, "No hay remedio."

"La puta gloria," she said. We did not have a great vocabulary and were not great conversationalists and had no need for an interpreter except on Kamba law and we went to sleep for one or two minutes with the Widow, fiercely, on guard. She had seen the Informer steal the off-shape bottle with the too white lion fat that we all knew well and it had been her cough which had called our attention.

At this time I called Msembi, the good rough boy who served as mess steward and was a hunting, not a crop-raising Kamba but was not a skilled hunter and was reduced, since the war, to servant status. We were all servants since I served the government, through the Game Department, and I also served Miss Mary and a magazine named *Look*. My service to Miss Mary had been terminated, temporarily, with the death of her lion. My service to *Look* had been terminated, temporarily; I had hoped permanently. I was wrong of course. But neither Msembi nor I minded serving in the least and neither of us had served our God nor our King too well to be stuffy about it.

The only laws are tribal laws and I was a Mzee which means an elder as well as still having the status of a warrior. It is difficult to be both and the older Mzees resent the irregularity of the position. You should give up something, or anything if necessary, and not try to hold everything. I had learned this lesson in a place called the Schnee Eifel where it had been necessary to move from an offensive to a defensive position. You give up what you have won at great cost as though it had not cost a dime and you become eminently defensible. It is hard to do and many times you should be shot for doing it; but you should be shot quicker if you did not make the adjustment.

So I had told Msembi that he would serve dinner in one half of an hour in the mess tent and that plates would be laid for Debba, the Widow and myself. He was completely delighted and full of Kamba energy and malice and went off to give the order. Unfortunately that was not how it turned out. Debba was brave and la puta gloria is a better place than most people ever reach or attain. The Widow knew it was a rough order and she knew that no one ever took Africa in a day nor on any given night. But that was the way it was going to be.

Keiti killed it in the name of his loyalty to the

Bwanas, to the tribe and to the Moslem religion. He had the courage and the good taste not to delegate to anyone his order and he knocked on the tent pole and asked if we might speak. I might have said no, but I am a disciplined boy. Not with twelve of the best as Pop disciplined but with the implacable discipline of all of our lives. He said, "You have no right to take the young girl violently. [In this he was wrong. There had never been any violence, ever.] This could make great trouble."

"All right," I said. "You speak for all the Mzees?"

"I am the eldest."

"Then tell your son who is older than I am to bring the hunting car."

"He is not here," Keiti said and we knew about that and his lack of authority over his children and why Mthuka was not a Moslem but it was too complicated for me.

"I will drive the car," I said. "It is not a very difficult thing."

"Please take the young girl home to her family. I will go with you if you like."

"I will take the young girl, the Widow and the Informer."

Mwindi was standing, in his green robe and cap, beside Keiti now since it was torture for Keiti to speak English.

Msembi had no business there but he loved Debba as we all did. She was feigning sleep and she was the wife that we would all wish to purchase, all of us knowing we would never own anything that we had bought.

Msembi had been a soldier and the two heavy elders knew this and were not unconscious of their treason when they became Moslems and, since everyone becomes an elder eventually, he threw quick against their complacence and with the true African litigational sense, using titles, which had been abolished, and his own knowledge of Kamba law, "Our Bwana can keep the Widow since she has a son and he protects her officially."

Keiti nodded and Mwindi nodded.

Putting an end to it and feeling too bad about Debba who in her sense of glory had eaten the meal and slept the night as we were not permitted to sleep but as we slept so many times without the judgment of the splendid elders who had attained their rank uniquely, no, that was not just, by seniority, I said, to the interior of the tent, "No hay remedio. Kwenda na Shamba."

This was the beginning of the end of the day in my life which offered the most chances of happiness.

16

HAVING ACCEPTED the decision of the elders and driven Debba, the Widow and the Informer home to the Shamba where I left her with the things that I had bought for her I returned to camp. The things that I had bought made a difference and they did both have the cloth for their dresses. I would not speak to my father-in-law and gave him no explanations and we all acted as though we were returning, a little late perhaps, from a purchasing expedition. I had seen the bulge of the Grand MacNish bottle containing the adulterated lion fat wrapped in the Informer's paisley shawl but that meant nothing. We had better lion fat than that and would have better if we wished and there is no minor satisfaction comparable to have anyone, from a writer on up, and up is a long way, steal from you and think that they have not been detected. With writers you must never let them know since it might break their hearts if they had them and some have them and who should judge another man's cardiac performance unless

you are in competition? With the Informer it
was another matter, involving, as it did, his
degree of loyalty which was already in dispute.
Keiti hated the Informer, with considerable
cause, since he had served under Keiti in the old
days and they had many old unresolved things
dating from when the Informer had served as a
lorry driver and off-ended Keiti with, then,
youthful insolence and with treasonable frank-
ness about the great nobleman who was, by
other accounts than the Informer's, a backward
man. Keiti had loved Pop ever since he had
taken service under him and with the Kamba
hatred of homosexuality he could not tolerate a
Masai lorry driver impugning a White Man and
especially one of such renown and when the bad
boys painted the lips of the statue that had been
erected to this man with lipstick, as they did
each night in Nairobi, Keiti would not look at it
when he rode past. Charo, who was a more
devout Moslem than Keiti, would look at it and
laugh the way we all did. But when Keiti had
taken the Queen's shilling he had taken it for
always. He was a true Victorian and the rest of
us, who had been Edwardians and then Georgians and Edwardians for a brief period again
only to become Georgians and now were
frankly and completely Elizabethans within our
capacity to serve and our tribal loyalties, had lit-

tle in common with Keiti's Victorianism. On this night I felt so badly that I did not wish to be personal nor think about any personal things and especially not to be unjust with someone that I admired and respected. But I knew Keiti was more shocked that Debba and the Widow and I should eat together at the table in the mess tent than he was worried about Kamba law because he was a grown man with five wives of his own and a beautiful young wife and who was he to administer our morals or lack of them?

Driving along in the night, trying not to be bitter, and thinking of Debba and our arbitrary deprivation of formal happiness which could have been overlooked by anyone regardless of their seniority, I thought of turning off to the left and going down that red road to the other Shamba where I would find two of our group and not Lot's nor Potiphar's, but a Masai wife and see if we could parlay yaws into true love. But that was not the thing to do either so I drove home and parked the car and sat in the mess tent and read Simenon. Msembi felt terribly about it but he and I were not conversationalists either.

He made one very gallant suggestion: that he would go with our lorry driver and bring the Widow. I said hapana to that and read some more Simenon.

Msembi kept feeling worse all the time and had no Simenon to read and his next suggestion was that he and I should go with the car and get the girl. He said it was a Kamba custom and there was nothing to be paid but a fine. Besides he said the Shamba was illegal; no one was qualified to bring us to trial and I had made my father-in-law many presents as well as having killed a leopard for him on this same day.

I thought this over and decided against it. Some time before I had paid the tribal price to sleep in the bed of my mother-in-law which is a rough thing to do. How was Keiti to know this? He was supposed to know everything but the outfit we had built up was very taut and just possibly rougher than he knew. I was not sure about this since I respected and admired him so especially since Magadi. He had tracked there, when he had no need to and with both his snakes out above his cheekbones and under his turban until I was beat and Ngui was having difficulty. He had done this tracking in a heat of one hundred and five degrees Fahrenheit in the shade on the good thermometer in camp and the only shade we had was when I, beat, would take a break under a small tree, taking the shade as a great gift breathing deeply and trying to compute how many miles we were from campi; that fabulous place with the wonderful shade of the fig trees and the rippling stream and the water bags sweating cool.

Keiti had whipped us on that day with no ostentation and I did not respect him without cause. But tonight I still was not sure why he had intervened. They always do it for your own good. But I knew one thing: Msembi and I should not go back as rummies do and resume the exercise.

Africans are not supposed to ever feel bad about anything. This is an invention of the whites who are temporarily occupying the country. Africans are said not to feel pain because they do not cry out, that is some of them do not. Yet not showing pain when it is received is a tribal thing and a great luxury. While we in America had television, motion pictures and expensive wives always with soft hands, grease on their faces at night and the natural, not the ranch, mink coat somewhere under refrigeration with a ticket like a pawnbroker's to get it out; the African, of the better tribes, had the luxury of not showing pain. We, Moi, as Ngui called us, had never known true hardship except in war which is a boring, nomadic life with the occasional compensations of combat and the pleasure of looting given as a bone is thrown to a dog by a master who cares nothing for him. We, Moi, who at this moment were

Msembi and myself had known what it was to sack a town and we both knew, although the subject was never to be talked about but only shared secretly, what the mechanics and the procedure was to implement what the Bible phrase meant when they put the men to the sword and carried the women into captivity. This was no longer done but anyone who had done it was a brother. Good brothers are difficult to find but you can encounter a bad brother in any town.

The Informer was my brother as he continually stated. But I had not chosen him. In the thing which we had now, which was not a safari and where Bwana was very close to a direct insult, Msembi and I were good brothers and on this night, without mentioning it, we both remembered that the slave raiders who had come up the different routes from the sea were all Moslems and I knew that was why Mthuka with the slashed arrow on each cheek would never, nor could ever, have been converted to the fashionable religion his father, Keiti, and dear honest Charo and Mwindi, the honest and skillful snob, had been received into.

So I sat there and we had a sharing of our sorrow. Nguili came in once, humble as a nanake should come, but wishing to weigh in with his sorrow if it was permissible. It was not permissible and I slapped him on his greenfrocked ass, lovingly, and said, *"Morgen ist auch nach ein tag."* This is an old German phrase which is the opposite of no hay remedio, which is a true and beautiful phrase but which I felt guilt for having implanted as though I had the guilt of a defeatist or a collaborationist. I translated it carefully into Kamba with the help of Msembi and then feeling the guilt of a phrase mutterer I asked Ngui if he would find my spears because I was going out to hunt when the moon rose.

It was more than a little bit theatrical but so is Hamlet. We were all deeply moved. Possibly I was the most moved of the three of us, having made the old mistake of not watching my mouth.

Now the moon was up over the shoulder of the Mountain and I wished that I had a good big dog and that I had not declared to do something that would make me a better man than Keiti. But I had and so I checked the spears and put on my soft moccasins and thanked Nguili and left the mess tent. There were two men on guard with the rifles and the ammo and a lantern on the tree outside the tent and I left these lights behind and left the moon over my right shoulder and started off on the long walk.

The spear shaft felt good and heavy and it was taped with surgical tape so that your hand would not slip if it was sweaty. Often, using the spear, you sweat heavily under your armpits and on your forearms and the sweat runs down the shaft. The grass stubble felt good under my feet and then I felt the smoothness of the motor tire track that led to the airstrip we had made and the other track we called the Great North Road. This was the first night I had gone out alone with the spear and I wished I had one of the old Honest Ernies or the big dog. With the German shepherd dog you could always tell if there was something in the next clump of bush because he fell back at once and walked with his muzzle against the back of your knee. But being properly scared as I was when out with the spear at night is a luxury that you have to pay for and like the best luxuries it is worth it most of the time. Mary, G.C. and I had shared many luxuries and some had been potentially expensive but, so far, all had been worth the price. It was the stupidities of daily life with its unflagging erosion that was not worth what it cost, I thought and I checked the various bushes and dead trees that had cobra holes in my mind and hoped that I would not step on any of them if they were out hunting.

In camp I had heard two hyenas but they were quiet now. I heard a lion up by the Old Manyatta and resolved to keep away from the

Old Manyatta. I did not have enough courage to go up there anyway and that was also rhino country. Ahead, on the plain, I could see something asleep in the moonlight. It was a wildebeest and I worked away from him or her; it turned out to be him; and then got back onto the trail again.

There were many night birds and plover and I saw bat-eared foxes and leaping hares but their eyes did not shine as they did when we cruised with the Land Rover since I had no light and the moon made no reflection. The moon was well up now and gave a good light and I went along the trail happy to be out in the night not caring if any beast presented himself. All the nonsense about Keiti and the girl and the Widow and our lost banquet and night in bed seemed of no importance and I looked back and could just not see the lights of camp but could see the Mountain high and square-topped and shone white in the moonlight and I hoped I would not run onto anything to kill. I could always have killed the wildebeest, maybe, but if I did I would have to dress him out and then stay with the carcass so the hyenas did not get him or else rouse the camp and get the truck and be a show-off and I remembered that only six of us would eat wildebeest and that I wanted some good meat for when Miss Mary came back.

So I walked along in the moonlight hearing the small animals move and the birds cry when they rose from the dust of the trail and thought about Miss Mary and what she would be doing in Nairobi and how she would look with her new haircut and whether she would get it or not and the way she was built and how there was almost no difference between the way she was built and the way Debba was built and that I would have Miss Mary back by two o'clock the next in a day and that it was a damned good thing all the way around.

By this time I was nearly up to where she had killed her lion and I could hear a leopard hunting in the edge of the big swamp to the left. I thought of going on up to the salt flats but I knew if I did I would be tempted by some animal so I turned around and started on the worn trail back to camp looking at the Mountain and not hunting at all.

17

IN THE MORNING Mwindi brought tea and I thanked him, drank it outside the tent by the remnants of the fire thinking and remembering while I drank it, and then dressed and went out to see Keiti.

It was not to be a completely quiet day nor one devoted to reading and contemplation as I had hoped. Arap Meina came to the open flap of the mess tent and saluted smartly and said, "Bwana, there are small problems."

"Of what type?"

"Nothing grave."

In what amounted to the reception room in the area beyond the cooking fires where there were several large trees there were the leading men from two Masai Manyattas. They were not chiefs since a chief is a man who has taken money or a cheap medal from the British and is a bought man. These were simply the heads of their villages, which were separated by more than fifteen miles, and they both had lion trouble. I sat in the chair outside the tent with my

Mzee stick and tried to make intelligent and dignified grunts when I understood or did not understand and Mwindi and Meina interpreted. None of us were Masai scholars but these were good serious men and the troubles were obviously legitimate. One man had four long grooves across a shoulder that looked as though they had been made by a hay rake and the other at some time had lost an eye and had an atrocious old wound that started a little above the line of his scalp and came down, over the lost eye, almost to the point of his jaw.

The Masai love to talk and to argue but neither of these men was a talker and I told them and those who had come with them and stood saying nothing that we would attend to the problems. To do this I had to speak to Mwindi who then spoke to Arap Meina who then spoke to our clients. I leaned on my Mzee stick which has a silver shilling pounded out and flattened into the head of it and grunted in the purest Masai which sounds a little like Marlene Dietrich when she is expressing sexual pleasure, understanding or affection. The sounds vary. But they are deep and have a rising inflection.

We all shook hands and then Mwindi who loved to announce the worst possible news said in English, "Bwana, there are two ladies with bubu."

Bubu is any form of venereal disease but also includes yaws about which the authorities do not agree. Yaws certainly have a spirochete much like that of syphilis but opinion is divided as to how one acquires them. People are supposed to be able to acquire the old rale from a drinking glass or from sitting injudiciously on the seat of a public toilet or from kissing a stranger. In my limited experience I have never known anyone so unfortunate.

Yaws, by now, I knew almost as well as I knew my brother. That is to say that I had much contact with them without ever being able to appreciate them at their true worth.

The two Masai ladies were both quite beautiful and this reinforced me in my theory that, in Africa, the more beautiful you are the more yaws you got. Msembi loved the practice of medicine and produced all the yaws remedies without being prompted. I made a general cleaning and threw the result into the still live ashes of the fire. After that I painted the edge of the lesion with gentian violet for psychologic effect. Gentian violet has a wonderful effect on the morale of the patient and it inspires the physician and the spectators with its lovely purple color tingeing into gold. I made a practice, usually, of making a small dot with it on the forehead of the husband.

After this, to take no chances, I would sprinkle the lesion, sometimes having to hold my breath to work with it, with sulfathiazole and then smear it with Aureomycin, and apply a dressing. Always I would give oral penicillin and, if the yaws did not clear up, after the daily cure I would administer as massive doses of penicillin as we could afford. Afterwards I took the snuff out from under my armpit and put half of it behind the ear of each patient. Msembi loved this part of the treatment but I asked him to bring a bowl of water and the good truly blue Nekko two percent soap so that I might wash my hands after shaking hands with each patient. Their hands were always lovely and cold and once you take a Masai woman's hand, even in the presence of her husband, she does not wish to give your hand up ever. This could be tribal or it could be personal to a yaws doctor. It was one of the few things I could not ask Ngui as we had no vocabulary to handle it. In return for the services performed a Masai might bring you a few mealies. But this would be exceptional.

The next patient was no inspiration even to an amateur physician. He was a prematurely old man if you could judge from the teeth and the genitals. He breathed with difficulty and his temperature was one hundred and four. His tongue was white and furry and there were white pockets and caves in his throat when I depressed his tongue. When I touched his liver lightly, the pain was almost unbearable. He said he had great pain in his head, in his belly, in his chest and he had not been able to evacuate for a long time. He did not know how long. If he had been an animal it would have been better to shoot him. Since he was a brother in Africa I gave him chloroquine for the fever in case it was malaria, a mild cathartic, aspirin to take for the pain if it continued and we boiled the syringe and laid him flat on the ground and gave him one million and a half units of penicillin in the tired, sunken, black cheek of his left buttock. It was a waste of penicillin. We all knew it. But if you go for broke that is the way you go and we all felt ourselves to be so fortunate in the religion that we were trying to be kind to all those outside of it and who should hoard penicillin when he is headed, self-propelled, for the Happy Hunting Grounds.

Mwindi, who had entered into the spirit of it all and was wearing his green robe and green skullcap and thought that we were all non-Islamic bums but also Kamba bums, said, "Bwana, there is another Masai with bubu."

"Bring him here."

He was a nice boy, still a warrior, and proud but shy from his defect. It was the classical. The chancre was hard and it was not new and after feeling it I added up the penicillin we had left in my mind and remembered that no man should ever panic and that we had an aircraft that could bring more and I told the boy to sit down and we boiled the syringe and the needle again, although what he could get from them that was worse than he had I did not know, and Msembi wiped off the buttocks area, with cotton and alcohol, this time hard and flat as a man's ass should be, and I made the puncture and watched the tiny oily ooze that was the mark of my inefficiency and the wastage of that which now was like the Host, and through Mwindi and Arap Meina I told the boy, upright now and with his spear, when he should come back and that he should come six times and then take a note to the hospital that I would give him. We did not shake hands because he was younger than me. But we smiled and he was proud of having had the needle.

Mthuka, who had no business there, but had wandered by to watch the practice of medicine and in the hope that I would undertake some form of surgery since I did surgery out of a book which Ngui held and which had fascinating colored pictures some of which folded over and could be opened so that you saw the organs of both the front and the rear of the body at the same time. Surgery everyone loved but there had been no surgery today and Mthuka came up, long and loose and deaf and scarred beautifully to please a girl a long time ago and said, wearing his checked shirt and his hat that had once belonged to Tommy Shevlin, "Kwenda na Shamba."

"Kwenda," I said and to Ngui, "Two guns. You and me and Mthuka."

"Hapana halal?"

"OK. Bring Charo."

"Mzuri," Ngui said since it would have been insulting to kill a good piece of meat and not have it legally butchered for the Moslem elders. Keiti knew only too well that we were all bad boys but now that we had the backing of a serious religion, and I had explained that this religion in its origin was as old if not older than the Mountain, Keiti would take it seriously. I think we could have conned Charo, which would have been a terrible thing to do since he had the comfort of his own faith which was much better organized than ours, but we were not proselytizing and we had made a great stride when Charo took the religion seriously.

Miss Mary hated what she knew of the religion, which was very little, and I am not sure that in our group everyone desired that she be a member. If she was a member by tribal right it was all right and she would be obeyed and respected as such. But on an elective entrance I am not positive she would have made it. With her own group, of course, headed by all the Game Scouts and led by the magnificent, well-starched, erect and handsome Chungo, she would have been elected to be the Queen of Heaven. But in our religion there was not going to be any Game Department and while we planned to abolish both flogging and capital punishment against anyone except our enemies and there was to be no slavery except by those we had taken prisoner personally and cannibalism was completely and absolutely abolished except for those who chose to practice it, Miss Mary might not have received the same number of votes that she would certainly have had from her own people.

So we drove to the Shamba and I sent Ngui to get Debba and with her sitting beside, one hand holding the carved holster of the pistol, we drove off, Debba receiving any salutes from children or old people as though she were taking the salute from any regiment of which she might have been Honorary Colonel. At this time she was patterning her public behavior after the photographs in illustrated weeklies I had given her and she had selected the dignity and grace of the better royalty as though she were going over the bolts of cloth in the duka. I never asked her who she was patterning her public behavior on but it had been a year of well-photographed pageantry and she had much to choose from. I had tried to teach her the lift of the wrist and undulation of the fingers with which the Princess Aspasia of Greece would greet me across the smoke-filled clamor of Harry's Bar in Venice but we had as yet no Harry's Bar in Laitokitok.

So now she was receiving salutes and I was maintaining a rigid amiability while we went off on the road that curved up the slope of the Mountain to where I hoped to kill a beast sufficiently large, fat and succulent to make everyone happy. We hunted diligently and lay until almost dark on an old blanket on the high side of a hill waiting for a beast to feed out onto the open hillside. But no beast fed out and when it was time to go home I killed a Tommy ram which was all we really needed. I lined up on him and with us both sitting down had her put her finger on the trigger ahead of mine and while I tracked him with the sight I felt the pressure of her finger and her head against mine and could feel her trying not to breathe. Then I said, "Piga," and her finger tightened as mine tightened on the trigger only a tiny cheating shade faster and the ram, whose tail had been switching as he fed, was dead with his four legs oddly rigid toward the sky and Charo was running out to him in his ragged shorts and old blue blazer and his dingy turban to cut his throat and make him legal.

"Piga mzuri," Ngui said to Debba and she turned to him and tried for her royal manner and couldn't make it and started to cry and said, "Asanta sana."

We sat there and she cried and then stopped it clean and well. We watched Charo do his business and the hunting car come down from behind the brow of the hill and drive to the beast and Mthuka get out and lower the tailgate and he and Charo, very small at the distance and the big car small too, stoop and lift and swing the carcass up into the back of the car. Then the car came up the hill toward us, larger every moment as it came. There had been a moment when I had wished to pace the distance of the shot. But it would have been a chicken thing to do and a man should be able to shoot at all distances giving the proper allowance for shooting downhill.

Debba looked at him as though it was the first antelope she had ever seen and put her finger in the hole where the solid had passed through the very top of both shoulders and I told her not to get dirty with the blood on the floor. The floor had strips of iron on it to lift the

meat above the heat of the car and let the air cir-
culate and although well washed always it was a
sort of charnel house.

Debba left her beast and we drove downhill
with her sitting between Mthuka and me and
we both knew she was in a strange state but she
did not talk at all and only held tight on to my
arm and held tight to the carved holster. At the
Shamba she became regal but her heart was not
in it and Ngui butchered out the ram and threw
the tripe and the lungs to the dogs and opened
the stomach and cleaned it and put the heart,
kidneys and liver in the stomach sack and
handed it to a child to take in to Debba's house.
My father-in-law was there and I nodded to
him. He took the white, wet sack with its red
and purple content and went inside the house
which was really quite a beautiful building with
its conical roof and red walls.

I got out of the car and helped Debba down.

"Jambo, tu," I said and she said nothing and
went into the house.

It was dark by now and when we got to camp
the fire was burning and my chair and the table
with the drinks had been set out. Mwindi had
bathwater ready and I took a bath, soaping
carefully, and then dressed in pajamas, mosquito boots and a heavy bathrobe and came out
to the fire. Keiti was waiting.

"Jambo, Bwana," he said.

"Jambo, Mr. Keiti," I said. "We killed a small Tommy. Charo will have told you he is OK."

He smiled and I knew we were friends again. He had the nicest, cleanest smile of anyone I ever knew.

"Sit down, Keiti," I said.

"No."

"I am very grateful for what you did last night. You acted correctly and exactly as you should. I have seen the father of the girl for some time and have made the necessary visits and presents. There was no way you should know this. The father is worthless."

"I know. Women rule that Shamba."

"If I have a son by the girl he will be educated properly and may choose to be a soldier, a doctor or a lawyer. This is exact. If he wishes to be a hunter he can remain with me as my son. Is this clear?"

"It is very clear," Keiti said.

"If I have a daughter I will give her a dowry or she may come to live with me as my daughter. Is that clear?"

"It is clear. Better, maybe, stay with the mother."

"I will do everything according to Kamba law and custom. But I cannot marry the girl and take her home because of stupid laws."

"One of your brothers can marry her," Keiti said.

"I know."

The case was now closed and we were the same good friends as always.

"I would like to come some night and hunt with the spear," Keiti said.

"I am only learning," I said. "I am very stupid and it is difficult without a dog."

"Nobody knows the night. Not me. Not you. Nobody."

"I want to learn it."

"You will. But be careful."

"I will."

"No one knows the night except in a tree or in some safe place. The night belongs to the animals."

Keiti was too delicate to speak about the religion but I saw the look in his eye of one who has been led up to the top of a high hill and seen the temptations of the world spread out before him and it reminded me that we must not corrupt Charo. I could see that we were winning now and that I could have had Debba and the Widow for dinner now with a written menu and place cards. So, winning, I crowded just a little for the extra point.

"Of course, in our religion, everything is possible."

"Yes. Charo told me about your religion."

"It is very small but very old."

"Yes," Keiti said.

"Well, good night then," I said. "If everything is in order."

"Everything is in order," Keiti said and I said good night again and he bowed again and I envied Pop that Keiti was his man. But, I thought, you are starting to get your own men and while Ngui can never compare with Keiti in many ways yet he is rougher and more fun and times have changed.

In the night I lay and listened to the noises of the night and tried to understand them all. What Keiti had said was very true; no one knew the night. But I was going to learn it if I could alone and on foot. But I was going to learn it and I did not want to share it with anyone. Sharing is for money and you do not share a woman nor would I share the night. I could not go to sleep and I would not take a sleeping pill because I wanted to hear the night and I had not decided yet whether I would go out at moonrise. I knew that I did not have enough experience with the spear to hunt alone and not get into trouble and that it was both my duty and my great and lovely pleasure to be in camp when Miss Mary should return. It was also my duty and my wonderful pleasure to be with Debba but I was sure that she would sleep well at least until the moon rose and that after the moon rose we all paid for whatever happiness or sorrow we had bought. I lay in the cot with the old shotgun rigidly comfortable by my side and the pistol that was my best friend and severest critic of any defect of reflexes or of decision lying comfortably between my legs in the carved holster that Debba had polished so many times with her hard hands and thought how lucky I was to know Miss Mary and have her do me the great honor of being married to me and to Miss Debba the Queen of the Ngomas. Now that we had the religion it was easy. Ngui, Mthuka and I could decide what was a sin and what was not.

Ngui had five wives, which we knew was true, and twenty head of cattle, which we all doubted. I had only one legal wife due to American law but everyone remembered and respected Miss Pauline who had been in Africa long ago and was much admired and beloved especially by Keiti and Mwindi and I knew that they believed she was my dark Indian wife and that Miss Mary was my fair Indian wife. They were all sure that Miss Pauline must be looking after the Shamba at home while I had brought Miss Mary to this country and I never told them that Miss Pauline was dead because it would have saddened everyone. Nor did we tell them of another wife they would not have liked who had been reclassified so that she did not hold that rank nor category. It was generally presumed even by the most conservative and skeptical of the elders that if Ngui had five wives I must have at least twelve due to the difference between our fortunes.

It was generally understood that I was married to Miss Marlene who on this safari, through photographs I had received and letters, was supposed to be working for me in a small amusement Shamba I owned called Las Vegas. They all knew Miss Marlene as the author of "Lili Marlene" and many people thought that she was Lili Marlene and we had all heard her on our first safari many times singing a song called "Jonny" on the old crank-up phonograph when *Rhapsody in Blue* was a new tune and Miss Marlene sung about mutts around the phlegm. This tune had always moved everyone deeply then and when I was gloomy or dispirited in those days on rare occasions, Keiti would ask, "Muts around flem?," and I would say to put her on, he would crank the portable phonograph and we would all be happy hearing the beautiful, deep, off-key voice of my beautiful non-existent wife.

This is the material from which legends are built and the fact that one of my wives was supposed to be Lili Marlene was no deterrent to the religion. I had taught Debba to say, "Vámonos a Las Vegas," and she loved the sound of it almost as much as, "No hay remedio." But she was always afraid of Miss Marlene although she had a large picture of her wearing what looked to me like nothing on the wall above her bed along with advertisements for the washing machine and garbage disposal units and the two-inch steaks and cuts of ham and the paintings of the mammoth, the little four-toed horse and the saber-toothed tiger that she had cut from *Life* magazine. These were the great wonders of her new world and the only one she feared was Miss Marlene.

Because I was awake now and I was not sure that I would ever sleep again, I thought about Debba and Miss Marlene and Miss Mary and another girl that I knew and, at that time, loved very much. She was a rangy-built American girl running to shoulders and with the usually American pneumatic bliss that is so admired by those who do not know a small, hard, well-formed breast is better. But this girl had good Negro legs and was very loving although always complaining about something. She was pleasant enough to think about at night though when you could not sleep and I listened to the night and thought about her a little and the cabin and Key West and the lodge and the different gambling places we used to frequent and the sharp cold mornings of the hunts we had made together with the wind rushing by in the dark and the taste of the air of the mountains and the smell of sage back in the days when she cared for hunting other things than money. No man is ever really alone and the supposed dark hours of the soul when it is always three o'clock in the morning are a man's best hours if he is not an alcoholic nor afraid of the night and what the day will bring. I was as afraid as the next man in my time and maybe more so. But with the years, fear had come to be regarded as a form of stupidity to be classed with over-drafts, acquiring a venereal disease or eating candies. Fear is a child's vice and while I loved to feel it approach, as one does with any vice, it was not for grown men and the only thing to be afraid of was the presence of true and imminent danger in a form that you should be aware of and not be a fool if you were responsible for others. This was the mechanical fear that made your scalp prickle at real danger and when you lost this reaction it was time to get into some other line of work.

So I thought of Miss Mary and how brave she had been in the ninety-six days she had pursued her lion, not tall enough to see him properly ever; doing a new thing with imperfect knowledge and unsuitable tools; driving us all

with her will so we would all be up an hour
before daylight and sick of lions, especially at
Magadi, and Charo, loyal and faithful to Miss
Mary but an old man and tired of lions, had
said to me, "Bwana kill the lion and get it over
with. No woman ever kills a lion."

18

IT WAS A BEAUTIFUL day for flying and the Mountain was very close. I sat against the tree and watched the birds and the grazing game. Ngui came over for orders and I told him he and Charo should clean and oil all the weapons and sharpen and oil the spears. Keiti and Mwindi were removing the broken bed and taking it to Bwana Mouse's empty tent. I got up to go over. It was not badly broken. One cross leg in the center had a long fracture and one of the main poles that held the canvas was broken. It was easily repairable and I said I would get some wood and have it sawed to measure and finished at Mr. Singh's.

Keiti, who was very cheerful that Miss Mary was arriving, said we would use Bwana Mouse's cot which was identical and I went back to my chair and the bird identification book and more tea. I felt like someone who had dressed for the party too early on this morning that felt like spring in a high alpine plateau and as I went over to the mess tent for breakfast I wondered what the day would bring. The first thing it brought was the Informer.

"Good morning, brother," the Informer said. "How is your good health?"

"Never better, brother. What is new?"

"May I come in?"

"Of course. Have you had breakfast?"

"Hours before. I breakfasted on the Mountain."

"Why?"

"The Widow was so difficult that I left her to wander alone in the night as you do, brother."

I knew this was a lie and I said, "You mean you walked to the road and caught a ride up to Laitokitok with one of Benji's boys in the lorry?"

"Something like that, brother."

"Go on."

"Brother, there are desperate things afoot."

"Pour yourself your pleasure and tell me."

"It is set for Christmas Eve and Christmas Day, brother. I believe it is a massacre."

I wanted to say, "By them or by us?" but I controlled myself.

"Tell me more," I said, looking at the Informer's proud, brown, guilt-lined face as he raised a shot glass of Canadian gin with a glow of bitters in it to his gray red lips.

"Why don't you drink Gordon's? You'll live longer."

"I know my place, brother."

"And your place is in my heart," I said quoting the late Fats Waller. Tears came into the Informer's eyes.

"So this St. Bartholomew's eve is for Christmas Eve," I said. "Has no one any respect for the Baby Jesus?"

"It is a massacre."

"Women and children too?"

"No one said so."

"Who said what?"

"There was talk at Benji's. There was much talk at the Masai stores and at the Tea Room."

"Are the Masai to be put to death?"

"No. The Masai will all be here for your Ngoma for the Baby Jesus."

"Is the Ngoma popular?" I said to change the subject and to show that news of impending massacres meant nothing to me, a man who had been through the Zulu War and whose ancestors had done away with George Armstrong Custer on the Little Big Horn. No man who went to Mecca not being a Moslem as another man might go to Brighton or Atlantic City should be moved by rumors of massacres.

"The Ngoma is the talk of the Mountain," the Informer said. "Except for the massacre."

"What did Mr. Singh say?"

"He was rude to me."

"Is he participating in the massacre?"

"He is probably one of the ringleaders."

The Informer unwrapped a package he had in his shawl. It was a bottle of White Heather whisky in a carton.

"A gift from Mr. Singh," he said. "I advise you to examine it carefully before drinking, brother. I have never heard the name."

"Too bad, brother. It may be a new name but it is good whisky. New brands of whisky are always good at the start."

"I have information for you on Mr. Singh. He has undoubtedly performed military service."

"It is hard to believe."

"I am sure of it. No one could have cursed me as Mr. Singh did who had not served the Raj."

"Do you think Mr. Singh and Mrs. Singh are subversives?"

"I will make inquiries."

"The gen has been a little shadowy today, Informer."

"Brother, it was a difficult night. The cold-heartedness of the Widow, my wanderings on the Mountain."

"Take another drink, brother. You sound like *Wuthering Heights*."

"Was that a battle, brother?"

"In a way."

"You must tell me about it someday."

"Remind me. Now I want you to spend the night in Laitokitok, sober, and bring me some information that is not bullshit. Go to Brown's Hotel and sleep there. No, sleep on the porch. Where did you sleep last night?"

"On the floor of the Tea Room under the billiard table."

"Drunk or sober?"

"Drunk, brother."

Mary would certainly wait for the bank to open so that she could get the mail. It was a good day for flying and there was no sign of anything building up and I did not think Willie would be in any hurry about getting out. I put a couple of cool bottles of beer in the hunting car and Ngui, Mthuka and I drove out to the airstrip with Arap Meina in the back. Meina would mount guard over the plane and he was smart and very sharp in his uniform and his .303 with the sling was freshly polished and oiled. We made a run around the meadow to put the birds to flight and then retired to the shade of a big tree where Mthuka killed the engine and we all sat back and were comfortable. Charo had come along at the last minute because he was Miss Mary's gun bearer and it was only proper that he should meet her.

It was past noon and I opened one of the

quarts of Tusker and Mthuka and Ngui and I drank from it. Arap Meina was under discipline for a recent drunkenness but he knew I would give him some later.

I told Ngui and Mthuka I had a dream last night that we should pray to the sun as it rose and again to the sun as it set.

Ngui said he would not kneel down like a camel driver or a Christian even for the religion.

"You don't have to kneel down. You turn and look at the sun and pray."

"What do we pray in the dream?"

"To live bravely, to die bravely and to go directly to the Happy Hunting Grounds."

"We are brave already," Ngui said. "Why do we have to pray about it?"

"Pray for anything you like, if it is for the good of us all."

"I pray for beer, for meat and for a new wife with hard hands. You can share the wife."

"That's a good prayer. What do you pray for, Mthuka?"

"We keep this car."

"Anything else?"

"Beer. You not get killed. Rain good in Machakos. Happy Hunting Grounds."

"What you pray for?" Ngui asked me.

"Africa for Africans. Kwisha Mau Mau. Kwisha all sickness. Rain good everywhere. Happy Hunting Grounds."

"Pray to have fun," Mthuka offered.

"Pray sleep with wife of Mr. Singh."

"Must pray good."

"Take wife of Mr. Singh to Happy Hunting Grounds."

"Too many people want to be in religion," Ngui said. "How many people we take?"

"We start with a squad. Maybe make a section, maybe a company."

"Company very big for Happy Hunting Grounds."

"I think so too."

"You command Happy Hunting Grounds. We make a council but you command. No Great Spirit. No Gitchi Manitou. Hapana King. Hapana Queen's Road. Hapana H.E. Hapana D.C. Hapana Baby Jesus. Hapana Police. Hapana Black Watch. Hapana Game Department."

"Hapana," I said.

"Hapana," Mthuka said.

I passed the bottle of beer to Arap Meina.

"Are you a religious man, Meina?"

"Very," said Meina.

"Do you drink?"

"Only beer, wine and gin. I can also drink whisky and all clear or colored alcohols."

"Are you ever drunk, Meina?"

"You should know, my father."

"What religions have you held?"

"I am now a Moslem." Charo leaned back and closed his eyes.

"What were you before?"

"Lumbwa," Meina said. Mthuka's shoulders were shaking. "I have never been a Christian," Meina said with dignity.

"We speak too much of religion and I am still acting for Bwana Game and we celebrate the Birthday of the Baby Jesus in four days." I looked at the watch on my wrist. "Let us clear the field of birds and drink the beer before the plane comes."

"The plane is coming now," Mthuka said. He started the motor and I passed him the beer and he drank a third of what was left. Ngui drank a third and I drank half of a third and passed what was left back to Meina. We were already putting up storks at full speed at the approach and seeing them, after the running rush, straighten their legs as though they were pulling up their undercarriage and commence their reluctant flight.

We saw the plane come over blue and silvery and spindle-legged and buzz the camp and then we were barreling down along the side of the clearing and she was opposite us, with the big flaps down, passing us to land without a bounce and circling now, her nose high and arrogant, throwing dust in the knee-deep white flowers.

Miss Mary was on the near side now and she came out in a great, small rush. I held her tight and kissed her and then she shook hands with everyone, Charo first.

"Morning, Papa," Willie said. "Let me have Ngui to pass some of this out. She's a bit laden!"

"You must have bought all Nairobi," I said to Mary.

"All I could afford. They wouldn't sell the Muthaiga Club."

"She bought the New Stanley and Torr's," Willie said. "So we're always sure of a room, Papa."

"What else did you buy?"

"She wanted to buy me a Comet," Willie said. "You can pick up quite good bargains in them now, you know."

We drove to camp with Miss Mary and me sitting close together in front. Willie was talking with Ngui and Charo. At camp Mary wanted the stuff unloaded into Bwana Mouse's empty tent and I was to stay away and not watch it. I had been told not to watch anything in detail at the aircraft either and I had not watched. There was a big bundle of letters, papers and magazines and some cables and I had taken them into the mess tent and Willie and I were drinking a beer.

"Good trip?"

"Not lumpy. The ground doesn't really heat up anymore with these cold nights. Mary saw her elephants at Salengai and a very big pack of wild dogs."

Miss Mary came in. She had received all the official visits and was beaming. She was well-beloved, well-received, and people had been formal about it. She loved the designation of Memsahib.

"I didn't know Mousie's bed was broken."

"Is it?"

"And I haven't said a thing about the leopard. Let me kiss you. G.C. laughed at your cable about him."

"They've got their leopard. They don't have to worry. Nobody has to worry. Not even the leopard."

"Tell me about him."

"No. Sometime when we are coming home I'll show you the place."

"Can I see any mail you're finished with?"

"Open it all."

"What's the matter with you? Aren't you glad to have me back? I was having a wonderful time in Nairobi or at least I was going out every night and everyone was nice to me."

"We'll all practice up and be nice to you and pretty soon it will be just like Nairobi."

"Please be good, Papa. This is what I love. I only went to Nairobi to be cured and to buy presents for Christmas and I know you wanted me to have fun."

"Good, and now you're back. Give me a hold hard and a good anti-Nairobi kiss."

She was slim and shiny in her khakis and hard inside them and she smelled very good and her hair was silver gold, cropped close, and I rejoined the white or European race as easily as a mercenary of Henry IV saying Paris was worth a mass.

Willie was happy to see the rejoining and he said, "Papa, any news beside the chui?"

"Nothing."

"No troubles?"

"The road at night is a scandal."

"It seems to me they rely a little too much on the desert as being impassable."

I sent for the saddle of meat for Willie and Mary went to our tent for her letters. We rode out and Willie took off. Everyone's face shone at the angle he pulled her into and then, when he was a distant silver speck, we went on our way home.

Mary was loving and lovely and Ngui was feeling badly because I had not taken him. It would soon be evening and there would be *Time* and the British airmail papers and for the bright receding light and the fire and a tall drink.

The hell with it, I thought. I have complicated

my life too much and the complications are
extending. Now I'll read whichever *Time* Miss
Mary doesn't want and I have her back and I
will enjoy the fire and we'll enjoy our drink and
the dinner afterwards. Mwindi was fixing her
bath in the canvas tub and mine was the second
bath. I thought that I would wash everything
away and soak it out with the bathi and when
the canvas tub had been emptied and washed
out and filled again with former petrol tins of
hot water from the fire, I lay back in the water
and soaked and soaped with the Lifebuoy soap.

I rubbed dry with my towel and put on pajamas and my old mosquito boots from China
and a bathrobe. It was the first time since Mary
had been gone that I had taken a hot bath. The
British took one every night when it was possible. But I preferred to scrub every morning in
the washbowl when I dressed, again when we
came in from hunting and in the evening.

Pop hated this as the bathi ritual was one of
the few surviving rites of the old safari. So when
he was with us I made a point of taking the hot
bathi. But in the other kind of washing yourself
clean you found the ticks you'd picked up in the
day and had either Mwindi or Ngui remove
those that you could not reach. In the old days,
when I had hunted alone with Mkola, we had
burrowing chiggers that dug into the toes under

the toenails and every night we would sit down in the lantern flare and he would remove mine and I would remove his. No bathi would have taken these out, but we had no bathi.

I was thinking about the old days and how hard we used to hunt, or rather, how simply. On those days when you sent for an aircraft, it meant you were insufferably rich and could not be bored by any part of Africa where it was at all difficult to travel or it meant that you were dying.

"How are you really, honey, after your bath and did you have a good time?"

"I'm well and fine. The doctor gave me the same stuff I was taking and some bismuth. People were very nice to me. But I missed you all the time."

"You look wonderful," I said. "How did you get such a fine Kamba haircut?"

"I cut it square at the sides some more this afternoon," she said. "Do you like it?"

"Tell me about Nairobi."

"The first night I ran into a very nice man and he took me to the Traveler's Club and it wasn't so bad and he brought me home to the hotel."

"What was he like?"

"I don't remember him terribly well, but he was quite nice."

"What about the second night?"

"I went out with Alec and his girl and we went someplace that was terribly crowded. You had to be dressed and Alec wasn't dressed. I don't remember if we stayed there or went somewhere else."

"Sounds wonderful. Just like Kimana."

"What were you doing?"

"Nothing. I went out to a few places with Ngui and Charo and Keiti. I think we went to a church supper of some kind. What did you do the third night?"

"Honey, I don't remember really. Oh, yes. Alec and his girl and G.C. and I went somewhere. Alec was difficult. We went a couple of other places and they took me home."

"Same type of life we've been having here. Only Keiti was difficult instead of Alec."

"What was he difficult about?"

"It escapes me," I said. "Which of these *Time*s would you rather read?"

"I've looked at one. Does it make any difference to you?"

"No."

"You haven't said you loved me or were glad to have me back."

"I love you and I'm glad to have you back."

"That's good and I'm so glad to be home."

"Anything else happen in Nairobi?"

"I got that nice man who took me out to take me to the Coryndon Museum. But I think he was bored."

"What did you eat at the Grill?"

"There was fine fish from the big lakes. In filets, but like bass or walleye pike. They didn't tell what fish. Just called it samaki. There was really good fresh smoked salmon that they flew in and there were oysters, I think, but I can't remember."

"Did you have the Greek dry wine?"

"Lots of it. Alec didn't like it. He was in Greece and Crete I think with that friend of yours in the RAF. He doesn't like him either."

"Was Alec very difficult?"

"Only about small things."

"Let's not be difficult about anything."

"Let's not. Can I make you another drink?"

"Thank you very much. Keiti's here. What do you want?"

"I'll take Campari with just a little gin."

"I like it when you're home in bed. Let's go to bed right after supper."

"Good."

"You promise you won't go out tonight?"

"I promise."

So, after the supper I sat and read the *Time* air edition while Mary wrote in her diary and then she walked on the new cut path with her searchlight to the latrine tent and I turned off the gaslight and put the lantern on the tree and undressed folding my things carefully and laying them on the trunk at the foot of the bed and got into my bed, folding the mosquito bar back under the mattress.

It was early in the night but I was tired and sleepy. After a while Miss Mary came in to the bed and I put the other Africa away somewhere and we made our own Africa again. It was another Africa from where I had been and at first, I felt the red spilling up my chest and then I accepted it and did not think at all and felt only what I felt and Mary felt lovely in bed. We made love and then made love again and then after we had made love once more, quiet and dark and unspeaking and unthinking and then like a shower of meteors on a cold night, we went to sleep. Maybe there was a shower of meteors. It was cold enough and clear enough. Sometime in the night Mary left the bed for her bed and I said, "Good night, blessed."

I woke when it was getting light and put on a sweater and mosquito boots over my pajamas and buckled my bathrobe around with the pistol belt and went out to where Msembi was building up the fire to read the papers and drink the pot of tea Mwindi had brought. First I put all the papers in order and then started to read the oldest ones first. The horses would just be finishing at Auteuil and Enghien now, but there were no French racing results in these British airmail editions. I went to see if Miss Mary was awake and she was up and dressed, fresh and shining and putting drops in her eyes.

"How are you, darling? How did you sleep?"

"Wonderfully," I said. "And you?"

"Until just this minute. I went right back to sleep when Mwindi brought the tea."

I held her in my arms feeling her fresh early morning shirt and her lovely build. Picasso had called her my pocket Rubens once and she was a pocket Rubens, but trained down to one hundred and twelve pounds and she had never had a Rubens face and now I felt her clean, freshly washed-ness and whispered something to her.

"Oh yes, and you?"

"Yes."

"Isn't it wonderful to be here alone with our own Mountain and our lovely country and nothing to spoil it?"

"Yes. Come on and get your breakfast."

She had a proper breakfast with impala liver broiled with bacon and a half of papaya from town with lemon to squeeze on it and two cups of coffee. I drank a cup of coffee with tinned milk but no sugar and would have taken another cup but I did not know what we were going to do and I did not want coffee sloshing in my stomach whatever we did.

"Did you miss me?"

"Oh yes."

"I missed you terribly but there were so many things to do. There wasn't any time at all, really."

"Did you see Pop?"

"No. He didn't come into town and I didn't have any time nor any transport to get out there."

"Did you see G.C.?"

"He was in one evening. He said for you to use your own judgment but adhere strictly to the scheme as outlined. He made me memorize it."

"Is that all?"

"That's all. I memorized it. He's invited Wilson Blake down for Christmas. They get in the night before. He says for you to be prepared to like his boss, Wilson Blake."

"Did he make you memorize that?"

"No. It was just a remark. I asked him if it was an order and he said no, that it was a hopeful suggestion."

"I'm open to suggestion. How was G.C.?"

"He wasn't difficult in the same way Alec was. But he's tired. He says he misses us and he's very outspoken with people."

"How?"

"I think fools are beginning to annoy him and he's rude to them."

"Poor G.C.," I said.

"You're both quite a bad influence on each other."

"Maybe," I said. "Maybe not."

"Well, I think you're a bad influence on him."

"Didn't we go into this once or twice before?"

"Not this morning," Miss Mary said. "Certainly not recently. Did you write anything while I was away?"

"Very little."

"Didn't you write any letters?"

"No. Oh, yes. I wrote G.C. once."

"What did you do with all your time?"

"Small tasks and routine duties. I made a trip to Laitokitok after we killed the unfortunate leopard."

"Well, we are going to get the real Christmas tree and that will be something accomplished."

"Good," I said. "We'll have to get one we can bring back in the hunting car. I've sent away the truck."

"We're going to get that one that is picked out."

"Good. Did you find out what sort of tree it is?"

"No, but I'll find it in the tree book."

"Good. Let's go and get it."

We started out, finally, to get the tree. Keiti was with us and we had shovels, pangas, sacking for the roots of the tree, large guns and small guns in the rack across the back of the front seat and I had told Ngui to bring four bottles of beer for us and two of Coca-Cola for the Moslems. We were clearly out to accomplish and except for the nature of the tree, which would make an elephant drunk for two days if he ever ate it, we were out to accomplish something so fine and so blameless that I might write about it for some religious publication.

We were all on our good behavior and we noted tracks without commenting on them. We read the record of what had crossed the road that night. And I watched sand grouse flighting in long wavering wisps to the water beyond the salt flats and Ngui watched them too. But we did not comment. We were hunters but this morning we were working for the Forestry Department of our Lord, the Baby Jesus.

Actually we were working for Miss Mary so we felt a great shifting in our allegiance. We were all mercenaries and it was clearly understood that Miss Mary was not a missionary. She was not even under Christian orders; she did not have to go to church as other Memsahibs did and this business of the tree was her shauri as the lion had been.

We went into the deep green and yellow-trunked forest by our old road that had become overgrown with grass and weeds since we had been over it last, coming out in the glade where the silver-leafed trees grew. Ngui and I made a circle, he one way and I the other, to check if this rhino and her calf were in the bush. We found nothing but some impala and I found the track of a very big leopard. He had been hunting along the edge of the swamp. I measured the pug marks with my hand and we went back to join the tree diggers.

We decided that only so many could dig at a time and since Keiti and Miss Mary were both issuing orders, we went over to the edge of the big trees and sat down and Ngui offered me his snuff box. We both took snuff and watched the forestry experts at their work. They were all working very hard except Keiti and Miss Mary. It looked to us as though the tree would never fit into the back of the hunting car but when they finally had it dug out it was obvious it would and that it was time for us to go over and help with the loading. The tree was very spiky and not easy to load but we all got it in finally. Sacks wet down with water were placed over the roots and it was lashed in, about half its length projecting from the rear of the car.

"We can't go back the same way we came," Miss Mary said. "It will break the tree in those turns."

"We'll go by a new way."

"Can the car get through?"

"Sure."

Along this way through the forest we hit the tracks of four elephants and there was fresh dung. But the tracks were to the south of us. They were good-sized bulls.

I had been carrying the big gun between my knees because Ngui and Mthuka and I had all seen these tracks where they crossed the north road on our way in. They might have crossed over from the stream that ran into the Chulu swamp.

"All clear now to campi," I said to Miss Mary.

"That's good," she said. "Now we'll get the tree up in good shape."

At camp Ngui and Mthuka and I hung back and let volunteers and enthusiasts dig the hole for the tree. Mthuka drove the car over out of the shade when the hole was dug and the tree was unloaded and planted and looked very pretty and gay in front of the tent.

"Isn't it lovely?" Miss Mary said. And I agreed that it was.

"Thank you for bringing us home such a nice way and for not worrying anybody about the elephants."

"They wouldn't stop there. They have to go

south to have good cover and feed. They wouldn't have bothered us."

"You and Ngui were smart about them."

"They are those bulls we saw from the aircraft. They were smart. We weren't smart."

"Where will they go now?"

"They might feed a while in the forest by the upper marsh. Then they'll cross the road at night and get up into that country toward Amboseli which the elephant use."

"I must go and see they finish properly."

"I'm going up the road."

"Your fiancée is over under the tree with her chaperone."

"I know. She brought us some mealies. I'm going to give her a ride home."

"Wouldn't she like to come and see the tree?"

"I don't think she would understand."

"Stay at the Shamba for lunch, if you like."

"I haven't been asked," I said.

"Then you'll be back for lunch?"

"Before."

Mthuka drove the car over to the waiting tree and told Debba and the Widow to get in. The Widow's little boy bumped his head against my stomach and I patted it. He got into the back seat with Debba and his mother but I stepped down and had Debba come and sit in the front seat. She had been a brave girl to come to the camp, bringing the mealies and to stay at the waiting tree until we had come in and I did not want her to ride back to the Shamba in any but her usual place. But Miss Mary being so nice about the Shamba had put us all on our honor as though we had been given our parole.

"Did you see the tree?" I asked Debba. She giggled. She knew what sort of a tree it was.

"We will go and shoot again."

"Ndio," she sat up very straight as we drove past the outer huts and stopped under the big tree. I got down to see if the Informer had any botanical specimens ready to transport, but could locate nothing. He probably has them in the herbarium, I thought. When I came back Debba was gone and Ngui and I got in the car and Mthuka asked where we were going.

"Na campi," I said. Then thought and added, "By the big road."

Today we were in suspense, suspended between our new African Africa and the old Africa that we had dreamed and invented and the return of Miss Mary. Soon there would be the return of whatever Game Scouts G.C. brought and the presence of the great Wilson Blake who could enunciate policy and move us or throw us out or close an area or see that someone got six months as easily as we could take a piece of meat to the Shamba.

None of us was very cheerful but we were relaxed and not unhappy. We would kill an eland to have for Christmas Day and I was going to try to see that Wilson Blake had a good time. G.C. had asked that I try to like him and I would try. When I had met him I had not liked him but that had probably been my fault. I had tried to like him but probably I had not tried hard enough. Perhaps I was getting too old to like people when I tried. Pop never tried to like them at all. He was civil or moderately civil and then observed them through his blue, slightly bloodshot and hooded eyes without seeming to see them. He was watching for them to make a mistake.

Sitting in the car under the tall tree on the hillside I decided to do something special to show my liking and appreciation for Wilson Blake. There was not much in Laitokitok he would care for and I could not picture him as truly happy at a party given for him in one of the illegal Masai drinking Shambas nor in the back of Mr. Singh's. I had grave doubts if he and Mr. Singh would get on too well. I knew what I would do. It was absolutely an ideal present. We would charter Willie to fly Mr. Blake over the Chulus and all of his domain that he had never seen. I could not think of a finer nor more useful present and I began to like Mr. Blake and to give him almost most favored nation status. I would not go along but would stay modestly and industriously at home photographing my botanical specimens, perhaps, or identifying finches while G.C. and Willie and Miss Mary and Mr. Blake worked out the country.

"Kwenda na campi," I told Mthuka and Ngui opened another bottle of beer so that we would be drinking while we crossed the stream at the ford. This was a very lucky thing to do and we all had a drink from the bottle while we watched the small fish in the pool above the long ripple of the ford. There were good catfish in the stream but we were too lazy to fish.

19

MISS MARY WAS waiting under the shade of the double fly of the mess tent. The back of the tent was up and the wind blew new and cool from the Mountain.

"Mwindi's worried about you hunting barefoot and going out nights."

"Mwindi's an old woman. I took my boots off once because they squeaked and the reason they squeaked was his fault for not dubbing them properly. He's too bloody righteous."

"It's easy to call someone righteous when they're looking after your own good."

"Leave it at that."

"Well, why is it that you take so many precautions and sometimes you don't take any at all?"

"Because sometimes they signal possibility of bad peoples and then you hear they're somewhere else. I always take what precautions we need."

"But when you go out by yourself nights."

"Someone sits up with you and the guns and

there are always the lights. You're always guarded."

"But why do you go out?"

"I have to go out."

"But why?"

"Because the time is getting short. How do I know when we can get back? How do I know we'll ever get back?"

"I worry about you."

"You're usually sound asleep when I go out and sound asleep when I come back."

"I'm not always. Sometimes I touch the cot and you're not there."

"Well, I can't go now until there's a moon and the moon gets up very late now."

"Do you really want to go so much?"

"Yes, truly, honey. And I always have some-body keep guard over you."

"Why don't you take somebody with you?"

"It isn't any good with anybody with you."

"It's just another craziness. But you don't drink before you do it, do you?"

"No, and I wash clean and put on lion fat."

"Thanks for putting it on after you get out of bed. Isn't the water cold in the night?"

"Everything is so cold you don't notice it."

"Let me make you a drink now. What will you have? A gimlet?"

"A gimlet would be fine. That or a Campari."

"I'll make us each a gimlet. Do you know what I want for Christmas?"

"I wish I did."

"I don't know whether I should tell you. Maybe it's too expensive."

"Not if we have the money."

"I want to go and really see something of Africa. We'll be going home and we haven't seen anything. I want to see the Belgian Congo."

"I don't."

"You don't have any ambition. You'd just as soon stay in one place."

"Have you ever been in a better place?"

"No. But there's everything we haven't seen."

"I'd rather live in a place and have an actual part in the life of it than just see new strange things."

"But I want to see the Belgian Congo. Why can't I see something I've heard about all my life when we are so close to it?"

"We're not that close."

"We can fly. We can make the whole trip flying."

"Look, honey. We've been from one end of Tanganyika to the other. You've been to the Bohoro flats and down the Great Ruaha."

"I suppose that was fun."

"It was educational. You've been to Mbeya and to the Southern Highlands. You've lived in the hills and hunted on the plain and you've lived here at the foot of the Mountain and in the bottom of the Rift Valley beyond Magadi and hunted nearly down to Natron."

"But I haven't been to the Belgian Congo."

"No. Is that what you really want for Christmas?"

"Yes. If it's not too expensive. We don't have to go right after Christmas. You take your time."

"Thanks," I said.

"You haven't touched your drink."

"Sorry."

"It isn't any fun if you give someone a present and you're not happy about it."

I took a sip of the pleasant unsweetened lime drink and thought how much I loved it where we were.

"You don't mind if I bring the Mountain along do you?"

"They have wonderful mountains there. That's where the Mountains of the Moon are."

"I've read about them and I saw a picture of them in *Life* magazine."

"In the African Number."

"That's right. In the African Number."

"When did you first think about this trip?"

"Before I went to Nairobi. You'll have fun flying with Willie. You always do."

"We'll gen the trip out with Willie. He's coming here day after Christmas."

"We don't have to go until you want to. You stay until you're finished here."

I knocked on wood and drank the rest of the drink.

"What did you plan to do this afternoon and evening?"

"I thought I'd take a siesta and catch up on my diary. Then we would go out together in the evening."

"Good," I said.

Arap Meina came in and I asked him about the setup at the first Manyatta. He said there was a lioness and a lion, which seemed strange this time of year, and that they had killed five head of stock in the last half-moon and the lioness had clawed a man the last time they had come over the thorn Boma, but the man was all right.

There is no one hunting in the area, I thought, and I cannot get a report in to G.C. before I see him, so I will have the Informer spread the word about the lions. They should work downhill, or across it, but we will hear of them unless they go toward Amboseli. I'd make the report to G.C. and it was up to him to deal with that end of it.

"Do you think they will come back to that Manyatta?"

"No," Meina shook his head.

"Do you think they are the same ones that attacked the other Manyatta?"

"No."

"I will go to Laitokitok for petrol this afternoon."

"Perhaps I could hear something there."

"Yes."

I went over to the tent and found Miss Mary awake reading with the back of the tent propped up.

"Honey, we need to go into Laitokitok. Would you like to go?"

"I don't know. I was just getting sleepy. Why do we have to go?"

"Arap Meina came in with some news of some lions that have been making trouble and I have to get petrol for the lorry. You know, what we used to call gas for the truck."

"I'll wake up and clean up and come along. Do you have plenty of shillingi?"

"Mwindi will get them."

We started off on the road through the open park country that led to the road that went up the Mountain and saw the two beautiful Tommy rams that always grazed close to camp.

Mary sat in the back seat with Charo and Arap Meina. Mwengi was in the back on a box and I began to worry; Mary had said I didn't have to go until I wanted to. I would hold out for three weeks after the first of the year. There was plenty of work to do after Christmas and there would be work all the time. I knew I was in the best place I had ever been, having a fine, if complicated, life and learning something every day and to go flying all over Africa when I could fly over our own country was the last thing I wished to do. But maybe we could work out something.

I had been told to keep away from Laitokitok but this visit for petrol and supplies and Arap Meina's news of the lions made our visit completely normal and necessary and I was sure G.C. would have approved of it. I wouldn't see the police boy but I would stop in for a drink with Mr. Singh and to buy some beer and Coca-Cola for camp since I always did that. I told Arap Meina to go over to the Masai stores and tell what lion news he had and pick up any news there was and to do the same at the other Masai hangouts.

At Mr. Singh's there were several Masai elders that I knew and I greeted them all and made my compliments to Mrs. Singh. Mr. Singh and I conversed in my phrase book Swahili. The elders needed a bottle of beer badly and I bought it and drank a symbolic gulp from my own bottle.

Peter came in to say the car would be down immediately and I sent him to look for Arap Meina. The car came down the road with the drum roped and three Masai women in the back. Miss Mary was talking happily to Charo. Ngui came in to get the cases with Mwengi. I handed my bottle of beer to them and between them they drained it. Mwengi's eyes shone with absolute delight as he drank beer. Ngui drank it like a racing driver quenching his thirst at a pit stop. He saved half for Mwengi. Ngui took a bottle out for Mthuka and me to share and opened up a Coca-Cola for Charo.

Arap Meina came up with Peter and climbed into the back with the Masai women. They all had boxes to sit on. Ngui sat in front with me and Mary sat with Charo and Mwengi behind the gun rack. I said good-bye to Peter and we started up the road to turn to the west into the sunlight.

"Did you get everything you wanted, honey?"

"There's really nothing to buy. But I found a few things we needed."

I thought of the last time I had been there shopping but there was no use thinking about that and Miss Mary had been in Nairobi then and that is a better shopping town than Laitokitok. But then I had just begun to learn to shop in Laitokitok and I liked it because it was like the general store and post office in Cooke City, Montana.

In Laitokitok they did not have the cardboard boxes of obsolete calibers that the old-timers bought two to four cartridges from each season in the late fall when they wanted to get their winter meat. They sold spears instead. But it was a home-feeling place to buy things and almost everything on the shelves and in the bins you could have found a use for if you lived around there.

But today was the end of another day and tomorrow would be a new one and there were no people walking on my grave yet. No one that I could see looking into the sun or ahead over the country and watching the country as we came down the Mountain, I had forgotten that Mthuka would be thirsty and as I opened the bottle of beer and wiped its neck and lips, Miss Mary asked, very justly, "Aren't wives ever thirsty?"

"I'm sorry, honey. Ngui can get you a full bottle, if you like."

"No. I want just one drink of that."

I passed it to her and she drank what she wished and passed it to me.

I thought how nice it was that there was no African word for I'm sorry, then I thought I'd better not think that or it would come between us and I took a drink of the beer to purify it from Miss Mary and wiped the neck and the lip of the bottle with my good clean handkerchief and handed it to Mthuka.

508 • ERNEST HEMINGWAY

Charo didn't approve of any of this and would have liked to see us drink properly with glasses. But we were drinking as we drank and I did not want to think anything that would make a thing between Charo and me either.

"I think I will have another swallow of beer," Miss Mary said. I told Ngui to open a bottle for her. I would share it with her and Mthuka could pass his to Ngui and Mwengi when he had quenched his thirst. I had not said any of this aloud.

"I don't know why you have to be so complicated about the beer," Mary said.

"I'll bring cups for us the next time."

"Don't try to make it more complicated. I don't want a cup if I drink with you."

"It's just tribal," I said. "I'm truly not trying to make things any more complicated than they are."

"Why did you have to wipe the bottle so carefully after I drank and then wipe it after you drank before you passed it on?"

"Tribal."

"But why different today?"

"Phases of the moon."

"You get too tribal for your own good."

"Very possibly."

"You believe all this."

"No. I just practice it."

"You don't know enough about it to practice it."

"I learn a little every day."

"I'm tired of it."

As we came down a long slope Mary saw a big kongoni about six hundred yards away, standing tall and yellow at the lower crest of the slope. No one had seen it until she pointed it out and then everyone saw it at once. We stopped the car and she and Charo got out to make their stalk. The kongoni was feeding away from them and the wind would not carry their scent to the animal as it was blowing high across the slope. There were no bad animals around here and we stayed back with the vehicle so we would not hamper their approach.

We watched Charo leading from one piece of cover to another and Mary following him, crouched down as he was. The kongoni was out of sight now but we watched Charo freeze and Mary come up beside him and raise her rifle. Then there was the sound of the shot and the heavy plunk of the bullet and Charo ran forward out of sight with Mary following him.

Mthuka drove the car cross country through the bracken and the flowers until we came to Mary and Charo and the dead kongoni. The kongoni or hartebeest is not a handsome animal in life nor in death but this was an old male, very fat and in perfect condition, and his long, sad face, his glazed eyes, and his cut throat did not make him unattractive to the meat eaters. The Masai women were very excited and very impressed by Miss Mary and kept touching her in wonderment and unbelief.

"I saw him first," Mary said. "The first time I ever saw anything first. I saw him before you did. Mthuka and you were in front. I saw him before Ngui and Mwengi and Charo."

"You saw him before Arap Meina," I said.

"He doesn't count because he was looking at the Masai women. Charo and I stalked him by ourselves and when he looked back toward us I shot him exactly where I wanted to."

"Low down in the left shoulder and hit the heart."

"That's where I shot for."

"Piga mzuri," Charo said. "Mzuri mzuri sana."

"We'll put him in the back. The women can ride up front."

"He isn't handsome," Mary said, "but I'd rather shoot something that isn't beautiful for meat."

"He's wonderful and you're wonderful."

"Well, we needed meat and I saw the best kind of meat we could get and fat and the biggest next to eland and I saw him myself and just Charo and I stalked him and I shot him myself. Now, will you love me and not go off alone by yourself in your head?"

"You ride up in front now. We won't be shooting anymore."

"Can I have some of my beer? I'm thirsty from stalking."

"You can have all of your beer."

"No. You take some too to celebrate me seeing him first and we being friends again."

We had a pleasant supper and went to bed early. I had bad dreams in the night and I was awake and dressed before Mwindi brought the tea.

That afternoon we went out on a ride around the country and found by their tracks that the buffalo were back in the forest by the swamp. They had come in during the morning and the trail was wide and deep cut like a cattle trail but cold now and the dung beetles were working rolling up the balls of buffalo sign. The buffs had headed into the forest where the glades and the openings were full of fresh new heavy grass.

I had always liked to see the dung beetles work and since I had learned that they were the sacred scarabs of Egypt, in a slightly modified form, I thought we might find some place for them in the religion. Now they were working very hard and it was getting late for the dung of that day. Watching them I thought of the words for a dung beetle hymn.

Ngui and Mthuka were watching me because they knew I was in a moment of profound thought. Ngui went for Miss Mary's camera in case she should want to take any pictures of the dung beetles, but she did not care to and said, "Papa, when you get tired of watching the dung beetles, do you think we might get on and see something else?"

"Sure, if you are interested, we can find a rhino and there are two lionesses and a lion around."

"How do you know?"

"Several people heard the lions last night and the rhino crossed the buffalo trail back there."

"It's too late for good color."

"Never mind. Maybe we can just watch them."

"They're more inspiring than dung beetles."

"I'm not seeking inspiration. I'm seeking knowledge."

"It's lucky you have such a wide open field."

"Yes."

I told Mthuka to try and find the rhino. He had regular habits and now that he was on the move, we knew about where we might find him.

The rhino was not far from where he should

have been but, as Miss Mary had said, it was too late to photograph well in color with the speed of film that was then available. He had been to a water hole in gray white clay and in the green of the brush and against the dark black lava rocks, he looked a ghostly white.

We left him undisturbed but magnificently and stupidly alert after his tick birds had left him and swung wide downwind of him to come out, finally, onto the salt flats that stretched toward the edge of the marsh. There would be very little moon that night and the lions would be hunting and I wondered how it would be for the game knowing the night was coming on. The game had no security ever but on these nights the least of all and I thought how it was on a dark night like tonight the great python would come out from the swamp to the edge of the flats to lie coiled and waiting. Ngui and I had followed his track once into the swamp and it was like following the single track of an over-size lorry tire. Sometimes he sunk so that it was like a deep rut.

We found the tracks of the two lionesses on the flat and then along the trail. One was very large and we expected to see them lying up but did not. The lion, I thought, was probably over by the old abandoned Masai Manyatta and he might be the lion that had been raiding the

Masai we had visited that morning. But that was conjecture and no evidence to kill him on. Tonight I would listen to them hunt and tomorrow if we saw them I would be able to identify them again. G.C. had said, originally, we might have to take four or perhaps six lion out of the area. We had taken three and the Masai had killed a fourth and wounded another.

"I don't want to go over too close to the swamp, so we won't give our wind to the buff and maybe they will feed out in the open tomorrow," I told Mary and she agreed. So we started back toward home on foot and Ngui and I read the sign on the flats as we walked.

"We'll get out early, honey," I said to Mary, "and there is a better than fair chance we'll find the buff in the open."

"We'll go to bed early and make love and listen to the night."

"Wonderful."

20

WE WERE IN bed and it was quite cold and I lay curled against the tent side of the cot and it was lovely under the sheet and the blankets. No one has any size in bed, you are all the same size and dimensions are perfect when you love each other and we lay and felt the blankets against the cold and our own warmth that came slowly and we whispered quietly and then listened when the first hyena broke into the sudden flamenco singing noise as though he were blasting into a loudspeaker in the night. He was close to the tent and then there was another one behind the lines and I knew the drying meat and the buffalo out beyond the lines had brought them. Mary could imitate them and she did it very softly under the blankets.

"You'll have them in the tent," I said. Then we heard the lion roar off to the north toward the old Manyatta and after we had heard him we heard the coughing grunts of the lioness and we knew they were hunting. We thought we could hear the two lionesses and then we heard another lion roar a long way away.

"I wish we did not have to ever leave Africa," Mary said.

"I'd like never to leave here."

"Bed?"

"We'd have to leave bed in the daytime. No, this camp."

"I love it too."

"Then why do we have to go?"

"Maybe there will be more wonderful places. Don't you want to see the most wonderful places before you die?"

"No."

"Well, we're here now. Let's not think of going away."

"Good."

The hyena slipped into night song again and took it far up past where it was possible. Then broke it sharply off three times.

Mary imitated him and we laughed and the cot seemed a fine big bed and we were comfortable and at home in it. Afterwards she said, "When I'm asleep, just straighten out good and take your rightful share of the bed and I'll get into mine."

"I'll tuck you in."

"No, you stay asleep. I can tuck myself in asleep."

"Let's go to sleep now."

"Good. But don't let me stay and you be cramped."

"I won't be."

"Good night, my dearest sweet."

"Good night, dear lovely."

As we went to sleep we could hear the closer lion making deep heavy grunts and far away the other lion roaring and we held each other hard and gently and went to sleep.

I was asleep when Mary went to her bed and I did not wake until the lion roared quite close to camp. He seemed to shake the guy ropes of the tent and his heavy coughing was very close. He must have been out beyond the lines but he sounded, when he woke me, as though he were going through the camp. Then he roared again and I knew how far away he was. He must be just at the edge of the track that ran down to the landing strip. I listened as he moved away and then I went back to sleep.

CAST OF CHARACTERS

The Narrator The author, who never in his whole life ever kept a journal, is writing, a year after the events that inspired it, a story in the first person. As he once remarked to his third wife, Martha Gellhorn, "We're just sitting cross-legged in a bazaar and if people aren't interested in what we're saying they'll go away."

Mary Ernest Hemingway's fourth and last wife.

Philip (Mr. P., Pop) Philip Percival, the longest lived and most knowledgeable of all white hunters, who guided, among many others, Teddy Roosevelt and George Eastman, and whose physical appearance Hemingway used to disguise Baron Bror von Blixen as the model for the white hunter in "The Short Happy Life of Francis Macomber."

Gin Crazed (G.C.) The game warden of the Kajiado District of the British administration of what was then Kenya Colony. This was a very large area comprising most of the game country south of Nairobi and north of the Tanganyika (now Tanzania) border with Kenya. At no time during their safari except for their taking the whole outfit down to visit their son and daughter-in-law in southern Tanganyika did the Hemingways hunt outside the Kajiado District.

Harry Dunn A senior police officer in the same administration.

Willie A commercial bush pilot. Like all pilots who do not bomb civilians, a very noble character.

Keiti The chief and the authority figure of the white hunter's safari crew. His Edwardian opinions as to what was appropriate behavior on the part of Europeans differed little from those of the butler in the movie many readers may have seen: *The Remains of the Day*, with Emma Thompson and Anthony Hopkins.

Mwindi Under Keiti, the person in charge of the safari household servants.

Nguili A steward and apprentice cook.

Msembi A steward.

Mbebia The safari cook, a highly skilled and important job. The daughter of the last Governor General of the Belgian Congo, whom together with her husband I was guiding on a month's shooting safari, told me that the roast wild duck that she had just eaten was better than the one she had enjoyed last at the Tour d'Argent in Paris. The first of these cooks learned their craft from European ladies who knew their cooking. There is a fine account of the training of such a cook in Isak Dinesen's *Out of Africa*.

Mthuka A black African driver. The generation of white hunters to which I belonged, who learned

their trade after World War II, drove shooting
breaks that they designed and owned themselves
and which were not part of the equipment provided
by the safari outfitter, but that was not the case with
the Hemingways' safari. Percival used a shooting
break supplied by the outfitter and it was driven by
Mthuka. Hemingway, when he took over the safari
crew from Percival, had Mthuka drive for him as
well.

Ngui Hemingway's gun bearer and tracker. No one
who liked big-game hunting and was fit enough to
do it would have ever let his rifle be carried by a gun
bearer. The term really meant a native guide as that
term was used in Maine or Canada. A gun bearer
was expected to have all the skills that General
Baden-Powell and Ernest Thompson Seton thought
a Boy Scout should. He had to know the animals
and their habits, the useful properties of wild plants,
how to track, especially how to follow a blood
spoor, and how to look after himself and others in
the African bush, in short, a Leather-Stocking or
Crocodile Dundee.

Charo Mary Hemingway's gun bearer. Hemingway is
at pains to point out, in this story, the space and
time aspect of ethical behavior in different cultures.
Western ethics allows polygamy and polyandry
sequentially by death or divorce but a person can
have only one spouse at a time. Mary is married to
a spouse at the time of this story who has, within
the ethical framework of the West, already had two
spouses by divorce and a third, Pauline, by both
divorce and death. Mary, who has been married
before twice herself, is protected from her husband

taking a second wife by the ethics of the West, but not from sequential polygamy, which troubles her a great deal. It is what lies behind her desire to kill a lion, not in the way Pauline did twenty years before, but in a new and superior way. Charo was Pauline's gun bearer on that other safari.

Mwengi Philip Percival's gun bearer.

Arap Meina A game scout. A game scout was the lowest ranked game law enforcement officer in Kenya. There were no white game scouts. At the time of this safari there were no black game rangers. It is perhaps just a coincidence that Arap Meina has the same name as the young Kipsigis warrior who took Beryl Markham on the spear hunt for warthog in *West with the Night* and who was later killed in the First World War.

Chungo A handsome, spit-and-polish head game scout who works for G.C. He might remind readers of Denzel Washington as the Duke in the splendid movie version of *Much Ado About Nothing*.

The Informer He is what he is called, a police informer. Hemingway did a lot of intelligence work, first in the Spanish Civil War, where he brought the term fifth columnist into the English and many other languages, and then in Cuba during World War II, where he helped to catch several German spies, one of whom was executed, who were sent over to Havana via Spain. Hemingway shows a sympathy and a pity for the Informer which is shared by nobody else in the story.

Bwana Mouse Patrick, Ernest Hemingway's middle son, a.k.a. "mouse."

The Widow The mother of Debba and under the dubious protection of the Informer.

Debba A young black African woman. Hemingway has been faulted as unable to realistically depict women in his fiction. This would be, if true, a serious fault in a major writer, similar to pointing out that an Old Master could not draw the human figure. Hemingway grew up in a household shared with four sisters so he certainly had an opportunity to learn. A different sort of criticism is now styled political correctness. Art is regarded by these critics as a tool in social engineering. In Hitler's Germany, it was politically correct to depict Jews as dirty polluters of a pure Aryan stream. Whatever the reader's opinions about artistic competence or purpose he or she should pay attention to Debba.

Mr. Singh In the old colonial Kenya, when the white people pronounced it to rhyme with "key" instead of the post-colonial rhyme with the first name "Kay," the population, for administrative purposes, was divided into European, Asian and African according to their continents of origin. Mr. Singh is an Asian and a Sikh. His people originate from the Punjab and their rage at the way the Indian government handled the Golden Temple crisis led to the assassination of Mrs. Gandhi. The Sikhs are a warlike and mechanically gifted people, many of whom are machine tool operators, airline pilots, police inspectors and electrical engineers. A Sikh policeman friend of mine had the unpleasant task of having to arrest a very cantankerous, fat and foulmouthed old European lady on a charge of having poisoned her husband for the insurance. Although she called him a curry-farting bastard to his face, my friend arrested her with the utmost care and professional courtesy.

Mrs. Singh The very handsome wife of Mr. Singh.

SWAHILI GLOSSARY

askari (noun) Soldier, a loan word from Turkish.

bili (adjective) Ungrammatical form of two. Should be mbili.

Boma 1. (noun) Fence, an area protected or sealed off by any sort of enclosure. 2. (noun) Buildings and grounds of a district government headquarters.

bunduki (noun) Gun, a loan word from Arabic.

bwana 1. (noun) Title prefixed to name of a European man having no other title. 2. (noun) Sir (used by an African addressing a European).

chai (noun) Tea.

chakula (noun) Food.

chui (noun) Leopard.

dudus (noun) English plural of word for bug: dudu.

duka (noun) Store.

dumi (noun) Male animal.

hapana (interjection) No.

Hiko huko (phrase) It or he is over there.

hodi (interjection) Hello (calling attention, or answering call).

jambo 1. (noun) Concern. 2. (interjection) Greeting: "Cool?" to which the correct response is "sijambo": "Cool, man." (Literally: "no concern.")

kanga (noun) Guinea fowl.

kidogo (adjective) Small.

Kikamba (noun) The language spoken by the Kamba tribe.

kongoni (noun) Coke's hartebeest.

kubwa (adjective) Big.

kufa (intransitive verb) To die.

kuhalal (transitive verb) To cut the throat of.

kuleta (transitive verb) To bring.

kupiga (transitive verb) To shoot, also to hit or strike.

kuua (transitive verb) To kill.

kwali (noun) Francolin, a pheasantlike upland game bird.

kwenda (intransitive verb) To go.

kwisha (intransitive verb) It is finished. A contraction of imekwisha.

mafuta (noun) Fat, lard.

Manyatta (noun) A masai word equivalent to Boma.

mbili (adjective) Two. (Note H's purposefully illiterate usage in conversation with Debba in Chapter 14.)

mchawi (noun) Witch.

memsahib (noun) Title prefixed to name of a European woman having no other title. A contraction of Madam Sahib.

mganga (noun) Wizard. A good witch.

mimi (personal pronoun) I.

mingi (adjective) Many.

moja (noun) One.

moran (noun) A Masai word equivalent to askari.

mtoto (noun) Child.

mwanamuki (noun) Woman.

Mzee (noun) Old man.

mzuri (adjective) Good.

ndege (noun) Bird, aircraft.

ndio (interjection) Yes.

Ngoma (noun) Dance.

nyanyi (noun) Baboon.

panga (noun) Machete, sword, cutlass.

poli poli (adverb) Slowly.

pombe (noun) Homemade beer.

posho (noun) Cornmeal.

risasi (noun) Bullet.

samaki (noun) Fish.

sana (adverb) Very.

shamba (noun) Small cultivated field.

shauri (noun) Affair, business, concern.

simba (noun) Lion.

tembo (noun) Elephant. Can also mean hard liquor.

tu (adjective) Only, just.

uchawi (noun) Witchcraft, in the bad sense.

Ukambani (phrase) In the country of the Kamba tribe.

wanawaki (noun) Plural form of mwanamuke,
    woman.

watu (noun) People.

EDITOR'S ACKNOWLEDGMENTS

Thank you, Michael Katakis, as Hemingway literary rights manager, for myself and my brothers, for sustaining our belief that this job was worth doing.

Thanks as well to the staff of the Kennedy Library and especially Megan Desnoyers and Stephen Plotkin, whose archival professionalism has been such a help to all who have had the privilege to work with the manuscripts of Ernest Hemingway.

Thanks also to the editorial staff of Scribner and especially Charles Scribner III and Gillian Blake for their help to a grateful amateur.

Special thanks to my wife, Carol, who shares my belief that writing is important and that one word is worth a thousand pictures.